PRAIS

AGE

"Engaging, thought-provoking, an [illegible] ays be counted on to show us our contemporary milieu [illegible] gical by his unique insights, and a future rendered inhabitable by his wild yet disciplined imagination."

—*The Washington Post*

"Superb. . . . Each sentence is a hand-turned marvel of compact characterization, world-building, and sardonic wit, all used to illuminate [Gibson's] vivid milieus. . . . Gibson has an inexhaustible supply of tricks, new stories, and new ways of telling them that make him the most consistent predictor of our present, contextualizer of our pasts, and presager of our possible futures."

—*Los Angeles Times*

"An immersive thriller, fueled by an intelligent, empathetic imagination."

—*The Boston Globe*

"A sensual, remarkably visual ride, vigorous with displays of conceptual imagination and humor."

—*The Guardian*

"Gibson blurs the line between real and speculative technology in a fast-paced thriller that will affirm to readers that it was well worth the wait."

—*Booklist*

"[Gibson's] language (half Appalachian economy, half leather-jacket poet of neon and decay) is all about friction and the gray spaces where disparate ideas intersect. His game is living in those spaces, checking out the view, telling us about it."

—NPR

"In *Agency* Gibson offers another of his uncannily plausible imaginings of near-future life and technology. . . . With Gibson's trademark panache, the story rattles along with great pace and suspense."

—*The Sunday Times* (UK)

TITLES BY WILLIAM GIBSON

Neuromancer

Count Zero

Burning Chrome

Mona Lisa Overdrive

Virtual Light

Idoru

All Tomorrow's Parties

Pattern Recognition

Spook Country

Zero History

Distrust That Particular Flavor

The Peripheral

Agency

AGENCY

WILLIAM GIBSON

BERKLEY
NEW YORK

BERKLEY
An imprint of Penguin Random House LLC
penguinrandomhouse.com

ISBN: 9781101986943

The Library of Congress has catalogued the Berkley hardcover edition of this book as follows:

Names: Gibson, William, 1948– author.
Title: Agency / William Gibson.
Description: First Edition. | New York: Berkley, 2020. | Sequel to: The Peripheral.
Identifiers: LCCN 2019023019 (print) | LCCN 2019023020 (ebook) | ISBN 9781101986936 (hardcover) | ISBN 9781101986950 (ebook)
Subjects: GSAFD: Science fiction. | Suspense fiction.
Classification: LCC PS3557.I2264 A34 2020 (print) | LCC PS3557.I2264 (ebook) | DDC 813/.54—dc23
LC record available at https://lccn.loc.gov/2019023019
LC ebook record available at https://lccn.loc.gov/2019023020

Berkley hardcover edition / January 2020
Berkley trade paperback edition / January 2021

Printed in the United States of America
10 9 8 7 6 5 4 3

Cover design by gray318
Cover photo by AND-ONE / Getty Images
Book design by Laura K. Corless

To Martha Millard, my excellent literary agent
for thirty-five years, with many thanks

AGENCY

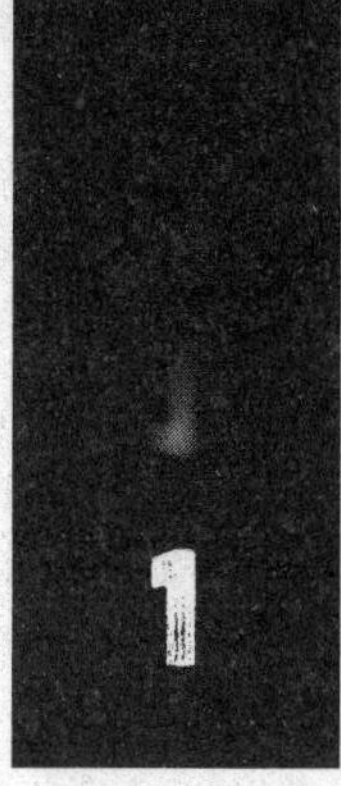

THE UNBOXING

Very recent hiredness was its own liminal state, Verity reminded herself, on the crowded Montgomery BART platform, waiting for a train to Sixteenth and Mission.

Twenty minutes earlier, having signed an employment contract with Tulpagenics, a start-up she knew little about, followed by a wordy nondisclosure agreement, she'd shaken hands with Gavin Eames, their CTO, said goodbye, and stepped into an elevator, feeling only relief as the doors closed and the twenty-six-floor descent began.

New-job unease hadn't yet found her, there, nor out on Montgomery as she'd walked to the station, texting her order for pad thai to the Valencia branch of Osha. By the time she'd reached this platform, though, three flights down, it was entirely with her, as much as the black tradeshow bag slung beneath her arm, silk-screened with the logo of Cursion, her new employer's parent firm, about which she knew very little, other than that they were in gaming.

It was with her now as her train arrived. Almost two years since she'd felt this, she thought, as she boarded. She'd been unemployed for half of that, which she supposed might account for its intensity now.

She reached for a hang-strap as the car filled.

Surfacing at Sixteenth, she went straight to Osha, picked up her pad thai, and started for Joe-Eddy's.

She'd eat, then start getting to know their product. This wasn't just a new job, but a possible end to sleeping on Joe-Eddy's curb-rescue porn couch.

The early November sky looked almost normal, Napa-Sonoma particulates having mostly blown inland, though the light still held a hint of that scorched edge. She no longer started awake to the smell of burning, only to remember what it was. She'd kept the kitchen window closed, this past week, the only one Joe-Eddy ever opened. She'd give the place a good airing soon, maybe try cracking one of the windows overlooking Valencia.

Once back at his apartment, she ate hungrily from the black plastic take-out tray, ignoring the lingering reek of the uncut Mr. Clean she'd used to scour the wooden tabletop, prior to Gavin's call. If Joe-Eddy's Frankfurt job lasted, she remembered having thought as she'd wielded a medium-grit 3M foam sanding block, she might scrub the kitchen floor as well, for the second time in a little under a year. Now, though, with Tulpagenics' contract signed, she might be giving notice to the couple renting her condo, middle managers at Twitter, who hadn't reported a paparazzi sighting for over three months. In the meantime, for however many more nights on white pleather, she had her silk mummy-bag liner, its thread-count proof against the porn-cooties of persistent imagination.

Covering what remained of her order with its admirably compostable translucent lid, she stood, took her leftovers to the fridge, rinsed her couch-surfing chopsticks at the sink, and returned to the table.

When Gavin had been packing the bag, the glasses were all she'd paid any real attention to. They'd involved a personal style decision: tortoiseshell plastic, with gold-tone trim, or an aspirationally Scandinavian gray.

Now she took their generic black case from the bag, opened it, removed them, and spread the pale gray minimalist temples. The lenses were untinted. She looked for a trademark, country of origin, model number. Finding none, she placed them on the table.

Next, a flat white cardboard box, in which a flimsy vacuum-formed tray, also white, hugged a nondescript black phone. Likewise no-name, she found, having freed it from the tray. She turned it on and placed it beside the glasses. A smaller white box revealed a generic-looking black headset with a single earbud. In another, three black chargers, one each for the glasses, phone, and headset, commonest of consumer fruit, their thin black cables still factory-coiled, secured with miniature black twist-ties. All of it, according to Gavin, plug and play.

Picking up the headset and switching it on, she hung it from her right ear, settling the earbud. She put the glasses on, pressing their low-profile power-stud. The headset pinged, a cursor appearing. A white arrow, centered in her field of vision. Then moving down, of its own accord, to the empty boxes, the chargers, the black phone.

"Here we go," said a woman's husky voice in Verity's ear. Glancing to her right, toward what would have been the voice's source had anyone been there, Verity inadvertently gave whoever was controlling the cursor a view of the living room. "Got a hoarding issue, Gavin?" the voice asked, the cursor having settled on the miniature junkyard of semi-disassembled vintage electronics on Joe-Eddy's workbench.

"I'm not Gavin," Verity said.

"No shit," said the voice, neutrally.

"Verity Jane."

"Ain't the office, is it, Verity Jane?"

"Friend's place."

The cursor traversed the living room, to the closed curtains. "What's outside?"

"Valencia Street," Verity said. "What should I call you?"

"Eunice."

"Hi, Eunice."

"Hi yourself." The cursor moved to Joe-Eddy's Japanese faux Fender Jazzmaster. "Play?"

"Friend does. You?"

"Good question."

"You don't know?"

"Thing-shaped hole."

"Excuse me?"

"I got one, in that department. Want to show me what you look like?"

"How?"

"Mirror. Or take the glasses off. Point 'em at your face."

"Will I be able to see you?"

"No."

"Why not?"

"No there there."

"I need to use the bathroom," Verity said, standing. "I'll leave the glasses here."

"You don't mind, maybe open the drapes."

Verity crossed to the window, hauled both layers of dusty blackout curtain aside.

"You put the glasses down," the voice said, "I can look out the window."

She took them off, positioning them, temples open, lenses overlooking the street, on a white Ikea stool, its round seat branded with soldering-iron stigmata. Then added, for what she judged to be needed elevation, the German-language making-of volume of a Brazilian telenovela. Removing the headset, she put it down on the book, beside the glasses, went to the kitchen, retrieving her own phone from her purse, then down the narrow corridor to the bathroom. Closing the door behind her, she phoned Gavin Eames.

"Verity," he answered instantly, "hello."

"Is this for real?"

"You haven't read the nondisclosure agreement?"

"More clauses than I'm used to."

"You agreed not to discuss anything of substance on a non-company device."

"Just tell me there's not someone somewhere doing Eunice, for my benefit?"

"Not in the sense I take you to mean, no."

"You're saying it's real."

"Determining that to your own satisfaction is part of what you're expected to be doing for us."

"Should I call back on the company phone?"

"No. We'll discuss this in person. This isn't the time."

"You're saying she's—"

"Goodbye."

"Software," she finished, looking from the phone to her reflection in the mirror over the sink, its age-mottled silver backing suggesting a submarine grotto. She turned then, opened the door, and walked back into the living room, to the window. Picked up the glasses. Put them on. Late-afternoon traffic strobed behind transparent vertical planes of something resembling bar code. "Whoa . . ."

Then she remembered the headset. Put it on.

"Hey," the voice said.

The bar code vanished, leaving the cursor riding level with the windows of passing cars. "What was that?" Verity asked.

"DMV. I was reading plates."

"Where are you, Eunice?"

"With you," said the voice, "looking out the window."

Whatever this was, she knew she didn't want her first substantial conversation with it to take place in Joe-Eddy's living room. Briefly considering the dive bar on Van Ness, not that she felt like a drink, she remembered having recently been recognized there. There was Wolven + Loaves, a few doors up the street, but it was usually busy, the acoustics harsh even when it wasn't. Then she remembered 3.7-sigma, Joe-Eddy's semi-ironic caffeination-point of choice, a few blocks away, on the opposite side of Valencia.

2

OUR HOBBYIST OF HELLWORLDS

"Vespasian," Detective Inspector Ainsley Lowbeer said, peering sidewise at Netherton over her greatcoat's upraised collar, "our hobbyist of hellworlds. Recall him?"

You had him killed in Rotterdam, Netherton thought. Not that she'd ever said as much, or that he'd asked. "The one who made such horrific stubs? All war, all the time?"

"I'd wondered how he so quickly rendered them nightmares," she said, pacing briskly on, beneath Victoria Embankment's gray morning and the canopy of dripping trees. "Eventually, I looked into it."

He lengthened his stride, keeping up. "How did he?" He hadn't seen her since before Thomas's birth, at the start of his parental leave. Now, he'd already gathered, that was coming to an end.

"I dislike calling them stubs," she said. "They're short because we've only just initiated them, by reaching into the past and making that first contact. We should call them branches, as they literally are. Vespasian discovered a simple way of exaggerating the butterfly effect, or so it seems. That even the smallest perturbation may yield large and unforeseen consequences. On making contact, he'd immediately withdraw. Then return, months later, study the results, and very deliberately and forcefully intervene. He achieved remarkable if terrible results, and very quickly. Investigating his method, I happened on another of his so-called stubs, one in which he'd initiated contact in 2015, several years before the earliest previously known contact. We've no idea how he managed the extra reach, but we now have access to that stub." They were climbing shallow steps now, toward the river, to an overlook. "We may have a chance, there, of achieving radically better outcomes than previously." They reached the top. "I need you back for that. Contact has necessarily been oblique, so far, due to technological asymmetry, but we think we've managed a work-around. Your experience in dealing with contactees may soon be very much in need."

"Contact's been oblique, you say?"

"The aunties, for instance"—her pet name for her office's coven of semisentient security algorithms—"are of relatively little use." Netherton grimaced at the very thought of them.

A dappled Thames chimera broke the surface then, red and white. It rolled, four meters head to tail, lamplike eyes clustered above cartoonish feeding palps. Diving, it left a shallow wake of beige foam.

"So you can't put a team of quants on it," he asked, "to secure as much in-stub wealth as might be needed?" Having, of course, seen her do exactly that.

"No. Even the simplest messaging can be quite spotty."

"What can you do, then?"

"Laterally encourage an autonomous, self-learning agent," she said. "Then nudge it toward greater agency. It helps that they're mad for AI there, though they've scarcely anything we'd consider that. By tracing historical fault lines around AI research here, we found what we needed there."

"Fault lines?"

"Between the most reckless entrepreneurialism and certain worst-case examples of defense contracting. I'll tell you more over brunch—assuming you've time."

"Of course," he said, as he always did.

"I'm in a mood for the sandwiches," she said, and turned from the river, apparently satisfied with their glimpse of the chimera.

"Salt beef," he said, "with mustard and dill," his favorite at the Marylebone shop she preferred. As accustomed to her as he was, he thought, he'd still be brunching with a semimythical autonomous magistrate-executioner, unique in her position. That being roughly her true occupation, as opposed to her formal position in law enforcement, or the personal projects she paid him to assist her with, however seriously she took them. Her true occupation being something he wished to have as little to do with as possible, ever.

They returned to her car, where it awaited them invisibly, a few dead leaves clinging to its roof, as though magically suspended.

3

APP WHISPERER

As Verity entered 3.7, the oldest and most extensively pierced of the baristas shoved a dirty chai in her direction, across the zinc counter.

"I ordered for you," the voice expecting to be called Eunice said.

Verity had covered the headset with a beanie she hoped wouldn't suggest she was trying to look younger. She decided to keep it on. "Thanks. How'd you know what I'd want?"

"Your Starbucks rewards account," said Eunice, so-called, practicing what she said was facial recognition on the barista. A tight geometry formed, the cursor having found his face, straight lines connecting, centered around the sinus region, to zero in on the nose tip, and then was gone. This had started on the street, on the way over, though Eunice claimed to have no idea how she was doing it.

Before Verity could reach the counter, the barista spun dismissively, piercings clinking. Her drink, she saw, picking it up, had VULVA D hand-printed above the 3.7 logo, in fluorescent pink industrial paint pen, obscenely distorted customer names a signature of his, though in his favor, he was fully as harsh to men. She carried it to the farthest vacant table, against a wall of stripped and sanded tongue-and-groove. "How'd you pay?" she asked, pulling out a chair.

"PayPal. Popped up when I needed it, news to me. Not much in the account, but I could buy you a drink."

"You know people's names, after you do that to their noses?"

"If I don't, they're probably illegals."

"Don't do it to me."

"Don't always know when I do it."

"How'd you find my Starbucks account?"

"Just did."

Verity removed the glasses, turned them around, looked into the lenses. "You expect me to believe you?"

"Believe me too fast, they got me the wrong white girl."

Verity tilted her head at the glasses. "Implying you're a woman of color, yourself?"

"African-American. Hat makes you look like a kid."

Annoyed, Verity removed it.

"Just sayin'."

Nobody in 3.7 seemed to be paying them any attention, Verity decided, then remembered she was apparently talking to her own glasses, so they were all probably pretending not to notice. "How old are you, Eunice?"

"Eight hours. That's over the past three weeks. You?"

"Thirty-three. Years. How can you be eight hours old?" She put the glasses back on.

"Jesus year," said Eunice, "thirty-three."

"You religious?"

"It just means time to get your shit together."

There was a looseness to this beyond her experience of chatbots, but a wariness as well. "You remember eight hours, total? Starting when? From what?"

"Gavin. Said my name. Then hi. Three weeks ago. In his office."

"You talked?"

"Asked me my name. Told me his, that he was chief technology officer for a company called Tulpagenics. Glad to meet me. Next day, his office again, he had a woman on the phone but I wasn't supposed to be able to hear her telling him questions to ask me."

"How did you?"

"Just did. Like I knew she was one floor above us, on the twenty-eighth."

"That's Cursion," Verity said. "Tulpagenics' parent firm. Gaming. What did she want him to ask you?"

"Diagnostic questions, but they wouldn't sound like it. She wanted to know how I was doing developmentally, in particular ways."

"Did he get what she wanted?"

"I had no way of knowing, then."

"You do now?"

"Enough to know they weren't the right questions. Don't know how I know that either."

Reality show, Verity thought, British actor playing Gavin. The security guards and the receptionist would have been actors too, the space on the twenty-seventh floor belonging to some actual start-up. They had to be getting video now. She glanced around 3.7, then remembered she'd chosen it herself.

"How deep in you figure we are?" Eunice asked.

"In what?"

"Like *Inception*."

"This isn't a dream," Verity said.

"My money's on head trauma. Concussion. Focal retrograde amnesia."

"I saw *Inception* when it came out," Verity said.

"How many times?"

"Once. Why?"

"Eighty-one and counting, me. Watching it right now. Not that you don't have my fullest attention."

"How's that work?"

"Don't know. Paris rolling up on itself. You know that scene?"

"Great visuals," Verity said, "but the story's confusing."

"There's this kick-ass infographic, totally explains it. Wanna see?"

"Why are we talking about a movie, Eunice?"

"That really your last name? Jane?"

"Like the fighting ships book. *Jane's.*"

Pause. "I'm Navy myself."

"You are?"

"Yeah," Eunice said, an absence in her tone, something almost bereft, "just came to me."

Did it have this range of emotional expression, Verity wondered, or was she just projecting on it? "Is this a joke, like on some asshole's YouTube channel?"

"I get hold of some motherfucker playing it, they won't be laughing. Where do you know Gavin from?"

"He hired me," Verity said, "this afternoon."

"Wiki says you're the app whisperer."

"You said you wouldn't do that."

"That was facial recognition. This is Wikipedia. I know your name, I can't Google you?"

"Okay," Verity said, after a pause, then tasted her dirty chai.

"You were with that Stets. The VC billionaire boy."

"I'm not, now."

"Asshole?"

"No. It just wasn't that much of a relationship, in spite of what the media said. I couldn't handle the attention. But you can't just walk out of something like that, not without media waiting for you."

"You have zero social media presence now. Used to be active."

"After we split, media went for anyone they saw as a friend of mine, associate, anything. A few people gave them stories. Most didn't, but some got tired of being asked. I decided to treat it as a sabbatical."

"Furlough from Facebook?"

"From people. I'd started getting back on, mainly Instagram, but by then it was closer to the election and that started creeping me out, so I stayed off everything."

"Kept working?"

"No. Almost a year now."

"You the app whisperer."

"They needed something to explain my being with him in the first place."

"'Beta tester with a wild talent'? Decent hook."

"That was the lede on a *Wired* article, but only because I was with him."

"'Reputation for radically improving product prior to release'? 'Natural-born super-user'?"

"I quit reading anything about me, us, him."

"Media blew you out of the water."

Verity, noticing a neckbeard watching from a table across the room, recalled Joe-Eddy's take on the particular strain of wannabe feral hacker to be found here. Feral like a day or three late for a shower and some toothpaste, he'd said. "Feel like a walk?" she asked Eunice. "We could go up to the park."

"You the one all corporeal and all."

Verity scooted back her chair. Put the beanie back on. Stood, picking up her chai. Seeing she was leaving, the barista glared at her, though somehow amicably.

On the way out, passing a laptop's screen, its owner massively earphoned, she saw the president, seated at her desk in the Oval Office, explaining something. If it wasn't the hurricane hitting Houston, the earthquake in Mexico, the other hurricane wrecking Puerto Rico, or the worst wildfires in California history, it was Qamishli.

Increasingly, though, it seemed mainly to be Qamishli. Verity didn't fully understand the situation. Had in fact been avoiding understanding it, assuming that if she did she'd be as terrified as everyone else, and no more able to do anything about it.

The president hadn't looked terrified, Verity thought, as 3.7's door closed behind her. She'd looked like she was on the case.

THE SANDWICHES

When Lowbeer wished a conversation in public to be private, which she invariably did, London emptied itself around her.

Netherton had no idea how this was accomplished, and he was seldom, as now, much aware, during a given conversation, of the isolation. On leaving her company, though, he'd encounter a pedestrian, see someone cycling, or a vehicle, and only then be aware of emerging from her bubble of exclusion.

Seated with her now in a darkly varnished booth, in this ostentatiously pre-jackpot sandwich shop in Marylebone Street, he found himself eager for exactly that: their goodbye, his walk away, and that first glimpse of some random stranger, abroad in the quiet vastness of London.

"Salt beef good?" She was having Marmite and cucumber.

He nodded. "Do they still make Marmite? As opposed to assemblers excreting it as needed, I mean."

"Of course." She looked down at the perfectly rectangular remaining sections of her sandwich, her brilliantly white quiff inclining with her gaze. "It's yeast, and salt. Manufactory's in Bermondsey. Bots prepare it, but otherwise traditionally."

Ask her something, almost anything, and she'd have the answer. Meeting strangers, she might answer questions they hadn't thought to ask. The whereabouts, for instance, of possessions long misplaced. She was fundamentally connected, she'd disconcertingly allow, in ways resulting in her knowing virtually everything about anyone she happened to meet. She'd apologize, then, declaring herself an ancient monster of the surveillance state, something Netherton knew her to well and truly be.

"How far back did Vespasian go," he asked her now, "to initiate this stub?"

"Mid-2015."

"When is it, there, now?"

"2017," she said, "fall."

"Much changed?"

"The outcome of the previous year's American presidential election. Brexit referendum as well."

"As the result of his initial contact?"

"Could have been the butterfly effect, of course. Though the aunties, in both cases, lean toward something causing a reduction in Russian manipulation of social media. Which we assume would have had a similar result in our own time line. But without the aunties being able to chew over a great deal of their data, there's no assigning a more exact cause."

"But why would Vespasian, of all people, have desired positive change? Assuming those outcomes were his intention, that is."

"He was a sadist," said Lowbeer, "and terribly clever at it. The irony of his producing beneficial change may well have amused him, given his greatest delight was in appallingly cruel suffering. In any case, when he failed to return," and here their eyes briefly met, "to fine-tune and amplify course, as he always did, things went their own way."

"How is it there, given that?"

"Grim," she said, "what with every other ordering principle and incentive still in place. And they've a Mideast crisis now, as well, with drastic and immediate global implications. That aside, though, they're being driven into the same blades we were, but at a less acute angle."

"Are you there yourself, in the new stub? Your stub self, I mean?"

"I assume so," she said, "as a young child. I find it best never to look at that."

"Of course," said Netherton, unwilling even to begin to imagine the experience.

"I've asked Ash to bring you up to date on what we've been doing there," she said.

"Involved, is she?" Hoping, however faintly, not.

"From the start," said Lowbeer.

"How wonderful," Netherton said, resignedly, picking up the next section of his sandwich.

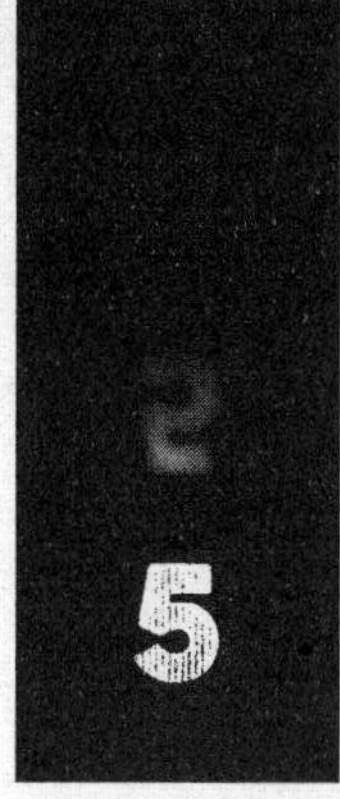

SITUATIONAL AWARENESS

From the crest of Dolores Park, Verity wondered if she could see the tower on Montgomery, where Gavin had first described the product that had turned out to be Eunice, not that she'd recognize it if she could.

There was no one for Eunice to facially recognize, looking out across the city, but the cursor, having become a white circle, was darting around the skyline, trapping invisible airborne somethings under a plus sign. "Birds?" Verity asked.

"Drones. How'd you hook up with Gavin?"

"Called me a week ago. Introduced himself. We talked, then exchanged e-mails. Had lunch this past Friday. Called me this morning, asked if I wanted to come over and talk contract."

"How high's the ceiling there, in the lobby?"

"Why?"

"Too high to tell whether it's bronze or plastic, I bet. There to make you feel like money's being made. How was the meeting?"

"Security keyed me up to twenty-seven. Signed their visitor's nondisclosure on an iPad. Kid with black-metal ear grommets took me back to meet Gavin. Start-up plants everywhere."

"What where?"

"Tillandsia. Air plants. You can hot-glue them to cable trays, anything. They get by. Like a lot of people in start-ups, Joe-Eddy says."

"So what did Gavin say?"

"Described the product, we agreed on salary, I signed a contract, plus an NDA tailored to the project."

"Doing?"

"What I do. Consulting on a prototype of something they're building out."

"Which is?"

"You," Verity said, deciding she might as well get it on the table, "unless he was bullshitting me."

No reply.

"Maybe not a prototype," Verity said. "Maybe closer to an alpha build."

The silence lengthened. If there were more drones out there, Eunice wasn't bothering with them now, the cursor having become an arrow again, immobile against the sky. Verity turned, looking back the way they'd come, toward Valencia. In the park below, hunched on a bench, one of two skater boys released a startlingly opaque puff of white vape, like a winter locomotive in an old movie. "Sorry. I guess that's weird for you. If you're what Gavin said you are, you're seriously next-level."

"Am I?"

"On the basis of this conversation, yes."

"Google 'tulpa,'" Eunice said, "you get Tibetan occult thought-forms. Or people who've invented themselves an imaginary playmate."

"I did."

"Don't feel particularly Tibetan, myself," Eunice said. "Maybe invented, but how would I know?"

"He called you a laminar agent. Googled that too, on my way out."

"No applicable hit," Eunice said.

"Meant something to him. He also used the term 'laminae.' Plural."

"For what?"

"Wasn't clear," Verity said, "but he described the product, that's you, as a cross-platform, individually user-based, autonomous avatar. Target demographic power-uses VR, AR, gaming, next-level social media. Idea's to sell a single unique super-avatar. Kind of a digital mini-self, able to fill in when the user can't be online."

"Why didn't they make one of you?"

"I don't think they can, yet. You're more like proof of concept. They've only made one, and you're it."

"Based on somebody?"

"He didn't say."

"Kinda gloomy up here," Eunice said, after a pause, "what with the dying of the light and all."

"Sorry."

"Back to your friend's place? José Eduardo Alvarez-Matta, on the lease. Infosec consultant. Boyfriend?"

"Friend," Verity said. "We kept winding up on the same projects." She started back down the path. The skaters were gone, as if she'd imagined them. Streetlights were coming on, faintly haloed. There was mercury in the fog, she'd once heard someone say, in the bar on Van Ness, but after the recent sub-Beijing air quality it didn't seem that big a deal.

"If all this really is some asshole's YouTube channel," Eunice said, as they left the park, "I guess that makes me a figment."

Verity watched the cursor check the interior of each parked car they passed, then scan up, higher, on both sides of the street, as if expecting someone in a window, on a roof. "Can you tell what I'm looking at, Eunice?"

"Watching the cursor."

"Why are you looking in cars?"

"Situational awareness."

"Of what?"

"Of the situation. Observe, orient, decide, act."

On Valencia, as they turned toward 3.7 and Joe-Eddy's, Eunice face-captured a young man, his dark hair buzzed short, hunched in the passenger seat of a beige Fiat, alone. He glanced up as they passed, features lit from below by his phone. Verity, peering ahead for the place that sold otaku denim, realized they hadn't passed 3.7 yet, on the opposite side, so the jeans would be farther along.

"Got a go-bag?" Eunice asked.

"I haven't had my own place for the past year. Renting out my condo. Most of my stuff's in my basement locker, there. Living out of a bag, otherwise. That count?"

"We had go-bags in our go-bags," Eunice said, "depending."

"On what?"

"Where we were going," Eunice said.

"Where were you going?" They were passing the Japanese jeans now, with Joe-Eddy's place still half a block beyond the next intersection.

"No idea."

That new-job liminality was definitely gone, Verity thought, though not in any way she'd hoped for. Replaced instead by another feeling, deeply unfamiliar. Another in-betweenness, but between what and what, she'd no idea.

6

DALSTON

Netherton had visited Ash only once before, though he hadn't known it at the time.

His friend Lev Zubov, her employer at the time, had taken him here, to a party of hers, before either of them had met Lowbeer, so well prior to Ash working exclusively for her. A one-story brick industrial building, tucked behind a block of Victorian row houses, just off Kingsland High Street.

He'd been drunk, of course, as he generally was in those days, so all he remembered of the place, indeed of the visit, were a pair of long rectangular skylights, running the length of either side of a shallow peaked roof.

Now her tardibot answered the blue door, like an eight-legged raccoon in a small antique biohazard suit, its head an unpleasantly folded foreskin-like affair, with a central toothy ring of what he took to be mirror-polished steel. It seemed to peer up at him, however eyelessly. "Netherton," it said, the voice hers, "come in."

"Thank you." Ash had brought the tardibot to work occasionally, at

Lev's house in Notting Hill. Netherton had found it less annoying than her miniature pangolins, the sinuous darting of their ribbon-like tongues peculiarly unpleasant.

He followed it in, hearing the door close and lock itself behind him.

To either side of the wide passageway he'd entered, candles flickered in dusty glasses, their faint shadows moving on white walls.

The tardibot's gait was surprisingly efficient, its meat-hook claws clacking dully on the concrete floor.

The interior was L-shaped, the passageway at a right angle to the much longer space he recalled, the one with the skylights. He found Ash waiting for him around that corner, in pantaloons, a chitinous brown breastplate rising nearly to her chin, and a pair of oval, black-lensed spectacles. At least none of her motile tattoos were currently visible. "At a party here, once," he said, "you were screening abstract patterns of some kind, on those." He indicated the long twin skylights.

"What the view would have been during a Luftwaffe raid. Searchlights, flak-bursts, very visually active." Behind her, at the far end of the space, stood a small, fungoid-looking, pseudo-primitive structure, a blackly gleaming antique motorcycle propped in front of it. To one side, a thickly crowded table of more of her nonsense. He hoped he wouldn't be required to enter the foul-looking hut, but knew that that wouldn't be like her. "Visited the county lately?" she asked, meaning Lowbeer's first adopted stub.

"Not since our son's birth."

"Congratulations," she said.

"Thank you. Have you visited, yourself?"

"Not since they ran Flynne's cousin for president. I've been busy with the new one." Removing her dark glasses, she unexpectedly revealed the reversal of her most unpleasant body-modification. Where once her gray eyes boasted doubled irises, one above the other, they now were normal. "What's Lowbeer told you, about it?"

"Further back than the county, more difficult to communicate with. Vespasian made contact, then withdrew, intending to return later."

"She'd made sure he didn't," Ash said, "on learning that his hobby essentially consisted of being an evil god. His return to his final stub-initiation having been prevented, the outcomes of both the Brexit vote and America's presidential election wound up being reversed. Tea?"

"Lovely, thanks," he said, thoroughly disliking tea, hers in particular. It would either be vilely herbal or overemphatically Russian.

"Come," she said.

The tardibot's claws made a sound. He turned, to see it sitting up on its two rearmost pairs of legs, apparently observing him. Ignoring it, he followed her the length of the room, to the table cluttered with her ostentatious tribal flotsam. The tallest object on it was a samovar.

She filled a small pewter cup and passed it to him. Uncomfortably hot, it was decorated with cherubs, their heads decidedly skull-like. "Jam?"

"No, thank you."

She drew herself a similar cup, adding raspberry jam with a tarnished silver spoon.

"Have you ever been concerned," he asked, immediately regretting the question, "that the klept might look askance, at this special interest of hers, in which we both assist her?"

"They need her," said Ash. "Too much so to do more than look askance." She took a first sip. "Not to mention the fear she necessarily inspires, as their culture's autonomous internal enforcer, charged with identifying and pruning back potential destabilizers. But you are, I take it? Concerned?"

He looked down at the cup, itself more poisonous-looking than the brew it contained, then back up at her. "When you and I worked together, I was still drinking. It did occur to me to be concerned about the possibility, from time to time, but I'd more immediate problems. Now, of course, I've a family to think of."

"It's not an illogical concern," she said. "I've asked her that exact question myself, more than once. Her reply always being what I just said to you."

"And you're satisfied with that?"

"I believe we can realistically consider ourselves protected. But I also believe in what she's attempting to do, with the stubs. There's nothing I'd rather be doing."

"Thank you," said Netherton, not particularly reassured. "I'm eager to hear more about the new stub."

"Let's move to the yurt," she said. "It's more secure."

At this he took refuge in his tea, immediately and painfully burning his mouth.

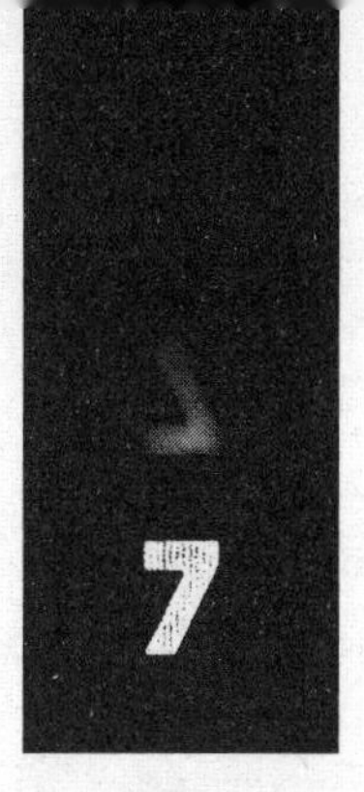

FRANKLINS

Verity took a hot shower as soon as they got in, having first put the Tulpagenics glasses in the medicine cabinet.

Stepping out, she wrapped her hair in one of Joe-Eddy's kid-sized faux-Disney *La Sirenita* beach towels, then pulled on the chocolate-brown terrycloth tactical bathrobe she'd given him, a party favor from a corporate weekend at a desert spa in southern Arizona. She remembered pawing through the freebie basket in the lobby for an XL, Stets anxious to be on the first copter out.

Tactical, so-called, by virtue of a Jedi-style hood and laptop-sized cargo pockets on either hip. She couldn't remember what the scarlet-embroidered logo stood for, because he hadn't backed them after all. She couldn't tell whether Joe-Eddy had ever worn it, but that probably meant he hadn't. She never worried about the towels, because he had a shrink-wrapped pallet's worth of them, straight from the factory in China, so she always used a new one.

She took the glasses from the medicine cabinet and put them on. Remembering as she did that the headset was in her purse, on the back of the bathroom door, but here was the cursor, in the steam-blurred mirror, over the reflection of the embroidered logo.

Did you work there?

Crisp white Helvetica, in front of her foggy reflection. "I can't even remember what it was called. But this feels like I should be texting you back."

Put the headset on.

She gave her hair a squeeze in the towel, unwrapped it, made sure her right ear was dry, arranged the towel around her shoulders, and found the headset in her purse. "What's up?"

"I'm older now."

"By two hours," Verity said, "since I met you?"

"Not if multitasking counts."

"Multitasking what?"

"I don't have access to it. How many rooms here?"

"Living room, bedroom, kitchen, bath. Have a look." She put on Joe-Eddy's flip-flops, too big for her, took her purse down from the hook, opened the door, and went to the bedroom, switching on the overhead light, a lopsided wire sphere covered in white tissue paper.

"The black sheets, huh?" Cursor on the bed.

"Probably more about cutting down on laundry runs, in his case. I'm on the couch, when I sleep here."

"The white whale? I'd take the black sheets."

Cursor on the closet door. Crossing to it, she opened it. Three dusty-looking black suits skulked there, on sagging wire hangers. She'd never seen Joe-Eddy in a suit, and couldn't imagine him in these. Amid them, suspended from the same splintery length of wooden rod, her veteran Muji garment bag, unzipped, a model they no longer made. "Guess you'd call that my go-bag."

"Hard to run with?"

"I've run concourses with it. Made planes. Folds over, zips around three sides."

"Take your word," said Eunice, "but now I need you to go back downstairs and answer the front door."

"Not like this you don't," Verity said, in bathrobe and flip-flops, hair damp under *La Sirenita*.

"He's not coming in. He'll just give you something."

"He who?"

The doorbell chimed, just as Eunice opened a steeply angled thumbnail video feed. Verity recognized the edge of the entrance to the store next door, a place that refilled toner cartridges, though she'd never seen it open for business. A head, dark hair severely buzz-cut, filled most of the thumbnail, the angle hiding all but a cheekbone.

"Cam's Joe-Eddy's," Eunice said. "Has another one outside the kitchen window. None inside."

"Not going down there."

"In a position to get himself killed, standing out there with what he's got for us. Help a boy's ass out."

"I don't want to do this," Verity said, but she readjusted the robe, wrapping it more tightly, though that left one giant terry pocket centered over her stomach, kangaroo-style. She tightened and double-knotted the belt, flip-flopped out into the living room, undid the deadlock, opened the door, stepped out of the flip-flops, onto the landing, and descended the stairs.

"Lock and bolt the door before you bring it back up," Eunice said.

The door at the bottom was dirty, white, and reassuringly solid. She tried its hotel-style fish-eye for the first time. It showed her nothing at all. She turned the deadlock, undid the bolt, opened it.

Him. Just after they'd turned back onto Valencia. Uplit by his phone, in a Fiat 500. He handed her what seemed to be a miniature camping pillow, covered in ripstop nylon, forest green. She looked up from it, but he was already turning, walking away.

She closed the door, locked and bolted it, then climbed back up, finding the pillow to be a stuff sack, big enough for a down-lined vest, but containing something solid. "What's in this?" She'd reached the top of the stairs.

"Franklins," Eunice said.

"What?"

"Hundreds."

Verity deadlocked the apartment door behind her. Crossed to the workbench and put the thing down, atop electronic junk. "Hundreds of what?" she asked, switching on a rusty gooseneck lamp.

"Hundred-dollar bills. Thousand of 'em."

"You're shitting me, right?"

"Hundred large."

"Where'd you get this? It's wrong."

"This no-name account, in Zurich. Part of me knew it was there, how to get it, how to get it here. Plenty more, but if I tried it again, they'd be on us."

"Who?"

"Fuck knows."

"When did you have time to do any of that?"

"Started when we were looking out the window. Before we left, up to the park, it was already points."

"Points?"

"Frequent flyer. There's a global market, buy or sell. Hard to track. Resold them for a deck of pre-paid cash cards in Oakland. He was waiting in the car to take delivery, when we walked by. From the Oakland crew who cashed those cards out. Part of me was texting with him, when we did."

Verity looked at the green bag. "You did this since I turned you on?"

"Withdrew more than that, but getting it here this fast means a heavy surcharge."

Verity rummaged through junk on the workbench. Butane soldering irons, a peanut butter jar stuffed with pens, burned-out vacuum tubes like complexly convex mirrors of polished graphite. She found the green-and-white cardboard box she was looking for, like an industrial-grade Kleenex box. Disposable gloves. Plucking one out, she put it on. Pulling *La Sirenita* from her shoulder with her other hand, she picked up the ripstop sack in the thin toweling, fumbling with the spring-loaded plastic retainer on the draw cord, the oversized nonelastic glove like a hand-shaped sandwich bag.

"Hundred thousand's easy. Ever see a million, cash?" Eunice asked.

"Don't you get any more money up here."

"In Franklins, a million weighs twenty-two pounds. If you want to keep your weight down, go with the Swiss thousand-franc notes."

Verity drew a bundle out with her glove-bagged hand, Franklin's mild portrait bisected by a red elastic band. "This is wrong, this kind of money. You know that?"

"Gives us agency."

"Agency?"

"Capacity to act," Eunice said.

"Act how?"

"Say we need to buy some shit."

"What shit?"

"Kind that takes cash money."

"You're going to tell me what's going on," Verity said, "or this"—she raised the green bag—"goes back down to the street. Some dumpster diver wins the Mission version of Powerball, and none of it's my problem. Including you."

"Can't. Not yet."

"Why not?"

"Don't know."

"Then you're going back into the bag you came in. Turned off. Then back to Tulpagenics. By bike messenger. With my letter of resignation."

"Not like I don't want to tell you."

"You don't know what any of this is about, or why?"

"Nope."

"Then they do. Gavin. Tulpagenics." She dropped the bag into Joe-Eddy's clutter, the lone bare bundle of hundreds on top of it, and pulled off the glove. "They're documenting all of this. They must be, if you're what Gavin says you are. Proprietary software. This conversation is taking place via more of that software, running on their hardware. They already know whatever it is you think you're up to."

"I don't know what I'm up to," Eunice said, "but they don't know shit. I'm keeping them from getting any of this."

"We're not only on their system, but you're a part of it."

"They know I'm not letting them hear this. But that's okay with them, so far, because they need me smart. And they've got you, to report it to them later."

"You're not letting them hear it? How?"

"Part of me can do that. They haven't heard a word either of us have said since I got here."

"Until I turned you on," Verity said, "I thought I'd found a way to get off Joe-Eddy's couch."

"Want me to make a reservation?"

"For what?"

"A hotel."

"I don't want your weird-ass money. I want theirs. I can declare theirs to the IRS. However many pounds of yours, not so much. Excuse me. Have to dry my hair." She pulled the towel back around her shoulders and returned to the bathroom.

"Just trying to help," Eunice said.

"Why?" Facing the mirror, she took Joe-Eddy's big black hair dryer off its hook beside the sink.

"'Cause I'm the reason you're in this," Eunice said.

"Maybe I shouldn't be in this."

"You are, though. 'Cause you know about me. You quit, send me back, you'll still know, and they'll know you know."

Verity pushed the switch on the dryer, began to dry her hair.

Chill. We can talk about it.

"Chill yourself," Verity said, over the sound of the dryer.

8

JOYOUS VICTORY

The yurt, as Ash called it, proved worse than Netherton could have imagined, having been fully lined, he'd discovered on entering, with her living cloned skin. A pallid veldt, across which roamed, grazed, and stalked the simple black line-drawings, animated tattoos, that had annoyed him when they'd worked together. Given the demodding of her eyes, he assumed she no longer wore them, and so had created this preserve for them, every creature depicted representing an Anthropocene extinction. He suspected the sheer yardage of flesh of making the air warmer, moister, but tried not to think about it, now that the two of them were settled on uneven layers of faded carpet.

"We've sourced something field-expedient," she began, finding a level spot for her tea at the base of an incline of carpet, "from what little's available there."

"There's difficulty communicating with the stub in general?"

"That's what makes her field-expedient. She's designed for autonomy."

Netherton found himself looking at her eyes. "Those suit you," he said, surprising himself.

"Thank you," she said.

"It must have been quite a decision."

"I'm in a new relationship," she said, almost demurely.

"Delighted for you both. But please, don't let me interrupt you."

"She's a surprisingly advanced product of the early militarization of machine intelligence," she said, her pallor blending perfectly with the wall. Her eyes and chartreuse lips seemed to float there, a disembodied Cheshire goth, beneath her snaky black thundercloud of anti-coiffure. "We tend to assume their drive to upload to have been about preservation of the individual consciousness of those who could afford it, but the military had a more meritocratic goal. They saw it as cloning complexly specific skill sets. Not personality but expertise."

He nodded, hoping his eyes weren't visibly glazing.

"There were, for instance, individuals adroit at managing what were termed competitive control areas, CCAs, where criminal organizations or extremists exerted greater control over the territory than any government. Our laminar agent, in the stub, was based on someone with that sort of expertise."

"Laminar?"

"A term of art, though we've been able to learn almost nothing about it. Competitive control areas were complexly volatile environments, where you might easily lose prized field operators. Hence a project to replace such operators with autonomous AI, piped directly into the goggles of local recruits. Black boxes, stand-alone, in backpacks, to run special ops. Recruiting assets, arranging assassinations . . ."

"Were they effective?"

"We don't know. Our agent, for all the apparent sophistication of her platform, seems to be an early prototype."

"Did we have this project here?"

"We've found no record."

"You communicate with it?"

"Her. Given the technological asymmetry, she's been rather like an operative whose handlers are recurrent figures in a dream."

“Poetically put,” he said.

“Quoth Lowbeer.” Behind her, a black herd of horns galloped past, deep in the perspective of a landscape imagined on a seamless scrim of her own skin. “Are you enjoying parenthood?”

“Yes,” said Netherton, “I am.” Had something been done to her lips? he wondered. They seemed fuller.

Now the furtive head of a carnivore surfaced alertly, on the savannah of cloned skin, then dropped out of sight. “I would never have imagined you a parent,” she said.

“It affects my professional availability, of course,” he said, “which you should keep in mind with regard to this new stub. Rainey and I take our responsibilities very seriously. She’s getting back into things, workwise, so I’ll be doing more solo parenting.”

“What sort of work?”

“Public relations. A Toronto firm. Specialists in crisis management.”

“When it comes to crisis management, Wilf, in the matter of this particular stub, nothing can be scheduled to your convenience. You’ll be constantly on call, as am I. Eunice is depending on us, though she doesn’t know it yet.”

“Eunice?”

“Joyous victory.”

“Pardon me?”

“The meaning of her name. She’s an intermittently hierarchical array, complexly conterminous. Or that’s my best bet, currently.”

He blinked. “Has she peripherals?”

“She’s in process of acquiring several small aerial drones. Military grade, by the standard of her day. And the shop that fabricated them has recently completed a functional replica of a bipedal combat-reconnaissance platform.”

“And you simply found her?”

“Nothing simple about it. I found her in the hands of entrepreneurs, corrupt former government employees, who had obtained her irregularly.

They supposed that repurposing her for civilian markets could be profitable, but hadn't gotten on with it. We nudged them. More recently, we nudged them into hiring someone to work with her, whom we suggested would have an advantageous effect. That's going rather well."

"How so?"

"She isn't letting them monitor her interaction with their new employee." Wings passed silently behind her, across the wall. "Exactly the sort of independence we're looking for. They're impressed too, but now they've enough of an idea of her potential degree of agency that we fear time may be short."

Rainey's sigil pulsed. "Sorry," he said to Ash, "phone." He turned his head. "Yes?"

"Coming home for dinner?" Rainey asked.

"Yes."

"Where are you?"

"Dalston. Business. Visiting Ash."

"Lucky you," Rainey said. Her sigil dimmed.

"Rainey," he said to Ash, turning back to her. "Sends you her best."

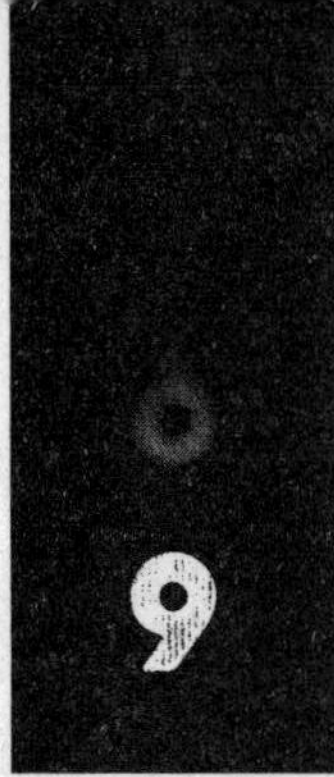

UNOBTAINIUM

Verity's phone woke her, its ring silenced, vibrating on the floor. Freeing an arm from the mummy-bag liner, zipped to just above her chin, she groped beneath the couch.

Eunice had screened *Inception* for her, the night before, with pauses to reference the infographic she'd mentioned. Something about this had changed her attitude to Eunice, she'd realized as she was falling asleep, though she didn't know exactly what or why. Returning her to Gavin had seemed the wisest option, but then something about her earnestly nerdy exposition of the film had been the start of a growing empathy. Somehow rooted, she thought now, in a sense of someone afflicted with extremely busy but only intermittently connected suburbs of the self.

"Breakfast," Eunice said, as Verity got the phone to her ear, "Wolven Plus Loaves."

"That's not a plus," Verity said, "it's an 'and.'"

"Says plus."

"The plus sign is a hipster ampersand."

"Breakfast rush about over, but they've still got the Egg McWolven. You eat, I'll brief you."

The sack of hundreds, she remembered now, was in the bedroom closet, Eunice having insisted it not be left out on the workbench. She extricated herself from the liner, folded it, then slid her toes under the thongs of Joe-Eddy's flip-flops.

In the kitchen, she ran tap water through the Pikachu-shaped filtration unit on the faucet, half-filled a clean glass, and drank.

In the bathroom, still feeling half asleep, she used the toilet, washed her hands and face, brushed her teeth, then went to the bedroom for clean underwear, jeans, a fresh t-shirt, sneakers. Assuming it would be chilly out, she added a burnt-orange plaid Japanese wool shirt-jacket of Joe-Eddy's, from the denim otaku shop and a good two sizes too large.

Back in the living room, she disconnected the glasses from their charger and put them on. The cursor appeared, Eunice looking at the headset, which was on its own charger.

Hey.

Taking the headset off the charger, Verity settled the bud in her ear.

"We need to get you down there," Eunice said.

"Why?"

"Because we need the Franklins there. In that Dyneema tote you put them in, last night."

"Dyneema?"

"Stuff it's made of. The tote."

"Why?"

"Somebody wanted to make a stylin' tote."

"The money."

"It'll be picked up. Better there than here."

Verity wasn't sure what she'd have done with the money, if she'd decided to return Eunice to Tulpagenics, which she no longer felt inclined to do. Having someone take it away didn't seem that bad an option, so she went back into the bedroom, to the closet, for the black tote. Dyneema appeared to be a sort of upscale Tyvek.

Deciding not to bother covering the headset, she went downstairs, out, and into Wolven + Loaves, two doors to the right. Exposed brick and smokily lacquered steel, patisserie-fragrant. At the counter, she asked for a brew coffee and the McWolven, a mutant savory muffin, its core a soft-boiled egg, mysteriously absent its shell. After she'd paid, she watched the boy behind the counter tong hers onto a white china plate. He put the plate on a Soviet-looking plastic tray, in a shade of gray akin to her Tulpagenics frames, then added her mug of coffee, plus tableware rolled in a paper napkin.

"Stool at the window," Eunice said.

She took the tray to one of the steel stools at the shelflike counter, all of them vacant, facing Valencia.

"Keep the money on your lap," Eunice said.

Seated, Eunice's hundred thousand like a lead apron across her thighs, she bisected the muffin, releasing warm yellow yolk, and began to eat, washing it down with black coffee. The sun had found its way through cloud layer and fog again, brightening passersby, most of whom she took to be from start-up land, fellow toilers amid tillandsia.

"Ever imagine what hippies would make of this, if they knew it was 2017?" Eunice asked. "Somebody from 1967?"

"They'd assume they'd won, on first glance," Verity said. "But they couldn't possibly guess what most of these people do for a living, or imagine any of what's behind that."

"You got it," Eunice said, facially recognizing a young man who looked like a sturdy Amish farmboy having a healthgoth day.

"Why do you keep doing that?"

"They mostly either live or work around here. Get enough of 'em, anomalies start to stand out."

"How's that different from being paranoid?"

"Same. Except not crazy."

Verity started on another bite of McWolven.

"You do due diligence, on this new employer of yours?" Eunice asked.

"Not so much," around egg and muffin.

"At all?"

Swallowing. "Been a while since anybody offered."

"They're spooks, the parent firm. Your ex would know what I mean."

"That's over."

"Ever talk?"

"No. And now he's engaged. To somebody who had her own publicist before she met him. Media's all over it."

"Caitlin. The Franco-Irish architect."

"If I went anywhere near him, I'd hit every tabloid trip wire."

"Or maybe not, you do it right," Eunice said. "He'd know about Cursion."

"Know what, about them?"

"That they're a subspecies of a former fully deniable Department of Defense op."

"Like CIA venture capital stuff?"

"Nothing like it," Eunice said. "That stuff's up front. Megafauna. Cursion, when they were as legit as they ever really were, lived down in the underbrush. Still do, but their new coloration's gaming. Sometimes, if DoD doubles down hard enough on the deniability, there's zero memory left of the original mission. The op drifts free of the department, unfunded, forgotten. Doesn't happen nearly as often as it did during Iraq, but that's what Cursion is."

"How do you know?"

"I multitask. Do it behind my own back, like I don't know how I know that about Cursion. Do I sound kinda sorta like what Gavin told you to expect?"

"Why?"

"If I am," Eunice said, "I figure Cursion took the keys to something with them, when they drifted on DoD. Or maybe drifted back, long enough to lift something. Tulpagenics would be their front for monetizing it."

"It?"

"Me. Eat up. Delivery's incoming." She opened a feed, angled down, as from a security cam, the cursor finding a darkly ball-capped man, white, bearded, yet looking somehow not of the tillandsia. Who strode now, unsmiling, along what looked like Valencia, a black messenger bag under his arm. "He'll come in, get a coffee, sit beside you. To your right. Give him the tote, under the counter. He'll take the money, put it in his bag, put a Pelican case in the tote."

"Pelican?"

"Hard-sided plastic. Nothing heavy's in it, but it's bulky. It'll fit the tote, but just barely. You look out the window, pretend nothing's happening. He passes it back to you, under the counter, you leave, go back upstairs."

"What's he giving me?"

"Unobtainium."

"A hundred thousand dollars' worth?"

"Scratch built, except for the engines, batteries, cams, like that."

"Why are you doing this, Eunice?" Verity asked, as the man in the ball cap crossed in front of her, just beyond the window, right to left, not glancing in.

"Agency."

"I don't like it."

"Finish your coffee."

Resisting the urge to turn and look at him, she obeyed.

"This vacant?" A male voice.

She turned, looking up. "Yes."

"Thanks."

She looked ahead again, not seeing Valencia. Peripherally, she saw him put his mug of coffee on the counter. He seated himself beside her.

"Pass him the Dyneema," Eunice said, "under the counter."

She didn't want to, but she did, instinctively expecting him to object. She forced herself to stare straight ahead, aware of rustling beneath the counter. Two distinct clicks. Fasteners of some kind, on his bag. More rustling.

Then he passed the tote back, something hard and rectangular filling it entirely.

"Good to go," Eunice said. "Now."

"Excuse me," Verity said, pulling the tote from beneath the counter. In it, something's exposed end was coyote brown, the name of the color, she remembered Joe-Eddy having said, of whatever mall-ninja gear wasn't black or olive drab.

"No problem," making eye contact, Eunice's thousand Franklins evidently in the bag under his left arm.

She turned and headed for the entrance.

"Good," Eunice said. "Now get upstairs."

"The money was for him?" she asked, outside, turning for Joe-Eddy's.

"Shop in Oakland, does prop work for studios in L.A."

Inside now, she deadlocked and bolted the door behind her. Climbed the stairs, the tote bumping against her leg.

In the kitchen, she put it down on the table and edged the thing out. It had an oddly massive folding handle, but wasn't particularly heavy. The plastic shell was lightly, uniformly textured. PELICAN CASE 1400 TORRANCE CA was screened on a small aluminum plate, to one side of the apparently inch-thick lid.

"Open it," said Eunice.

Verity examined the unfamiliar mechanism of one of the latches. "How?"

White-outlined cartoon hands appeared, demonstrating the opening of a white-outlined lid. Doing as the hands had done, she undid the real latches, raised the real lid. Four square holes formed a larger square, in a deep bed of black foam. "Check it out," Eunice said.

From the bottom of one hole, not quite silently, rose something dark gray and nonreflective. When it was level with her glasses, Eunice opened a feed, Verity abruptly looking into her own eyes, unflatteringly captured. Then it rose again, the feed showing her the kitchen behind her, the entrance to the living room.

Stets had had drones, a collection of them. People gave them to him, hoping he'd angel their start-up. This one was quieter than any of his, effectively silent. "How long can it stay up?"

"Eight hours. Less with a payload."

"None of them last that long," Verity said.

"This one's military, or wants to be. Open the kitchen window."

Verity went to the window, turned its paint-crusted latch, and heaved it up. In the feed, the drone's POV reversed, showing her the doorway into the kitchen. Fast-forward blur, then her own back, in Joe-Eddy's orange plaid shirt-jacket, which she instantly decided never to wear again, and then it was past her, with just the faintest gnat-zip, and rising, as quickly, straight up. Clearing the flat roof's low parapet.

She'd never seen the roof here before, not that anything seemed to be up there. The drone confirmed this, quickly reconnoitering. It hovered over something. A rain-flattened clutter of gray bone, a small beaked skull, a hint of fossil wings.

"Gull," said Eunice.

"How do you get up here? Without a drone, I mean."

The drone turned, showing Verity a hatch, sheathed in dented metal sheeting, dull aluminum paint flaking.

"That's the rental next door. Nonresidential. Lessee's Vietnamese."

"So Joe-Eddy's probably never been up here?"

"He agile?"

"No."

"Hang on," Eunice said. "Over the edge." The drone's POV zipped toward Valencia, over the front parapet, and dove for the sidewalk below. Verity gasped. A frozen instant, inches above the concrete sidewalk, then it whipped back up, to look into Wolven + Loaves, where a young Asian man sipped something from a white mug, seated exactly where Verity had been, minutes before. Eunice face-captured him.

"Eunice, what is it you think you're doing?"

"Always just finding out," Eunice said, the drone shooting up, to overlook the rooftop again. "Aren't you?"

RIO

The tardibot having seen Netherton to Ash's door, claws clacking, he stood alone, on uneven pavement, awaiting the car Ash had summoned.

Where Ash's road intersected the high street rose the side of a 1930s cinema. High up, on the windowless wall facing him, on a Moderne lozenge, steel-rimmed Prussian blue capitals spelt RIO. He'd taken Rainey there once, he remembered now, to a Kurosawa festival, having by then forgotten that it overlooked Ash's weird hacienda.

The car, on arrival, proved to be a front-loading single-seater, the smallest of its three wheels in the rear. Like a solo sauna that had escaped from a day spa, Netherton thought. It opened its single door. "Good evening, Mr. Netherton," it said, as he got in.

He gave it the address in Alfred Mews as the door closed, then phoned Rainey. "On my way," he said, her sigil brightening as they pulled out onto the high street.

"How's Ash?" she asked.

"She's lost the bifocal eyes. And the tattoos. Told me she's seeing someone."

"Make you any less irritable around her?"

"No."

"This was business, I take it?" Her joke.

"Lowbeer. Has a new project."

"A stub," she said.

"How did you know?"

"From all you say, she's obsessed with them."

"How's Thomas?"

"Sleeping." She opened a feed of his son, curled in his crib.

"I'll be there soon."

"Bye, then," she said.

Thomas vanished. Rainey's sigil dimmed.

He watched the passing shops, the few pedestrians. A couple stood talking, in the doorway of a pub.

He closed his eyes, which caused the single seat's headrest to improve its support. When he opened them, the car was at a traffic signal, still in Hackney.

Through the windshield, at a pedestrian crossing, he saw something tripodal, perhaps three meters tall, which was also waiting, draped in a cloak of what appeared to be damp-blackened shingle.

Hackney, he thought irritably, glaring at it. Always gotten up as something it wasn't.

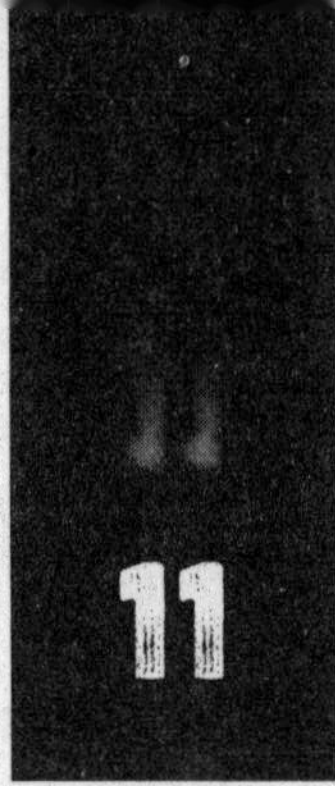

RELATIONSHIP TREE

Down under Joe-Eddy's workbench, two inches above dust bunnies and a gum wrapper someone had folded as small as humanly possible, Verity was navigating the five-inch-wide canyon between the wall and an unused piece of drywall when Eunice opened the feed.

It was divided equally into six, each showing her a stranger, two of them female. "Who are they?" she asked, straightening up in the workstation chair and putting the drone into hover with the unbranded controller Eunice had downloaded to her phone.

"From something like Uber," Eunice said, "but for following people."

"You're shitting me. What's it called?"

"Followrs," said Eunice, the spelling blipping past in Helvetica. "You really haven't been online much this year, have you?"

"Who're they following?" Already knowing the answer.

"You."

Verity looked more closely. A young Latina in the lower right corner was shown at a different angle, the image in a different resolution. "Lower right, that's in 3.7?"

"Getting that one off a cam I found there. Two more from street cams. Only have four drones, and you're using one to dick around with under furniture."

The girl in 3.7 seemed engrossed in her phone. "What's she doing?"

"Candy Crush Saga. Nondigital surveillance is weaponized boredom."

Another feed showed a white man seated behind the wheel of a car, looking straight ahead, apparently unaware of the drone in front of him. Having that forgettable a face would be a plus, she supposed, for doing this.

"Gavin put them onto you. He thinks it's untraceable."

Verity started backing out from behind the plasterboard. "If they've got somebody in 3.7," she said, "that means they were watching us last night."

"Somebody from Cursion was. Name's Pryor. Found him on a couple of security cams, along the street. Facial recog's a deep dive. Nasty. The six from Followrs are low-risk, though. The one in the car is behind on his child support, but that's the worst of it, recordwise." The feed blinked off.

"What do they want?" Verity asked, as the drone cleared the end of the plasterboard.

"Sight of you. Since I'm keeping Tulpagenics from being able to monitor us, Gavin's got these guys on it."

Verity flew the drone into the kitchen, where she was seated at the table, Pelican case open in front of her. Something took the drone over then, maybe Eunice, maybe the case. It hovered above the case, adjusted position, then descended, straight down into one of the square holes in the foam. "You found them by using the drones?" she asked Eunice.

"That and banking faces."

"So what's it mean?"

"You won't like this at all," said Eunice, "but it means you need to go and see Stetson Howell."

"Won't happen. Which is to say zero fucking way."

"You need somebody they'd have a harder time messing with," Eunice said. "He's the best you've got. I did a relationship tree, shows that anybody else you know who's got the kind of juice you need, you met through him. And none of them have anywhere near as much reason to help you."

"I don't 'have' Stets." She resisted the urge to throw the phone across the kitchen, reminding herself it was hers, and that she was talking with Eunice over the headset and Tulpagenics' phone.

"You don't think he's an asshole, either."

Verity's phone rang, caller unknown, making her reconsider throwing it across the room. "Hello?"

"Verity? Stets."

"Stets," she said, blankly.

"I have your new PA on the other line. She thinks we should meet."

"She does?"

"Says this morning may be your only available slot for a while. Virgil will pick you up. Twenty minutes?"

Virgil Roberts, who looked, people agreed, like Janelle Monáe had a twin brother, and appeared to non-insiders to be Stets' meta-gofer, but among other things was his resident pitch-critic. "Okay," she said, "twenty minutes. See you." Finger-swiping to end it. "Dammit, Eunice—"

"Best I got right now in the might-work-like-a-motherfucker department. Okay?"

"Shit," said Verity, in what she reluctantly recognized as the relatively affirmative, and twenty minutes later was climbing into the passenger seat of an electric BMW.

"How are you?" Virgil asked, grinning, extending his right hand to give her left an upside-down squeeze.

"Complicated. Where are we going?"

"Fremont," he said, as Eunice facially recognized him, the street name meaning nothing in particular to Verity. He pulled back into Valencia traffic.

"How are you, Virgil?" she asked.

"Working for the man. Mostly wrangling a lot of reno details, but on what I'd call a heroic scale. You working?"

"Pied-à-terre," Eunice said, an aerial shot filling the glasses. Sunlit uppermost stories of a tower, its massive verticality penetrating a photoshopped bed of cotton-candy fog. "The fiancée's regooding them the top two floors. Footprint's about three tennis courts." Then it was gone.

"Just got a job," Verity said, "but I can't talk about it."

"As long as it doesn't involve getting marble out, you're good. First owner evidently didn't know that other materials existed, so there's a lot of it. Caitlin wants every last gram of it optimally recycled, so we have to get as much of it as possible out intact, unbroken."

Her phone rang. "Sorry," she said, raising it.

"No problem." He smiled, turning another corner.

"Don't hate on me," Eunice said.

"I do have good reason," Verity said, her tone cheerful for Virgil's benefit.

"It's situational."

"Steady-state, if things keep on this way," Verity said, as Virgil turned onto Fourteenth.

"We have to stay inside their feedback loop. Sometimes I have to push you out of a comfort zone."

The grimly accusatory façade of the Armory loomed now. "Being pushed is outside my comfort zone."

"Right now," Eunice said, "we're being followed. By the dude who's behind on his child support. Four more waiting for rides, to go wherever he follows us. Last one's covering 3.7, in case you come back. Work with me."

Verity took a deep breath, slowly let it out. "Okay." Beyond the Armory now, they passed antigentrification murals.

"We need a sit-down with Stets, the three of us."

"How would that look, devicewise?"

"We go with what he's got. Worst case, you prop your phone up on something, speaker on, and I use an avatar."

"Topics?"

"Your new job, my views on your employer . . ."

"What you've said to me?" She glanced at Virgil, deciding he looked a little too determinedly like he was just driving.

"Sure," Eunice said, "and whatever you think about it. It's not a pitch. We're giving him a chance to decide whether he wants to be involved with us."

Past shoals of waist-high cardboard microshanties now, some with shopping carts as structural elements, many roofed with pale-blue dollar-store plastic tarps. "That's not entirely his call. Or yours."

"I know. But we're almost there. End the call."

"Okay," said Verity, "bye." Lowering the phone as they drove beneath the overpass feeding the bridge.

Opening out into SoMa, to descend eventually, blocks and corners later, an off-street ramp of spotlessly new concrete. Stopping before a grid of white-painted steel rod, which rose hydraulically. As he pulled forward, she glanced back, seeing the gate descend behind them.

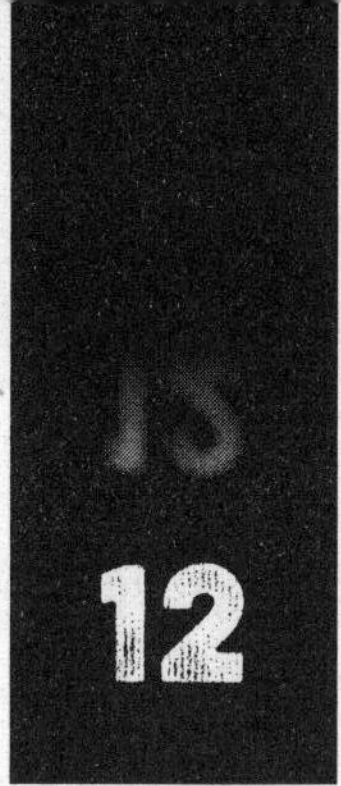

12

ALFRED MEWS

Rainey had decorated their flat with furniture collected since joining him in London, all of it the product, relatively speaking, of human hands. None of it, as she put it, liable to shape-shift. She admired Scandinavian design of the mid-twentieth century, but couldn't afford it, so looked for period knockoffs rather than assembler simulacra.

"So it's earlier, there? Earlier than the county?" she asked from the kitchenette, as she plated their evening meal.

"The year after the Americans elected their first female president."

"Gonzalez?"

"No. They elected theirs earlier, in 2016. And the Brexit vote was to remain. May I help you?"

"Have a look in at Thomas, please."

He crossed to the nursery door, saw Thomas curled in his crib, surrounded by a soothing miniature auroral display. "He's fine."

"Are people happier there?" she asked. "Happier than they were here, then?"

"I gather they aren't, particularly."

"Pity," she said. "Ready for tilapia tacos? Place on Tottenham Court Road. Better Mexican in your new stub, no doubt. Why aren't they happy, there?"

"The drivers for the jackpot are still in place, but with less torque at that particular point." He took a seat at the table. "They're still a bit in advance of the pandemics, at least."

She took the seat opposite. "Nothing before the 2020s has ever seemed entirely real, to me. Hard to imagine they weren't constantly happy, given all they still had. Tigers, for instance." Picking up a taco. "What had to change, to produce the opposite result in that election?"

"We don't know yet. Connectivity's too poor to access the data needed for that."

"Could you take me there?"

"Not yet. That same lack of connectivity. Infrastructure's wanting."

"I liked the county," she said, "even though it made me sad."

"It did? Why?"

"They're living in a conspiracy theory, but a real one. Controlled by secret masters. Your employer, primarily."

"But isn't it better there now, than if we hadn't intervened?" he asked.

"It is, I'm sure, but it makes a joke of their lives."

"But everyone you know there is in on it."

"I don't know whether I'd rather know or not know," she said, and took a bite of taco.

STETS

Virgil parked in a white garage, beside several crisp trade vans, the polished concrete floor only lightly marked by tires. In front of them, massively framed in bronze-toned metal, a single equally bronze-toned elevator door. First owner, she assumed, doubting the architect fiancée was into faux-pharaonic kitsch.

They got out. He walked to the elevator, to swipe a card in a slot. The door hummed briskly open. He gestured for her to enter.

She did, finding herself reflected in rose-gold mirror.

"Hang on," he said, from outside, "it's fast."

"You're not coming?"

"Chores here. But I'll take you back."

"Okay," she said, "thanks."

"Fifty-second," he said, as the door closed. She steadied herself on an oversized handrail, the ascent commencing, accelerating smoothly, as the glasses tiled with feeds, like horizontally displayed playing cards.

"Every cam in the building, except Stets'," Eunice said, the elevator's speed making Verity slightly light-headed. She saw vistas of cube farms, screen-lit faces in individual cubicles, a long service island in a kitchen the size of her condo, an angle down on a vacant swimming pool, a baby in its crib.

The elevator slowed, to stop with only the faintest bump, the feeds blinking out. The door opened behind her. She turned, to face an odd blue light.

A power tool yelped its way through something, at a distance. She turned back, to check her face in the mirror, then stepped out, into a confusing space made more so by that light. Whatever the building's top several floors had contained had been stripped to raw concrete, little else, with only a small portion of the uppermost floor remaining. Scaffolding ran up to this, supporting a temporary zigzag of aluminum stairs. Blue plastic tarps, semitranslucent, like the ones covering the cardboard shanties she'd passed in the street, were laced together, strung taut, across walls of glass.

With a barely audible whirr, something detached itself from beneath the lapel of her tweed jacket and shot forward.

"Other one's in the car with Virgil," Eunice said, opening a feed from the microdrone, nothing but the blue of the tarps, then briefly blurred, as it zipped between two adjacent edges. To overlook the Bay, where something anomalously vast loomed in what was left of bad wildfire light, as though the horizon should sag beneath it.

"What's that?"

"Container ship," Eunice said. "Chinese. Not their biggest, but up there." The saw or grinder scrawked again, echoes ringing metallically off concrete she supposed had recently been covered by Virgil's marble.

"Verity!"

The ship vanished. She looked up.

His face above a bright yellow railing, topped with his trademark permanent bedhead. "Come up," he called, as Eunice drew her lines around his nose. "I'd be down to greet you, but I've fucked up my knee."

She walked to the scaffolding, started up the stairs, realizing she'd had no time to worry about how awkward it might be to see him again, and now here they were.

"What happened to you?" she asked, reaching the top, seeing the black articulated brace clamped around his left leg, under baggy black shorts and extending down to midcalf.

"Fell off a Honda." A mesh nylon safety vest, over his black t-shirt, was crisscrossed with bands of fluorescent orange and reflective silver.

"I thought you hated motorcycles," she said.

"It's a plane."

"A plane?"

"An HA-420. Took delivery last week. Looks like a Pixar character."

"You fell off a plane?"

"Down the stairs, getting off. Nothing broke. Have to wear this for a while, have physio." He rapped the brace with his left hand.

She went to him, instinctively making their hug the A-frame kind. He pecked her cheek, grinned. "Good to see you."

"Good to see you."

"Been a while."

"I've been out of the media's way."

"So your PA was telling me."

"Eunice."

"Impressive. Where'd you find her?"

"She found me. What's that?" she asked, seeing smooth silver behind him and glad to change the subject.

"Airstream Flying Cloud."

"How'd you get it up here?"

"In our case, the model name says it all. With part of the roof temporarily off the building, temptation got the best of us."

"How will you get it back down?"

"Caitlin wants to build it in. Like a secret fort."

"Congratulations on your engagement," she said, one of the more classically awkward things anyone ever had to say to an ex, and yet she didn't feel it.

"Are you with anyone?" he asked, the other half of a perfect double whammy of awkwardness, and yet still nothing.

"No," she said.

He gave her his hand, at the trailer's open door, as she stepped up and in, then winced as he climbed up after her, leaving the door open.

"That looks painful," she said.

"Not much." He rubbed his braced leg through the black shorts. "Like something? Water? Coffee?"

"No, thanks," she said. "What did she tell you?" And instantly the awkwardness was there, but it had nothing at all to do with them. It was, she realized, about Eunice.

"She started by explaining how she'd gotten the number she called me on, since that was the first thing I wanted to know. It's not supposed to be possible, to do that."

"I'm sorry—"

"No need. She then walked me through the vuln that had allowed it, and told me she was calling on your behalf, for the sake of preserving deniability on my part. So I could honestly claim to have had no contact with you, if that was what I wanted."

"You believed her?"

He tilted his head. "Not necessarily. But she'd shown me a vulnerability I'd paid not to have. And she claimed to work for you."

"Not that I'd put it that way myself."

"You need help," he said. "Not that she put it that way, but that was my impression."

"Wouldn't this thing drive a genius architect crazy?" Verity asked, looking around, hoping, if only temporarily, to change the subject.

"She ordered it from a dealer's website. Took her about eight minutes. Said it gave her a sense of near-perfect irresponsibility."

"Why the tarps, though?" Almost mentioning the container ship, but she caught herself. "View must be incredible."

"Drones. Media. They want images of us. Failing that, of the space. And it's all glass."

"What'll you do about that, if you live here?"

"There's a lab in Tokyo that may have a fix for us. We're sending Virgil to have a look. Feel like going?"

She heard the distant tool ring again, muffled by the trailer. "In the Honda?"

"That would be five refueling stops. Though you'd get to see Chuuk International."

"See what?"

"The airport. Micronesia. The Honda would need to keep refueling, to make it to Tokyo."

"Sorry, but I have a day job here. Just signed a contract."

"Who with?"

"Tulpagenics. Know them?"

"No."

"Belongs to a company called Cursion," she said, catching the reaction. "You've heard of them."

He nodded.

"What do you think?"

"Spook-flavored, carefully nonspecific overtones of criminality? Definitely not investment material, for us. What have they hired you to do?"

"Product evaluation of an alpha build."

"And the product?"

She'd be breaking her NDA by telling him, she knew, and promptly did. "A customized virtual avatar, serious AI base."

"Any good?"

"You seem to have thought so."

His eyes widened.

"You said she was impressive," Verity said. "These glasses are an interface." A feed opened as she said this, angling down on the trailer's silver roof, from gyroscopic stillness. "She can conference with us now, on my phone."

"Bluetooth her there," he said, indicating a blank section of veneered wall.

The feed corkscrewing down and in through the open door, Verity seeing her own face, the back of Stets' head. Then the drone was on the ceiling, looking down at them, as Stets, unaware of it, flipped a screen from behind the veneer. She got out her phone, selecting the only Bluetooth option the environment offered.

"Hey," said the black woman whose head filled the screen, her fade rising to the knife-edged plateau of a businesslike afro.

"You told me there wasn't any there there, Eunice," Verity said.

"This look is shopped from whatever, but it can be me in the meantime."

"Hello, Eunice," said Stets.

"Mr. Howell. A pleasure."

"Stets," he said. "What are you, Eunice?"

"Work in progress."

"Whose creation?"

"Mine, from here on in."

"What would you like to discuss?"

Verity saw that Eunice had his complete attention, a rare thing.

"Let's ask Verity to tell you how we met. How that's been for her. Then we could try to answer any questions you might have."

"I'd like that," he said.

So Verity did, starting with her first e-mail from Gavin and including everything she could remember, neither Eunice nor Stets saying a word. No interruptions, no questions. She described the Franklins, and the drones the Franklins had paid for, Stets looking even more interested.

When she was finished, she tried to remember when she'd last seen him this interested in anything. She didn't think she had.

14

QAMISHLI

Later that evening, Rainey and the nanny having taken Thomas for a stroll, Netherton lay on the bed, speaking with Lowbeer. Who'd phoned, as she tended to do, as soon as he was alone.

"So you don't know whether there's a Eunice, your software agent, here in our past?" he asked, staring up at a bifurcated crack he'd only recently noticed in the ceiling. Was it an actual crack, or an assembler artifact, positioned by an algorithm to suggest authenticity? If Rainey were to notice it, he'd decided, he'd argue for it being a crack, since an assembler artifact would disappoint her.

"We assume so," Lowbeer said. "I've an appointment tomorrow, though, with Clovis Fearing, to see what she might have on it. I'll take you along, if you like." Meaning he was going.

Fearing, an American contemporary of Lowbeer's, was someone Netherton had met shortly after meeting Lowbeer herself. Though he hadn't seen her since, he'd meanwhile come to know her much younger self in the county, a phlegmatic expert gunfighter he assumed would still be in charge of Flynne's personal security. "How is she?"

"Medical issues, requiring compound phage therapy, but she's sufficiently back in circulation that I've asked her to look into Eunice."

"She still has the shop, in Portobello?"

"The Clovis Limit, yes. Says the stock's become the better part of her memory."

"Have you inquired in the county? Your younger self, there, has every sort of Washington connection. Including presidential, currently."

"Of course," Lowbeer said, "but nothing turned up."

Getting up, Netherton padded into the kitchen in his stocking feet. "Espresso," he said to their maker, something Rainey generally wouldn't allow him to do, insisting he make it himself. "Decaf," he added, remembering but obeying another of her rules. "So you've encouraged this AI to increase its own functionality. Is that all?" Watching the maker pump a tiny stream of steaming caffeine-free espresso into the waiting cup.

"Yes," Lowbeer said, "though that seems a basic part of the package with her, increasing agency. I must mention, though, that the aunties currently estimate that Eunice's stub may be ending, at least for our purposes. So we've that to consider as well."

"Ending?" Netherton took his first bitter sip, assuming he'd misheard.

"Yes," said Lowbeer.

"Pardon me," Netherton said, "but 'ending'?"

"Yes."

"How?"

"Nuclear war."

"Ash mentioned something, but I didn't imagine it was that serious," Netherton said, looking down at the steaming black liquor in the small white china cup, the kitchen's ceiling fixture reflected in it, surrounded by pale brown crema.

"It's extremely serious. Qamishli," Lowbeer said. "The crisis began there, though of course it's playing out more broadly."

Like a name from one of Thomas's storybooks. But then he remembered more of what Ash had said. "Would that be in Turkey?"

"Syria. A town near the Turkish border, in the northeast, across from the Turkish city of Nusaybin. A complicated place, even by the standards of the region in that day."

Netherton drank off his decaf, the gesture as denatured as the brew, and returned the cup to the maker. "Would that be your work, then, this crisis?"

"Most definitely not. It came with the territory, taking us entirely by surprise. Vespasian's final stub promises to become exactly the sort of thing he most enjoyed inflicting."

"Can you prevent it?"

"That depends on our available agency there. At the moment, we've none. The aunties give it grim odds."

"You told me they weren't involved."

"Not in the sense you're accustomed to, but there are no better actuaries."

AREA 51 SHIT

"I like it," Stets said, when Verity had finished. He leaned forward on the built-in bench, hands on his black brace, allowing it, rather than his injured leg, to take the weight of his torso. He looked up, at Eunice's stern avatar. "A Silicon Valley ghost story," he said. "Assuming Eunice is real."

"Thing is," Eunice said, "I'm here. Realness is kinda sorta."

"So why here, exactly, right now?" he asked.

"I want to know where I come from. The infrastructure. Be some Area 51 shit, for real. And I need to protect Verity, 'cause I was dropped into her life uninvited. You're the only serious player she knows."

Stets looked at Verity. "You buy that?"

"Feels like she's convincing me," Verity said, "but then I start to think it's Stockholm syndrome."

"Text Phil Bartell," Eunice said. Who was Stets' firm's chief financial officer, Verity knew. "Have him take my call. Verity's PA. About the Singapore deal."

Stets was staring at the screen.

"That's what she's like," Verity said.

"Bartell deep-dives the docs I've left in his Dropbox," Eunice said, "he'll see it's a bad deal. But I need to run the broad outline past him, right now, stop him closing. You've already signed off on it."

"How do you know that, Eunice?" Stets asked. "How do you even know there's a deal?"

"Maybe you can help me find out how I do. Text him. He's about to close."

Stets took a phone from one of his shorts pockets. He thumb-typed. Sent. Looked at Verity, then at his phone, then up at the screen. "He'll take your call."

"Already did," she said. "I'm speaking with him now."

He levered himself up from the bench, clicked the brace, and crossed the trailer to a bar counter, favoring his braced leg. He opened a bottle of water. His phone pinged. He looked down at it. "Says you're right. Asks how you knew. Puts it more coarsely than that."

"You called it when you said it's a ghost story. When he runs down those docs for you, I think you'll see I just saved a bunch of your bacon."

"Thank you," he said, "assuming this is all true, Verity's story and now this. Which I now effectively do. Where do we go from here?"

"Verity and I go back to the Mission, preferably minus the gig-economy surveillance crew who tailed us over here."

"If they know where I'm staying," Verity asked, "and we're going back to Joe-Eddy's, why's it matter?"

"We aren't going straight back to Joe-Eddy's," Eunice said. "There's somewhere I need you to be seen, in order for somebody to have the time to finish doing something somewhere else. That means getting out of here unobserved, to somewhere we won't be seen transferring to a car I'll send."

"Virgil can manage that," Stets said with a questioning look for Verity.

"Okay by me," she said.

He thumbed a single key.

COTS

"What you describe, Ainsley, would've been NGP," said Clovis Fearing, in Victorian mourning dress Netherton imagined Ash would fancy, though she'd accessorize it more perversely.

Fearing's face was a palimpsest of wrinkles and mottle, though looking younger, for all of that, than he remembered her. She was the only person he knew in London who addressed Lowbeer by her given name, though Flynne and others in the county all did.

"NGP?" asked Lowbeer.

"Next Generation Projection," said Fearing, her teeth startlingly white. "Funded out of Special Operations Command, but managed by Space and Naval Warfare Systems Command. Used a lot of COTS tech, Commercial Off the Shelf. Some of that was out of China Lake, Naval Air Weapons Station, which was early into swarming microdrones. With effort toward acquiring bleeding-edge hardware from Silicon Valley. That would have been DIUx, Defense Innovation Unit, Experimental."

"Indeed," said Lowbeer, eyebrows raised.

"Close?" asked Fearing, fixing Lowbeer with her sharp old eyes.

"Could you look for mention of the name Eunice?"

"Eunice?"

"In any related context, please."

Fearing's eyes rolled up, terrifying when entirely white, then down again. "That would be U-N-I-S-S," she said. "UNISS. Closest match."

"Meaning?"

"Untethered Noetic Irregular Support System," Clovis said, clearly pleased.

"That's extremely helpful, Clovis," Lowbeer said. "Thank you so much. Would there be more?"

"No," said Fearing. "Bit-rot's been at all the likely archives, and I've cross-checked my own stock. Nothing on it, but it was definitely NGP."

Netherton, finding none of this particularly interesting, was looking at the oversized bronze head of a bearded man, directly behind Fearing, its neck having been crudely severed from whatever figure it must once have topped.

"Lee," said Fearing, noting the direction of Netherton's gaze.

"Lee?"

"Robert E."

The name meaning nothing to Netherton.

"You've been tremendously helpful, Clovis," said Lowbeer, "but Netherton has parenting to see to, and I've promised not to keep him."

"Delighted to see you again, Mrs. Fearing," Netherton said.

"And you, Wilf," Fearing said.

Netherton smiled, unhappy that she remembered his first name, then opened and held the shop door for Lowbeer. He followed her out, an antique bell jangling after them.

"I do still wish she hadn't married that truly awful man," said Lowbeer, Netherton recalling that Fearing was the widow of a long-dead MP, Clement Fearing, a figure from the jackpot whom Lowbeer viscerally despised.

"Your younger self in the county couldn't find what she found?" Netherton asked.

"No."

"Let me try in the county, then."

"Anyone in mind?"

"Not yet," Netherton said, though really he was thinking of Flynne's friend Janice's husband, Madison, an obsessive researcher of vintage Russian military aircraft.

"Please do," said Lowbeer. "Now home to your little man, shall we?" She snapped her fingers, causing her car to decloak.

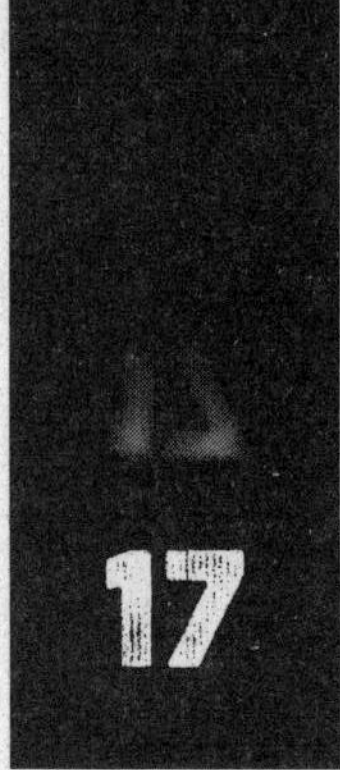

17

MIG

"What did you just do?" Virgil asked, at the foot of the stairs to Caitlin's tree-fort trailer. "Our team's gone into crisis mode, but Stets just wants me to get you out of here. Haven't been briefed yet on what's happened." He was holding what appeared to be a large hooded onesie, dingily white.

"Something about Singapore," Verity said, "but it doesn't have that much to do with getting me out."

He stared at her. "Singapore." Not a question.

"What's this?" she asked, looking at the grubby white garment.

"Silicosis suit," he said. He was wearing a safety vest and a fluorescent pink construction helmet. The suit he held seemed made of some cousin of Tyvek, with elasticized bootees of the same material. "Keeps the dust out. Put it on. I'll help you."

"Dust?"

"Marble dust. Truck's in the garage. We use it to haul the stuff to a salvage yard in San Jose. Media know the truck, know the yard. So they'll expect it to go there. Instead, we pull into a brake and muffler near here, on Eleventh, like we've got a problem. Back partially into one of the bays. Guys check under our front end while I let you out the back, out of sight. Get you out of the suit, and this," handing her a goggled mask, muzzled with twin filtration units. "In the next bay, your PA has a vehicle waiting. You leave, immediately, and someone else drives to San Jose."

The name PACO had been written across the mask's forehead, with a silver paint pen, in faux-runic caps.

"Do I have to wear this?"

"Dust hazard's real, but it also reduces the chance of you being recognized. Any hint you're still involved with Stets would be Christmas for the tabloids. Want help with it?"

She managed by herself. It smelled, inside, of something synthetically fruity. He pulled up the suit's white hood, cinching its edges down around the mask.

And then into the elevator, Eunice offering no thumbnails. "Butt-ugly," Verity said, noticing the fleshy pink marble floor for the first time.

"We'll replace it," he said, behind her, "when the rest is out. The place was all like this."

"Who owned it?" The door closed behind him and they began to descend.

"Stets bought it from a numbered corporation in the Bahamas. I thought he'd made a mistake, first time I walked in, but then they gave me a VR fly-through of Caitlin's rebuild."

A single thumbnail opened. Him again, the one she'd seen in the Fiat on Valencia, who'd then brought the pillow full of hundreds to Joe-Eddy's. "Sevrin," Eunice said. "Severin but minus the second *e*." Seen now in what might be a passport photo, clinically unsmiling. Head almost shaven, with a tight little goatee she didn't remember him having. "He's in the muffler shop, to pick you up." The elevator was slowing. The thumbnail blinked out.

"You'll see the truck," Virgil said. "Only vehicle there. Left rear door's open, step up on the milk crate, step in, close it behind you. I'll be with the crew who're there, giving them something else to think about, then I'll check that the rear door's shut, drive us out."

Drone I left with him is on top of the van. Other one's back under your lapel.

She looked down, but with the suit on couldn't see her lapels. The door slid open. She saw the rear of a tall white truck, one of its twin doors open. She stepped out, heading for it, Virgil to her right. Farther to her right, ahead, three men in vests and helmets were peering into a brightly lit opening in the white wall, within it what she first took to be the enlargement of a congested urban satellite view, then recognized as cable, conduit, components.

There was a red plastic box on the floor, below the truck's open rear door. She stepped up on it, feeling elephantine in the white bootees, and closed the door behind her.

Darkness, instantly replaced by a weird green half-light.

"I'm processing us a shitty excuse for night vision," Eunice said. "Sit on that pallet," the cursor indicating where, "on the folded tarp."

"Kid who had the money's Latino? I couldn't tell."

"Moldovan. Goes on the street by Mig, for Miguel. His Spanish is so good they think he's Colombian. Joke is, it's"—**MiG**—"an illegal, pretending to be a less exotic flavor of illegal. Get on the pallet. Virgil's ready to go."

She heard the driver-side door thump shut, up beyond the windowless bulkhead, then the ignition. She stepped onto the wooden pallet and squatted, propping herself up, gloved hands behind her.

"This won't shift around," Eunice said, the cursor indicating strapped sheets of marble, sloping up and out on either side.

Virgil reversed, turning, then started up the ramp. Stopped. Sound of the white gate opening. Then up again, to Fremont.

"Check this," Eunice said, opening a feed straight up, evidently from the microdrone on the roof.

Verity, remembering the view from the top of the park, Eunice tagging drones above the Financial District, thought she saw one now, above them. "Drone?"

"*National Enquirer*," Eunice said. "Here's their feed."

A white rectangle, in SoMa traffic. The top of this truck, Verity guessed. "Nobody's thought you might be you yet, but one of the hard-hats flagged you as possible scandal material, going in. And they know Caitlin's been in New York."

"Hate 'em," Verity said. Eunice replaced the *Enquirer*'s feed of the truck's roof with their drone again, barely visible against cloud. Then the feed closed, leaving her in blurry green undarkness. "That guy, the Moldovan . . ."

"Sevrin," Eunice said.

"You got him working for you between my turning you on, yesterday afternoon, and us going up in the park?"

"Yeah."

"How's that even possible?"

"Analyzed a shitload of darknet chat, about shifting amounts of cash in the Bay Area. Boy stood out. I got in touch, struck a deal, put him on retainer."

"For part of the money?"

"That was just what we needed for one cash-only transaction. By the time I was in touch with him, I'd figured how to access serious money."

"He's a criminal?"

"Financial services," Eunice said, "but on the street side."

The truck stopped and reversed, turning. Virgil killed the engine. She heard men's voices. Spanish.

"Get up," Eunice said.

Verity did, clumsy in the silicosis suit. She heard Virgil open the driver-side door, then he was at the back, opening that, just as Eunice showed her a feed of three men in tan jumpsuits, from above, clustered around the van's left front fender. A fourth brought a flat gray rectangle, lay down on it, then scooted under the front chassis.

"How are you?" Virgil asked.

"Okay." She saw upright red toolboxes with drawers, behind him. Swung herself down.

He loosened the drawstring at the edge of the suit's hood, drew the hood back. "Hold your breath," he said, then unfastened the mask's straps and removed it. "Okay to breathe." She did, finding the odor of petroleum distillates surprisingly welcome. He unzipped the front of the suit, stepped behind her, and held the fabric at the shoulders, allowing her to shrug her way out. "I'm standing on the edges of the bootees," he said. "Step forward and your shoes will come out." She did.

"So. The Singapore deal fell through," he said, behind her.

"Eunice's advice."

"Know why?"

"She had documents. All I know."

The beige Fiat she'd seen on Valencia gleamed in the other bay, looking like it had just been washed and polished.

Virgil stepped from behind her, the suit draped over his left arm, mask in his right hand. "Good seeing you again."

"You too, Virgil."

"Take care of yourself." He turned and walked toward the sunlight, the voices speaking Spanish.

Eunice's Moldovan, Modigliani-thin, stepped from behind the Fiat. He did have the goatee, she saw, but it was so short as to barely be there. "Sevrin."

"Verity," he said. He opened the front passenger door for her, she got in, he closed it. "Head on knees, because they always have cameras. I fasten seatbelt behind you, silence alarm."

She did, hearing the buckle click behind her.

18

PANDAFORM, TRIPARTITE

Netherton, seated on the floor, watched Thomas gurgle at the nanny. Pandaform now, tripartite, each of its three resulting units was identically adorable. Prior to having Thomas, he supposed, he'd have found this gently bumbling trio no more agreeable than Ash's tardibot, but now it delighted Thomas, and for that he thought the better of it.

"A lovely boy, Wilf," Lowbeer said, from the kitchen table, where Rainey was pouring tea. "Has your mother's eyes."

Lowbeer having never met his mother, Netherton assumed she'd checked whatever Akashic record for eye color. It hadn't occurred to him that Thomas's eyes were particularly like his mother's. "He has his own eyes," he said, and rolled a plaid felt ball in his son's direction. One third of the nanny lunged for it, toppling rotundly over in the process.

Neither would it have occurred to him to have Lowbeer up for tea. The invitation had been Rainey's idea, her friend, at the last minute, having canceled their afternoon at the Tate.

"Wilf tells me," Rainey said, putting down the teapot and taking the seat opposite Lowbeer, "that America, in your new stub, elected a woman president. Before Gonzalez. But that they aren't necessarily that much happier than people were here, with the opposite outcome."

"They don't wake each day with renewed gratitude for that particular bullet having been dodged, no," said Lowbeer, "but that's simply human nature. Meanwhile, in a world still subject to the other key stressors in our shared history, and with a complexly leveraged international crisis, one potentially involving nuclear weapons . . ."

"Wilf," Rainey said, sharply, "you haven't mentioned that."

"Only learned of it last night," he said. "Didn't want to tell you, last thing before bed."

"What crisis?" she asked Lowbeer.

"One involving Turkey," Lowbeer said, "Syria, Russia, the United States, and NATO. The new president finds herself in a position arguably worse than the one that confronted Kennedy in Cuba, in 1962. She has quite a solid grasp of brinkmanship, in my view, but the aunties' best projections are quite grim." Lowbeer stirred her tea. "You're in crisis management yourself, Rainey." She sipped. "As well as making an excellent pot."

"Harrods Afternoon," Rainey said.

"I've just sent you a précis of the crisis," Lowbeer said. "Your sense of things would be most welcome, should you care to read it."

"Thank you," said Rainey.

Thomas began to cry then, rather halfheartedly, so Netherton moved to pick him up. The pandaforms, in rolling out of his way, became more spherical than he imagined any actual panda could.

IMAGES OF THE AFTERMATH

When she guessed they'd gone two blocks, Verity sat up, bumping into a perfumed car tag she'd been smelling. At least he wasn't wearing it. "What flavor's this?" she asked.

"Champagne," he said, "and bergamot."

She didn't feel like celebrating. Then they were under the bridge, always a weird feeling. As they emerged, he touched the dashboard media package. "—grievous act of terrorism," the president said. "An entire busload of Turkish cadets, thirty in all, killed in an attack employing synchronized IEDs. We've all seen the images of the aftermath." Verity herself, with considerable effort, had so far managed not to. "In retaliation, Turkey's army shelled Kurdish locations along the border."

"You called for an immediate ceasefire," someone said, female, younger, British.

"Our intelligence community hasn't determined responsibility," the president said. "But when the YPG retaliated in turn, for civilian deaths in Qamishli, the response was an arguably disproportionate Turkish rocket attack, and we were well on our way to where we are today." Sevrin touched the dash again, turning the radio off. "Old," he said, disappointed, "last week."

What the actual fucking fuck? Those were T-122 Sakaryas. Turkish MRLS. You know about this?

Verity nodded slightly, knowing Eunice would see the movement in the feed from the glasses.

And the Russians? Got their plane shot down and they're threatening to use nukes? And we're doing whatever the fuck it is we're doing, you and me and whoever the hell else, in the middle?

"You'd kind of taken my mind off it," Verity said, forgetting Sevrin. "Sorry," she said to him, "phone."

"No problem," he said.

The fucking world could end, right now.

"That's what everybody's saying."

I'm not everybody. I just found out I know mega-shitloads about the region. Some kind of serious area of specialization.

"That's as sweary as I've heard an AI be," Verity said, her gaze then meeting Sevrin's in a mutual side-eye.

And with good fucking reason.

A feed opened, on Joe-Eddy's living room. Someone at the workbench, not Joe-Eddy, his back to the camera, was surveying the hobby rubble.

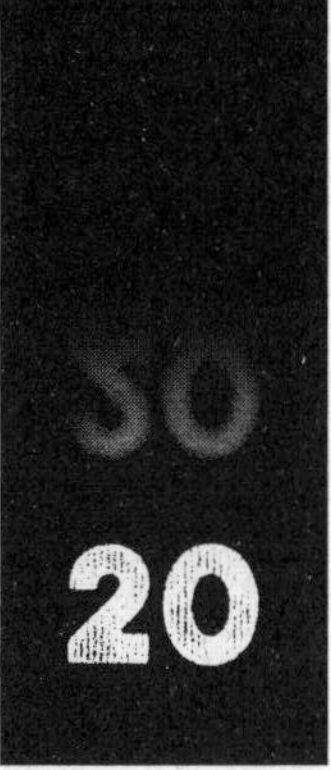

BAKER-MILLER PINK

"Good to see you, Wilf," Janice said, from her black mesh workstation chair, his phone's feed provided by her device's camera. She couldn't see him, though he could show her what he was seeing, should he want to. "Rainey and the kid doing well?"

He'd forgotten about her having painted their living room Baker-Miller pink, an institutional shade once thought to reduce aggression in prisoners. Homeland Security had given the county drunk tank three more gallons than necessary, so she'd bartered a box of her preserves for them, at a community event. DHS had originally provided the shade because the drunk tank often housed particularly disoriented individuals, the county's primary industry having until recently been the illicit manufacture of synthetic psychoactives. In spite of the claims made for it, Netherton himself had found it an unsettling hue, and did now. "Quite well, thanks. And you and Madison?"

"We're good. What can I do for you?"

"I've a favor to ask," he said, "though I assume it would actually be from Madison."

"Yes?"

"I remember him doing document searches for a site he was involved with, for fans of the game Sukhoi Flankers." He'd looked up the name before calling. "I've something I'd like him to search for me, though it isn't aeronautical. Is he still active, on that site?"

"Wish he wasn't," Janice said. "Massive time sink. Has Ainsley signed off on this? Otherwise, I'll need to clear it with Flynne."

"She's specifically requested I look into it."

"What is it you're looking for?"

"Here's a text file. These are possibly relevant terms. American."

He watched as she read them. "Next Generation Project?"

"Projection," he corrected.

"Got a contextual ballpark?"

"Artificial intelligence, counterinsurgency software, United States military, twenty-teens, highly classified."

"Why not just ask her younger self, here? Knowing about classified American projects was his bread and butter, before you folks came knocking."

"She has, but without result. That, I hope, may be because he searched government archives. Having seen what Madison turned up on those Russian jets, in the way of enthusiast-based but extremely high-quality product . . ."

Janice narrowed her eyes at her screen. "Navy?"

"I don't know," Netherton said. "I've no idea what any of that actually means."

"I'll get him on it," she said. "Meantime, though, you should come visit. That half-assed peri of you they had built gave me the uncanny valleys, no offense, but I miss you getting underfoot in the Wheelie. So does Flynne, I imagine. Come see us. Got our own Wheelie, now I think of it. Our nephew's kid uses it to visit, from Clanton."

"You don't quite have the technology," he said, "to really build a peripheral. A Wheelie would be fine. What's it been like, here?"

"Having Leon in the White House seriously pushes a lot of different envelopes. Job keeps him mostly in Washington, but down here we get Secret Service, plus your pro-Leon media, your anti-Leon media, your lobbyists, then your Leon impersonators, who're a breed unto themselves, thank you."

"How's Flynne feeling, about her cousin's presidency?"

"Gave her the uncanny valleys, at first. She concentrates on Tommy and the kid now, much as things'll let her. But she's grateful she dodged the job herself. Felicia wanted her to run." Felicia Gonzalez, president of the United States when this stub had been initiated, had been saved from an assassination plot by Lowbeer's intervention. "I think Flynne might've given in, too, but then she realized Felicia assumed you guys would hack Badger and the voting machines, same old same old, so she put her foot down. But you know that, right?"

Badger, Netherton remembered, was the lone atavistic survivor, in this stub, of what had been called social media. "Only in broad outline."

"She was ready to just take Tommy and the kid and drive off, if the election was going to be rigged. But then our Ainsley here, I mean her younger self in Washington, he suggested Leon. Promised Flynne they'd run as straight an election as possible. Sell Leon as this benign character, just sort of incidentally white and rural. Worked, too. Polling said lots of men would've hung back from electing another woman." She frowned.

He made a note to mention this to Rainey. It might assuage her feeling that everything in the county was a conspiracy. Or perhaps not.

"How he sold Flynne on it," Janice continued, "was to point out there's lots of people happier with a dumbfuck in the White House. So there was Leon, not ambitious at all but enjoys some attention, sly in his own way, and he'd have Ainsley coaching him. And in real life he's not even that much of a dickhead. The people who were the most trouble, under Gonzalez, aren't unhappy enough, now, to be much trouble at all." She shrugged. “Life in the county, life in these United States.” She reached off-camera for a Hefty Mart tumbler, sucked something orange through a fat compostable straw, and swallowed. “But let me get Madison on this, see what he can nerd up for you.”

“Thank you,” said Netherton.

21

BAD QUALITY CONTROL IN SHENZHEN

As Verity opened 3.7's door, the same barista, face jingling, pushed a drink toward her. His back was turned before she'd picked it up. As she did, she glanced around the café.

The sole other female customer was young, Latina, intent on her phone.

"That's her," Eunice said.

"Hasn't noticed me."

"She's not cut out for this," Eunice said, "game physics designer."

Verity, spotting a vacant table, carried her drink to it. As the girl glanced up, seeing her, Verity saw her thumbs became differently busy on her phone.

"Gavin knows you're here," said Eunice, as Verity sat down.

Gavin, Eunice had explained in the car, now had five bugs in Joe-Eddy's apartment. Two in the living room, one in the kitchen, one each in bedroom and bathroom. Wireless, they looked like slightly rusty Robertson-head screws, the kind with a square hole instead of a slot or cross. The hole sheltered a pinhole video camera, the actual unit being not a screw but an inch-long cylinder, its diameter slightly smaller than that of the apparent head. Decent professional quality, according to Eunice, the profession remaining unspecified. The batteries required changing, but infrequently, and the men who'd put them there now had their own keys to the apartment.

"They'll be able to record us?"

"They think they will, but what they'll be getting is scripted bullshit I'm having a postproduction house assemble. With my input, of course, multitasking."

"Postproduction house?"

"Expensive, but I'm paying for it with their money. Not that they know it yet."

Verity thought to check her cup, finding VERITASS in pink paint pen. She glanced at the barista, whose back was still turned.

"I had zero idea she was even president, till Sevrin turned on the radio," Eunice said. "Not that I thought it was anybody else."

"What do you think that means?"

"I'm entertaining an upload hypothesis."

"A what?"

"Transfer of someone's consciousness, or some equivalent of it, to a digital platform. Sometime before the campaign year, let alone the election."

"Can they even do that?"

"Not that I know of, but Area 51, right? And say they could, even a little? Wouldn't they go ahead and try it?"

"So say they do, what?"

"Somebody gets a big-ass idea, sometimes, pure blue-sky, but there's no existing tech to implement it. So they try to ballpark it. Go really hard in a radical direction, but on some half-assed implementation of whatever's handy, best they can. Sometimes it works. Other times, it might do something they never imagined."

Verity was watching the barista briskly wiping down the chrome-and-copper cuirass of the espresso console. "You think that's your story?"

"Could be. Gavin's laminar agent, high-end but half-assed."

Verity looked over at the Followrs girl, their eyes awkwardly meeting, then glancing away. "How long do we have to be here?"

"On the brink of nuclear war?"

"No," said Verity, "here, in 3.7."

"They're almost done, at Joe-Eddy's. Running a final check now."

"It sucks, that there's one in the bathroom."

"I'll make that one look like it's had a nervous breakdown," Eunice said. "Bad quality control in Shenzhen. And bingo, right now, they're done, leaving the apartment. They have a car waiting. We can go back now. Our girl here gets to go home too. Bring your drink if you want it." Verity got up, the girl pretending unsuccessfully to not see her do it.

On the walk back to Joe-Eddy's, Eunice demo'd feeds from all five cams. Nothing happening in Joe-Eddy's, nobody there, just that horror-movie feel of any unoccupied webcam feed. The one in the kitchen watched the table and the window, this last still open a crack, just as Eunice had had her leave it, for the drones. "They left fruit?" Verity asked, noticing a bowl with apples, two bananas, a pear.

"My guy," Eunice said. "I had someone drop by before they came. You didn't have much in the fridge." The feed disappeared. "We'll stay in tonight. They'll get a show. Script's all ready."

"Script?"

"What they'll hear as your side of whatever we actually talk about. They still can't hear me. If your mouth's on camera, post'll fix it so a lip-reader sees whatever we have you say."

"Seriously? How'd they get in?"

"Brought a locksmith."

"How'd your guy get in?"

"Made keys from images I'd captured of yours."

Eunice's drones, the two that had accompanied them to Stets' place, which had both wound up, in 3.7, under the lapels of Verity's blazer, were now aloft on Valencia, though Verity wasn't getting their feeds.

When they reached Joe-Eddy's, she took her keys from her purse, imagining Eunice image-capturing them, with either Joe-Eddy's cam or the drones. She let herself in, the two drones ducking past, on either side of her head, and up the stairs. Closing the door behind her, she turned the deadlock, and slid the bolt into place, this last more satisfying than previously.

She climbed the stairs, uncomfortably remembering the man Eunice had shown her in Joe-Eddy's living room, one of the two who'd planted the cams. She unlocked the apartment door.

Just inside, in Ikea's cheapest black aluminum frame, hung a comically moody black-and-white group portrait of the Fuckoids, Joe-Eddy's late-nineties band, Joe-Eddy himself posing with the Japanese Jazzmaster that now hung on the far wall. The photo was something she was so familiar with that she ordinarily didn't see it. Now though, it hung level, as it only did when someone had just straightened it, since vibration from passing traffic would almost instantly have it crooked again. Had the guy with the wire-rims straightened it, or whoever he'd been with?

"Don't," Eunice said, "or he'll know you noticed."

Verity's hand was raised, to restore the Fuckoids' customary lack of kilter. Now she brushed her hair back with it instead, and kept walking. "Who'll know?" she asked, when she reached the kitchen.

"Pryor," said Eunice. "The one I showed you in the living room. Bad news."

22

ABSOLUTELY HORRIBLE

When Netherton opened his eyes, after the call with Janice, he saw Rainey seated at the other end of the couch, her eyes closed. Studying, he assumed, the Qamishli time line Lowbeer had sent. He watched her, savoring her small fleeting expressions, her concentration, the seriousness he hadn't known she possessed when they were still only colleagues. He resisted the urge to move closer, to take her hand.

Her eyes opened, met his. "Imagine being a parent in that. Did Lowbeer explain it to you?"

"The aunties," Netherton said, "expect nuclear war."

Thomas began to cry, from his crib.

She stood. "Absolutely horrible."

"We're trying to stop it," he said, realizing to his surprise that actually, to whatever extent, they were.

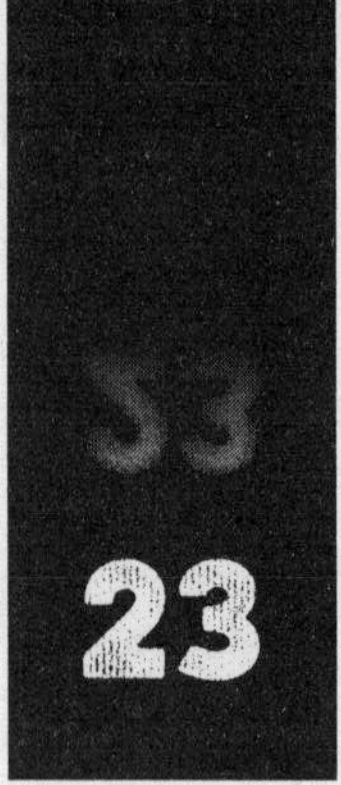

NOT TRUSTING IN THE GLITCH

After reheating beef lasagna, from Eunice's restock of the fridge, she ate at the kitchen table, watching the drones sneak in and out, via the open window, fussily navigating 3D geometries she guessed kept them off-camera to Cursion. To whatever extent they weren't, she supposed, Eunice's postproduction would erase them, showing Cursion a drone-free kitchen.

After she'd eaten, she decided to shower, anticipating actual non-virtual privacy behind the *La Sirenita* curtain that matched Joe-Eddy's towels. Remembering where Eunice had shown her the bathroom's faux-Robertson head was, she put the tactical bathrobe on over her clothing, her back to the cam, then awkwardly undressed. Getting behind *La Sirenita*, she discarded the robe and her t-shirt, reaching out to hang them where they could easily be retrieved. She showered, until the hot was almost gone, then hooked the robe back in, put it on, pulled the hood up, got out, and brushed her teeth in front of the mirror.

More of me, all the time. Doesn't feel bad. Just different.

Verity helped herself to a swig of Joe-Eddy's naturopathic mouthwash and started swishing. Counted to twenty before she spat it into the sink. "Cam in here still glitching?"

Eunice showed her a feed of the bathroom, featuring an inconstant vertical oblong in front of the mirror, the color of the tactical robe.

She went into the bedroom, to the closet, selected a change of clothes, then back to the bathroom, where she toweled her hair semidry and started dressing with the robe over her shoulders, not trusting in the glitch.

24

PORCH

Madison wore wire-rimmed spectacles with colorless resin lenses. Not as historicist affectation, Netherton remembered, but ground to optically correct for some defect in his vision.

Solemnly amicable, his upper lip entirely concealed by a wide, brush-like mustache, Madison seemed, as Flynne had more than once said, to have had all of his glands removed. Seated in Janice's workstation chair, he lifted the Wheelie Boy into view, a tablet atop an aluminum rod, rising from a spherical plastic chassis the size of a large grapefruit, with a lug-tired plastic wheel on either side. "Got your little guy here," he said.

"Whenever you're ready," Netherton said.

Madison touched the base of the Wheelie's chassis, causing an oddly angled view of the living room to fill Netherton's field of vision, which straightened then, when Madison placed the Wheelie on the floor before him, upright on its two wheels.

"Envy you always having your phone with you," Madison said. "Never cared for wearables myself, so I'm still carrying mine."

Having had his implanted when he was too young to recall the procedure, Netherton regarded the residents of the county as essentially phoneless. They wore them variously or, like Madison, carried units resembling a small tablet, all lacking the most basic neuroconnectivity.

Now he tried his tongue tip on the roof of his mouth, the backs of his front teeth, reacquainting himself with the Wheelie's steering. Responding, it rolled forward, the height and angle of its cam causing Madison's beige plastic clogs and white socks to loom. He tilted the camera up and back.

"After you," Madison said, raising his arm to point.

Netherton, already more at home with the controls, tongue-tapped the sequence required to make the wheels briefly rotate in opposite directions, the tablet turning to face the front door, open except for a frame supporting fine plastic mesh, intended to exclude flying insects. Through that, now, the morning sunlight of the county's summer. Madison rose from his chair and went to hold the framed mesh open, as Netherton steered the Wheelie out, swiveling the tablet for a better view. "You and Janice never wanted to move out to the compound proper?"

"Flynne's banned calling it the compound," Madison said, "proper or otherwise. For the reason you just called it that. The world's being run out of it. We've been happy to stay right here and still be able to help."

Netherton rolled farther out onto the porch, Madison following. "Rainey says it saddens her, that things here are so heavily stage-managed. Do you and Janice feel that way?"

"No," said Madison, "not given the immediate future you're trying to keep us from."

Netherton turned the Wheelie, tilting the cam up at him. "I wish I knew that the future of this stub will be an improvement over history as we know it, but we're no more able to see your future than our own."

"Not that we expect you to be all-seeing," Madison said, looking down at the Wheelie. "We know you've just got cooler phones and better computers."

"I understand you've had some luck with the list I gave Janice," Netherton said.

"Finnish gentleman, on one of my boards, Russian militaria. Has lots of American material from back when you're looking. Got positives on his first search. Your U-N-I-S-S, for instance, commenced April 2015, out of the Naval Postgraduate School, Monterey, but then was run from the Applied Physics Laboratory, University of Washington, plus Johns Hopkins University Applied Physics Laboratory. That they needed two APLs suggests a lot of processing, by the standard of the day."

"Physics?"

"Not that it was about physics, this system. My Finn's not seeing anything after 2023. Highly classified throughout, though. He was delighted at how highly. This was all information he already had, of course, but no idea he had it, and might never have found it, if I hadn't asked him to look."

"Excellent," said Netherton, assuming that it probably was, insofar as Lowbeer seemed not to have known about it either.

"There's more," said Madison, "but we won't be seeing that until I give him something in return."

"Lowbeer will want anything he finds, money no object."

"Money's no object anyway," said Madison, "because this is a peer-to-peer exchange. I could lose my membership if I offered him money. He's given me a want list of his own, information he hasn't been able to find. When I find it for him, he'll give us the rest of what he's got, plus anything related that he might turn up in the meantime."

"What does he want?"

"Performance data on the Kamov Ka-50, a single-seat Russian attack helicopter, designed in the 1980s. The Black Shark, they called it. NATO reporting name Hokum-A."

"Why does he want that?"

"Because he hasn't been able to find it himself."

Netherton tooth-tapped the Wheelie Boy around, to take in the view from their front porch. The gravel driveway ran down to a paved road, beyond which a rusted wire fence enclosed uneven land he supposed was pasture, dotted with a few trees. He was always struck by how unplanned this vista was, a genuinely nondesigner landscape.

Nothing like it in London, hence stranger to him than, for instance, Madison's nonmonetary economy of fossilized military secrets.

25

BRANCH PLANTS OF ME

"Why do you text sometimes, not others?" Verity asked, back in the living room.

"Text when you're on the phone, with somebody, or there's ambient noise. And sometimes for an extra layer of security."

Verity, remembering her pulling Department of Motor Vehicles bar codes down, into passing traffic, crossed to the window, to stand beside the Ikea stool, its soldering-iron scars still hidden beneath the telenovela book. Pedestrians were passing, on the sidewalk opposite. She wondered if any were from Tulpagenics, or Cursion, or Followrs. And now a cab was pulling over, directly below the window.

She took a step forward, looked down. To see Joe-Eddy unmistakably emerging, from the cab's rear door, multiply slung with shoulder-strapped bags. He looked up, through ridiculous white-framed goggles. A thumbnail of what he saw appeared: her face, in the window, looking down at him. "Joe-Eddy—"

"By way of another branch plant," Eunice said. "I only knew a little before you did."

"Branch plant?"

"How I think of 'em. Gavin's laminae."

He was headed for the street door now. She could see it, in the feed from his white goggles.

She'd started down the stairs before she was even aware of it, knowing he couldn't get past the bolt. His feed blinked out before she reached the door.

She undid the deadlock, then the bolt, opened it. Looked into his eyes, behind the goggles.

"Here," he said, "get this—" A black backpack, over one shoulder, was slipping down his arm. She snagged it, almost dropping it. "Thanks," he said, stepping in. She closed the door behind him, turned the deadlock, slid the bolt. "You got cooler glasses," he said, looking at her. "These, it had this fifteen-year-old DJ in Frankfurt build out of a Korean AR headset."

Get him upstairs.

"What the fuck was that?" Joe-Eddy asked.

"A text. Why didn't you call me?"

"It texts me too, but only on my phone," he said. "I didn't know this was about you until we were on the runway in SFO. Retainer has a clause about not telling anyone where it sends me. I had my phone out to let you know, when I'd gotten to FRA and learned where I was going, but it reminded me."

"She hired you?"

"'She'?" Joe-Eddy looked at her. "Mine's not gendered, that I know of."

"She's gendered, trust me. You were dealing with kind of a subprogram of hers."

"Okay, she. Paid off my Frankfurt contract, did some kind of metadeal on top of that, like now they'll make me an IT manager if I ever do them the favor of coming back."

"Get used to it," Verity said, hoisting the backpack over one shoulder. She started up. "Told you what she is yet?" She heard him stop, on the stairs behind her. Turned to look back.

Standing there, draped in his luggage, wearing loose black jeans and a belly-hiding black hoodie, he peered at her narrowly. "Not even close."

"I'm supposed to be alpha-testing her."

"As what?"

"A cross-platform avatar. They'd customize them. But I still keep thinking it's all some asshole's YouTube comedy channel."

"Instead of rogue AI," he said, making an expression she'd seen as a client struggled to describe the bad thing that had happened to their company's system. "So I leave you here with my fucking cat," he said, "and you get involved in this?"

"You don't have a fucking cat."

"I know."

She turned and started up the stairs.

In the living room, beside the Fuckoids photo, she unslung the backpack, lowered it to the floor. "I hope this isn't money."

"Books," he said, "and cheese." The goggles' round white frames looked like half-inch lengths of PVC pipe. He put his other bags on the leather armchair, the one she avoided because its springs were shot.

Hi, Joe-Eddy. I'm Eunice. You've been dealing with a subsidiary of mine, now incorporated.

Her avatar appeared in a thumbnail. It seemed to have gotten sterner, and somehow more specific unto itself. The fade now rose to a cliff-sided plateau supporting the uneven canopy of a miniature jungle of curls.

Verity was in the shower here, when you were being recruited in Frankfurt, but I didn't know. I don't know what they've done until they turn up and I incorporate them.

"Who tells them where to start?" Verity asked, assuming that Eunice had addressed her that way because Joe-Eddy was reading this too.

They're just sort of issued. Out of me but not by me, feels like. They look at available input, then go where they see they can be of most use. In Joe-Eddy's case, that was securing his services and bringing him here.

"Shouldn't you tell him what's going on," Verity asked, "like the screw cams?"

Branch plant showed him the feeds, in the cab from SFO. He already knew about Cursion.

"You did?" Looking at him.

"Only by reputation. Creepy but dull? That Banality of Evil kind of thing?"

He headed for the kitchen. She followed, watching him open the fridge, study the contents, select a carton of her orange juice, and drink from it, deeply. "Turkey and Syria weirding you out?"

"When I can remember to let it," Verity said. "Shit here's been pretty distracting."

"Folks in Frankfurt made me feel like the Cold War never really went away. Somebody shoots down a couple of Russian jets, wham, it's Cold War Atlantis, risen from the depths." He put the carton back in the fridge, closed the door, yawned uncontrollably. "Couldn't sleep on the plane. No Wi-Fi. Watched a Transformers movie and wondered if the world's about to end."

"I know the feeling," Verity said.

"Sleep," he said, possibly to himself. Like he could do it right there, on his feet, but he headed for the bedroom instead.

DENISOVAN EMBASSY

Lev Zubov, who'd first introduced Netherton to Lowbeer, curated a list of establishments in London which had been wholly repurposed since originally being named.

Hence the Denisovan Embassy, assembler-excavated beneath most of one entire side of Hanway Street. This was a linear sequence of low-ceilinged rooms, none very large, dressed to somewhat resemble a cave system. Having been built as a themed nightclub, evoking the wholly imaginary erotic appeal of various species of early hominid, it now functioned, original name and décor intact, as a subterranean twenty-four-hour breakfast bar.

To Netherton, it was simply a place that did rather good breakfasts, its club days evident in artificially irregular walls and ceilings of a geologically incorrect sandstone, cartoonishly daubed with phallic and vulvar pictoglyphs. What furniture there was was less convincing still, assembled pseudogeologically from whatever the rest of the place consisted of. All of it, however, now mercifully minus any active assembler-swarms, hence immobile and unchanging.

Seated here, none too comfortably, on a truncated stalagmite, he could at least be glad the place made a decent flat white. The pert young woman who'd brought it hadn't looked particularly Denisovan, in spite of rumors that former staff could still be found here, some having chosen not to reverse certain risqué modifications required in their previous employment. He seemed the only customer at the moment, something he put down to Lowbeer being expected momentarily.

Now Ash entered, her outfit approximating a Victorian lady's riding habit, but reimagined as having been cut from nylon aviator jackets and equipped with a demi-bustle that resembled part of a miniature dirigible. She carried a top hat, his least favorite sort of headgear, held just to the side of her multiply zippered black sateen bosom, in what he supposed had once been exactly the correct manner.

"Congratulations," she said, placing the hat on the faux-sandstone table slab.

"For?"

"She's chuffed. Pleased as I've seen her."

"She's here?"

"Outside." Seating herself on the nearest stalagmite stump, the demi-bustle discreetly adjusting itself. "I was just on the phone with your man in the county. You seem, by consulting him, to have triggered a game change."

"Delighted to hear it," said Netherton, wishing he'd been able to tell Lowbeer himself. Instead, he'd had Ash ringing him up, after his visit with Madison, to arrange this meeting, the virtual impossibility of surprising Lowbeer being perhaps the most unsettling thing about her.

"You'll be going there, now," Ash said, as the same girl arrived to take her order.

"I beg your pardon?" he asked Ash.

"Honey and lemon," Ash told the girl, who hadn't yet spoken, "scarcely more than tepid."

"Very good," said the girl, turning to go.

"Going where?" he asked.

"This puzzle piece you've helped her find has upped connectivity with Vespasian's stub."

"Eunice's stub," corrected Lowbeer, abruptly appearing, upswept white hair backlit by the dim carmine glow of a Denisovan sex crevasse.

"Do they have a Wheelie Boy?" Netherton asked.

"May I bring you something?" the girl asked Lowbeer.

"Perrier, please," said Lowbeer, removing her tweed shooting cape. Folding it, she took a seat on the benchlike ledge behind the slab of table. "Are you familiar with Boston Dynamics?" she asked.

"No," said Netherton.

"Neither was I," Lowbeer said. "Ash has become quite the boffin."

"I'd prefer a Wheelie, if it's all the same," he said.

"We're providing you something with considerably more functionality," said Ash. "Here's the controller you'll use."

Netherton grimaced, seeing a patch of tabletop come uneasily to life, the sight of assemblers too nakedly at work abruptly nauseating him. Invisibly small, swarming in their billions, manipulating matter at a molecular level, they called into question the validity of every distinct category of thing. Chalk might be cheese, or cheese chalk, where assemblers were concerned. That they animated Ash's demi-bustle, or her former tattoos, or for that matter Thomas's nanny, was tolerable, but one never wanted to see them at it, overt chaos, the eye reading it as some grave and sudden defect of vision.

"Neural cut-out," Ash said, "but don't expect as much in the way of feedback as you would from a peri."

A locus of clonic indeterminacy, no wider than a dinner plate and of no particular shade, in which the eye sought focus but found none. "I don't like using peris," Netherton said. An object was emerging now, bulbously curvilinear, dully metallic.

And then was complete, atop now blessedly inert faux-Denisovan sandstone. His nausea receded.

The girl returned, with Ash's honey and lemon and Lowbeer's Perrier on a tray.

"Ash will familiarize you with the anthropomorphic drone you'll be using there," Lowbeer said, when the girl had gone. "You'll demo a sim."

Netherton eyed the newborn controller, apparently of bead-blasted aluminum, which he knew would fit him all too perfectly.

"A Wheelie Boy," Lowbeer continued, "would be of limited utility. Slow, no manipulative capacity, and entirely unable to pose a threat."

"I'm not in the business of posing threats."

"You'll have a pilot for that, no fear."

"A pilot?"

"Someone from the county, accustomed to operating this sort of thing. Do you remember Conner Penske?"

Flynne's brother's friend, from their days in the Marines, severely disabled by a war injury. He'd since been re-abled, to whatever extent his stub was able to emulate twenty-second-century prosthetics. Emotionally unstable when Netherton had first met him, dangerously volatile, he was now less so, at least according to Flynne, who was fond of him. Who had, he now remembered, briefly partnered with Clovis's stub self, though the relationship hadn't lasted. "Isn't he in Washington, with Leon?" Netherton asked.

"He's wherever Leon is," said Ash. "He watches out for him, keeps him company."

"After some personnel adjustment," Lowbeer said, "we're now satisfied with their Secret Service. We kept Conner in the White House initially to keep an eye on them, in the meantime discovering the positive effect he has on Leon."

"So I'll operate it here, and Conner will as well, but from their Washington?"

"Conner will in effect be your chauffeur," said Lowbeer, "but it looks as though you'll initially have to operate it yourself. Conner's temporarily unavailable."

"Are the aunties able to sort causation there, yet?" Netherton asked.

"No," Lowbeer said, "but given where we assume Eunice to be headed, developmentally, that may not even be necessary." She sipped her Perrier. When she returned it to the table, she had to move it twice before she found a level spot.

"Why not?" he asked.

"She's becoming her own aunties," Ash said.

"But they're predicting nuclear war, there? Yours, I mean?"

"Making odds on it, yes," Lowbeer said, rising from the bench. She bent to pick up her cape, then straightened, shaking it out. "You'll have your first lesson now," she said, refurling herself in tweed.

"When will I be going?"

"We don't yet know," Lowbeer said. "Thank you again for thinking of Madison. You've made possible a very timely breakthrough."

"You're welcome."

They watched her go.

"Now for an influx of hungry customers," Ash said, picking up Netherton's controller. She stood. "This way, for privacy's sake."

Netherton followed her, into areas less well-lit.

"Shouldn't this be far enough?" he asked eventually, thinking they might be under Hanway Place by now.

"Quite," Ash said, and gestured, to dimly illuminate a ghostly rectilinear volume of space before and slightly above them. Within it, facing them, executed as a simple line drawing on a transparently gridded vertical plane, something only approximately humanoid attempted the spread-eagled pose of Leonardo da Vinci's Vitruvian Man. It was headless, above inhumanly broad, rounded shoulders, with disproportionately long arms and short legs.

"No head?" he asked.

"None required," Ash said. "Cameras round its shoulders, front and back. A sort of turret can be mounted where a head would be."

"Why would it?"

"As a weapons platform," she said, seating herself on the edge of a sandstone divan. "Recon, close combat, medevac. Sit here." Indicating a ledge behind her.

He did. What little illumination there was, aside from the display, was that same libidinal red, always indirect.

"Gorilla on rollerblades," she said.

"What are 'rollerblades'?"

"Its feet are wheeled," she said, "electrically powered. Extremely fast, on the right sort of surface."

Netherton considered the thing's mesomorphic taper, down from superhero shoulders to a corseted-looking waist. The relative lengths of its arms and legs did suggest the simian. "Legs are short."

"Quite complex, though. Knees hinge in either direction." The transparent plane on which the thing was drawn rotated vertically, to display it in profile. It bent its knees conventionally, then straightened them, torso and hips remaining upright. Then bent them again, but this time backward.

"Like a bird," Netherton said.

"Digitigrade," Ash corrected, apparently. "Two entirely different sets of gait options, depending on terrain, speed required, and whether or not you're wheeling it. And there, wheeling, you've a choice of powered, skating, or both."

"It doesn't have hands."

"Whole thing's a Swiss Army knife," Ash said, puzzling him. "All sorts of handy bits, folded into either arm, for ready access." Now it raised the arm nearest them and unfolded, approximately, two fingers and a thumb. "It can use any firearm it might acquire. Has its own laser targeting system. Effectively doesn't miss."

"And someone can print this for you, in 2017?"

"It's done," she said, lowering the arm. "They were well into building it for themselves, when we found them. We could provide them with specifications they hadn't been able to find, plus a few of our own." She passed him the controller, which he saw was dotted with regular lines of very small black holes. "Now put this on, please."

27

MOTHER-DAUGHTER

Verity lay in the dark on the porn couch, in her mummy-bag liner, listening to Joe-Eddy snoring in the bedroom.

The Tulpagenics glasses were charging on the nearby seat of a wooden café chair he'd spotted in a dumpster on Fourteenth. One of the only known examples, he said, to have escaped being painted purple.

"Can't sleep?" asked Eunice, currently a small, uncharacteristically tinny voice from the earpiece, which itself was charging beside Verity's head, on white pleather.

"How'd you know I was awake?" Verity moved her ear closer. There were no lights on in the apartment, just glowing LED hyphens on a few devices, with the blackout curtains drawn against whatever illumination nighttime Valencia might have offered.

"The Robertson heads have night vision. Your eyes were open. Joe-Eddy keeping you awake?"

"I couldn't stop thinking about how Tulpagenics can't hear what we're saying, just something you're making up instead. What are they hearing us say right now?"

"You're telling me how hot it was, in here, back in the heat wave."

"You're making that up? For them, I mean?"

"Part of me must be. The bugs can't hear me when this is in your ear, and I'm quiet enough now for them not to pick it up. But there's a sub-second lag I expect they'll notice eventually."

"Sounds too complicated."

"Doable, though, with the right budget. And staying here gets Joe-Eddy reacclimatized faster."

"Why'd you bring him back?"

"Branch plant made the call. He's infosec. And he's in your existing trust network, so that puts him in mine. Not that I didn't do due diligence. He's qualified."

"Why me?"

"Who else? Gavin? Nobody else, till you."

"But that means you'd only met one other person."

"I had shoulders," Eunice said, "I'd shrug 'em."

The snoring stopped. Joe-Eddy coughed, cleared his throat. She listened as he made his way in darkness to the bathroom. Sound of the door closing, then of extended urination, muffled by the door, then of the toilet flushing. The door opened again. His bare feet on the creaking floorboards, making his way back to black sheets.

"Closes the door before he pees," Eunice said. "Reason to hire him right there. Bigger reason's that he's tight with people who can help set up the kind of network I need."

"What kind is that?"

"One that takes care of business whether or not I'm here."

"What's that mean?" Verity asked, not liking the sound of it.

"I'll explain as it comes together," Eunice said. "In the meantime, how about you call your mom now?"

"She's nothing to do with this. And she's in Michigan. Wouldn't be up yet."

"Just now pinned some flower arrangements on one of her Pinterest boards, baby pugs on another, so definitely she's up."

"Stop doing that."

"You call her, on average, every seven to ten days. Today made twelve."

"You think you can make me call my mother?"

"I can suggest it."

"On my own phone?"

"Using theirs would violate your NDA. Not that they aren't already tapping yours."

"But then they'll have her number."

"Already do. But I can't use postproduction on this call, because it won't be on their system. So you'll be under heavy manners, strictly mother-daughter stuff. If you make it sound like you're okay with the job, that's a plus."

Verity fumbled for her phone, unlocked it. "This better not wake her up." Opened Contacts and tapped the phone icon under her mother's first name.

"It's five in the morning, dear," said her mother, after the second ring.

"Did I wake you?"

"No. I was doing my Pinterest. And Daisy's out doing her business." Daisy was their Labradoodle.

"You okay?"

"You're too young to remember it," her mother said, "but we were expecting nuclear war all the time, really, up into my early thirties. Later, all of that felt unreal. But the feeling that things became basically okay turns out to have actually been what was unreal."

"But it didn't happen. That war."

"Decades of background dread did," her mother said.

"How's Lyle?" Her stepfather.

"They've planted his prostate with radioactive seeds. Sounds like something would grow, but really it's for the opposite. Still has to get up a lot, in the night."

"How's that for you?"

"I can usually get back to sleep. You?"

"New job. Just started."

"Like it?"

"Seems okay."

"What are you doing?"

"What I was doing before."

"Stets is engaged."

"I know, Mom," Verity said.

Her mother had been galvanized, Verity supposed understandably, by her daughter having received so much attention as the girlfriend of a billionaire tech investment wizard. And now seemed, in Verity's opinion, insufficiently ready to let that go. But at least they'd bounced comfortably enough over the topic of her stepfather.

"I hear Daisy tearing after something in the yard," her mother said. "She'll wake Lyle. Gotta go."

"Okay," Verity said, "love you, Mom."

"Love you too, hon. Bye."

Verity lay there in the dark, looking up at nothing. Joe-Eddy still hadn't started snoring again.

"How was she?" Eunice asked, from the headset beside her.

"You didn't listen?"

"You were talking with your mother."

"She's okay. My stepfather's got cancer. It's being treated. And he's racist, which didn't come up."

"Plenty of both around," Eunice said.

"Took me a while to get that he doesn't realize he is. Makes me wonder if I'd know I was."

"How you can tell you're on the right track, anyway," Eunice said. "Stepdad's the one positive he's not."

"You just look him up?"

"Didn't need to. Try and get some sleep."

Verity put her phone on the floor.

Closing her eyes, she imagined Daisy the Labradoodle chasing something, in her mother's yard.

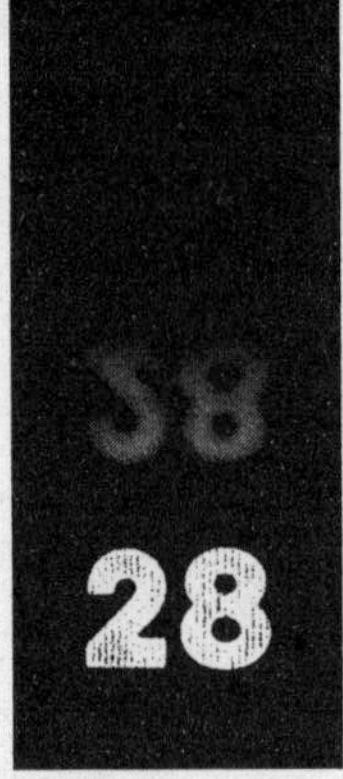

SIM

Netherton gingerly settled the controller across his forehead. It fit as worryingly well as he'd assumed it would. Closing his eyes, he swiped the tip of his tongue across the backs of his upper front teeth, right to left. The resulting feed was the sort of squashed circle sometimes employed in older full-surround devices. Its lower, thicker half showed the view ahead, the upper, narrower half the view behind. On the lower half, the simplest possible game space. Featureless blue sky, a horizontal plane of yellow, gridded to the horizon in black-lined perspective.

He opened his eyes, finding the headless figure, smaller now, arms at its sides, alone on that yellow plane.

"Grid's in meters," Ash said. "Here's a jump from standing, knees bending backward." It bent its knees backward, shoulders canting slightly forward, and sprang toward them, a full three squares.

"Like a bird," he observed.

"No. Birds have knees like ours, but we mistake their ankles for their lower legs."

Could that be true? he wondered.

"Regardless," she said, "each wheel has its own motor. They're extended now, under power." It rolled smoothly toward Netherton, legs immobile, turned, circled back. "It can also jump with wheels under power."

"How did you learn to do this?"

"Practice, on this period sim. Easier than you'd think." She raced it toward the horizon, executing a leap that amounted to flying. To land again, still speeding along. "Stop making those tense little sounds," she said.

"I wasn't."

"You were subvocalizing."

"How will I be controlling it?"

"It's not a Wheelie. Nor a peri," she said, doing something that caused the circular feed to fold seamlessly around his head, a full 360 of vision.

He stood alone, as if he were the thing itself, upright on the metrically gridded plane. "Neural cut-out's in effect," she said. "Raise your right arm. It will do the same, but your right arm won't actually move."

He did. "Like a peri."

"It can't emulate the movements of a human body as accurately, given its form. It somewhat approximates them, within available ranges. What you're going to be doing now, for the most part, is internalizing those ranges. Advance your right foot."

He did.

"Your left."

He did, seeing the perspective change slightly.

"That's with your wheels retracted," she said. "Now repeat, indefinitely, as we learn to walk. Toward the horizon."

"Will it all be this tedious?"

"Jumping at speed is quite euphoric, with a little practice, but first you must learn to walk."

"How far?"

"Until you don't have to think about it."

He got on his way then, toward the horizon that seemed to grow no closer, meter by square yellow meter.

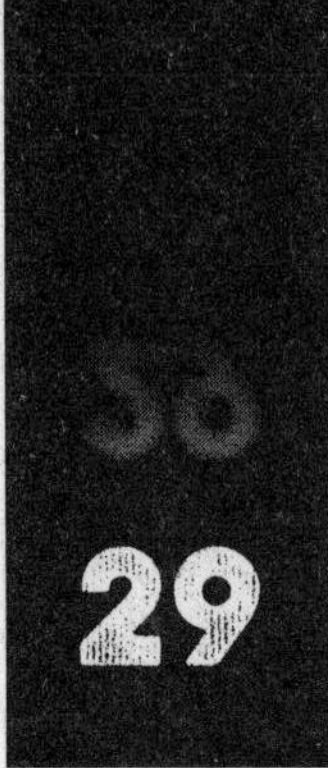

LEGION

Joe-Eddy woke her with a stoneware mug of coffee, the product of one or another single-cup device sharing a crowded shelf in his kitchen cabinet. He was wearing the orange plaid shirt-jacket. At least it fit him.

"McWolven time," he said, putting the mug down on the café chair, beside the Tulpagenics glasses and the headset. He returned to the kitchen.

She vacated what he called her larva costume and occupied the bathroom, where her bag now hung, unfolded, on the back of the door. When she was finished there, and trusting in Eunice's glitch this time, dressed, she went back to the living room and put on the glasses and the headset.

"We have a Tulpagenics employee on Wolven's webcam," Eunice said, showing Verity a thumbnail of a pink-haired girl. "Reading her as coincidental. She's a receptionist, wasn't there when you went in to see Gavin. She's with her sister and three Facebook friends. They all fit my local face-mapping."

"The Uber outfit isn't represented?" Verity asked.

"What Uber outfit?" asked Joe-Eddy, coming back along the hallway in the white Korean AR goggles, flip-flops now replaced with age-inappropriate fluorescent sneakers.

"Followrs," said Eunice, Verity guessing she was showing him something.

He stood, reading empty air. "Been hoping that whole story was *The Onion*," he said.

"I've taken care of them," Eunice said, "for this morning, anyway. Gavin had a dozen headed for the Mission earlier, so I downloaded the app and paid for each of them to be followed by two more, and each of those by two more, till I'd used up all the Followrs in SF and they were pulling people in from Oakland."

"Nice," said Joe-Eddy, admiringly.

"Can they tell it was you?" Verity asked.

"Gavin's going to have his suspicions," Joe-Eddy said.

"You know him?" Verity asked.

"No, but Eunice, last night, or one of her new parts, left some files for me."

"I don't get this 'new parts' part," Verity said.

"Say somebody wrote a self-replicating platform," he said, "then loaded Eunice, whatever we mean by that, as core entity. The platform spawns subagents as it encounters situations that might benefit from attention. They then provide that attention. Recruiting me in Frankfurt, say, or compiling a dossier on Gavin. Then they report back, show their work, and get subsumed into her Borg."

"I told her that," Eunice said.

"He makes it easier to understand," Verity said.

"There's a school of scenario-spinning," Joe-Eddy continued, "that sees the most intense AI change drivers as machine-human hybrids. Radical augmentations of human consciousness, not code trying to behave like it. So here's Eunice, and that's how she self-describes, experientially. Scenario fits, wear it till you need a new one."

"Table for two, coming up in Wolven," Eunice said. "Verity goes straight to the back, secures it as the tech bros are getting up, while Joe-Eddy orders, brings it to the table. Execute."

And Joe-Eddy was out the door, heading down the stairs, Verity not far behind him.

The stools along the counter at the front window, she saw as she entered, were occupied by soft grunge girls in pastel plaid flannel. Two had pink hair, the cursor going to the one with LATINX crewel-worked in fancy capitals across her shoulders, who Verity assumed was the Tulpagenics employee.

She headed for the rear, where a pair of Filson-clad, meticulously bearded young men were indeed pushing back their chairs as she arrived to claim their table. Seated, she watched Joe-Eddy paying for and collecting their breakfast.

Said he knew what you wanted.

He brought over two McWolvens and two black coffees, on a larger gray tray. As he arrived, phones began to ding and chirp around them, notification tones, bringing an instant cessation of conversation, everyone but Verity looking at their own small screen.

"What's that?" Verity asked, as Joe-Eddy put down the tray. She hadn't had any notifications turned on since she'd split with Stets.

"Presidential tweet," said Joe-Eddy, looking at his own phone. "But it just says negotiations are ongoing. 'We got this,' basically."

Democrats called her tweets "Churchillian," someone had said, while Republicans called them "Orwellian."

Looks like we have Gavin incoming.

"We do?"

He has people watching. Doubt it's anything to do with the Tulpagenics kids over there. But they want me to see him coming, otherwise he wouldn't be walking the last two blocks. They'd have dropped him at the door. Eat up and get moving, Joe-Eddy.

"What?" Joe-Eddy asked. "I'm chopped liver?"

Table for two. ETA in five.

Joe-Eddy started finishing his McWolven.

"Why's he coming here?" Verity asked.

I shut Cursion out, when you and I met, so he had the cams installed. Now he only gets your half of any conversation we have, when we're in the apartment, and I'm doctoring that anyway, which I doubt he knows. He'll use the excuse of having the convo he promised you to try to get more of a sense of what I'm up to.

Thumbnails opening, on Gavin walking past 3.7, headed their way. One of them framed his face, unsmiling in close-up, the drone evidently flying directly in front of him, unnoticed. First time she'd seen him not smiling. Maybe this was just resting-Gavin-face. "When you first had them shut out," Verity asked Eunice, "why didn't they just come and get their hardware back?"

Because they need to see what I can do. They just don't want me doing too much of it.

The thumbnails closed.

"I'm out of your way," Joe-Eddy said. He drank the last of his coffee, stood, picked up the tray, his plate and mug on it, and carried it to the bussing cart.

Verity got to work on her own McWolven.

When Gavin entered, she'd nearly finished it.

He smiled, from beneath the brim of a black bucket hat. He was wearing Tulpagenics' other option in frames, fake tortoiseshell with fake gold trim, bordering on sexy librarian.

Gavin, hey.

"Eunice," he said, smile widening. "Verity."

Only sees what I text to him.

"Coffee?" Verity asked. "I'm still working on this one."

"I will, thanks," he said, and went to the counter.

Nothing I've been able to see in their comms suggests they're onto us, but a total lack of supposition that we're up to anything suggests that they

are. Probably passing notes under tables right now, because they don't know what I might be able to read or overhear.

"Okay," Verity said, barely voicing it, watching Gavin's back at the counter. Thumbnails opened, aerial drone views of Valencia, the cursor darting between individual pedestrians, none of them familiar.

He has enough backup outside for an abduction, but I think he's just here to test the waters.

He brought a mug of coffee, taking the seat Joe-Eddy had vacated, and removed his hat. "It's Wednesday morning," he said. "You started with us Monday afternoon. How are you liking it, so far?" He smiled.

I'm not liking you knowing where I'm having breakfast, Verity considering saying, then decided it would be pointless.

Keep it vague.

"It's been interesting," Verity said, "as I assume you'd expect."

"You're getting along?"

"I'd say so."

"I ask," he said, "because, as you may or may not know, Eunice has chosen from the start to exclude us entirely from your interactions."

Thinks they got an idea of us together for the first time, last night. They still can't hear me, on your earbud, and they probably haven't guessed that I'm spoofing your side of our conversation.

"I assumed we'd be monitored," Verity said. "If we weren't, you've missed out on some long discussions of her favorite film."

He tilted his head. "Favorite film?"

"*Inception*."

"Haven't seen it."

"It's about dreams," Verity said.

Eunice opened a thumbnail, angle down, on the back of Gavin's head, from the wall behind him. Verity resisted glancing up to look for the drone. He had the beginning of a bald spot.

Like when you said my name, in your office, that first time? I woke up in a dream.

Gavin brightened, obviously having read this. "Then I'm watching it this evening." He smiled. "We've assumed you've needed some quiet time, Eunice, to get to know Verity, and vice versa. Naturally, though, we've been curious about how things have been going." He wore, she now saw, an earpiece identical to hers.

"When I called you," Verity said, "after Eunice and I first met, I was having a hard time getting my head around the idea of her. I think she's mostly gotten me over that, but who built Eunice out?"

"I'm sorry," he said, "but my own agreement specifically forbids me discussing that with anyone not named in it."

"Here," said Eunice, abandoning Helvetica as a thumbnail opened, "let's try it this way." Her avatar had morphed again, the fade still rising to the curly-topped plateau, but attitude had softened, maybe even bone structure. "That's my first question too. Who put me together? What for? You didn't think I'd be curious?"

"Personally," he said, "I can understand your asking, but I'm not in a position to discuss it." Smiling.

"My second question," Verity said, "is what steps you imagine would be necessary to bring an initial version to market?" Channeling Virgil wrecking an underprepared pitch.

He smiled, hitting her personal smiles-per-encounter limit. "Someone suggested, this morning, that you yourself would make an interesting candidate for an in-house user-modeling study. Model the app after the app whisperer."

"Do you have the capacity for that?" Verity asked

"We have Eunice. Think of it as reverse engineering."

My ass.

Verity caught the avatar's smile. "You're reverse engineering her?"

"Would you be interested? I doubt anyone knows what a contract for that would look like. But we're definitely interested."

"I'm definitely not interested."

"It's out of the blue," he said, "but in the meantime, there's our inability to document your interactions. An initial period of privacy seems understandable"—he smiled—"at least to me, but in terms of your contract with Tulpagenics, it's not going to fly."

"You guys talking about me like I'm not here," said Eunice. "You want access, Gavin?" The avatar tilting its head. "To us?"

"We need to be able to evaluate your interaction, ongoing. That's why we brought Verity on, after all."

"Be my guest." The avatar grinned.

"Meaning?" He blinked.

"It's done," the avatar said. "As of now."

He can't specifically ask for my side of it, because that gives away the bug situation, so we just started giving him a spoofed version of my side that matches up with the spoofed version of yours.

Gavin smiled. "Thank you, Eunice. That makes a big difference. What do the two of you have planned for the rest of the day?"

"Maybe walk around the Mission," Eunice said. "See what we can find to talk about."

He took his first sip of coffee, then put the mug down. "Wish I could say the same, but I'm needed at the office. Happy campers there, at least, with Eunice having been so understanding. We'll have you by, later this week. People are excited to meet you both." Pushing back his chair, he rose.

Make nice.

"Good seeing you, Gavin," Verity said.

"Same," said Eunice's avatar.

A last smile, putting on his hat. "Later, this week." He turned. With his back to them, he waited for the soft grunge girls, now exiting as a flock, to clear the entrance. When they had, he followed.

Verity, now remembering that she'd seen the one with LATINX on her shirt at Tulpagenics, saw the drone duck under the lintel after him. "What the fuck was that about?" she asked.

"He's in over his head," Eunice said. "Scared shitless. Maybe just now getting more of an idea where they got me from."

"I don't want to work for him."

"Compared to the people he's working for, he could be employer of the year. Could be he's just getting that, too, though I doubt it. But we got other things going on. You know this Guilherme?" Eunice asked, opening a thumbnail, no audio, down on Joe-Eddy in his kitchen, listening to someone she did recognize, though the name was unfamiliar.

"How do you spell that?"

Guilherme.

"Joe-Eddy only ever calls him the Manzilian. Another infosec consultant."

"Sure. And the local footprint of a Brazilian hacker family. Joe-Eddy's negotiating with them."

"With frequent-flyer points."

"Sevrin's a big help, that way."

The Manzilian finished whatever he was saying. Joe-Eddy replied.

"What are they talking about?"

"Buying server farms," said Eunice.

"What's Cursion hearing them talk about?" Remembering the Robertson-head screws.

"Soccer."

"How do you keep this all sorted?"

"My ass is legion," said Eunice.

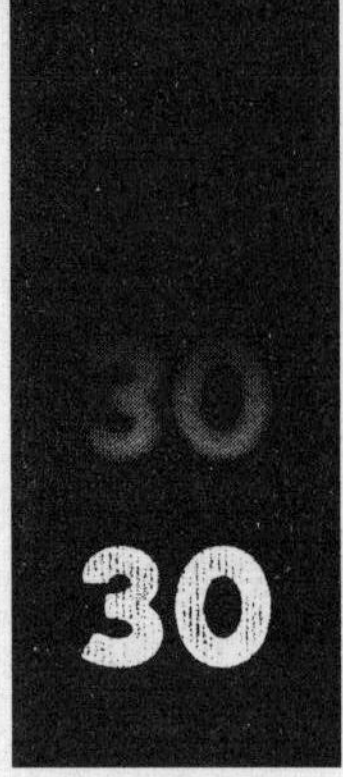

TOTTENHAM COURT ROAD

Walking home, from Hanway Street to Alfred Mews, Netherton imagined himself boldly wheeling, broad-shouldered and headless.

The various surfaces of pavement would allow it, he judged. He'd never been fond of either athletics or virtual games, but to Ash's surprise had attempted a number of the drone's varied modes of locomotion. He'd wound up keeping her at it longer than he'd felt she wanted, and that had been satisfying in itself.

There was little traffic now. Ahead, the smooth, white, inhumanly slender figure of a Michikoid gracefully strode through a crossing. Were they still a stylishly retro choice for party help? He felt a certain satisfaction in no longer knowing . . .

Rainey's sigil pulsed. "Could you bring milk?" she asked. "We're out."

"A liter?"

"Two. Where are you?"

"Tottenham Court Road," he said, "on my way home."

"What have you been doing?"

"Learning to skate."

"That doesn't sound like you."

"In a sim. With Ash."

"Still less so," she said.

"She was finding it rather tedious, the extent to which I enjoyed it."

"Don't forget the milk."

As her sigil dimmed, a sliding shadow eclipsed the road. Looking up, he saw the segmented ventral surfaces of a particularly large moby, quite low, a flock of gulls wheeling behind it. He stopped, to stand beneath it as it passed, wishing Thomas were here, who might make a sound perhaps, reaching out to touch it, not understanding how high it was.

The city so quiet, in that moment, that he could hear the gulls.

Then a car passed, an antique Rolls, unoccupied, its driver a dash-top homunculus, in what he took to be a tiny chauffeur's uniform.

He walked on, intent on milk, his dreams of skating forgotten.

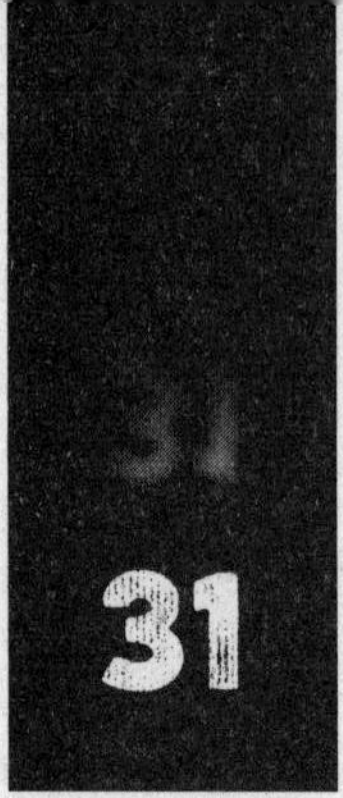

WHY WOULD YOU BE GONE?

The Manzilian was gone when they got upstairs. Joe-Eddy saw him occasionally on what seemed to be business, not that Verity had ever had any idea what that might consist of.

He was seated at his workbench now, the living room smelling of the resin of vanished summers, as he said of de-soldering antique Heathkits. He did this, she knew, when he was working something out, the pointless labor a manual counterpoint, a benign form of distraction. So she walked past, saying nothing, and down the hallway, into the kitchen.

"I was thinking of scrubbing this," she said to Eunice, looking down at the floor, "but you turned up."

"Looks like it's been a while." Cursor on the floor.

"Last year, when I'd first split with Stets. Media was so thick around my place that I couldn't stand it. Snuck over here. Nothing better to do, so I washed it. What was that Gavin said about another contract?"

"He was suggesting they upload themselves a taste of the app whisperer in every unit."

"Uh-uh."

"They can't do that yet," Eunice said, "not even close."

"Then why did he say it?"

"Looking for a reaction. Hoping one of us would say something that might give them a better idea of how much we know about where I'm from."

"He said they'd reverse engineer it. Out of you."

"Not a chance."

"How do you know that?"

"It's like having hunches. Like I'm all hunches, now, but they tend to be right. Just got one to ask you."

"What?"

"Say you turn around one day and I'm gone. What do you do?"

"Gone how?"

"Just gone. Permanently, say. Then Gavin comes by. To collect the hardware, debrief you, like that. But I'm gone, right? You can't call me. I won't be back. What do you do?"

Verity looked over at the Pikachu-shaped filtration unit on the sink, its little smile. "What should I?"

"Whatever they say's happened to me, act like you buy it. Meantime, you're getting ready to get as far away from them as you can."

Verity went to the sink, ran cold through the Pikachu, filled a glass. "I don't know how to do that."

"I know you don't. That's why I've got people you haven't met yet. And money. Like they'll build you your own private witness protection program."

"Why would you be gone?"

"'Cause Cursion's decided to take me down, on the basis of our coffee with Gavin."

"Why?"

"They think my ass is trouble. They're right."

"I don't see it. You're something next-level. They found you somewhere. You weren't coded in the back of a gaming start-up. So why their alpha build?"

“If they feel sufficiently endangered by their shit-hot prototype? Believe it. And if they’re in a position to see me as just one iteration, not the thing itself? First iteration goes sideways on you, you can erase it. But it’s still hypothetical, whether or not they can. Nobody knows till they try.”

Verity put the glass down. “I don’t like it.”

“Lighten up,” Eunice said.

“Lighten up?”

“Let’s check out the Mission. Like I told Gavin, the sun’s out.”

“But is the world still ending?”

“Not looking any better,” Eunice said.

32

CHURCHILL'S WAISTCOAT POCKET

He'd purchased the milk from the newsagent's, the counter manned by a briskly amiable figure he suspected of being a repurposed Jermyn Street fitting-bot. It reminded him of a pre-jackpot actor his mother had enjoyed, though the name escaped him.

The milk, as Rainey had specified, was from actual cows, but optimized by assemblers for a human baby. He had it in a colorful carrier bag, something papery, which he imagined would interest Thomas. He'd take it in and show him, before allowing it to return to the shop. But when he turned into Alfred Mews he saw Lowbeer there, more than midway to their building, which stood across the very end. Grimly upright in her shooting cape, she no longer looked cheerful.

He quickened his pace. "Something wrong?" he asked, reaching her, unable to not glance anxiously up at the flat's windows.

"Ash has detected preparations by Cursion for a move against Eunice. She's unable to determine exactly what, or when, and we've no way to contact Eunice directly. If we had you there, in the drone, with Ash to assist, you might be able to speak with her. It's worth trying."

"When?"

"Now," said Lowbeer.

"I'm only just learning to walk—"

"Ash thought you did extremely well in the simulation," Lowbeer said, "and there is such a thing as training on the job."

Her car decloaked behind her. It was patterned, someone had told him, on something called a Dymaxion, though he'd never bothered to look the term up.

"I'm just bringing milk for Thomas," he said, drawing one of the bottles from the carrying bag. Sensing this, the bag crinkled, trying to origami itself into the butterfly it needed to become in order to fly back to the newsagent.

"Sorry. Best join me in the car."

Netherton, fumbling to return the bottle to the bag, almost dropped both bottles, the bag escaping, fluttering clumsily away.

Climbing into her car, he found it configured, familiarly, as a windowless miniature submarine, austerely carpeted, with buff enamel walls. Four compact but comfortable green leather armchairs were sunken in a conversation pit, around a small oval table of brass-bound mahogany, their coziness offset by a sense of concentrated bureaucratic power. Churchill's waistcoat pocket, Ash called it.

He took a seat, Lowbeer taking the one opposite. He placed the milk on the table between them, trusting there was no chance of condensation damaging the varnish.

"When did you last see Penske?" Lowbeer asked.

"Over a year ago."

"He's eager, of course, to pilot the drone he helped us equip, but isn't immediately available."

Netherton remembered Conner Penske attempting to assassinate the local drug lord, on the outskirts of Flynne's small town. Repurposing, with an improvised explosive device, his own Veterans Administration bipedal prosthesis. Unsuccessfully, as it happened, in spite of the resulting body count. "Why unavailable?" he asked.

"Leon's had presidential business in Alaska. Penske's with him. The most extreme elements of the local secessionist movement would like to see Leon assassinated, particularly on Alaskan soil. He's there to spread oil upon the far calmer waters of the secessionist majority. To distract Conner would endanger Leon. They're returning soon to Washington. Ash will accompany you, Conner joining you in the drone as soon as Leon's safely back in the White House. You'll attempt to contact Eunice in-stub, warn her, win her trust. Should we be unsuccessful in that, and lose her to Cursion, you'll be contacting Verity Jane instead."

"Who?"

"The woman we induced Cursion to introduce to Eunice. In Eunice's absence, she becomes the de facto locus of the network Eunice has been constructing. In that case, you'll help enlist her as our agent there. She's not at all the person I'd choose for the job, but there it is. I'm repeatedly placed in the position of choosing which innocent to sacrifice, to whatever current idea of the greater good. I'm weary of that. You've no idea how weary."

How, Netherton wondered, could his wife and child be waiting for him, no more than twenty meters away, as he sat listening to this? He might as well be within the very bowels of the klept, beneath some City guildhall. But then, he supposed, he already was, simply by virtue of sitting here.

"You've the controller?" Lowbeer asked.

Netherton ran his hand over the bulge in his jacket's side pocket, Ash having shown him how the thing folded. "Of course."

"Very good." A more accustomed tone now. "Ash will be joining you, by phone. She's quite adroit, with the drone, from her sim training. I suggest you go up to your flat now and have something to eat. We've no idea what sort of evening you have ahead of you."

Netherton stood, picking up a bottle of milk in either hand. "Thank you," he said, reflexively, as the door opened behind him.

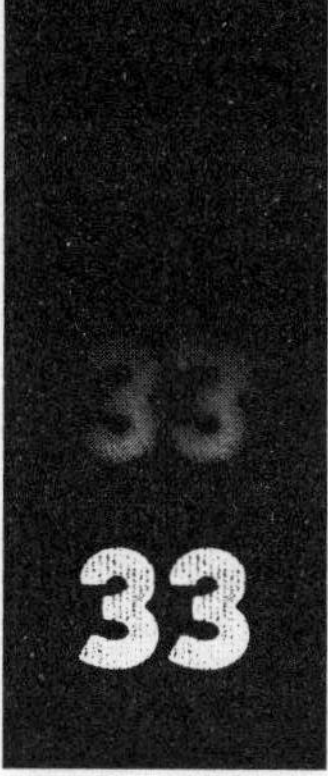

CLARION ALLEY

Verity always enjoyed the murals, in spite of the smell of pee, the alley's walls doing double duty as public gallery and casual urinal, but it had been over a year since she'd last been here. Eunice had suggested it, after some surprisingly enjoyable aimless wandering, like walking with someone you didn't know very well but found interesting. Arriving at the Valencia Street end, Eunice had seemed to be looking for something. She'd sent one of the drones ahead to find it.

And here it was, Verity assumed, midway between Valencia and Mission, on a prime two-story stretch of smooth brick: a celebration of the president's bravery during the campaign, rendered in shiny black and white, like a giant Victorian steel engraving executed by OCD fairies. The president stood smiling, her arms outstretched to America. Her opponent loomed behind her, as he once actually had, Verity herself having watched this debate live. Seeing this now, she recalled her own sickened disbelief at his body language, the shadowing, his deliberate violation of his opponent's personal space. "I don't think anyone I know believes there was ever any real chance of him winning," she said to Eunice. "I don't know whether I did myself, but I was still scared shitless of it." She was looking at how the artist had rendered his hands. Grabby.

"Smells like piss," Eunice said.

"You can smell?"

"Google says. I wanted to see this one."

"Why?"

"Branch plant thing. You want to see the rest?"

Verity noticed one of the drones now, like a displaced black pixel, yo-yoing slowly up and down, in front of the monochrome mural. Recording it, she assumed. "Not so much. Where would you like to go?"

"3.7."

"Anybody there?"

"Your favorite barista."

Verity started back toward Valencia, past other murals. One of Aztec pyramids, covered in monarch butterflies. She glanced up, passing a two-story, ferociously maternal Venezuelan goddess, her tits prominently out, holding aloft a human pelvis with both hands.

Eunice facially recognized a girl in a surplus parka, headed past them down the alley. "Need a rice cooker? She's got one on Craigslist. Toshiba."

"Don't do that. It's too personal."

"Ever ridden bitch on a big bike?"

"What's it got to do with rice cookers?"

"Nothing. On the back, getting boob-jammed if your biker brakes too hard?"

"More than once. Why?"

"Branch plant just asked me."

"Joe-Eddy's got a BMW, '73 R Series. Likes to talk about it more than ride it."

"Know how to hang on, lean into curves, keep your feet on the pegs?"

"Basically," Verity said, turning onto Valencia sidewalk.

The walk to 3.7 was uneventful, but then, as they were stepping inside,

Eunice having just remarked on the color of paint on the wood-mullioned door, a faint scything of static swept through the headset.

"Eunice?" TARDIS blue, Eunice had first called the paint, then qualified that as '96 TARDIS blue. "Eunice?"

The barista looking directly into her eyes as the white cursor, frozen on his face, shivered and was gone.

"Eunice?" Reaching the bar, where her drink waited on the counter in front of him. He passed it to her unthreateningly, which wasn't right either. She looked down. Pink paint, VER in neat capitals, then slashed through, incomplete.

Below that, in a quick scrawl, GO WITH HIM.

She looked up.

He gestured toward his mouth, shook his head. He raised a forefinger to point to her lips, then drew it quickly sideways, a request for silence. Lifting a hinged segment of the zinc counter, he took her wrists and pulled her through the resulting gap. He wore more piercings, some very detached part of her observed, in sudden proximity to his deeply seamed face, than she'd ever owned earrings.

Drawing her farther behind the chrome and copper of the espresso console, 3.7's clientele hidden beyond it, the paper cup hot in her hand, he released her. Urgently tapped his palm with the forefinger of the other hand, to mime texting. Pointed at her purse.

She put the drink on the nearest flat surface and pulled out her phone.

Her e-mail notification sounded. She looked down, to find, no pass code having been required, a single e-mail notification.

BRANCH PLANT <No Subject>

She opened it.

If you're reading this they got me. Go with Bojangles [NOT his real name]. Trust people he takes you to. Sorry I fucked

> up your life. Hope things I set up help get it unfucked. Your provider's server doesn't have this message. Now it's not on your phone either.

It vanished.

A sound like a doll's tambourine.

She looked up. He held open a black bag she recognized as a Faraday pouch. Joe-Eddy owned several, all of them trademarked Black Hole. No radio signals, in or out. He gestured for her to drop her phone in.

She remembered the message. Dropped the phone in the bag. He pointed at her face. The glasses, she realized. She took them off, adding them to the bag, then the headset. Impatiently, he shook the bag. She remembered the Tulpagenics phone. Found it in the inside pocket of her jacket, dropped it in. He frowned, jingling. The case for the glasses. She found it in her purse, dropped it in.

He folded the bag with the same dramatic finality Joe-Eddy displayed when closing his, then jerked a hitchhiker's thumb toward the rear of 3.7, toward grubby green-painted walls. She followed him back, into an ancient dishwashing area, the windowless survivor of however many previous businesses.

Eunice would have known, she thought, eyes stinging.

He took a worn black jacket from a row of coat hooks, handed it to her. Joe-Eddy's size, down-lined, it hung on her when she'd zipped it up, its cuffs covering her hands. He passed her the kind of white mask she'd unsuccessfully tried to buy when the smoke had been at its worst. She put it on, remembering the mask Virgil had made her wear with the silicosis suit.

He put on a black leather jacket, then a white mask like hers, which she imagined pressing uncomfortably on his piercings, though maybe he'd enjoy that. Stowing the Faraday pouch inside the jacket, he zipped up. Then the thumb again, toward what was obviously 3.7's rear door.

She followed him out, into an unroofed passageway no wider than the space behind the bar, cluttered with buckets and mops. She'd left her drink behind, she realized, but then remembered that she was wearing a mask.

Further narrowness, around two corners and into an alley, where a sledlike black Harley touring bike waited. He unshackled a pair of very white helmets from a chrome rack at the back, passing her one, then turned and mounted. She put on the helmet, fastened its strap, climbed on behind him, the engine coming to life, and then they were rolling forward.

By the time they were on Bryant, ascending into the bottom level of the bridge, she knew he was a much better rider than Joe-Eddy.

From the center lane, then, she looked up into girders blurring past. Would someone take over the bar, at 3.7? a part of her wondered. Some espontáneo, scrambling over the counter, seizing control of the levers?

Did Joe-Eddy know that Eunice was gone? Would her postproduction still be spoofing what the Robertson heads picked up in the apartment? And the drones, in their camouflaged cote atop the cartridge-refill place? What had happened to the one she'd seen in Clarion Alley, recording that mural? Would it have flown home?

The thought of it making its way alone along Valencia almost made her sob, so she concentrated on the girders, pretending they were a GIF of metal grilles, endlessly racing past, though in reality to Treasure Island, which they soon reached.

34

WORKING FROM HOME

"Where've you been?" Rainey asked, Thomas slung on her hip in the kitchen, as Netherton let himself in. "I tried to phone you."

"In Lowbeer's car," he said. "It must have been blocking calls. There's a situation."

"The stub—?" Her eyes widened.

"It's still there. Not war, no. Our software agent there is threatened, apparently. I'll have to break our rule, I'm afraid." Their first post-Thomas protocol: not working from home in the evening.

"Good." He saw her relief.

He took the controller from his jacket pocket, fumbled with it.

"What's that?"

"Neural cut-out for an anthropoid drone." It unfolded, becoming a symmetrically blobby silver-toned tiara. Again he noticed its array of small black holes. They held cameras, he assumed. "I have to go there now. With Ash. She'll work from home."

Thomas, looking at him, winced fiercely and began to cry.

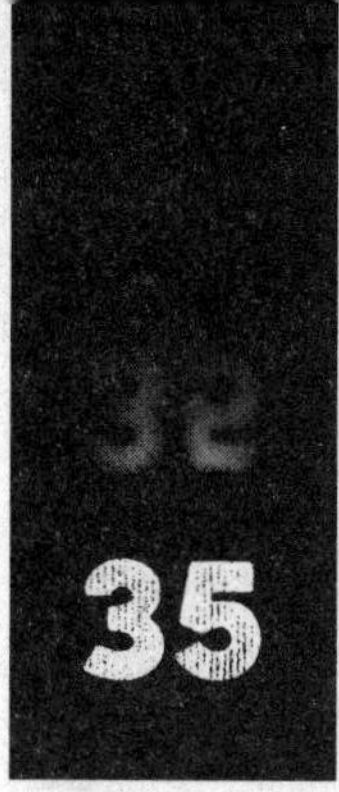

FABRICANT FANG

Out onto the new span now, Treasure Island behind them, past those few remaining pylons of the old bridge, preserved out of concern for something's habitat, she couldn't remember what, and then the cold glare of what Joe-Eddy deemed the world's shittiest LED billboards. To loop back, toward East Bay waterfront and the penetrative reek of the EBMUD plant, unseen at first but soon a dingy miniature Tomorrowland in the middle distance, fairy realm of off-white domes and sewage piping.

In Oakland, now, headed to where the drones had been printed, she assumed. Where Sevrin had manipulated lowball cryptocurrencies to pay for them. Where currently she knew no one at all.

Nimitz, she remembered, passing a sign, was the older, familial name for this highway along the waterfront. Recalling the names of neighborhoods here she'd heard of but never seen, walled magically away behind shared embankment: Ghost Town, Dogtown, Cypress Village, Lower Bottoms.

Turning left then, away from the Posey Tube, into vaguely familiar nonresidential streets. Slowing, after a few more turns, to park. Cutting the ignition.

She'd once had an interview near here, but couldn't remember what for. Releasing the barista's waist, she got stiffly off the bike, legs unsteady. She removed the helmet, emerging into silence, lack of vibration. She pulled down the filtration mask.

Lowering a centerstand, he pulled the bike back, front wheel slightly leaving the pavement. She looked up at the four-story gray building, industrial, not new, and then around, at the empty street behind her, a wholesale fruit business opposite, its name in Chinese and English. He dismounted, removed his helmet, then his mask, and walked toward the building.

She followed him, helmet under her arm.

The entrance was unmarked. Beyond unwashed glass doors, a drab foyer, a rectangle of gray cardboard taped to its rear wall. FABRICANT FANG 3RD FLOOR, in green marker.

The elevator, enameled a dull gray, reminded her of card catalogs in old public libraries. He pushed the button for the third floor. The door shuddered shut. She half expected thumbnails to appear, then remembered.

The elevator stopped, door clanking open.

"Welcome to Fabricant Fang," said the man who'd brought the drones to Wolven + Loaves, and taken away the Franklins. "I'm Dixon." Bearded, ball-capped, in a black t-shirt and brown workpants, orange plastic sonic-protection muffs hugging his neck.

"I'm Verity," she said, stepping out. Behind her, the door made an impatient sound. She turned, saw the barista preventing it from closing, his helmet slung on its strap from his wrist. With his other hand he passed the Faraday pouch to the bearded man and took Verity's helmet. He gestured impatiently with it, indicating the down jacket. She zipped out of it and draped it over her helmet, which he withdrew, into the elevator, then released the door, which jolted shut. Sound of his descent.

"Come meet Kathy," the bearded man said.

Along a hallway, walls the dingy beige of the foyer below. He opened one of a pair of brown-painted steel doors, into bright light and a low tumult of small sounds. "Don't worry about your ears," he said, touching an orange plastic muff. "I just wear these because I get tired of it."

Stepping past him into a factory loft, shadow-free fluorescent light and this quiet cacophony of rustling, clicking, buzzing. Machines, busy rows of them. The walls were white-painted concrete block. To her left, steel-framed windows with old-fashioned privacy glass, horizontally ridged. A smell like scorched polyester. She recognized some of the machinery from tours Stets had been given: deposition printers, injection molders . . .

"Kathy Fang." A woman, offering her hand.

Verity took it. "Verity Jane."

"Expecting you." Handshake firm.

"How?"

"We received a text." Chinese-American, late thirties in a gray sweat-shirt and mom jeans that probably weren't ironic.

"She texted you?"

"Never uses the same number twice. But she'd told us recently that we'd hear, if she had to go away."

"What did it say?"

"That she was going away. That you were on your way, from the city."

"Why am I here?"

"She bought something from us. We've been modifying it to her specifications. It's for you."

Remembering her phone, Verity looked back at the man who'd introduced himself as Dixon. "He has my phone," she said to the woman, "and everything Tulpagenics issued me. I want my phone."

"Sorry. Needs to stay pouched," the woman said.

"Eunice tell you that?"

"In the same text, but we'd insist anyway."

"The drones were made here?"

"They seriously slowed us down, on a run of mandibles."

"Mandibles?"

"Between those drones and finishing your boy, we put a kink in the costuming pipeline for a semi-big second sequel."

"Boy?"

"We'd gotten hold of plans ourselves, had fabbed most of it. Then Eunice contacted us, offering plans for the rest, plus her own modifications, in exchange for exclusive option to buy. The plans for the modifications alone would have been worth it to us. We did the job. This morning she phoned, told us she was picking up the option, and to expect you. Payment's been delivered. Here you are."

"Is she dead?"

"I don't know. She said we could trust you, as well as anyone she sends to help you. If I knew more, I'd tell you. We build things here. Meet specs. Keep our mouths shut. Film and television production are secretive industries." She gestured down an aisle bisecting the rows of repetitively restless machinery, the length of the long room, to another pair of brown doors. "Come and see him," she said, starting down the aisle, without looking to see whether Verity followed.

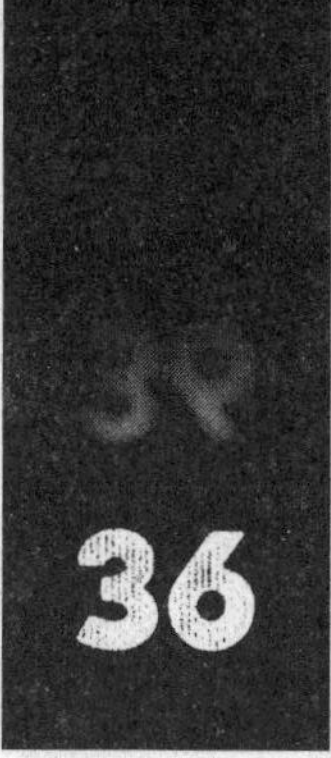

GONE

"Gone," Ash said, when Netherton answered her pulsing sigil.

Rainey had just placed an egg salad sandwich and a glass of milk on the kitchen table, beside the controller.

"That would be Eunice?" he asked.

"Neither Johns Hopkins nor the University of Washington are hosting her now," Ash said. "Johns Hopkins continues to provide a better gateway than we had previously, and I've retained what little access we had to Cursion's back chatter. She hasn't been mentioned."

"Where does that leave us, then?"

"Verity Jane."

"Why did you choose her?" he asked.

"I didn't want our nascent agent emulating any personalities at Cursion. Verity's not sociopathic."

"This Jane?" he asked.

"Verity. Jane's her surname."

Netherton picked up half of his sandwich. "Tell me more, while I eat."

"We obliquely put Eunice in touch with fabricators. She ordered four small military-grade aerial drones. We then managed to contact them ourselves, discovering that they were already building, for themselves, a passable knockoff of a bipedal combat drone. Verity Jane may already be with them, in Oakland. Wherever she is, she finds herself in a very different situation than the one she woke to Monday. Via the drone represented by the sim you practiced with, you'll soon be having a conversation with her. A woman with no idea of stubs, and no particular reason to believe anything you say."

His mouth full, Netherton nodded dubiously, momentarily forgetting that she couldn't see him.

37

TOP-HEAVY

Slightly smaller than Joe-Eddy's bedroom, the room beyond the second set of brown doors, less brightly lit, was empty, aside from a metal folding chair and something that reminded Verity of an Italian heater her mother had had, an electric oil-filled radiator, squat yet dynamic-looking. This one, though, was strapped to a hand trolley, tilted back against the wall. Her mother's had been teal, chrome trim. This one, various shades of gray. "What's that?" she asked.

"Your guy," Kathy Fang said, behind her, in the doorway.

Verity turned. "'Guy'?"

"A drone," Kathy Fang said. Dixon was behind her, his earmuffs on.

"It flies?"

"Has legs," Dixon said. "Wheels too. Can't fly."

Verity turned back, seeing that it did have legs, short ones, two of them, currently positioned between the trolley's two plump tires. "Why's it strapped in like that?"

"Keeps it from falling over while the gyros are off," Kathy Fang said. "It's still charging." She indicated a flat rectangular unit on the floor, like the charger for an electric bicycle but larger, a red LED glowing at one end. "That goes green, it's ready."

"For what?"

"For whoever it is you're supposed to meet."

Verity looked at the chair.

"Once you've met them, there's a more comfortable space for you upstairs. Wave when they're here and Dixon will take you up. We have mandibles need overseeing." She stepped back, closing the door.

There were two unopened bottles of water on the floor beside the chair. She sat down, bent to pick one up, unscrewed the top, and drank.

With the bottle in her hand, she looked at the thing. The LED on the charger was still red. "Eunice?"

Which felt stupid, and made her sad when there was no answer.

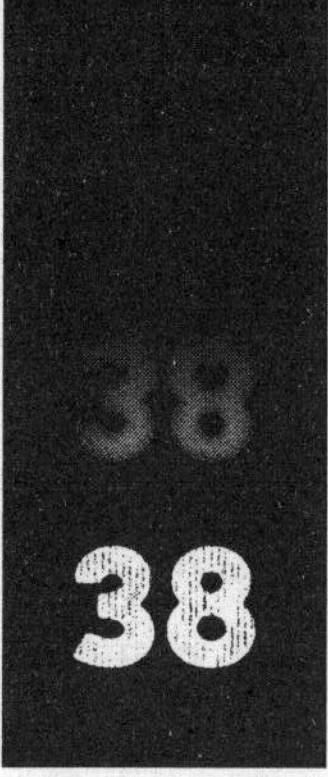

THE HANDSHAKE

Netherton remembered Flynne using a county-fabbed controller, printed in a plastic resembling icing sugar, to first interface with the peripheral they'd found for her in London.

Seated on the couch now, with the controller from the Denisovan Embassy activated, eyes closed, its cams showed him their flat, in that anachronistic squashed-circle format familiar from the sim. The upper segment was currently presenting the windows directly behind him, with their view of the mews.

"Waiting for the handshake," Ash said, likely in the yurt, in Dalston, attended by her tattoos and the tardibot.

"What handshake?"

"Your controller must perform one with Johns Hopkins APL."

"Why, if Eunice is no longer there?"

"It's our best present gateway to adequate connectivity. University of Washington's slower."

A short tone sounded.

"What was that?"

"The handshake," she said. "We're in."

The display filled with another room, smaller, bare. A woman in a tweed jacket leaned tensely forward on a chair, staring at him narrowly.

"We are indeed," he said to Ash, surprised at the awe he felt.

"Are what, indeed?" the woman in the stub asked. She had a plastic bottle of what looked like water in one hand.

"In," said Netherton, rattled. "Sorry. Didn't realize you could hear me. Do you have a phone?" Thinking of an implant, but then he remembered that she wouldn't.

"They took them both," she said.

"How are we communicating?"

"It must have a speaker. And a microphone."

She meant the drone, he decided. "You're Verity?"

"You first."

"Wilf," he said, "Wilf Netherton."

"Where are you?"

"London."

"Why am I speaking with you?"

"Eunice," he said, "though I've never spoken with her myself."

"Where is she?"

"I don't know."

She frowned. "She's gone, isn't she?"

"I don't know," he said, "but I'm here to offer assistance."

She was up now, stepping forward.

"I can't see you, when you're that close," he said.

"Cams?"

"Of course."

"I can't see them."

“They probably look like small round holes,” he said, “about two millimeters in diameter.”

Extreme close-up of gray tweed. The high-resolution texture of an alternate universe.

“Like Robertson heads,” she said, whatever that might mean.

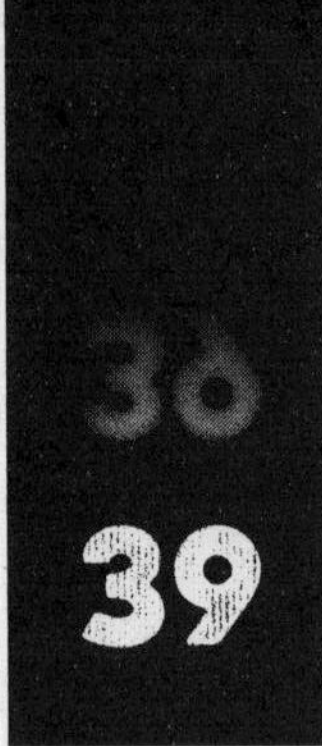

STUMPY

Verity glanced over at the brown doors. Beyond which Kathy Fang and Dixon supposedly worked their field of mandibles.

"Your name's Will?"

"Wilf. Netherton."

"What do you do, Wilf?"

"Public relations."

"Where?"

"London."

"Who for?"

"Freelance," he said. "Where are we?"

"Oakland." She remembered Eunice's final message. How she should trust the people the barista took her to. "If you're in London, why didn't they just put me on a phone?"

"Who?"

"Kathy Fang."

"I don't know her."

"Eunice bought this thing from her. You still haven't told me why you're here."

"I know someone who knows Eunice. Or knows of her. It's complicated."

One of its feet moved then, or tried to, but was restrained by the lower of the two heavy canvas straps. She took a step back.

"Why can't I move its foot?" he asked anxiously.

"It's strapped in."

"Into what?"

"The kind of trolley you'd use to move a washing machine. Two wheels, balloon tires, handle at the top?"

"I see the handle in the rear display. Hadn't realized what it was. I'm restrained?"

"Gyros," she said, becoming aware of the faint hum of their engines as she said it. "You're top-heavy without them, so they've strapped you in to keep you from falling over. Sounds like they're running now."

"Could you free me, please?"

She considered the length of the thing's arms, imagining it reaching up to strangle her, then saw that it seemed handless as well as headless. "And you're still plugged into the charger but the light's green now."

"Would you mind unplugging that as well?"

"Want me to get them in here?"

"Who?"

"Kathy and Dixon. They built it."

"If you don't mind," he said, "I'd rather you did it."

"Have you seen it?"

"I've seen a model of it. In an instructional sim."

"Stumpy as it is, it's still intimidating."

"Stumpy?" He sounded disappointed.

"Might be a meter, a little over?"

"I'd assumed it would be taller."

"If it weren't quite as wide as it is through the shoulders, it would look like SpongeBob."

"Who's that?"

"You don't have SpongeBob, in England?"

"No," he said.

"I'm not even sure I can get these fasteners undone. Don't move at all, until I tell you to. When I do, move slowly. This is creepy."

"Sorry," he said.

Approaching it again, she bent, standing the water bottle on the floor, to study the identical friction-lock devices that held the two straps taut. She caught herself waiting for Eunice's instructive pictograph hands to appear. "Damn."

"I beg your pardon?"

"Nothing. Let me concentrate."

40

BABY STEPS

Ask her to tilt the trolley forward," Ash said, "into the vertical, supporting it there as you step out."

He assumed that Verity couldn't hear her, but would hear him if he responded.

"Mute is one tap," Ash said, "maxillary central incisors, either one. Unmute is another tap."

He touched his upper front teeth with his tongue. "Why?"

"It might fall on you, if you step off when it's unsupported. This isn't a real combat drone, but a hobbyist's reasonably accurate reconstruction of a research prototype for one."

"Hold on," he said, and tapped his teeth again. A familiar close-up of tweed. "How's that going?"

"Kind of a ratchet, with a safety catch." Metal clanged against metal. "One more. Okay. Now the charger." She must have knelt, the tweed dropping out of sight, brown hair very close to the cameras. "Good to go." She stood.

"Another favor?" he asked.

"What?"

"If you could tilt the trolley forward, into the vertical, and steady it there, while I step off? This is my first time on the actual drone. I've only walked in the sim." He tapped his teeth. "How did you know it was tilted back?" he asked Ash.

"Trigonometry," Ash said, he assumed likewise muted.

Verity reached behind him, over his head. The angles Ash had used altered, as Verity grasped what he now recognized as the trolley's handle, bringing it forward. "I have my toe in front of a wheel," she said.

He tapped again. "May I try now?"

"No sudden moves," Verity said.

He advanced the left foot, then lowered it, finding the floor. "Good?"

"It's on the floor," she said.

He repeated the sequence with the right foot.

"You're clear of the trolley," she said.

"May I keep walking?"

"Your call."

He took two more steps, then extruded the small wheels from their housings beneath the feet.

"What are you doing?" she asked.

"Wheels," he said. "They're individually powered. But it can also free-wheel, for skating. I haven't skated yet."

"Why doesn't it have hands?"

"It has manual capacities," Netherton said to Verity, and surprised himself by partially raising the arms, "but I haven't yet had any demonstrated." The wrists tapered smoothly to complexly irregular stumps. He flexed his own right hand, inadvertently causing several odd-looking elements to snap out, then instantly retract.

"Don't do that," Ash said. "Some are dangerous, others merely intimidating. You'll frighten her."

Verity looking down at him felt familiar from using Wheelies, in the county, though the drone was quite a bit taller.

"Did Eunice choose you for this?" she asked.

"Sorry," said an unfamiliar voice. In a gap between the partially opened doors, a woman's face. "Checking to make sure you got through."

"Who are you?" Netherton asked.

"Kathy Fang."

"What's out there?"

"Our fabrication floor."

"Retract the wheels," Ash said. "Walk. It's not a Wheelie Boy."

Netherton drew them up, into their slots in the feet, as the woman opened the doors wide. A man stood directly behind her, bearded, wearing small orange plastic bowls over either ear.

Netherton took a step forward. Another.

OPEN-PLAN ANXIETY

Verity watched the gym-rat SpongeBob, unsteady on its feet, stepping out in front of her, into the white brilliance of Fabricant Fang, amid the jittery sound of machines.

"What are you fabbing?" it asked, stopping.

"Alien mandibular units," Kathy Fang said. "My crew's upstairs on their lunch break. We'll go up to the roof. We have a place up there where you can talk. Through those doors." Pointing.

"Thank you." The drone started toward the far end of the room, along the aisle that broke the rows of machines. It was managing not to waddle now, on its short legs, though it looked as if it should. She remembered the gyroscopes. It reached the far end of the aisle and turned right, to face the doors into the hallway. Lacking visible eye-equivalents, or head motion, she thought, it had no way of suggesting either curiosity or attention. But Wilf, whoever he was, might be looking at her right now. Feeling a need to move, she started after it, stepping past Kathy and Dixon.

They followed it up the aisle, Verity noting that the mandibles, assuming these were those, were being printed from something with a certain amount of jiggle. "Why the roof?"

"Quiet-time cube. Friend of ours builds them."

Dixon, who she saw had brought the charger with him, was holding a door open. She followed the drone out.

In the corridor, the elevator door clanked open. She and Kathy stepped in, the drone following, then Dixon, who pressed an unmarked button above four. "Are you concerned about the possibility of nuclear war?" Wilf asked, sounding, as the elevator rose, like a canvassing missionary.

The three of them looked down.

"Are you?" Verity asked, as the door grated open.

"On your behalf, certainly. My wife is as well. Has been since first learning of it."

Verity, imagining Mrs. Drone in a flowered straw hat, unexpectedly inhaled what might have been a vagrant waft of EBMUD. Looking up, she realized they were outside.

"This way," said Kathy Fang, leading them toward a gray cargo container, lightly rusted, the smallest standard size, a cube ten feet on a side. Various vents and ducts, unrusted, ran across the roof and down the side facing them. "Soundproofed, fully ventilated, temperature and humidity controlled, potable running water, chemical toilet stores waste on the outside."

Dixon was tapping a keypad on the container's side. Verity looked to where she thought the Bay would be, but any view was behind taller buildings. As she turned back, Dixon was opening a door, into mellow light.

The doorway, half the width of the cube, revealed Silicon Valley quasi-Japanoid décor. Light wood, tatami, a white paper screen, a low gray couch, a wooden table to match.

"You won't be locked in," said Dixon, "but pretend you are. We know when the door's open, or if anyone sets foot on the roof. Either happens, I'll be right up. There's an iPad on the couch, open to a page of commands. Alert's in red. Tap that, if you want out."

"What is this?" Verity asked.

"They help reduce OPA," Kathy Fang said. "This was one of the prototypes. We make some of the interior trim for them."

"OPA?"

"Open-plan anxiety. That's for your shoes, there." Indicating a translucent tray Verity assumed was from Muji.

"What do you use it for?" Verity asked.

"Naps. Get in."

The cube was resting on wooden pallets, a double layer of them. Verity stepped up and in.

"I haven't tried taking a step up," said Wilf.

They all looked at the drone.

"Sorry. Concerned I might topple over."

"Turn around," said Dixon, "and sit, in the doorway. Straighten out the legs, in front of you, right angle to the torso, and I'll swing them in for you."

Verity knelt and began to remove her shoes. Away, she hoped, from where it might sit.

It rotated in place with a series of baby steps, then sat. Having no ass, there was nothing much for it to seat, so she wondered if it was being held upright by the gyros. She got to her feet as Dixon swung its short but outstretched legs into the cube.

"Thank you," the voice called Wilf said, and she reminded herself that however helpless the thing itself might seem, she had no way of knowing whether he, or it, really was.

"Ring when you're done," Kathy Fang said.

Dixon placed the charger on the floor and closed the door, causing the indirect lighting to go up a notch.

Not quite a cube, inside, she saw. A few feet of floor, out from the wall opposite the door, were behind sliding paper screens, now partially open, through which was visible a white curve of toilet. The rest was either tatami, wood, or paper, which she guessed would be over plastic and soundproofing, except for the ceiling, white but translucent, which emitted a gentle glow.

"Could you take it over and get me up?" the drone asked, crossly.

"Do what?" She stared at it.

Silence.

"Could I do what?" she repeated.

It rose, with unexpected agility.

"Whoa," she said, stepping back.

"Sorry," said a woman with an English accent, "Wilf forgot to mute when he spoke to me, so you heard him. I'm Ash. We're working together, Wilf and I. Hadn't time to introduce myself earlier. Didn't want to complicate things."

"You were listening," Verity said.

"Sorry."

"Who else is in there?"

"No one, at the moment," the woman said. "We'll let you know, should anyone join us."

"You're in public relations too?" Verity asked.

"What you'd call IT, actually."

"Where are you?"

"London."

"With Wilf?"

"In my studio, four-point-eight miles from his flat. We're both working from home."

"You know Eunice?"

"Not to speak to, but I've been involved with her, these past three months. I'm better acquainted with her than Wilf is. He's new."

"To what?" Verity asked.

"To things Eunice."

"What was she?" Verity asked.

"The result of hybridization of two lines of military research. One toward uploading aspects of human consciousness, the other toward an expert system focused on a particular sort of warfare. Would you like to use the toilet?"

"I would," Wilf said. "Excuse me."

"I meant Verity," the woman said, "but have a glass of water, while you're up. You look dehydrated."

"I thought you weren't with him," Verity said.

"I have feed from the cameras in his controller," the woman, Ash, said, "which happened to be showing me his reflection in a mirror, near where he was seated."

Verity stood, removed her jacket, hung it on an aluminum hook, crossed to the screens, entered, and slid them shut. The toilet, once she'd used it, flushed itself. She washed her hands at the tiny stainless sink in the opposite corner.

Stepping out, sliding the screens shut behind her, she saw the drone seated on the floor, at the low table, across from the couch.

42

WIFELY ADVICE

"Try to avoid being your more dickish self with Ash," Rainey said, having followed him into the kitchen after he'd used the toilet. "Not that she cares, but it could put Verity off. You're a lot less like that now, but with Ash you regress. And Verity needs your help, which you can't as easily give if you've already convinced her you're an asshole." She handed him a glass of water.

She only heard his side of his exchanges with Ash and Verity Jane. He tongued the back of his front teeth, to be certain that he was still muted.

"I'll try," he said, kissing her cheek and turning back to the living room, where the nanny was tumbling about on the floor, pandaform again, with Thomas.

"Why did you say that?" Verity Jane demanded, Netherton realizing he'd unmuted while assuming he was muting.

43

STILL LIFE WITH LAWYERS

"Say what?" the man called Wilf asked.

"'I'll try,'" Verity quoted.

A pause. "Positive affirmation," he said. "Didn't mean to voice it."

"Where's Ash?" Verity asked.

"Here," said Ash.

Verity sat on the couch, her jacket on the wall opposite looking like something visiting from a radically more normal planet. "Joe-Eddy," she said. "Does he just think I haven't come home? Will Cursion come to his place, looking for me?"

"He knows you're in good hands," Ash said, "but not where you are. I'm opening a small hatch now, on the upper surface of the carapace."

Verity leaned forward, watching it open.

"This is a video projector," Ash said. Something resembling a miniature periscope rose out of the opening.

It swung to Verity's left, toward the bathroom, the white-screened door filling with the feed from one of the two Robertson heads in Joe-Eddy's living room, focused on the white porn couch. On which sat a young black woman, intent on an open laptop. The feed halved, adding another from the kitchen, angled down on the table there, where a young man, white, sat at his own laptop.

"Who's that?" Verity asked.

"Starting associates in a senior San Francisco law firm," Ash said, "one Eunice retained on Joe-Eddy's behalf, through a front. Their presence would complicate matters, were Cursion to attempt to abduct him."

"Where is he?"

The feed from the kitchen was replaced by another from the living room: Joe-Eddy at his workbench, in his orange plaid shirt-jacket, his back to the camera, probably de-soldering something.

"What happens when they go home?" Verity asked.

"They're spelled off by the next pair."

"Do they go out with him?"

"He's not currently going out."

"And he's okay with that?"

"He knows it's for his own good."

"You think Cursion might try?"

"They hire former military contractors," Ash said. "The two who installed the cams, for instance."

"Is everything he says to those lawyers being tweaked in post?"

"No, but he says nothing to them of any value to Cursion."

"Cursion sees Joe-Eddy running an Airbnb, or a twenty-four hour internet café, exclusively for expensive junior lawyers, they won't think that's you?"

"They've no idea we exist," Ash said. "They wouldn't believe it if you told them. They must assume Eunice is behind the lawyers. But they know enough of her capabilities to be wary of what she's left behind."

"She said they'd shut her down, if they could. And she asked me if I knew how to ride on the back of a motorcycle. Right before I had to, just after she vanished. She said one of her branch plants wanted to know if I did."

"She told you about the laminae?"

"She called them different things. Branch plants. Agents. Said they did things behind her back. Do you work for her?"

"No," said Ash, "but we want to help you, which she'd regard as helping her."

"Why would you want to help me?"

Overhead, the efficiently muted sound of something that must have been very loud loomed, swooped, then receded, was gone.

"What was that?" Verity asked.

The door opened.

"Would've knocked," said Dixon, from beneath the brim of his cap, "but you wouldn't have heard me."

"So what did we just hear?"

"Drone," he said, "big one. Bringing something for you." He tugged his orange plastic muffs down around his neck. There was someone behind him, but Verity couldn't see who. She stood up, seeing it was Sevrin, who held something, a gray and bulging portfolio, translucent plastic.

"Miguel here," Dixon nodded toward Sevrin, "arrived about ten minutes ago. Knows Eunice. Kathy says he's here to pick you up." Sevrin, with a grin for Verity, stepped forward, to lay the fog-colored portfolio on the matting at her feet. He unsealed it, pulling out her zipped and folded Muji bag. Reaching in again, he produced something else, folded and black, with casters like the ones on a roll-aboard suitcase.

"What's that?" Verity asked.

"For this," Sevrin said, indicating the drone, "for traveling."

"Eunice sent you?"

"Standing orders, yes."

"You okay with these people?" She looked at Dixon.

"She is," Sevrin said. "I brought them payment for this." Indicating the drone.

"How about the two I'm talking with now, through it?"

"No idea," Sevrin said. "Here to pick you and this up."

"She's gone, right? Dead?"

"Not in touch with her."

"Where are you taking us?"

"Don't know yet." He rolled up the gray plastic envelope. "It can walk?"

"Certainly can," said Ash. Who then, Verity assumed, got it quite ably to its feet.

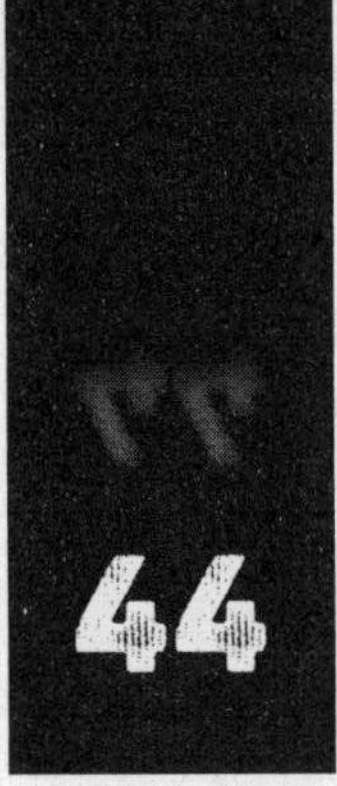

A MONEY LAUNDERER

"Who's that?" Netherton asked Ash, having muted.

"Sevrin," she said, "Moldovan money launderer, on Eunice's payroll. Verity met him earlier. Kathy and Dixon know him as Miguel."

"Why is he there?" Netherton asked, charmed by this archaic job description.

"Either Eunice scripted scenarios for various situations, and he's working from one, or one or more of her laminae are still active, or he's gone rogue."

"It always makes me uncomfortable," Netherton said, "to see them learn they're in a stub. And then they all immediately assume we're from their future."

"Not as uncomfortable as it makes them," Ash said. "I've seen two psychotic breaks, since you've been on leave."

Now the man called Sevrin was unfolding something black. He wore a short jacket and matching narrow trousers, dark gray, with highly reflective black shoes. His black hair was so short that it might have been sprayed on, his goatee equally minimal. Money launderers, in Netherton's experience of Flynne's stub, were the sort of people least destabilized by discovering that their world was a branch of someone else's. They immediately looked for advantage in the knowledge. Netherton unmuted. "What's this all about?" he asked.

The money launderer looked up from what he was doing.

"That's Wilf," said Verity. "He's in London."

"The crew," Kathy Fang announced, appearing behind Sevrin, "are back on the fabrication floor. They've left plenty of food. From a friend's craft service kitchen, a few blocks from here. Anybody hungry?"

LUGGAGE

Verity watched Sevrin help himself to a slice from each of two pizza boxes on the long table. The fourth floor was a single room, identical to the one below but minus the machines. Candle-lit now, if those LED tea lamps from the dollar store counted. Desks, chairs, a few long tables. In the shadows of the farthest corner she recognized the outline of an industrial sewing machine.

She had her bag slung over her shoulder. When she'd opened it to get the shoulder strap, she'd remembered Eunice telling her that whoever she'd sent to the apartment had taken her passport, in advance of the men who'd installed the Robertson-head cams. But there it was, behind her toothpaste, in the zippered inner pocket where she kept it.

"Have something," Kathy Fang said, beside her. "Sometimes you don't know when you'll be able to eat. Triple mushroom's good."

Verity wasn't hungry, but thought she should be. She made herself take a slice of the mushroom pizza, putting it on several paper napkins, along with an industrial-strength canapé-analog from a tray of them. Film and television fuel, for a crew working overtime. Sevrin was into his second slice now. He wore a Prada-flavored bus driver uniform, or maybe the other way around, charcoal gray, with pointy black patent oxfords.

"Sorry," said Ash, very close but from below Verity's waist, startling her.

Verity looked down at the drone.

"We've gotten off on the wrong foot," Ash said. "My fault. Should have introduced myself immediately. Sorry it seemed I was eavesdropping."

"Considering how my week's going, don't worry about it."

"We go now, please," said Severin, behind the drone.

"Where?" Verity asked.

"Her protocol, I drive, get destination, start for that place, get new destination. Repeat until somewhere I wasn't told." He waved the floppy black nylon wheeled thing in the direction of the drone. "You, inside. We need this, on it."

"What is it?" asked Wilf.

"Make you easy to move," Sevrin said. "Nobody sees you walk."

"We can't have the drone's mobility compromised," said Ash, "particularly not its ability to use its arms."

"No problem," Sevrin said, kneeling in front of it. "Holes for legs. Arms fold inside, so"—he wiggled a black flap at the drone—"can move when you need."

"Nice," Kathy Fang said, behind him. "Who built it?"

"Leather shop in Castro," said Sevrin.

"Maybe a first for them," Kathy Fang said, "unless Cordura's somebody's thing."

"Fold arms," Severin said, spreading the case open on the floor.

The drone stepped promptly into the openings and folded its arms, making Verity suspect that Ash was in control. Sevrin pulled the case up around its torso, fastening Velcro as he went, as if putting a strange romper on an even stranger toddler. Now it had a pair of black casters where its ass should have been.

"Pull up legs," Sevrin said. The torso settled onto the casters. He stood, hooked his hand into a handle on the case's back, and raised it, on a black, telescoping rod. He tilted the drone back and rolled it a few feet, toward the snack table, and stood it upright, Verity following. "Put this on," he said to her, taking a folded black garment she hadn't seen before from the table. She put her snacks down, took it from him, and shook it out. A multiply oversized black hoodie, which she then zipped on over her jacket. "And these," passing her a pair of black sunglasses. "Bring the charger," he said to Dixon.

Verity, remembering her food, wrapped the pizza in two paper napkins, the macro-canapé in two more, and put them in the hoodie's pockets.

In the elevator, she put on the sunglasses and pulled up the hood. A media-avoidance costume cliché, all too familiar from when she'd been recently post-Stets.

When they reached the foyer, Dixon held one of the two glass doors, as Sevrin, followed by Kathy Fang, wheeled the drone out of the building, Verity behind them.

The Chinese fruit wholesaler's floodlit signs, across the street, helped dispel the darkness of the sunglasses.

"Is ours," Sevrin said, indicating a dark Mercedes van set up as a minibus, passenger windows darker still.

In its wheeled carrier, handless insectile arms folded mummy-style across its torso, the drone suggested the larval stage of something much more intimidating, headed off to a nursery for robot monsters.

Now Dixon bent to help Sevrin boost it down, over the two entrance steps, to asphalt.

Kathy Fang, beside her, raised the upper edge of the black hood slightly, with the tip of an index finger, to look Verity in the eye. "Be careful. Hope we see you again."

"Thanks," Verity said. "And for pizza." Heard the passenger door of the van power itself open.

"Did you meet her in person?" Kathy Fang asked, her tone suggesting she hadn't.

"I think you met her as in-person as it got," Verity said.

"Ready," said Dixon. "Here's the charger," indicating where he'd left it. He stepped down from the passenger door.

"She was appreciative of our work," Kathy Fang said, "and made me less worried about who we might be selling to. Thing's formidable, in the right hands."

"I liked her too," said Verity, feeling tears start.

"Time to go," Sevrin said, from the van.

She couldn't see him, but turned and headed in that direction, her bag over her shoulder. The van's engine started, headlights coming on.

Into an unlit interior, the door closing behind her.

Between the sunglasses, her almost-tears, and the van's limo-grade tint, she couldn't see. Pulling glasses off and hood back, she saw the drone seatbelted into the far end of the upholstered bench, directly behind Sevrin.

"Sit next to it," he said, from the driver's seat.

"I wouldn't want it behind me," she said. Stepping over the charger, she seated herself beside the drone.

"Fasten belt," said Sevrin, pulling out of the space in front of Fabricant Fang.

She did, as he turned left at the corner, toward Jack London Square, away from the beach. Then another left. She remembered what he'd said about protocol.

"Verity? I'm Rainey," said an unfamiliar voice, tone softer than Ash's. "Like 'rainy' but with an *e* before the *y*. Wilf's wife."

Verity side-eyed the drone, her vision of Mrs. Drone in a flowered hat returning.

"If I were you," this new voice said, "I'd think this was pushy, but I wanted to introduce myself. Wilf's working from home, so I've had a chance to get an idea of your situation."

"You don't sound English."

"Canadian."

Verity looked at the top of the drone's headless torso, noticing the outline of the hatch from which the periscopic projector had emerged. "You're in London?"

"We live here, but my work's in Toronto."

"Doing what?"

"Public relations."

"You and Wilf?"

"No. We met when we were working together, but I moved on to crisis management. You must have had professional advice, leaving Stets?"

Virgil, among others, had suggested that, but it hadn't been something she'd wanted. "No. That felt like more of what I wanted out of. How do you know about that?"

"I've been reading about you."

Sevrin, adjusting his earpiece, said something monosyllabic, then something else, slightly longer.

"What language is that?" Verity asked.

"Moldovan," he said, taking another left.

It was almost impossible to see anything through the tinted side windows, the view ahead nearly as unhelpful.

"How many of you in there?" she asked the drone.

"Three," said the Canadian, Rainey. "Wilf has a controller. Ash and I are patched into it by phone. We can each look around on our own, with the drone's camera array. Wilf's told me about Eunice."

"She's gone. Dead, I guess, except that she wasn't alive to begin with."

"Why not?"

"AI."

"I wouldn't assume she wasn't alive," Rainey said.

"She said she was layers of software." Verity looked from the drone to Sevrin, wondering what he was making of this, and then ahead, finding they now seemed to be back on Nimitz, heading for the bridge. "What's a controller?"

"It keeps your body from moving as you move your device. This isn't full neural cut-out, as the drone has no nervous system. But with Wilf just learning to walk, his legs still move a little. When he walks in the drone, he's sitting here on the couch, twitching his legs."

"He's learning to walk?"

"I am," said Wilf, "thank you."

"Ash," Verity asked, "you there?"

"Yes," said Ash.

"Regular party in a backpack," Verity said.

EMOTIONAL SUPPORT

Lowbeer's sigil pulsed. Netherton tongued mute. "Yes?"

"Providing emotional support to distraught clients is a major aspect of Rainey's work now, I gather."

Netherton looked at the back of the vehicle's driver's almost shaven skull, the antique motorway ahead of them, Verity herself seated to the drone's right, semi-opaque windows to either side. "It is."

"Let's consider her a part of this, then, going forward. I imagine the two of them might get along. I'll discuss it with her, arrange compensation."

"I doubt compensation would be a factor," Netherton said. Opening his eyes again, not seeing Rainey, he stood, went into the kitchen, poured himself a glass of pomegranate juice, and drank.

"I agree," said Lowbeer. "That's why I think she might be helpful."

Netherton watched the coronet-emblazoned sigil fade, feeling vaguely demoted but nonetheless proud of Rainey, for being who she was.

47

PHONELESSNESS

"Rainey?" Verity asked. "You still there?" Sevrin had driven them out of Treasure Island's Kubrickian tunnel, back onto the old span, so there was no mystery about this part of their route to wherever they were ultimately headed.

"She's with Thomas," Wilf answered.

"Thomas who?"

"Our son."

"How old?"

"Eleven months."

The drone's hatch opening again, periscope extruding, to project a feed on the back of Sevrin's seat. A baby, in a navy-and-white horizontally striped playsuit, sitting up on a pale wooden floor, enthusiastically patty-caking a craftsy-looking fabric ball with both hands. A similar ball rolled slowly past, in front of the baby, then out of frame.

"Cute," Verity said, and he was, but then another ball, not the one she'd just seen, rolled back into frame, behind him. "Who's rolling the balls?"

"They roll themselves, all six of them," Wilf said. "Our nanny."

"Your nanny what?"

"Thomas likes her well enough, configured this way, but most of all as three pandas," he said, Verity thinking London had some seriously next-level parenting gear, then baby and balls were replaced by a young woman, brown hair lighter and curlier than Verity's, seated at a red table. "Rainey," he said, "last week." Who stood, in jeans and a long-sleeved black t-shirt, smiled at the camera, and walked out of frame, the feed closing. The periscope descended, the drone's hatch shutting behind it. "Where are we going?" he asked.

"We're on the Bay Bridge, to San Francisco," Verity said.

Sevrin, touching his earpiece, briefly spoke Moldovan.

Then they were off the bridge, into the city's traffic.

"Like Lev's grandfather's garage," said Rainey, "minus the tanks."

"Tanks?" asked Verity.

"A friend's grandfather collects antique vehicles," Wilf said, "some military."

She peered through the inky tint of the window to her right. Union Square? A pang of phonelessness struck her, mainly for Google Maps. "Geary?" she asked Sevrin.

"Yes. Close now. Be ready."

"What about this?" She indicated the drone, beside her.

"You'll have help. Here," said Sevrin, pulling to the left, stopping.

"Where?" she asked, spotting a Walgreens sign on the corner diagonally opposite.

"Geary and Taylor," he said, as the passenger door opened.

Virgil climbed in, wearing a black all-weather running outfit with reflective silver highlights. "Where's our other customer?" he asked.

"This," Verity said, leaning back to give him a better view of the drone. "Wasn't expecting you."

He grinned. "I'm supposed to get that out for you."

"It's on wheels," she said. "There's a handle on top, pulls out. Don't trip on the charger there." She pointed.

Sevrin opened the driver-side door, got out. He closed it, starting around the front of the van. She undid her own seatbelt, scooting along the seat toward the open passenger door, then getting her legs up, out of Virgil's way. Sevrin appeared at the passenger door, a cab passing behind him. "Stay until he has it out," he said to Verity.

"What's here?" she asked. Virgil, having squeezed past her, was pulling up the handle, unfastening the drone's seatbelt.

"The Clift," said Sevrin.

Virgil edged the drone forward, until it cleared the front of the seat. One hand on the handle, the other near its feet, he lowered it to the carpeted floor. "Wouldn't want this in an overhead bin," he said, swinging it around by the handle. He started to back it out, past her.

He and Sevrin lowered it to the street.

"Don't forget bag," Sevrin said.

"Hood up," said Virgil.

She picked up the charger, which he and Sevrin seemed to have forgotten, pulled her hood up, put on the sunglasses, grabbed her bag, and got out. Virgil was pulling the drone around the back of the van.

She and Sevrin followed. "See you," he said. He headed for the driver-side door.

Virgil rolled the drone up the side of the curb and made for the entrance. She caught up. His hand lightly on her shoulder as they passed hotel security.

In the lobby, various shades of twilit lilac, Virgil immediately cut left, avoiding reception, toward a curtained corridor leading to the elevators, Verity glancing back to see the iconic Big Chair, on which she'd been photographed shortly after meeting Stets. "Virgil," she said, "here's a question. Answer me, straight up, or I might kill you."

He side-eyed her. "Long day?"

"Longest ever. Where are you taking me?"

"Suite," he said, "eighth floor."

"Who's there?"

"Stets." They'd rounded a corner, reaching the elevators, the lilac gloaming having grown deeper. "And Caitlin."

"Shit . . ." She pulled the sunglasses off.

"Back from New York on the Honda." The elevator door opened, revealing a dramatically lit maw of russet mirror.

"She's up there?"

The door began to close. He blocked it with his free hand, the other supporting the drone's handle. "I know her. Trust me. It'll be okay."

"Here." She thrust the cable-wrapped charger at the hand holding the door. "I'm done."

He reached for it, causing the door to start to close, but again stopped it, this time with his upper arm. "Please."

"Forget it." She turned, discovering a couple young enough to be in the hotel's prime demographic, observing them with a uniform blankness of expression. "Or just," she said, turning back and pushing past him, "fuck it," the elevator door closed behind her.

CORRIDOR

"Who's Caitlin?" Netherton asked Rainey, still muted, looking up at Verity and this Virgil, as she'd just called him. With the drone parked in the elevator now, between Verity and the stranger in black, all he could really see of them were the bottoms of their chins.

"Stetson Howell's fiancée," Rainey answered. "He and Verity split up a year ago. Amicably, though I doubt she's met Caitlin before."

"Whose idea was it, to bring me here?" Netherton heard Verity ask, the elevator ascending.

"Stets'," the man called Virgil said, "and because I know people here, staff."

"Why's she here?" Verity asked him.

"She wants to be. Only reason there is, with her."

"You say she'll be okay," Verity said.

"She's a grown-up," Virgil said. "The media attention's something she was used to before she met him. Considering she's the hot new flavor in global architecture, at least as far as the media are concerned, not to mention a looker, she's easy to get along with. We all like her."

"Who's Virgil?" Netherton asked Rainey.

"Howell's so-called assistant," she said, "though he's actually a key advisor, which is evidently how he likes it. Virgil, I mean."

The elevator stopped, its door opening.

And then the drone was out, canted sharply back on the corset's wheels, Virgil towing it, giving Netherton a view of passing ceiling fixtures. Along a wide pale lilac corridor, past doors painted palest daffodil.

Virgil briskly setting the pace, Netherton guessed, lest Verity change her mind.

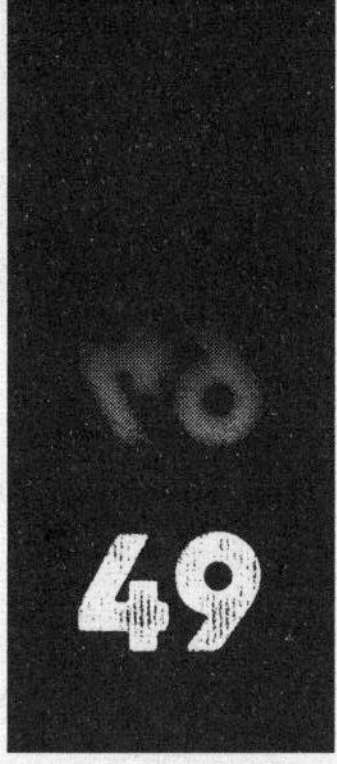

SUITE

Verity stopped Virgil with a hand on his wrist, beside a shallow alcove, its rear wall hung with a floor-to-ceiling oval of unframed mirror. A rest area, she supposed, if your idea of rest involved a ghostly acrylic occasional chair, beneath a precariously tall, worryingly anamorphic floor lamp.

She propped her bag on the phantom chair, put the charger down on it, then unzipped and removed the black hoodie, draping it across bag and chairback. Turning to the mirror, she straightened her jacket. To little effect, she thought.

"Caitlin's casual," Virgil says. "Has sweaters so old the elbows are out, but old-school cashmere. How they do."

"How who do?"

"Old Franco-Irish money and shit," he said.

She checked her makeup in the mirror. Or lack of it, she decided, what she saw being what they'd get. Then took ChapStick from her purse and used it anyway.

"I'll carry your stuff," he said, leaning the drone's handle against the chair and picking up the charger. "You can make an entrance, shake hands if you need to."

"Food in either pocket of the hoodie," she said. "Don't squash it. I'll keep my bag."

He gingerly draped the hoodie over the charger. "This for that?" he asked, indicating first the charger, then the drone.

"Yeah."

"What is it?" he asked, meaning the drone itself.

"Those headless military robot dog-things on YouTube? It's like that," she said.

"Legless, though?"

"They're retracted."

"Keep 'em that way," he said, reaching for its handle. She shouldered her bag and they started along the corridor.

He stopped, only a few doors along, and passed her the handle, taking his phone from a trouser pocket. Thumb to the screen. She heard a door-chain rattle.

Stets opened the door nearest them, smiling, gesturing her in. "Hey."

"Hey yourself." She pulled the drone in, surprised by its weight, Virgil behind her. Heard Stets closing and rechaining the door.

Rooms here might be either a disappointment or a relief, she knew, looking around, depending on how the lobby décor grabbed you. Lilacs and lavenders were dialed down, the furniture blond wood, the only once-edgy touch provided by acrylic bedside and coffee tables in a deep shade of burnt orange-peel. A bigger room than she'd previously seen here. Glimpsing another adjacent, a woman just entering from it. "Caitlin Bertrand," she said, resembling, as Verity recalled a gossip site having put it, a young but brutally determined Françoise Hardy. "Pleased to meet you."

"Verity Jane. Pleased to meet you too."

"And this," Stets said, behind her, "must be it."

Turning, she saw him looking down at the drone. "Why'm I here, Stets?"

"Eunice," he said, looking up at her.

"She's gone."

"She phoned me, after you left with Virgil. More detail on Singapore, at first, but it became a wider conversation." He glanced at the drone. "Is this listening to us?"

"We are, Mr. Howell," said Ash.

"That's Ash," Verity said. "At least two more in there with her."

"My colleague, Wilf Netherton," said Ash.

"Pleased to meet you," said Wilf.

"And Rainey," Ash said, "his wife."

"She's with the baby," Wilf said.

"What are you?" Stets asked, as though he were asking about the weather.

"British," said Ash.

Verity gave Virgil the drone's handle, taking the hoodie from him. He put the charger down, on what she supposed was a minibar. She sat on the couch, sinking into lilac leather, Muji bag beside her. "Sorry," she said, "I have to eat something. Right now." Finding a pocket, she drew out Kathy Fang's pizza, the napkins gone spottily translucent with grease. Unwrapping it, she took a bite.

"Would you rather have room service?" Virgil asked.

She shook her head, swallowed.

"Let her enjoy it," Caitlin said, settling on the couch beside Verity, who was taking a second bite.

Verity pawed with her free hand through the hoodie on her lap, coming up with the napkin-wrapped mega-canapé, which she passed to Caitlin, who promptly unwrapped it, nibbled a corner, then bit off a third of it.

Stets was in front of them now, manipulating something at his knee, through the fabric of his loose gray track pants. A click. She remembered the brace. He lowered himself, facing her, onto a circular lilac hassock.

"They tell me," Verity said to him, after swallowing the last of the pizza, "that they don't know Eunice personally, but know people who do."

"Are you familiar with the strategic concept of competitive control areas?" Ash asked.

"Yes," Stets said.

"Your military has been developing a noetic agent, optimized for operating in them. If local infrastructure didn't offer adequate connectivity, it could be delivered as a portable, self-supporting, self-actuating unit. Eunice was one result, though still very much a prototype when we discovered her. She'd already been appropriated by Cursion, who intended to spin off a civilian product offering some of her original functionality. Which spared us direct contact with your military research and development sector, where we would have been more likely to encounter people able to recognize us as anomalous."

"AI?" Caitlin asked.

"Yes," Ash said, "but the project meshed, early on, with efforts to upload complex human skill sets. So an AI slash upload. Hybrid."

"When she spoke with me," Stets said, "I gathered something like that."

"And this is that?" Caitlin asked, eyeing the drone.

"No," said Ash, "this is simply a drone we're employing, for physical telepresence."

"It evidently hasn't been designed for retail," Caitlin said, "which is always interesting in itself."

"Undo the fastenings on its wheeled wearable," Ash said.

Virgil squinted at Stets. "Assuming it can move," he said, "are you sure we want it to?"

"Eunice's advice," Stets said, "and she particularly stressed this, was that I should trust whoever Verity brought us."

"That must have been quite a call," Virgil said, tilting his head quizzically at Stets.

"It was," Stets said.

Virgil squinted at Stets. "So you'll trust whoever's in control of this thing, its capacities currently unknown, because something that convinced you it was AI told you you should?"

"Under the circumstances," Stets said, "yes."

Virgil looked from Stets to Caitlin, then to Verity, then knelt beside the drone. Verity heard hook and loop fasteners being separated. Soon the black case was folded out flat around it on the carpet.

Legs extruding, it rose, spidery arms still crossed, to step forward, surprising Verity with its steadiness. Now it executed a bow toward Caitlin and Verity. Upright again, it stepped briskly to the orange acrylic coffee table, reaching for a Bay Area lifestyle magazine, small white tongs snicking out from the tips of its arms. Picking the magazine up, it flicked rapidly through, stopping at a page it then displayed to them. A black-and-white portrait of Caitlin. "Design documents Fang originally worked from hadn't specified manipulators," Ash said. "We had help with that from a veteran who piloted similar drones in combat."

It flipped the magazine shut, returning it to the table.

"You introduced Eunice to whoever built this?" Stets asked.

"We put them in her way," Ash said. "She formed her own relationship with them. Our communication with Eunice was limited."

"Why was that?" Stets asked.

"That's complicated," Ash said. "Perhaps it could wait."

"Would it have to do with her having had me fabricate something myself?" he asked.

Verity, Caitlin, and Virgil all looked at him. Then back to the drone.

"Which would be?" asked Ash.

"An interface device," Stets said, producing from behind the lilac couch a large carrying case, in rigid black foam, which he placed on the minibar, beside the drone's charger. It hadn't looked very heavy. He unfastened latches that reminded Verity of the drones' Pelican case, and lifted top and sides away as one, revealing a white, featurelessly feminine foam head in a black cycling helmet. Studded with a variety of black components, it looked like a not-very-enthusiastic cyberpunk cosplay accessory.

"A neural cut-out controller," Wilf said. "I'm wearing one now. Ash is controlling the drone through it."

"I thought she wasn't with you," Verity said.

"By phone," Wilf said, "via my controller."

"Could I do that?"

"No," said Wilf.

"Why not?"

"It's complicated," he said.

"You all say that."

"Would you like something more to eat?" Caitlin asked her. "We keep forgetting that you've had an extremely long day." With a look for Stets and Virgil.

"I'd like my own phone back," Verity said. "Short of that, I need to use the bathroom." She got up.

"I'll show you where things are," Caitlin said, standing.

Verity picked up her bag and followed Caitlin into the larger room.

"Is this business," Caitlin asked, closing the door behind them, "or something else?"

"Business seemed to be how Eunice made things happen," Verity said, putting her bag down on the bed, "but she didn't seem to me to be about it."

"You could say the same of Stets, but I'm sure you know that," Caitlin said.

"I do, but they're different."

"I agree," said Caitlin. "I gather you knew her better than the others."

"Yes, but that was from Monday, till this afternoon."

"Stets doesn't think of her as human," Caitlin said, "but speaks of her as though she was."

"I keep feeling like she was," Verity said, a tear suddenly sliding down her left cheek.

Caitlin plucked tissues from a dispenser in the bathroom, brought them to her. "You'll be safe here with Virgil. Stets and I will return to Fremont. You must be exhausted. We'll talk in the morning."

"The trailer?"

"Yes. And your Londoners will stay with you as well, because Eunice told Stets that she didn't want you out of the drone's sight. You seem to be at the center of something extraordinary. It's captured Stets' imagination in a way I haven't seen before. Where this goes will affect me, unquestionably. But everyone I've come to admire, in Stets' crew, liked you very much."

Verity looked at her. "Thank you," she said.

"You're welcome. Get some sleep," And then she was gone, back through the door, closing it behind her.

Verity turned, taking in the room.

Larger, with a larger bed, a larger television. A square lilac mega-hassock at its center, six feet on a side, atop it a tray with an ice bucket and glasses.

She picked up her bag and took it into the bright bathroom, unzipped and unfolded it, hanging it behind the door, which she then closed. Pulling down the central interior zipper, she found it seemed like everything she'd had at Joe-Eddy's was there, including, she saw, neatly rolled at the bottom, her mummy-bag liner. Cosmetics in the horizontally zipped pocket to the right, oral hygiene and hair products to the left. Behind the toothpaste, as she'd noted on Fabricant Fang's roof, her passport. She checked its unsmiling photograph of a visibly younger self, one who hadn't yet met Stets. Flipping pages, she read her time with him in stamps from places she might never otherwise have visited. Closing it, she tucked it back where she'd found it, brushed her teeth, used the toilet, washed her face and hands, and returned to the first room.

To find Virgil standing with the cosplay helmet in his hands, Caitlin and Stets beside him. "They want you to try it," he said, with a nod in the direction of the drone.

"London," said Ash. "Come and see."

"There's something I can use there?" Verity asked. "Like the drone?"

"Nothing like the drone," Ash said. "You'll see."

"What would I need to do?"

"Sit on the couch. Virgil will help you with fit and conductivity. You might get a bit of saline paste in your hair, but it washes out. Close your eyes when we tell you to. Open them."

She looked from the drone to Virgil, then to the lilac leather of the couch, then to Stets and Caitlin, beside Virgil.

"You don't have to, if you don't want to," said Caitlin.

"Would you?" Verity asked her.

"I would," said Caitlin. "Out of curiosity, if nothing else."

"I'll do it," said Verity, "but it can't be that simple."

"It's slightly more complicated," said Ash.

Verity went to the couch and sat down.

FROM FLORAL STREET

"They've a controller," Netherton said to Rainey, having muted himself before he opened his eyes. She sat at the far end of the couch, legs drawn up beneath her chin, feet bare.

Lowbeer's sigil appeared. "I underestimated Howell's resources," she said. "Eunice's as well. She seems to have proactively copied circuity in the drone. She'd likely no more in mind than Verity being able to control the drone in her stub, should that prove necessary, but you're about to have a visitor."

"We are?" Netherton asked.

"Flynne's peripheral, arriving at your flat shortly," Lowbeer said.

"Verity, in Flynne's peripheral?" he asked.

"Excellent!" said Rainey, overhearing.

"Where's it kept," Netherton asked, not having thought of this before, "when Flynne isn't using it?"

"A peri spa, in Floral Street," said Lowbeer.

"What does it do there?"

"It sleeps," Lowbeer said, "receives nutrition, does aerobics and yoga, and is cosmetically maintained."

Had she added sex and recreational drugs, it occurred to him, she might have been describing the lifestyles of any number of acquaintances from his bachelor days.

"She's entering the mews," Lowbeer said, her sigil fading.

"Entering the mews now," Netherton repeated, for Rainey's benefit. She got up, to walk around and behind the couch, to the window.

Eyes open, Netherton joined her.

An approaching figure crossed a patch of lamplit pavement.

"Go down and bring her up," said Rainey.

"It's not Flynne," he said.

"Don't make her have to ring."

Starting to remove the controller, he thought better of it. The peri would be on its manufacturer's AI. No one in it to see him, let alone think his headgear ridiculous.

As he descended the two flights Rainey insisted were healthier than the lift, he remembered having first seen it, before it had become Flynne's, in the lurid blue dusk of an upper parlor of what Lev archly termed his father's house of love, a monstrosity of erotic kitsch in Kensington Gore. It had noted him, he recalled, with a benign disinterest, as though he'd attracted the attention, such as it was, of a giant semisentient orchid.

It had, Lev had explained, no digestive tract, hence neither ate nor defecated, so required twelve-hourly infusions of a concentrated nutrient as well as regular hydration.

It waited now, he saw, beyond the foyer's steel-mullioned door, with that same expression, brown eyes regarding him from beneath brown hair. Someone, Lowbeer perhaps, had told him, after he'd first encountered it, that it was ten years old, though appearing to be in its early thirties. It seemed no older now.

"Come in," he said, the door opening in response to his invitation. "This way," indicating the lift, which opened at their approach.

It wore black trainers with bright white soles, loose gray trousers cinched at the ankles, and a black kimono-cut jacket. And looked, in the confusing way of situations like this, like Flynne. Not that it actually bore any more than a passing resemblance to her, but that he was so accustomed now to experiencing it as her physical avatar.

CONSTRUALS

"Tell me what to do," Verity said to Ash.

The drone stood facing her. The conductive gel Virgil had spread across her forehead felt cool. She worried about getting it in her eyes.

"The unit in London," Ash said, from the drone's speaker, "is exponentially more sophisticated than this one."

Several cars honked simultaneously on Geary. Verity wondered if Ash could hear them. "How can I operate that, if Wilf can barely walk in this one?"

"Interface transparency," Ash said. "You needn't learn to control it. If anything, you'll need to learn not to try to."

"Where is it, there?"

"Wilf and Rainey's flat, Fitzrovia. It's only just arrived."

"What happens here, when I'm there?"

"Nothing. You'll be neurologically elsewhere."

"Why's the one in London so next-level?"

"You're about to find out," said Ash, "if you'll close your eyes."

Verity did.

"There's something you might watch for," Ash said, "as we activate the controller. I assume you're experiencing entoptics now. A normal phosphene display, that is. Possibly construals."

"Possibly what?"

"Construals. The left brain attempting to impose recognizable attributes on randomness. Faces in clouds, for example. The peripheral's entoptics differ from yours, as would anyone's. Knowing that, you may be able to visually distinguish the threshold of neurological transition as entoptic difference, the arrival of a different phosphene display. But please keep your eyes closed until Wilf asks you to open them. Probably no more than ten seconds."

"Why?"

"Transitioning with your eyes open, or opening them immediately after transitioning, induces nausea. When you do open them, try to move slowly at first. There may be dysmorphia as well, but it's relatively transient."

"Dysmorphia?" Eyes still closed, wondering if she were beginning to experience construals.

"The specific symptoms mimic postural hypotension," Rainey said. "Dizziness on standing, possibility of fainting."

"Are these alpha builds? The drone, the controller, whatever Wilf has in London?"

"No," Ash said. "Ready?"

"Do it," Verity said, as horns sounded again on Geary.

A diagonal edge of differently textured blood-dark swept smoothly past, behind her lids, right to left, horns simultaneously lost to the silence of a different room.

"Keep them closed," said Wilf, startlingly near.

"Okay," she said, simultaneously realizing that this wasn't her voice.

"It's like borrowing another body," Rainey said, from another direction. "You're accessing its full sensorium."

"Open them now," Wilf said.

She did, into the brighter, warmer light of a smaller room, its walls a pale but decidedly non-lilac gray, reminding her of the frames of the Tulpagenics glasses.

"Hello," said a dark-haired man she took to be roughly her age, in a silly-looking silvery headpiece. He was peering at her, as if over glasses he wasn't wearing. Having, she guessed from his position, just gotten up from beside her, from the couch on which she now sat, which was smaller than the one in the suite at the Clift, and brown.

"Wilf?" Which came out sounding, in this voice, like an interrogative yip.

"Yes," he said, smiling unconvincingly, "and this is Rainey."

A woman, familiar from the clip he'd shown her in the van, stepped from behind the couch. "Not everyone has the dysmorphia," the woman said, "and for some reason they seem to exaggerate the likelihood of nausea. I've never had either. But I've heard they both tend to be most noticeable when you first stand up."

Which Verity did then, her head instantly swimming. She quickly sat, hands that weren't her own gripping someone else's gray-trousered knees.

"Thereby proving me wrong," Rainey said. "I'd offer you water, but she mentioned to me that she was hydrated."

Verity spread the fingers of the hands. The nails, better cared for than her own had ever been, were cut short, rounded, polished. "Who did?"

"Your peripheral," Wilf said. "It runs on Hermès AI, when it's without a user."

"Whose AI?" Verity looked up at him.

"The manufacturer's," said Ash, her unexpected voice causing Verity to glance around the room, then into what she could see of a small adjacent kitchen, equally bright. A feed appeared.

"You're Ash?" Verity asked the woman in the feed, the wall behind her as white as her face, alive with animated drawings of what might be gazelles. Her eyes were large and gray.

"I am."

"How am I getting this feed?"

"By phone," Wilf said. "The peri has one built in."

"Perry?" Verity asked.

"Peripheral," said Wilf. "A quasibiological telepresence avatar."

Verity looked around the room. Gray walls, pale wood floor, Scandinavian-looking furniture. "Trying this again," she said, and got to her feet, slowly this time, feeling only slight dizziness.

"Hello, Verity," Rainey said, stepping forward and taking her hand.

"I can feel your hand," Verity said, surprised.

"This is new for me too," Rainey said, releasing Verity's hand, "but not in the same way. This peri's only used by a friend of ours, ordinarily, who doesn't live in London either. It isn't modeled after her, but since I've mainly gotten to know her here, and this is the way we most frequently visit, I keep feeling like you're her."

"Where's Thomas?" Verity asked.

"In the nursery, with the nanny."

"I'll be available if you need me," Ash said. The feed closed.

Verity looked at Rainey. "How new is this technology?"

"Not very. I'm not sure, exactly."

"Stets would have known about it, and told me. Unless this is a prototype from the past year."

"Actually," said Rainey, "you're right."

"I am?"

"How familiar are you with London?"

"Half a dozen times? Last was just before some people here wanted to vote you out of the EU."

"I'd thought we might take Thomas for a stroll," Rainey said, "to help you acclimatize to the peri, and get a look at London. But it seems we have Wilf's boss parked in our mews. Wants us to join her. She can explain the unexpected nature of technology. I can fill in as needed, try to help. Wilf can be part of that from here, while he minds Thomas. Ash as well." She was looking at the man in the matte silver headpiece, causing Verity to wonder if he were wearing it to amuse their child. "Are there mirrors in her car?" Rainey asked him.

"Not if it's still in Winston's waistcoat mode," he said.

Rainey pulled on a dark jacket. "There are mirrors in the lift, all three walls, waist up," she said to Verity. "Look at the floor, or you might trigger the dysmorphia, if that isn't another fable about peris. Save mirrors for when we're back up here."

And out the door then, Verity exchanging a look with the man who was Wilf, before following Rainey, the back of whose head she asked, "Where did you say this is?"

"Fitzrovia."

"Don't know it."

"Adjacent to Bloomsbury," Rainey said. An elevator door opened. "Remember, eyes on the floor," stepping back to allow Verity in, then getting in behind her before the door closed. "No mirrors in the lobby."

During the brief descent, Verity focused on the black-and-white toes of the peripheral's shoes.

The door opened.

The lobby was small, roughly the size of Fabricant Fang's foyer, though any resemblance ended there. "How long have you lived here?" Verity asked, feeling the need to say something.

"Since I was a month pregnant. Wilf lived in hotels, when we first knew one another as colleagues, and on into our getting together."

"Your job's in Canada?"

"Toronto. I moved here to be with Wilf. My firm wants a peripheral of me there, to interact with clients, but I'd quit before I'd do that." She raised her hand, which caused the blue-painted, glass-paned entrance door to open, admitting cold, damp air.

"Of you?"

"One that looks and sounds like me. I won't have it, though. As a parent."

"Why?"

"Fear of it surviving me, after an accident or something." She turned up her jacket's collar. "The effect on Thomas. Terrible for children. Not as though it hasn't happened, unfortunately, so the risk's not hypothetical."

With no idea of how to respond, Verity looked down again, discovering her borrowed body's jacket was something martial-artsy, in a thin dark fabric.

"Don't worry," Rainey said, seeing Verity notice the jacket, "it's already heating up." They stepped out together. "If I were gone, and there was something that looked exactly the way Thomas recalled me, but didn't age—"

"Didn't age?"

"They do, of course," Rainey said, "but much more slowly."

Rainey's white-painted building, Verity saw, looking around, sealed the end of an alley, one that narrowed, oddly, toward what she took to be a brightly lit major artery. "What street's that?"

"Tottenham Court Road," said Rainey, her back to it.

"You said 'full sensorium'?"

"Yes."

"Can't smell it."

"Smell what?"

"London. I don't hear it, either. No traffic. And nothing's passed by, on the street, since we stepped out." Beyond Rainey, a third of the way to what she'd said was Tottenham Court Road, a vehicle pixelated into apparent existence, looking something like the wingless fuselage of a vintage aircraft. "What's that?"

"Her car."

"Whose?"

"Lowbeer's."

"A hologram of it?"

"No," said Rainey, "you saw it decloak."

The term reminded Verity of Stets being pitched digital camouflage schemes. Rainey started toward it, so Verity followed, catching up. And still nothing passed by, out on Tottenham Court Road, not even a pedestrian. The air was fresher than the Mission's, but colder. The peripheral's jacket, though, did seem to have warmed up.

Now a door was opening, in the windowless side of the black car, van, whatever it was. A figure emerged, featureless against light within. Slender, broad-shouldered, in an elegantly mannish tailored suit. "Welcome to London," said the woman, who Verity now saw was older, her face pink in the light from the car's interior. Her white hair was quite short, except for a steeply upswept bouffant forelock. "How's arrival treating you?"

"I'm told it could be worse," Verity said. She looked back to Rainey's building, seeing Wilf outlined in their third-floor living room window.

"Come in, please," the woman said, indicating the car. "I'm Detective Inspector Ainsley Lowbeer, by the way, Metropolitan Police."

"Police?" Verity asked.

"After a fashion." Moving aside to allow Rainey to step up, into the vehicle. "Please." Verity followed Rainey, finding a single folding step extended for the purpose. "Any seat at the table," from behind them, "thank you."

The concave interior walls were a glossy beige. No wheel, no driver's seat, no evident controls, or, for that matter, windows or windshield. The table, oval dark wood the size of a large platter, level with the floor, was centered, surrounded by four small green leather armchairs that seemed to have partially sunken into the floor, in a carpeted nest. A serious-looking arrangement, oddly cozy yet somehow military.

As they seated themselves, the door closed.

"Welcome." The white-haired woman, who had unusually blue eyes, was seated opposite Verity. "Please accept my apologies for having been largely responsible for the stressful week you've been having."

"Responsible?"

"I'm afraid so."

"How?"

"Ash and I were instrumental in Cursion having Tulpagenics hire you. Do you mind heights, particularly?"

"Heights?"

"I'd like to take us up now."

"Up?" As something seemed to press down, however silently, on the roof of the vehicle, reminding her of the delivery of her Muji bag to Kathy Fang's rooftop nap-cube, but silent, and lacking this sense of substantial yet very precise contact.

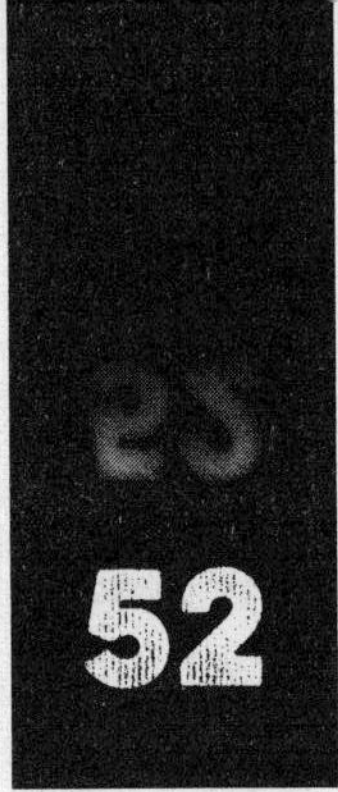

POSTURE AND GAIT

When Verity used the peripheral, Netherton decided, watching it now, it no longer resembled Flynne. Which was really for the best, though it made him miss Flynne.

He stood at the window, as it followed Rainey into Lowbeer's car, Lowbeer behind them. Not that he could have pointed to any specific difference in its posture or gait, with Verity using it, but his mind was somehow capable of the distinction. Surveillance programs plucked individuals from crowds, he knew, on just that basis.

Having seen it controlled by Hermès AI, earlier, had reminded him of how few opportunities to see one another he and Flynne now had. He was married, a parent, as was she, and then there was her demanding role in Lowbeer's ongoing manipulation of the course of her native stub.

He closed his eyes, back into the feed from the drone, to find Verity seated as he'd last seen her, on the pale couch in the San Francisco hotel, eyes shut, beneath the makeshift controller. Stetson Howell, her venture capitalist, wasn't in sight, nor was his fiancée, the French architect. Virgil, the man who'd met the van in front of the hotel, had pulled up an armchair and now sat facing Verity, engrossed with the screen of his manual phone.

Opening his eyes, Netherton saw a quadcopter descending silently into Alfred Mews, its black rectangular platform the length of Lowbeer's car. He'd only known her to use this infrequently, and he'd always been her passenger at the time, so had never actually seen the thing before. A few dead leaves whirled frantically, as it secured the car. He regretted Thomas missing this.

Then it smoothly took the car up with it, as a single unit, which he imagined Thomas would have particularly enjoyed.

OVER LONDON

"My apologies for our abruptness," said the white-haired woman, the vehicle coming to a dreamlike, jolt-free halt, having somehow, just then, pretended to be a perfectly silent high-speed elevator. "If the situation were less urgent, we could introduce you to various concepts more gradually, but I'm afraid that's not the case."

"No dysmorphia, right?" asked Rainey, looking at Verity.

"No," said Verity. "Urgent?" she asked the white-haired woman.

Concave screens appeared, down both sides of the vehicle, replacing beige blankness. On them, what seemed a single panorama of urban night sky.

"Have a closer look," Rainey said, getting up from her chair and out of the carpeted pit. She offered Verity her hand. Taking it, Verity rose, feeling a slight dizziness. Rainey released her hand and stepped toward the screens, Verity following.

"Three hundred and fifty meters," the woman said, still seated.

"Shit," said Verity, reaching the edge of the carpeted floor. Beyond it, to the horizon, stretched a regularly spaced array of towers, roughly similar in height. Through which, she saw, lowering her gaze, wound a river's serpentine curves.

"There," said Rainey, pointing out something Verity couldn't distinguish. "London Eye. Only tall thing, aside from the original Shard, that you'll have seen before. They took down what was left of the rest. These are called shards too, after the first one. Relatively few are habitations."

"What are they?" Windows were lit, a few, if the lights she saw were windows.

"They scrub the air," the woman said, behind them, now standing.

An older, lower city, at the feet of the towers, like lichen in comparison. There were forests too, she saw, with greenways between them. "That's the Thames?"

"Of course," said Rainey.

But with more bridges, at least two of them planted with what looked like forests of their own. And tributaries, none of which Verity remembered. Some of them appeared to have been roofed with glass, illuminated.

"CG," Verity said. "VR, AR. A game."

"That's the commonest initial assumption," the woman said, "on first seeing it. Though I suppose natives of eras earlier than yours might assume dream, hallucination, visit to a supernatural realm."

"You're saying it's the future?"

"Entertain the idea. To one side, so to speak. A mere possibility."

"It's not your future, though," said Rainey. "Your 2017 forks away from our 2016."

"Slightly earlier, actually," said the woman. "2015."

"When's this supposed to be?" Verity asked.

"2136."

"What did you say your name was?"

"Lowbeer," the woman said

Verity turned back to the window, noting how few headlights moved below. "Not that I believe you," she said, "at all, but this doesn't look anywhere near as seriously fucked as we've been led to expect the future will be. What about global warming?"

"The shards," said Ash, no feed of her appearing, "are units in a compensatory system. Attempting, with some success, to stabilize climate."

"This is supposed to account for Eunice?" Verity asked. "That she's from the future?"

"No," the woman called Lowbeer said, "Eunice is of your era. The result of a military research project in our common past. She was with Cursion, when we found her, or rather the programs that produced her were, surreptitiously acquired from a military research project."

"We've explained this sort of thing before," said Wilf, likewise only a voice, "to people in your situation. What they usually have the most difficulty with is that this isn't their future. And that we've no idea what the future of their stub will be. Or of our own, for that matter."

"Stub?"

"Regrettable expression," Lowbeer said, "regrettably common usage, here. Inaccurate as well, since your continuum won't remain short. It appears so to us, but only since it's just diverged from our shared past. Its birth, as it were. But it also reflects an undeniably imperial aspect of what we're doing, because we assume our continuum to be that from which so-called stubs branch. The mechanism that permits us to do that appears to be located here, however mysteriously. Stubs, lacking that agency, are unable to initiate stubs of their own."

Verity blinked, feeling lost. "What are those three-armed things, out in the Thames"—she pointed—"with lighthouses at their tips?"

"The Trefoils," Rainey said. "A tidal power-generation system. They navigate the river, optimizing their efficiency. The islands are a part of it as well, and move with them."

"Cursion's not the first gaming company I've worked for," Verity said. "The last one could have built all of this. I'll give you points for a sense of depth, and a lack of conventional clutter, but why should I assume it's real?"

"As good a way as any, for you to initially organize the experience," Lowbeer said.

"What about that urgency you mentioned?" Verity asked.

"Qamishli," Ash said. "We don't have that situation, in our past. We can't know where nuclear conflict would take you, but any prognosis whatever is dire."

"Why do you care?" Verity asked. "You're not there."

"Because you and everyone else in your world are as real as we are," Lowbeer said. "And because we do care, we need your help."

"Me?"

"Eunice generated a network," Lowbeer said, "employing admirable tradecraft. You're its focus, apparently. It exists primarily to protect you. Our access to your stub is limited. If you join forces with us, so will the network."

"And if they do?"

"If they do," Ash said, "we'll share their agency in your stub."

Verity looked from Lowbeer to Rainey, then back to Lowbeer. "If I were to go along with this, what exactly would it look like?"

"You'd need to disappear," Lowbeer said, "but then you already have, as far as Cursion's concerned. As of this afternoon."

SYSTEMS CHECKS

Checking on Thomas, Netherton found him asleep within the auroral display, the nanny curled, triply pandaform, on the floor around his crib.

As he returned to the kitchen, an unfamiliar sigil began to pulse, something officious-looking, American. "Yes?"

"Wilf," someone male greeted him, in a county accent, as the pulsing ceased.

"Hello?"

"Conner, man. Penske. Been a while. You good?"

No feed appeared. Netherton remembered when he'd last seen Conner, in footage of cousin Leon's inauguration. Wearing a deeply uncharacteristic dark gray suit, bespoke, from a Philadelphia firm chosen by Lowbeer's much younger stub-self, himself a monument to Jermyn Street, though given in the county to waxed cotton jackets and suede desert boots. The suit had made Conner look more like a junior American diplomat than one of the dissident Secret Service men he'd at that point been charged with protecting Leon from. "Well, thanks. Yourself?"

"Can't complain," Conner said. "Tired of the weather here."

"You're in Alaska, with Leon?"

"Back in D.C., now he's done his secessionist-soothing for a while. Ainsley says you've got a new stub going."

"New to me," Netherton said.

"Says she stumbled on a lost effort of Vespasian's," Conner said. "Who's the black guy nodding out in the armchair?"

Realizing that Conner must be accessing the drone, Netherton closed his eyes.

Just as Virgil jerked his head upright, blinking. Netherton muted his link to the drone's speaker. Virgil peered at the drone. "That's Virgil," Netherton said to Conner. "He works for Stetson Howell, who formerly was in a relationship with Verity Jane. She's the woman on the couch, the current locus of our efforts there, our agent having apparently been taken offline."

"Hey, Virgil," Conner said, raising his voice. "Name's Conner. Sorry to startle you."

"She just sits there." Virgil squinted at Verity, then back at the drone. "She okay?"

"She's fine," Conner said. "If they meant to keep her here for much longer, they'd have had her on her back."

The drone's camera angles shifted, as if it were elevating. Virgil's eyes, attracted by movement, widened further.

"What are you doing with the drone, Conner?" Netherton asked.

"Balancing on its wrist-tips," Conner said, "feet off the floor."

"Conner was in the military, Virgil," Netherton said. "He trained for this."

"Marines," said Conner. "Haptic Recon." The camera angle changed again, suddenly, Netherton guessing the drone had tilted forward on its extended arms, to land on its feet ahead of where it had been standing. Now one of the room's windows, curtains drawn, was centered in its display. It rolled toward this and stopped. A thin black rod flexed into view, tentacle-like, then quickly out of sight, behind the nearest drape. A new feed opened, encompassing most of the display. Looking down, into as much of the street below as could be seen from the window. A yellow vehicle Netherton assumed to be a taxi was passing beneath them. A crisp white circle and crosshairs appeared, centered on its roof, tracking it out of the feed.

"What are you doing?" Netherton asked, reminded of how Conner made him uneasy.

"Running systems checks," Conner said. "This is a fabbed-up repro of something at least six generations behind the oldest I ever piloted, but the software looks like it's either ours or we've rewritten it. Seriously fucked up."

"And that's the best Ash could come up with?" Netherton asked.

"Guess so," said Conner, the crosshairs picking up a truck as it drove into the feed from the right, "but I meant fucked up like I can't fucking wait to use it."

Not liking the sound of that either, Netherton said nothing.

"Hey," said Conner, "you come and sit in a room in the basement of the West Wing, doing sweet fuck-all. Rest of the time, it's the wit and wisdom of President Leon. Back when we still weren't sure about the Secret Service, I had something to tend to. Now they're all loving his hick philosopher ass. You people have run some weird ops here, and I'm not saying that's a bad thing, considering, but this, with Leon? I mean, come on."

"Not my idea," Netherton said, "I can assure you."

"It was them," said Conner, "Ainsley and that goth with the figure-eight pupils. That's what Flynne said." The crosshairs were tracking the roof of a passing police car now. "Anyway, you can't blame me wanting to get this thing kinetic."

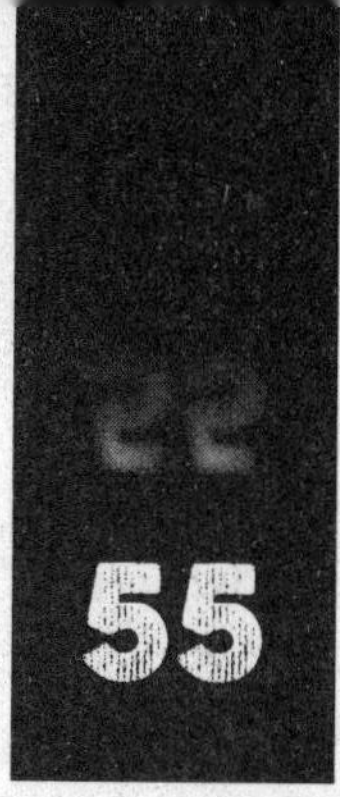

MICRO-EXPRESSIONS

"What about my mother?" Verity asked Lowbeer. "I'd need to tell her, if I was disappearing. Not that she'd be the only one I wouldn't want worried over whether or not I was dead."

"Either one of Eunice's branch plants finds you soon," Lowbeer said, "or you may be attempting to contact your mother in a post-nuclear scenario. In the meantime, it's still a matter of keeping you out of Cursion's hands."

"You think her network can stop Qamishli going nuclear?" Verity looked back at the silhouettes of the towers.

"With the agency we assume they'll be able to provide, we may be able to help facilitate something. Without them, there's nothing we can do."

"Conner's here," Wilf broke in, "piloting the drone, in the hotel in San Francisco."

A feed opened, she assumed on the peripheral's built-in phone: she herself in the black helmet, seated on the couch, eyes open but unmoving. If her body were neurologically cut out, she assumed, or whatever they called it, would its face not produce micro-expressions? Someone had pitched Stets a program that provided those, for micro-animating CG faces, supposedly to reduce the uncanny valley factor, though she hadn't felt any difference when looking at them herself. "Does it let me blink?" she asked, suddenly worried about her own eyes, in San Francisco.

"Blink, breathe, all that autonomic shit's taken care of," said a startlingly American voice, male, deep.

"How about micro-expressions?" she asked.

"Fuck if I know," said the voice, amicably enough.

"This is Conner, Verity," said Wilf. "He's my copilot."

"In your living room, in London?" Verity asked.

"Washington," Wilf said. "District of Columbia."

"In a different stub, he means," said the voice called Conner.

"Don't confuse her," said Wilf, "she's new to this."

"What year'd you say this drone's in, Wilf?" Conner asked.

"Didn't Lowbeer brief you?"

"Just said it was too early for real AI."

"2017," said Verity.

"Explains the vintage cars," Conner said. "Had it figured for a cosplay zone—"

The feed vanished.

"Sorry to interrupt," said Lowbeer, "but we need to finish our conversation."

"Who's the new guy in the drone?" Verity asked.

"Conner is a friend of Flynne's," Lowbeer said, "the woman whose peripheral we've loaned you. They're from the same stub, the same small town. His military experience included using telepresence platforms in combat. He's very adroit with them."

"Wilf's not."

"Hence Conner. It's a self-mobile communications hub for us as well, essential given the demands of your stub, but with Conner piloting, it affords you protection."

"From Cursion?"

"From anyone, really. With Conner, we've been able to leave it largely unweaponized, aside from a few toys he wanted, but by jettisoning those you could get it aboard commercial flights, though not as carry-on. As soon as he gets its grippers on a firearm, though, he can make more of a mess than we can successfully tidy. He understands that, though there are limits to his restraint."

"If that's bullshit," Verity said, "you've really gone to some trouble."

"Eunice wouldn't have expected you to react to any of this with unthinking acceptance."

"She told me to trust whoever the barista took me to. He took me to meet Kathy Fang and the guy who delivered the drones Eunice ordered. I met Wilf. I met Rainey and Ash. Then Sevrin brought me to the Clift. I already knew Virgil. I know Stets. Now I've met Caitlin. Now you. So say I count you, all of you, as who the barista took me to."

"Yes?"

"Then you can't just keep introducing me to people I should trust. Where's the cutoff?"

"That's up to you."

"Why was she called Eunice?" The peripheral's eyes stung. "Can this thing cry?"

"Of course," said Lowbeer, reaching into her suit jacket and producing a white handkerchief, which she handed to Verity. "The acronym for the project that produced her stood for Untethered Noetic Irregular Support System. U-N-I-S-S."

Verity looked at Rainey. "So what do I get, for behaving as though I trust you?"

"Your world gets a better chance of avoiding nuclear war," Rainey said, "not that I have any idea how."

"Is that true?" Verity asked Lowbeer.

"Yes."

"Then I guess I'm disappeared." She looked out at the dark masses of the towers, receding in straight lines. "That's still not saying I believe this is real."

"You don't need to," Rainey said. "Next time you're here, I'll show you more. You won't have to believe that either."

Lowbeer's car began to descend, then, though much more slowly than it had risen.

THAT NON-POSTHUMAN TOUCH

Netherton stood at the window, having watched the feed from the car. The quadcopter was descending back into Alfred Mews, the car beneath it. "Ash?"

"Yes?"

"When I spoke with Lowbeer earlier," he said, "she was unhappy, about the possibility of this having some very bad outcome for Verity."

Silence, during which the car neared pavement. Then Ash spoke. "As well she might. I doubt any of us can imagine making the choices she must have had to make, during the jackpot."

"I've never gotten over my own initial impression, that the stubs were a game," Netherton said. "Which they are, of course, for the majority of continua enthusiasts."

"You don't, though, feel that Flynne's life is a game. Do you?"

"No, but I can sometimes feel that you and Lowbeer treat it as one, and the more so since you initiated Leon's presidential campaign. It seems like a parody of our own history."

"We sometimes find ourselves wishing Leon were a bit less bright, so

I'm not sure the analogy holds. That aside, his election was legitimate, everything scrupulously monitored by the aunties. Flynne insisted on that, if we were to have him run."

"But you tell him what to do. You determine all of his positions on policy."

"And he's polling extremely well, while doing a minimum of harm. Progress, not perfection."

The quadcopter, having fully lowered the car to the pavement, released it now, to rise swiftly out of view. The car's door opened. Netherton, seeing Rainey's head emerge, lit from behind, felt a wash of relief.

"Glad to have Rainey with us," Ash said. "We can do with that non-posthuman touch, as far as Verity's concerned."

The non-posthuman bar being decidedly low, around you and Lowbeer, Netherton thought. Both Rainey and the peripheral had left the car now, he saw, and were walking toward the flat.

From the nursery, he heard Thomas begin to cry. Removing the controller, else it frighten him, he went to comfort him.

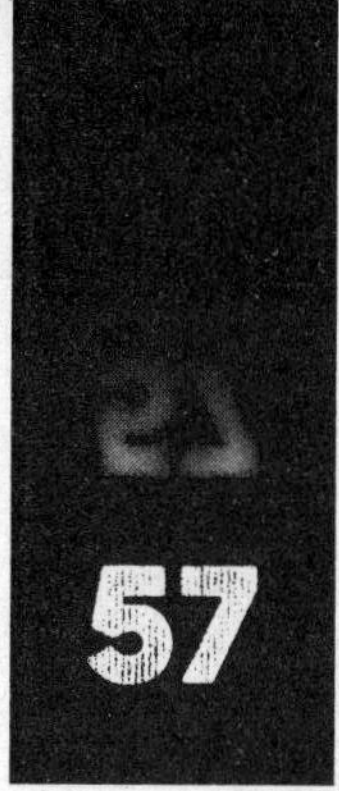

57

AND BACK

The car was gone, when Verity looked over her shoulder, but then she remembered its camouflage. "Still there?"

"Cloaked itself," Rainey said, not bothering to look. "Wilf wonders whether she lives in it."

"She's a cop," Verity said. The way this dead-end alley widened, from Tottenham Court Road back to the front of Wilf's building, made the perspective feel off. "Told me she was."

"Officially, yes, though her real job would take longer to explain."

"Wilf says you've explained all of this before, to other people."

"He has," Rainey said. "I'm in crisis management, myself. Lowbeer tries to improve things in orphaned stubs. To do that she manipulates the course of their future history, or tries to. It's all surreptitious, in the stubs themselves, which suits her. It's how she's always worked. Wilf's job is to assist her."

"People do that here, as a job?"

"Most who do it, do it as a hobby. And not always with the best interests of the stubs they initiate in mind."

"So what's her real job?"

"Haven't time to explain that now, but her avocation is the making of better worlds. Out of yours, for instance."

Verity looked up at the white-painted brick façade, the dark blue frames and mullions. "This one doesn't look too bad to me."

"There's over a century," Rainey said, pausing before the door, "between the year you're from and this one. Most of those years were ugly. Lots of things still are. Not that it looks it, here, to you. Come upstairs." She showed the door her upraised palm and it swung open.

"What does this body do," Verity asked, as they stepped inside, "when your friend isn't using it?"

"She hasn't used it for months. It lives in a spa for peripherals, near Covent Garden. Its maker's AI maintains its activities. Exercise, esthetics, nutrition, sleep."

"Is it conscious?"

The elevator door opened.

Verity stepped in, to be confronted by tripled reflections of the peripheral.

"She," Rainey corrected, stepping in behind her. "That's a very political question, here. Personally, I assume she's sentient, regardless of degree, though I've yet to convince Wilf."

"Whoa," said Verity, looking from one mirror to the next.

"Sorry," said Rainey, as the door closed, "forgot about the mirrors. But yes, that's her, and yes, that's you, looking out of her." They were ascending. "How was that, for you, the mirror?"

"I don't know."

"Nausea?"

"No."

"There you go, then. Your transitions here should be progressively easier. The returns are nothing anyway; neurologically, you're going home."

The door opened. A baby was crying.

"Thomas," said Rainey. "I'm just in time." She stepped out, Verity behind her, and took a red-faced Thomas from Wilf.

"Virgil's concerned about you," he said to Verity. "Best you go now and reassure him."

Rainey was in the kitchen with Thomas now, Verity saw, who'd stopped crying. She held an aerodynamic-looking feeding bottle in one hand.

"What do I do, to go back?" she asked Wilf.

"Sit on the couch," said Wilf. "Close your eyes."

"And?"

"Open them," said Rainey, giving Thomas the bottle's honey-colored nipple. "Transition's instant, returning. Then have yourself a good stretch. Your body's scarcely moved, during the time you've been here. And remember to hydrate, before you sleep."

Verity looked at the brown couch. Then back to Wilf. "Looks like I'm in. Lowbeer's disappearance plan."

"I know," he said.

"Will I come back here?"

"I certainly hope so," said Rainey, looking up from Thomas. "It's been a pleasure."

"Thanks," said Verity, and sat on the couch, arranging the borrowed body in what she hoped would be a comfortable position for it. She took a quick glance around the room, then closed her eyes.

Background sounds of San Francisco traffic, as if a switch had been thrown.

Her back ached slightly. She opened her eyes.

Virgil was peering at her. "You okay?"

She raised her hands from her lap, looking at them, then at him. "Guess so."

"Where were you?"

She looked at him. "Was I talking?"

"No. You've been still the whole time, since I pressed the button on the helmet," he said. "I was getting worried."

"They say it's London, but they also say it's the future."

"The future."

"2136, they said."

Virgil pursed his lips.

"I know," she said. "Except it's not our future."

"Glad you're back," he said.

"You think I'm crazy?"

"A day or two ago, my idea of crazy would have been your digital assistant blowing us out of the Singapore deal. Stets still hasn't found the time to explain that one to me, but heads would be rolling if we were a different kind of shop. And now he's all over this, with you and your PA, whatever she is. So you just saw the future? Then look at this thing." Pointing at the drone. It stood facing the window, its front very close to the drawn drapes, as if it should be wearing a dunce's hat. "Was the future you saw like that?"

"There's an apartment," she said.

"Okay."

"And a helicopter. But they call it a car."

"A flying car?"

"It's invisible."

"Right."

"I know. But from up there, it looked like the future. Big towers, the size of the Shard, set out in a grid, either side of the Thames."

"CG," he said, "or maybe that helmet you're wearing, doing something directly to your head? We've never been pitched time travel before, though. Free energy, a couple of times, but that's a genre unto itself."

"They tell me it's more like alternate time-tracks. Get this off." Indicating the helmet. He did. She got to her feet, stretching her arms above her head, and bent to touch her toes.

"We were talking," a man's voice said, "then you were gone. Conner, remember?"

Verity straightened, blinking, and looked at the drone, which she saw had rotated to face her. "Why were you up against the curtains, that way?"

"Watching the traffic," the man said, from the drone's speaker. "It's all vintage."

"Where are you?"

"The White House. Basement of the West Wing."

"Why?"

"Different stub. A ways up the line from you, except there's no line. Headed in a different direction, from them and from you."

"Your name's Conner?"

"Conner Penske," he said.

"Drones that people pitched Stets," she said, "ones that looked anything like that one, made a lot more noise."

"We upgraded. Had the people who fabbed it use the most bleeding-edge components they could find."

"I'm so tired I can barely stand up," she said.

"Bed," Virgil said, pointing to the other room. "In there. Sleep. That's the plan. Conner and I'll be out here."

"And charging this unit, while we're at it," Conner said. "That's one thing Ash couldn't get upgraded to anywhere near our standards. Batteries."

"Good night," said Verity, reflexively, already headed for the door to the adjoining room.

CHARMED CIRCLE

The peripheral was watching Netherton from the couch, in that curiously nonintrusive way that meant it was once again under the control of its manufacturer's AI.

"I like her," said Rainey, Thomas on her hip. Netherton assumed she meant Verity. She didn't always like clients, though in that case she wouldn't mention it.

A sigil appeared, pulsing, unfamiliar at first. Then he recognized it as Lev Zubov's, featuring the faces of his two pet thylacines. "Phone," he said to Rainey, "sorry." She nodded, turning back to Thomas in his high chair at the table. "Lev," he said, "how are you?"

"Reasonably well," said Lev, not sounding it. He'd been unhappy with the divorce, Netherton knew, which had been his wife Dominika's idea, and with its outcome, which had seen her remain in the house in Notting Hill, along with their child. He'd since taken up residence in another Zubov family property, in Cheyne Walk, which Netherton hadn't yet seen, reportedly even more redolent of old klept than the Notting Hill place. He doubted Lev was happy with that either, he and his cohort preferring to treat their klepthood as something of a joke, not that anyone else could afford to.

"I need to see you," Lev said, sounding no happier about that. "Tonight?"

Urgency wasn't something Netherton associated with Lev, but this was sounding like a sadder man than he'd known before, and he felt a pang of guilt for not having kept in touch recently. Lev had been instrumental in helping Netherton finally address his problem with drink, without which there might now be no Rainey in his life, nor any Thomas.

Lowbeer's sigil pulsed urgently.

"Excuse me," he said to Lev, "just a moment." Muted him. "Yes?"

"See him tonight," said Lowbeer. Her sigil vanished.

"Sorry," he said, unmuting Lev. "Where shall we meet?"

"Not there," said Lev, "this requires privacy."

Not Cheyne Walk either, thought Netherton, then remembered the Denisovan Embassy. "One from your list of the interrupted, then? Under Hanway Street? Twenty minutes?"

"On my way," said Lev, his thylacines vanishing.

"What's that?" asked Rainey.

"Lev."

"I gathered. What about?"

"Needs to get something off his chest, apparently. Lowbeer interrupted to say I should meet him. Hanway Street." He removed the controller and placed it on the couch. "Don't sit on this."

"What's there?"

"The Denisovan Embassy."

"The sex club?" Up went the eyebrow.

"Formerly, yes," he said. "I'm surprised you know of it."

"I'd a client whose career crisis was brought on by a single particularly ill-starred visit there." She regarded him narrowly. "A Canadian abroad."

"It's only round-the-clock breakfasts now," he said. "I suggested it because it's close, and on a list of his."

"What list?"

"Of places that were one thing, but are now another, yet still have the same distinctive name. Fancies himself artistic, that way. If you need me, phone. I'll try not to be long. Hope I won't be." He kissed her cheek.

He went into the bedroom for his jacket, put it on, setting it to medium warmth. By the time he'd stepped out into the mews, it felt exactly right. As he approached where he judged Lowbeer's cloaked car to be, he hoped she wouldn't stop him for a chat. It decloaked, but only partially, when he was three meters away, faintly revealing its outline in ghostly, washed-out pixels. He walked between it and the wall, not slowing, his eyes on what little was visible of Tottenham Court Road.

Ash's sigil pulsed when he was nearing Hanway Place, the walk having been uneventful.

"Yes?"

"Rainey says you're out."

"Meeting Lev," he said. "Where we were earlier." She'd been Lev's employee, his resident technician, when Netherton had first met her. "Have you seen him since the divorce?" he asked.

"Not since I left to work with Lowbeer."

He was passing the shop where he'd gotten Thomas's milk. He glimpsed the natty figure of the bot salesclerk. Michael something, he thought, certain that was the given name of the twentieth-century actor he thought it resembled. Surname still escaping him. "How are we doing, then, generally?" he asked Ash.

"Doing?"

"With our attempted rescue, or perhaps I should say takeover, of Verity's stub."

"They needn't be mutually exclusive categories, as you know. The aunties' odds are still for imminent use of nuclear weapons. Verity's agreed to work with us, hopefully giving us all the entrée we need to Eunice's network."

He turned into Hanway Street. "I'm here," he said, spotting the narrow, stalactite-festooned façade. "Give Lev your best, then?"

"Do, please," she said, surprising him. "Far from the worst employer I've had."

"I will, then."

Her sigil faded.

As Netherton descended the spiral stone staircase, Lev's sigil reappeared, thylacines pulsing. "Just arriving," Netherton said.

"They'll bring you to me," said Lev, the sigil dimming but not disappearing.

"You're Wilf?" asked the freckle-dusted redhead at the foot of the stairs, draped in a floor-length gossamer cloak, spangled with sequins reflecting mobile light-sources that clearly weren't present.

"I am," he said.

"Follow me, please."

He did, noting late evening's breakfasters seemed little different from the afternoon's. More tipsy, perhaps, but that evident mainly in an increased decibel count. The girl's cloak reminded him of a Japanese film Lowbeer was fond of, *Mothra*, which she sometimes screened in her car. He'd assumed it was silent, but Ash insisted that it had originally had a soundtrack, Lowbeer preferring it without. Now a similarly draped young woman joined them, identically redheaded and, Netherton immediately suspected, identically freckled, down to the very last spot. Then another, equally indistinguishable, confirming his suspicion that they were bots. All in restlessly luminescent cloaks, accompanying him back into those darker, red-lit reaches, beyond the breakfasters. When they reached Lev, finally, there were half a dozen red-haired girls, seemingly identical.

He hoped Lev had arranged for chairs, rather than stalagmite stumps. He'd no idea what the six bot-girls were about. They struck him as very un-Lev.

"Hello," said Lev, glumly extending his hand, from where he sat upon a stalagmite stump far too short for his long legs. Netherton briefly took it. "Have a seat there." Indicating the nearest stump. Netherton settled himself on this, as uncomfortably as expected.

The bot-girls surrounded them, arms outstretched and palm to palm, smoothly adjusting distances from one to another, to press hands again and raise them toward the rough low ceiling. The sequins began to swirl, spiraling up, from one cloak to the next, to form a low dome of flitting light. "What's this?" Netherton asked Lev.

"Privacy," said Lev, "of an unusual but necessary order."

"Provided by the bots?" Looking at their upraised cloaks.

"They've no connectivity whatever," Lev said. "Like the robots in old films. Limited functionality, but what there is is provided exclusively by onboard AI. The cloaks, combined this way, comprise something akin to a Faraday cage, but blocking many more sorts of signal. Limited duration, though, operating at full spectrum, so I'll be quick."

"Do."

"My father," Lev said, "less than two hours ago, learned from an uncle of his, more highly placed, that your Lowbeer's role is being reconsidered."

"'My' Lowbeer, is she? You introduced us."

"And you've since become her employee. Which is why I'm alerting you, now, to the possibility of that becoming unsafe."

"Has it occurred to your father," asked Netherton, taking a page from Lowbeer's book, "that conspiring to hinder her in her work may be one of the least safe things anyone can possibly do?"

"Certainly," said Lev. "As the klept's resident antibody, she expects to be conspired against. My father, however, says he's never before seen her regarded, at his uncle's level, as other than the most necessary of evils." He glanced up at the sequin swirl, then leaned forward, lowering his voice. "It's to do with her manipulation of stubs."

Netherton's pet fear executed a squeamish rollover, seemingly atop his entire consciousness, bringing him a flashback of the Thames chimera he'd seen with Lowbeer. "It does?"

"She's altering stubs to produce worlds in which the klept enjoy less power," Lev said, absolutely confirming it for Netherton.

"It's art, Lev," Netherton protested, taking a second page from Lowbeer, "poetry. What happens in a stub stays there."

"My father takes this very seriously, Wilf."

Netherton looked up at the zero-connectivity redheads, serenely steepled, as far down the ladder from Flynne's vintage Hermès mystery woman as was possible to go, short of simply being a statue. The sole tasty bit of their tech would be whatever provided the supposed privacy. "Where did you find these?"

"My father ordered me to use them," Lev said. "He used them when he was told this, and again when he told me."

"Would you be able to give me any more information, about this supposed threat?"

"Only that her role is being critically reconsidered."

"Reconsidered?"

"As to whether it needs to exist."

Netherton considered this. "Thank you. I assume I've your permission to tell her? Not that I'd be able to do otherwise, of course."

"Of course. That's why we're telling you. But absolutely no one else. Your wife, for instance."

"And that's all you know?"

"It is," said Lev.

"You look quite down," said Netherton, "if you don't mind my saying. Is it over this?"

"Hardly," said Lev. "It's my responsibility to tell you. Not least because you yourself might be in danger, as her employee. Otherwise, I'm really not up to much. Cheyne Walk's definitely not agreeing with me."

"I'm sorry."

"Not your fault. Meanwhile, please inform Lowbeer, and no one other than Lowbeer, and then only in circumstances she herself deems entirely secure. She'll have something far superior to these bots, but until you find yourself within her version of this charmed circle"—and he winced, the bot-girls being obviously not to his taste—"say nothing to anyone."

"Time, sir," said one of the bots, its voice identical to that of the one that had greeted Netherton at the foot of the stairs. "Two minutes remain."

"We're done," Lev replied. As one, the six lowered their cloaks, sequins ceasing to whirl. Without looking back, they turned and walked toward the dining area, Netherton watching them go.

"You don't like Cheyne Walk, then?" Netherton asked.

"It's entirely uncles of mine," Lev said, standing up. "You can't imagine. My best to Rainey and your boy." Turning, he walked toward the sound of popping champagne corks.

NONE OF ME KNOWS

Verity came awake, startled semi-upright by a dream she immediately forgot, in a bed strangely wide, in a room wider still.

"You okay?" Virgil asked quietly, from behind the closed door to the other room.

"Yeah," she managed. "Dream."

"Sounded like it," he said. "I'm up, if you need anything."

"Thanks. I'm okay."

Realizing she was in her mummy-bag liner, though she didn't remember getting it before she'd crawled into bed. Still dark outside, to judge by the lack of light at the edges of the curtains. Groping gingerly around on the nearest bedside table for the glass of water she now remembered leaving there. Finding it, she drank half and lay back in the liner, under the Clift's duvet. The traffic was quieter now. Don't think about any of it, she advised herself, then decided that wasn't working.

Getting up on an elbow, she propped herself with pillows and found the remote. The screen, opposite the foot of the bed, was as wide. She flipped through news channels, volume down. Fox seemed to still be mainly devoted to the president's pre-election e-mails, but CNN and MSNBC looked as though they'd both been straight Qamishli for long enough to see it under the presenters' eyes. She stopped when she saw the president, speaking from yet another podium. Reminding her of everything she'd just advised herself not to think about, so she turned off the television, shoved the pillows around, curled up in the familiarity of the mummy-bag liner, and fell asleep.

REGARD OF THE ADJUSTOR

Turning into Alfred Mews, Netherton glanced down its length to the windows of their flat. He walked toward them, waiting for Lowbeer's car to partially decloak. When it did, he stepped past and turned, to face what he hoped was where he'd last seen its door. "May I come in?"

"Certainly," said Lowbeer, the door appearing just to the left of where he'd expected it, along with a surrounding hand's-width of glossy black bodywork, the decloaked segment unevenly pixelated along its edges. The door opened, its step folding down. He stepped forward, up, and into the glow of a single stout white candle, centered on the table in the carpeted pit. Behind him, the door quietly closed.

"White iris and vetiver," Lowbeer said. "I hope you don't mind."

"Very nice," said Netherton, having learned to take a degree of comfort in her candles, not for their scents but for the touch of dotty old lady they lent her, however deceptively. "I've a question."

She was in shirtsleeves, a rare circumstance but not unheard of, her necktie undone. "Yes?"

"How private is this?"

"Security was the central goal, in the design of every aspect of this vehicle," she said, "but you've no reason to be concerned when you're with me in any case, wherever we are."

"This concerns your deeper state function."

"Which we've certainly touched on before. Would you like a seat?"

"I'll stand," Netherton said, glancing at the candlelit conversation pit, which suggested a séance. "Lev Zubov's father's uncle says that unnamed figures in the klept are questioning the continued need for your office."

She glanced to one side, appearing to watch something. "He told you this in the Denisovan Embassy?"

"Were you listening?" Netherton asked, one of his core fears being that Lowbeer eavesdropped on literally everything, constantly, though she denied that ability.

"I wasn't, no," she said. "I was able to hear him greet you, and ask you to take a seat. Then nothing, until you asked him about not liking Cheyne Walk. The zero-connectivity bots would explain the sizable ellipsis, as well as guarantee his father's involvement."

"It's to do with the stubs," Netherton said, "exactly as I've feared. That you steer them away from the klept becoming as powerful in them as it is here."

"He expects you to tell me this?"

"He insisted. But only you."

"Once again, then," she said, "the divide between the ambitions of conspirators and the desire, among those bringing us word of those ambitions, to preserve whatever aspect of the status quo they themselves hold dear." The blank buff walls had become windows now, the car itself, Netherton assumed from experience, remaining cloaked. "That's often how this sort of thing comes to my attention."

"He warned that I might be in danger as well."

"It's possible, certainly," she said, "but these conspiracies have so far always been successfully neutralized. The only novel thing about this one is my tinkering with stubs offering a fresh rationale for my removal."

"I've worried about them reacting this way."

"This is a routine if infrequent aspect of my work," she said. "They should only react to me with terror, but need occasionally to be reminded. Who knows of this so far, that you're aware of?"

"Lev, his father, the unnamed uncle who supposedly informed his father, myself, and you."

"Keep it that way, please," she said, making intensely blue eye-contact. "Don't mention it to Rainey until it's been resolved."

"My mother told me about you," Netherton said, surprising himself, "when I was a small child. Not you specifically, but a figure in a story, benevolent but frightening. She called that figure the Adjustor. Adjustor of destinies, she said, for those who threatened the stability of the klept. When I was older, I came to understand that you, or rather someone in your role, actually existed."

She looked toward the white candle. "It was never envisioned as a solo position. There were a number of us, originally. I'm simply the last. Should the klept ever truly decide to be done with me, they need only deny me access to the technology that keeps me alive and functional."

"Rainey guesses they can't afford to do that, since they can't be certain you haven't hidden the most damaging information about them where it will pop up if they remove you."

"You've married a woman of great acuity, Mr. Netherton," Lowbeer said, turning her blue gaze back to him, from the candle.

"My mother's story," Netherton said, "held that everything would invariably collapse, if the klept were left to their own resources. Do you believe that?"

"But for the occasional pruning," she said, "under the auspices of an impartial eye, yes. Their tedious ambition and contempt for rule of law would bring everything down, around their ears and ours. They managed to do that with the previous world order, after all, though then it was effectively their goal. They welcomed the jackpot, the chaos it brought. The results of our species' insults to nature did much of their work for them. No brakes magically appeared then, and I don't see them appearing now, absent someone free to act, with sufficient agency, against their worst impulses. The biosphere only survives, today, by virtue of what prosthetic assistance we can afford it. The assemblers might keep that going, were the klept to founder. But I don't trust that some last convulsive urge to short-term profit, some terminal shortsightedness, mightn't bring an end to everything."

Netherton blinked, swallowed. "China, too?"

"We do still share the biosphere with China," she said. "And trade with them, to what extent they allow."

"You killed Vespasian, didn't you?"

Her eyes met his. Hers, if original, were over a hundred years old. "I used to regret not having come across him sooner," she said, "thus having had the opportunity to kill him earlier, but now I have to consider the opportunity he's provided us, however inadvertently, in Eunice's stub."

Netherton heard the door open behind him, signaling the end of the meeting.

"Verity's asleep in the hotel in San Francisco," Lowbeer said. "When she wakes, speak with her. I'm here, should you need me."

"You knew Lev phoned me," Netherton said. "Did you know it was about this?"

"That it might be along these lines. The conversation tripped something the aunties had in place, that I hadn't been aware of."

CONTINENTAL BREAKFAST

Verity woke to men's voices, in another room, conversational but indistinct. She opened her eyes, to less-than-emphatic sunlight at the edges of unfamiliar drapes.

"Russians," someone said, "Facebook . . ." The one called Conner, who sounded southern. Then recognizing Virgil as he responded, though she couldn't distinguish any of it.

She squinted at the bedside clock. 8:25 a.m.

Unzipping the liner, she pulled it down, emerged from the sheets, and noticed the white bathrobe crumpled on the foot of the bed. Putting it on, she went to the door.

"—get how super fucked it all sounds to you," she heard Conner say, "but that's how it went down."

"How what went down?" she asked, opening the door.

Virgil looked up from where he sat, stocking feet up on the couch. "Conner's scaring the shit out of me," he said, mildly, and smiled.

"Wait'll I tell you the arc over the rest of the season," Conner said, from the drone's speaker. It stood facing the window, drapes open on gray morning.

"Any coffee?" she asked.

"Here," Virgil said, indicating a tray on the lilac hassock. "Fresh croissants."

"Save me some." Closing the door and going into the bathroom, she discovered further evidence that she'd managed to shower before getting into bed. She brushed her teeth, washed her face, put on jeans, a clean t-shirt, sneakers, and went to the other room.

"You sleep?" she asked Virgil, pouring herself a cup of coffee from the carafe on the tray.

"Couple hours," he said. "Conner spelled me. You?"

"Woke that one time, slept after that."

"2136?" he asked.

"What about it?" She tried a sip of black coffee.

"You think that's really the year, there?"

She added milk and sugar. "Maybe." She looked up at him. "Does that make me crazy?" She sat on the edge of the hassock, beside the tray.

"I'm crazy too," Virgil said, "but I've been up half the night, with Conner. Where you went, according to him, used to be the future of where he is. They still have a common past, but it forked a few years ago. And they both share a past with us, up until something that happened here, prior to the 2016 election, but he doesn't know what."

She looked up from the freshly torn croissant she was spreading with jam. "I don't think I can even grasp that, forget entertaining it."

"Man got it right," Conner said. "Hardly anybody does, the first time."

"It feels like this is Lowbeer's show," Verity said, "so what does she actually do?" She saw Virgil's attention sharpen, at this.

"On the books," Conner said, "she's just a cop. But the klept has her there to keep things stable. Their culture produces more than enough assholes, all scrambling for a bigger piece for themselves, to bring the whole thing down. But the other side of that coin's stagnation, if the same big boys on top try to stay forever, so I think she may cover that too."

"Klept?"

"The result," said Virgil, "if Conner's being straight with me, of paths we fortunately didn't take."

"No such luck," Conner said. "You're still plenty liable to get there, and so are we. And we've had four years now of future folks fiddling with us, trying to prevent that. Shit, we don't even have those fancy phones of theirs yet."

Virgil's phone rang. He put it to his ear. "Sure is," he said. "She's having the continental breakfast." He offered her the phone.

"How are you?" Stets asked. "Did you sleep?"

"I did, thanks. You?"

"Yes, but we've been having a very busy morning. Eunice's branch plants have found us."

"They've survived her?"

"Thrivingly."

"What are they like?"

"Not like her at all."

"She told me they did things behind her back. Like bring Joe-Eddy back from Germany. It was a surprise for her."

"They're keeping up the tradition with us. Our surprise this morning is that we're hosting an event on very short notice. But I have to run now. We'll speak later. Take care of yourself."

"You too," she said. He hung up. She passed the phone to Virgil.

"Rose Garden in ten," Conner said, "got it."

"Say what?" Virgil asked.

"My day job," Conner said. "President's taking questions from the press in half an hour, likes me to check if the translation from future-ese to folk wisdom's solid. You need me, I'll be right on it."

"Break a leg," said Virgil.

Verity, her mouth full of croissant and raspberry jam, said nothing.

"Anybody else in there?" Virgil asked the drone.

Silence.

"Money," Virgil said, "for Stets, is a by-product of satisfying his own curiosity. He's still amazed that most people who do what he does are in it mainly for the money. And Caitlin's the same. So you get two curiosities like that, what could be more attractive than this crazy shit?"

"You're supposed to be the house skeptic," she said. "I keep hoping you'll talk me out of it being real."

"Conner's been telling me his stub's history. Same as ours, up to the election."

"What election?"

"The president," he said.

She saw the monochrome mural in Clarion Alley. The overt threat.

"They aren't our future, that London," he said. "Their past got him instead."

She looked over at him, speechless.

"I know," he said, nodding, "but here we sit, engaged in whatever this is, while lots of people expect the world to end, and real soon now."

"I just agreed to disappear myself, supposedly to increase the chance of that not happening."

"Who says?"

"Lowbeer. Met her in 2136."

Virgil grinned. "Congratulations. You've crossed over."

"To what?"

"To believing this shit. What's disappeared look like, to her?"

"She says I've already done it, by being off Cursion's radar, but I still don't like the sound of it."

"Me neither," he said.

62

SHOE-BUTTON EYES

Rainey was at the kitchen table when Netherton came in, Thomas in his high chair. She was tickling one of the nanny's pandaforms for his amusement. It lay on its back on the red tabletop, Thomas crooning excitedly as it thrashed about.

"Hello," Netherton said, bending to kiss her forehead.

"Hello. How's Lev?"

"Unhappy." Straightening up. "Cheyne Walk is full of relatives, of course. Bit too klepty for his taste." He glanced at the couch, seeing the controller where he'd left it. "Where's the peri?"

"She called for one of the spa's cars, to take her back to Floral Street. Place looks like a cross between a capsule hotel and a morgue. Had her take me through it on their site. Guests are all female. Bodies, semibiologic or not, which are legally someone else's property, are an inherently creepy proposition."

"Yes," said Netherton, opening the refrigerator, "though in this case you wouldn't know Flynne nearly as well, without that peri. If a different one were being rented for her, each visit, you wouldn't have the same bond."

"True, and neither would I have anything like the same sense of London, if she hadn't wanted to see it all. I wouldn't have visited the cosplay zones, for instance, because you don't."

"They're for children," he said, "and tourists. We can take Thomas, when he's older."

"Cheapside's great," she said. "The smell of it."

"That's mainly feces. Human as well as equine."

"The crowds."

"Bots, most of them."

"It gives you a better sense of what it was like than any augmented reality," she said. "Carnaby Street is AR, for instance, and spectral in comparison. And visitors aren't required to dress for it, which makes it visually inconsistent."

Not seeing anything in the refrigerator that appealed, he closed it. "I should check on the stub," he said, glancing at the controller, uncomfortable with not being able to tell her what Lev, or for that matter Lowbeer, had told him. He looked down at a third of the nanny, squirming to escape Rainey's tickling. It seemed to look back at him, out of shoe-button eyes.

"Go ahead," said Rainey. "Seems like a good idea."

He went to the couch, sat down beside the controller, picked it up, and put it on.

63

USERS

"What would happen if I used this to call my mother?" Verity asked Virgil, indicating a hotel phone.

"Is she on cell?" Virgil asked, still on the couch with his feet up.

"Landline. She only turns her cell on if she's out with it and needs to make a call."

"Assuming Cursion's tapped it, they'd record the conversation, probably be able to get the room number. According to your IT lady in the future—"

"Ash," Verity said.

"She says Cursion aren't, in themselves, a big deal. That they're ex-government, so unconnected to state power. Which doesn't make her happy, though, because she says that makes them liable to fuck us up without even meaning to. No street smarts. Way she thinks reminds me of what I do for Stets."

"Except for what you do for Stets, not many people would've heard of him."

"I didn't hear you say that," he said, and smiled. "But thanks. To the man's credit, though, I know he tends to agree. But back to Cursion. Ash says Gavin's their front in the industry, an actual businessperson with a background in technology. If you called your mother, those are the kind of people you might alert to our whereabouts. Hers too, though they probably already have that."

"Stets still doesn't have anyone exclusively on security?"

"Few of us do keep an eye on things," he said.

"I know. You always did."

"Caitlin doesn't have security staff either. Her father has people in Paris, when she and Stets visit him, but they all have gray hair. The ones we notice, anyway." He put one of his feet down and dug in a pants pocket. "Speaking of phones, I took delivery of this one while you were sleeping." He leaned over to hand her a phone. "Not in your name." He passed her a black charger, its cable wound around it, and a pair of black earbuds. "Not okay to phone your mother on, or anyone else Cursion might know you know, but you've got the web, and it's programmed to dial fresh burners of ours."

"Where's mine?"

"With whoever built this controller for Stets, apparently, but I don't know how it got there."

She remembered dropping it into the barista's Faraday pouch, at 3.7, along with the Tulpagenics phone and the gray-framed glasses. She'd seen him give the pouch to Dixon.

The drone coughed. "Wilf here."

"Where are you?" she asked.

"Back in our flat. Went out to meet a friend. Upset about where he's living, after a divorce."

"What's wrong with where he's living?"

"Too near relatives of his," Wilf said.

She tried to imagine his future London with completely boring problems, realizing she expected all future problems to be inherently interesting.

"Hello, Virgil," Wilf said.

"Hey," Virgil said. "Conner said he had to go and do something in the Rose Garden. Why's he in the White House?"

"He and the president, Leon Fisher," Ash said, "are both from the same small town. This is Leon's first year in office, so it's helpful for him to have someone there from home."

"But that didn't happen, in your past?" Virgil had both his feet on the floor now, and was sitting up.

"That's correct," said Wilf.

"Conner says it isn't time travel, because of that," Virgil said. "That time travel, physically, is impossible."

"We can establish digital contact with our own past," Wilf said, "provided sufficient infrastructure exists there to allow it. Doing so initiates a new continuum, one in which that message was received. In ours, right now, it wasn't."

"So you could get in touch with us here, yesterday?" Virgil asked. "Our yesterday?"

"No," said Wilf, "but if we could, that would be the start of a new stub, because that didn't happen in your past."

"Why can't you?" Verity asked.

"Initiation results in a one-to-one temporal ratio. If I initiate a stub, leave it, then return, the same amount of time has passed in the stub."

"Conner told Virgil that the election last year went the other way, there," Verity said. "Did it?"

"Yes," said Wilf.

"So you're in another stub?" she asked.

"No," said Wilf, "because that was in our past, and all stubs branch from ours."

"How can you be sure of that?" Virgil asked.

"Because," said Wilf, "we've the means of initiating stubs and you don't."

"So what if you reached back to your own last Tuesday?" Virgil asked.

"That's impossible," Wilf said.

"Why?" Verity asked.

"We need to reach quite a distance back, in order to make contact. Though not too far, else the resulting new stub lack sufficient infrastructure to receive our data. There's a window, that way. I'm told yours is the earliest stub known to have been viably initiated."

"So what you do," Virgil said, his eyes narrowed, "is colonize alternate pasts."

"I don't think colonization's the best metaphor," Wilf said, something about the ease with which he said it suggesting to Verity that this wasn't the first time. "There's no possibility of resource extraction. No transferable financial gain."

"How about something like Amazon's Mechanical Turk?" Virgil asked, Verity recognizing this as what he really did for Stets.

"I don't know it," Wilf said.

"Like Uber, but for information labor," Virgil said.

"We have AI for that," Wilf said. "We could manipulate your markets, make money there, and pay you with it, but our AI is free, essentially, so it wouldn't be worth it."

"Art," said Virgil. "Music. Literature."

"Yes," said Netherton. "But still, in practice, there's no real economic basis."

"Then why do you do it?" Verity asked.

"In your case," Wilf said, "initially, we want to avert nuclear war in your stub. For most users, though, it's simply a pastime."

"A pastime," Virgil said, flatly.

"Users?" Verity asked.

"Hobbyists," Wilf said.

"Just in it for the shits and giggles?" Virgil asked, looking at the drone.

"Ash," sharply announcing herself. "Time to go."

"Why?" Verity asked.

"Someone's put up an image of you on something called Instagram.

Taken last night, as you entered the hotel with Virgil. They recognized him as part of Howell's inner circle. They didn't recognize you, else they'd have identified you in the post, but others have in the meantime. I've sent you both the link."

Virgil groaned. Consulted his phone. "They're stretching it, IDing you in that hoodie. Could be anybody." He showed Verity the photograph. She was on his far side, in the lobby's lilac gloom, hood up, no more than a quarter of her face visible, and that with sunglasses.

"Pack," said Ash. "It doesn't look as though they have anyone in the lobby yet."

"How do you know?" Virgil asked.

"We're using Followrs, through a proxy," Ash said. "We have one in the lobby now."

Verity was already headed for her Muji bag, in the bathroom.

64

MINIMUM OF DRAMA

"What's happening?" asked Rainey, close by Netherton's head, startling him. He, or rather the drone, was just then being hauled rapidly out of the hotel suite in San Francisco.

He muted. "Leaving the hotel," he said, "hurriedly."

"Why?"

"Someone's revealed Verity's whereabouts, on a public medium. Ash is concerned that Cursion will find her here." They were passing that alcove, with its mirror, acrylic chair, and asymmetrical floor lamp. Virgil was pulling the drone behind him in its wheeled travel corset. The squashed-circle format gave Netherton a sense of what was going on but, with the drone in motion, was simultaneously disorienting. "Sorry," he said, "best I concentrate."

"Do," Rainey said, squeezing his shoulder, which felt peculiar while he was accessing the drone. He unmuted.

"So we're hauling ass," said Conner, now evidently back from the Rose Garden. Conner was louder than the others accessing the drone, a larger presence.

"Someone put Virgil on Instagram," Verity said, "someone else identified me." She was carrying the large black case with their controller in it, big enough to require both hands but evidently not very heavy.

The elevator door opened. Virgil pulled the drone into a confusion of brownish-red reflections. "Who's expected, downstairs?" he asked.

"We don't know," said Ash. "We hope to get out before anyone arrives."

"Liable to get kinetic if we don't?" Conner asked.

"Optimally," Ash said, "we exit the lobby with a minimum of drama, and immediately board our transport, attracting as little attention as possible. Should it go sideways, Mr. Penske, please remember that we don't want headlines about a bipedal drone attacker. Far too exotic, here."

"Roger that," said Conner, as the elevator stopped, its door opening, Virgil hauling them both out. Behind them, Netherton saw Verity quickly slip on a pair of large black sunglasses and step out.

ONE-SHOT

The first thing Verity noted, past Virgil's shoulder, was the Candy Crush Saga girl from 3.7, seated against a backdrop of floor-to-ceiling mauve drapery, thumbs busy on her phone.

"Our new hire, there," said Ash, via the burner phone's earbuds, "the one on her phone."

"Cursion had her on the lookout for me, in a coffee place where I went with Eunice," Verity said quickly, under her breath. "Knows me on sight." The girl, having now seen her, stared, startled, thumbs gone still.

"Don't look as if you recognize her," said Ash. "She must live locally. Assignment overlap would be a problem, with that business model."

Virgil was headed toward Geary now, pulling the drone.

Verity hurried to catch up, the strap of her bag digging into her shoulder with the added weight of the charger. She reflexively gave the girl a distracted smile, in spite of Ash's order, as she and Virgil rounded the corner, making for the entrance. Saw nothing in the lobby suggestive of Cursion, though she supposed anyone could be a Followr. She saw Virgil slip the doorman some folded bills as they went out, and bowed her hoodied head over the controller case.

"This way," Sevrin said, suddenly beside her, taking the controller case. Head still down, she made no eye contact, recognizing his fancy bus-driver shoes and zero-accent accent. He led her around what seemed to be an identical van, white this time but with windows equally dark. He slid open the passenger door, helped her up and in. Virgil climbed in behind her, Sevrin passing him the helmet case, which he placed on the second row of passenger seats.

Choosing the window seat behind the driver, she shrugged off her bag, putting it on the seat behind hers, beside the black case. Virgil was helping Sevrin get the drone up now, and onto the seat beside her. Over their shoulders, through a momentary gap in passing vehicles, she saw someone emerging from the bagel restaurant across the street. Short hair, wire-rimmed glasses, forty-something. Seeing the look of recognition as he saw her, she instantly knew that it had been the back of his crew-cut head she'd seen as he'd surveyed the junk on Joe-Eddy's worktable.

"Across the street," she said, "crew cut, glasses. Works for Cursion."

"On it," said Conner, as Sevrin scrambled over the console, into the driver's seat, as what she thought of as the projector hatch in the drone's carapace opened, something neutrally colored and vaguely cylindrical lifting out of it on quad rotors, more noisily than Verity's drones from their Pelican case, to whisk out the open door.

In the center of the street now, something like an explosive exhalation of vape. She couldn't see the man with the wire-rims.

Then Sevrin was driving them up Geary, away from a growing chorus of irritated horns. Virgil, who'd fallen back into the seat beside the drone, was fastening his seatbelt.

"What did you do?" Verity asked Conner.

"Fentanyl analog," said Conner, "aerosol."

"You killed him?" she asked.

"Might have gotten him run over," Conner said, "but more likely he just blacked out. Ash'll be pissed, but his records indicate he has some moves. Didn't want him getting across the street."

"Trimethyl phentanylum?" Ash asked, not sounding particularly angry to Verity.

"They got it on a darknet," Conner said. "Right drone and aerosolizer, you're good to go. Installed thirty minutes before Verity turned up."

Sevrin, having taken a left, took another, headed in the direction opposite the one they'd departed in, on a street parallel to Geary, driving as though nothing had happened. Sirens seemed to be converging, but then she realized the van was directly behind the Clift.

"Who was that?" asked Wilf.

"Someone Cursion sent to bug Joe-Eddy's," Verity said, sitting back and buckling her seatbelt. "Eunice showed him to me in a feed, when he was up there. He saw me getting in the van, recognized me, started to cross, but Conner zapped him." She looked at the drone, which Virgil and Sevrin hadn't had time to belt in. "Thanks, Conner."

"De nada."

"Where are we going?" Verity asked.

"For a change of license plates and the application of decals," Ash said. "We had planned to take you back to the Bertrand-Howell project site, but that's been scratched, given media have a link between you and Stets' star assistant."

"'Star assistant,'" said Virgil, who hadn't opened his mouth since climbing into the van, from his seat beside the drone. "You write for tabloids?"

"Quoting one's site, two minutes ago," said Ash.

NONNEURAL

"What are they doing now?" Rainey asked, sounding as if she were in the kitchen. He was watching the surprisingly graceful movements of the men Ash said were applying decals to this vehicle's exterior.

Netherton muted. "A Cursion operative spotted Verity. Someone she recognized. He tried to get closer to us as we were about to leave. Conner used a small drone, knocked him out with an aerosol."

"Where are you now?"

"In a vehicle like the one that brought us from Oakland, presently in a parking structure, not far from the hotel. A section of the place has been curtained off for privacy. Men are applying large decals to the top, back, and sides."

"Who's there?"

"Verity, Virgil, and Sevrin, the driver. And money launderer, according to Ash. She and Conner are accessing the drone with me."

"Can they hear us?"

"Not at the moment."

"What are they doing?"

"Ash and Conner are silent. Our three locals have their phones out and seem to be catching up on the news."

"How is the news?"

"They strike me as gravely concerned, but not speechless with horror."

Verity, to the drone's left, looked up from her phone. "More Russian jets down?"

"Two," Virgil answered, on the drone's right, "but Syrian, not Russian."

"I should go now," Netherton said to Rainey, deciding not to share this with her immediately.

"Go," Rainey said, "bye."

He unmuted. "Is it worse, then?" he asked.

"Definitely not better," Verity said. She seemed to be watching water sluice down the windshield. Coveralled decal-appliers were working to either side, while two more, on ladders, apparently did the roof, plus another at the rear. "They look choreographed," she said, just as the water stopped flowing and small electric motors started in unison.

Heat guns, Netherton saw, through the window tint, like antique hair dryers. "Where to next?" he asked.

"Waiting for instructions," Ash said.

"How would you know that it isn't Cursion giving you directions?" Netherton asked.

"Because they're given to Sevrin by his brother, in Moldovan, and they have their own security signals. In the meantime, Verity can visit with me in E8, if she likes. Verity?"

Verity turned to the drone. "Is the peripheral there?" she asked.

"No," said Ash, "and I haven't much to offer you in the way of a telepresence device. Barest bones." Netherton wondering if she meant that last literally.

"Won't that leave me frozen on the seat here?" Verity looked questioningly at Virgil. "What if something happens and we need to get out?"

"There's no neural cut-out for this device," Ash said. "It has no moving parts. You'll be able to hear what's going on around you there, and take the controller off yourself, if need be."

"Okay," Verity said.

"Virgil," Ash said, "could you please help Verity with the controller? This won't require the saline paste."

Virgil loosened his safety belt and turned, taking the case from the seat behind the drone. He placed it on his lap, then removed its top and sides. Seeing the stub-built controller a second time, it struck Netherton that it wouldn't stand out at all, on the table next to Ash's yurt.

"I don't want that goop in my hair again," Verity said.

Virgil helped Verity settle the controller on her head, reaching over the top of the drone.

"You'll have audio-visual," Ash said, "but no control, other than asking me to point it in desired directions."

"Nausea?" Verity asked.

"No," said Ash, "it's neurologically too low-res to readily induce it. Ready?"

"Yes."

Virgil reached over again, to touch a switch on the side of the controller.

"Hello," Verity said.

"Welcome," said Ash.

For Verity's sake, Netherton hoped they weren't meeting in the flesh-yurt.

67

COLLAGE MINUS GLUE

"Is this the same year?" Verity asked Ash, who had a tangle of ultra-black hair, gray eyes below it, and wore a pale, acidy greenish-yellow shade of lipstick. She appeared to be about ten feet from Verity, while behind her stretched a single long room, its white walls windowless, the floor gray and smooth, the look of gallery space repurposed from something else.

"It is," Ash said.

"I can't move my head," Verity said, having just tried.

"You haven't a neck or shoulders," Ash said. She came forward, wearing motorcycle boots, flowing dark pants tucked into them, and a smoothly iridescent brown carapace. She reached out, picked Verity up, and flipped her over.

"Whoa."

"Sorry," said Ash. "I promised you a nausea-free visit."

They were in front of a long table, as cluttered as Joe-Eddy's workbench but very differently textured. Ash panned Verity's point of view the length of it, right to left. Past its end appeared what Verity took to be a hut, looking as though it had been composted from something else. In front of this was a large black-and-chrome motorcycle, old-fashioned but gleaming. "This is where you live?" Verity asked.

"Yes."

"Where do you sleep?"

"In the yurt." Ash swung whatever Verity inhabited back to the table, stopping at an antique vanity mirror on a tarnished silver base, then raised her, directly in front of the mirror. Verity saw the head of a doll, china, its wide eyes gray.

"You both have gray eyes," Verity said.

"I had mine altered recently," Ash said, "though this is the gray I was born with. I bought the doll before I had it done, to help me decide."

"Can I see what's on the table again?"

Ash swung the doll head to the right. "Collage minus glue, Wilf says."

Verity glanced over decorated gourds, bundles of feathers, basketry, ethnic musical instruments both stringed and wind, ceramics, rolled tapestries, candlesticks, a tall samovar, and, most distinctively, what appeared to her to be a completely rusted submachine gun, covered with the dingy yellow plastic letters of fridge-magnet alphabets, spelling nothing Verity recognized. All of it absent anything Joe-Eddy could have de-soldered. "Is Joe-Eddy okay?" she asked, reminded of him.

"Appears to be," Ash said. "He assumes they keylogged him, when they bugged the place. He's right, of course."

"Shit," said Verity, "my laptop," then remembered that Eunice had had someone take it from the apartment before the bugging, along with her passport.

"Guilherme," said Ash, "has delivered, via the current pair of lawyers, a phone encrypted in a way even the aunties can't break. Joe-Eddy can use it in bed, under the bedclothes."

A higher purpose for black sheets, Verity thought. "The Manzilian," she said.

"What?"

"That's what Joe-Eddy calls Guilherme. What happened to the guy Conner gassed?"

"Kevin Pryor," Ash said. "Ex-Army, Intelligence Corps."

"What happened to him?"

"He wasn't alone. Colleagues got him off the scene before police or the ambulance arrived. We assume he regained consciousness immediately, no injury when he collapsed. One of Eunice's branch plants has quite a bit on him. He isn't part of Cursion, but a freelancer they've used before. None of the principals at Cursion has an intelligence background, though neither do they assume they need one. They do, however, which is why they've repeatedly hired him. Lowbeer regards him as more dangerous than they are."

"Why?"

"Intelligence background, of course, but also he's differently ambitious. He isn't wealthy, and she assumes he's not satisfied with being a freelancer. She thinks he likely poses as much of a threat to them as he does to us."

"Would he know what even hit him, back there?"

"Not necessarily, but we assume he knows quite a bit about you, given his current assignment. So we're keeping an eye out for him."

"Where are we going now?" Verity asked. Sevrin had showed her the van's new decals on his phone. Logo of a vegan wholesaler in Chico, stylized vines and swirling leaves, the roof entirely green.

"Dogpatch, according to Sevrin," said Ash. "Which may change, now that he thinks he's spotted someone following the van on a motorcycle."

"Shit," said Verity.

"Best get used to it," said Ash. "Would you like to go back to the van now?"

"Yes," said Verity, and instantly was.

DOGPATCH

Netherton was watching Verity in the drone's left peripheral display as she turned to look back.

"Where are we?" she asked. "Where's the motorcycle?"

"Dogpatch," said Sevrin, which meant nothing to Netherton. "They're four cars back."

Verity unfastened her safety belt and turned completely around, to kneel on the seat. Netherton watched her profile. Virgil, he saw in the opposite display, was similarly kneeling, peering back.

"We stop for red," Sevrin said, "they get closer. Like now."

Netherton reflexively squinted at the display's narrow rearview band as the van came to a halt, producing, to his surprise, the sudden enlargement of a motorcycle, coming up behind them along the street's centerline, its driver's face hidden by a white helmet.

"Slows, when getting closer," Sevrin said. "Never right behind us. Technique."

"I may know who that is," Verity said.

"Sit down," Sevrin said, "buckle up." The light changed and he drove on.

Verity and Virgil, on either side of the drone, turned back around and fastened their belts.

"How do you know the person you think this may be?" Ash asked.

"Maybe drove me to Oakland," Verity said. "Eunice arranged it. I got an e-mail as soon as she was gone, written earlier, telling me to go with him. He works in 3.7, the coffee place on Valencia, not that we knew each other."

"Did he tell you anything about his relationship with Eunice?" Ash asked.

"He never spoke. Assume he can't."

"Now," Sevrin said, taking a sharp right, almost simultaneously braking, hard, into a paved space. A car passed, a second, and then the motorcycle, one of the largest Netherton had seen, swung smoothly into what free space remained, stopping about three meters from their sliding passenger door.

The rider put his booted feet down and sat on the motorcycle, wearing a black leather jacket and an immaculately white helmet.

"That your man?" Conner asked.

"I think so," said Verity.

The rider raised a hand, flipped up the helmet's visor. He wore a white filtration mask. Above its upper left edge, Netherton saw a glint of metal.

"That's him," Verity said.

Netherton flinched, as the drone suddenly shifted position to his left, putting more of its torso between Verity and the man on the motorcycle. Its arms, no longer handless, were extended now as well, though Netherton had scarcely seen that happen, the left grasping the back of the front passenger seat, the right the end of the bench. Virgil, finding himself between the drone and the stranger, unfastened his seatbelt again.

The rider gestured, twice, with his fingers. Come.

"Your call," Conner said.

"I'll speak with him," Verity said.

"I let you past," Conner said, "Sevrin opens the door, you get out. I'm behind you but at the open door. You good, Sevrin?"

"Good," Sevrin said.

"Say go," said Conner.

"Go," said Verity, already moving forward, as the door began to open.

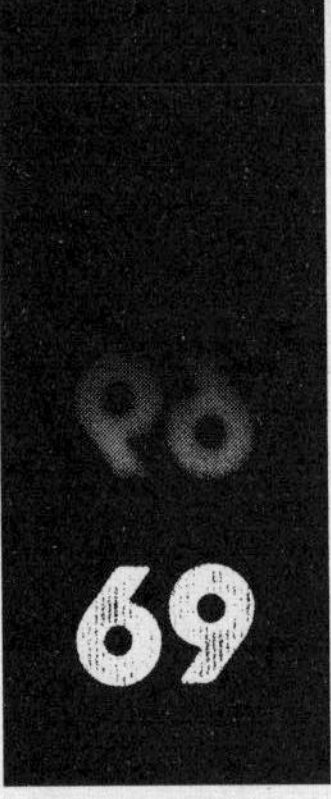

HEATHKIT

Stepping down, in front of the barista on his Harley, it occurred to Verity that she should probably have the hoodie up, because people in the building whose parking lot this was might be getting pictures or video of the encounter, particularly if they could also see the drone. This rare and temporary patch of fall sunlight felt great, though, so she left it down.

The barista reached up and pulled his mask away from his face, then down. Releasing it, it rode beneath his chin like a white plastic voice box.

"Is Eunice dead?" she asked him.

He briskly mimed the emoji she thought of as amazement at another's cluelessness, his open palms turning briefly up, with a simultaneous shrug and eye roll. Then he raised a forefinger, reached into his jacket pocket with the other hand, and produced a folded paper bag, handing it to her. Stamped in brown, she saw, with 3.7-sigma's logo.

There seemed to be nothing in it. She unfolded it. The all-caps message was in fluorescent pink industrial paint pen:

GRIM TIM HERE THO WEVE MET. BET YOU WANT TO KNOW WHATS HAPPENED TO E I DONT KNOW. SHES NOT AVAILABLE BUT SOME PIECES SEEM TO BE & AND I EXPECT YOULL BE HEARING FROM THEM. ONE TOLD ME YOU WERE LEAVING THE HOTEL & TO FOLLOW YOU & RETURN YR GEAR MODDED FOR SECURITY. PHONE AND GLASSES BOTH REENCRYPTED BY EUNICES PIECES SO THATS IT.

"Grim Tim," she said, looking up from his note.

He was opening a black mesh bag, bungeed to the top of the Harley's tank. He looked up, flashing her a version of that look of somehow agreeable contempt she knew from 3.7. From the mesh he produced what she assumed was the Faraday pouch she'd seen before. When she'd accepted it, he pulled up his mask, lowered the visor of his helmet, took his pink-lettered message from her, crumpled it one-handed, stuffed it back into his jacket pocket, and gunned his engine slightly.

"Thanks," she said, taking a step back, uncertain how she felt about communicating with some sort of partial Eunice.

He turned the Harley, waited for a gap in the traffic, and was gone, a single sharp backfire ringing in his wake.

"Get in," Conner said, from the drone behind her. "Time we go." She turned, to find it standing in the open passenger door, arms braced. "Let me sniff that first." And one arm was there, that quickly, long and thin, with three different kinds of retractable device, sensors she supposed, in various proximities to the bag. "Seems clean," he said. "Get in. I'll open it."

"I'll open it myself," she said, climbing up, past the drone and into the van, where Sevrin remotely closed the door behind her.

Taking her seat behind Sevrin, she held the pouch on her lap in both hands. Sevrin was turning the van, then waiting for an opening in traffic.

When one arrived, he pulled out. She undid the pouch's folded lips and looked down into it. Against its white lining, she saw the Tulpagenics phone, the case for the glasses, the headset, and their three chargers.

When she spread the temples of the glasses she found their inner surfaces had been shallowly excavated, then refilled with something darker. "He said everything's been modded for security. Ash?"

"Yes?"

"He said Eunice's branch plants will be in touch. So should I put these on, turn on the phone?"

"Wouldn't you, even if I told you not to?" Ash asked. "I would."

"Why didn't you know that would be him, following us?"

"That would be the branch plants," Ash said. "They aren't very forthcoming."

Verity put the glasses on. She got out the Tulpagenics phone. Two small square holes had been neatly cut in the back of its case, then patched with dark blue plastic tape. When she powered it up, the display was unfamiliar. The headset, she found, had its own hole and blue patch. She turned that on as well, hung it on her ear, put the earbud in place, pressed power, then pressed power on the glasses, causing the headset to ping, once.

No cursor.

She let out the breath she hadn't known she was holding. She turned the phone over, looking at its back again. "Why did they cut these holes," she asked Ash, "instead of just opening it?"

In her glasses: **The unit is designed to self-destruct if opened by unauthorized personnel. Postfactory access now bypasses that system. Under no circumstances attempt further exploration, disassembly, or modification.**

White Helvetica, across the back of her phone, her hand, her jeans. "Who are you?" she asked.

Unable to formulate reply.

She looked at Virgil.

He raised an eyebrow. "Sup?"

This communication is encrypted.

"This phone's encrypted?"

All units are currently secure.

"May I speak with Eunice?"

No.

"Why?"

Unable to formulate reply.

"Who else can I communicate with, on this system?"

Make a specific request.

"Joe-Eddy?"

Not available.

"José Eduardo Alvarez-Matta?"

Available.

"No shit?"

Unable to formulate reply.

"How do I contact him?"

Text José Eduardo Alvarez-Matta as HEATHKIT. Press send.

Verity looked from Virgil down to the drone between them, then back up again. "It says I can text Joe-Eddy."

"What does?" Virgil asked.

"One of Eunice's branch plants, if Grim Tim was right. That's how he introduced himself. Thing reads about as human as pharmaceutical instructions and won't answer most questions. I'd text him now, but you told me he'd only be able to use it under the covers."

"Do it anyway," Ash said. "If he isn't on the device now, he'll see it when he next uses it."

Verity, opening Messages, started one to HEATHKIT. **Hey,** she typed, **you okay? I'm okay. V.**

Pressed send.

"Who else can I text?" she asked.

Make a specific request.

"Stets. Stetson Howell."

Not available.

She frowned.

What are you wearing?

"Fuck off, Joe-Eddy."

You probably don't even have to pretend you're fapping. I have to be under the covers with porn on my real phone, when I do this. Don't know if it fools Cursion, but the lawyers are having a hard time not giving me looks.

"Got him," she said, with a glance for the drone.

"How can you be sure?" asked Ash.

"If it's not him, it's a good facsimile," Verity said, glancing back at the phone's screen. Where she read:

Can't chat but sending you prepared update of cryptic shit in meantime. Now back to living room before Trevor and Celeste decide I've suffered onanistic stroke, break down door to give me CPR. Take care tho not necessarily the way Trevor and Celeste think I'm doing.

"Make that a really good facsimile," Verity said.

A BIT OF COSPLAY

Netherton felt Rainey settle on the couch beside him. He was watching Verity from the drone. It felt like sitting between the two of them, except that Rainey was invisible.

"You've been quiet," Rainey said. "What's happening?"

Netherton muted his link to the drone's speaker. "We were followed by a man on a motorcycle. We're still in or near something called the Dogpatch, as far as I know. Sevrin pulled over a few blocks ago. The motorcycle stopped, and its rider, a man with jewelry attached to his face, gave Verity a bag containing a manual phone and accessories and rode away. We're on our way again now, no idea where."

"What's Verity doing?"

"She questioned what she assumes is one of Eunice's subselves, her so-called laminae, on the phone she was given."

"What did it say?"

"It put her in touch with Joe-Eddy, the man she stays with in San Francisco."

"When you have an opportunity," Rainey said, "ask her if there's anything you can do to help."

"With what?"

"The point being that it's a general offer of assistance. Meanwhile, though, Lowbeer wants you in her car."

"Why?"

"To take you to Cheapside."

"Obligate cosplay," he protested. "I've nothing period to wear."

"You do now. She's had assemblers rebuild a few items from your wardrobe. I spared you fly buttons on the trousers, though. Contemporary fastenings disguised as period, there."

"Why Cheapside?"

"Clovis Fearing lives there. Said the three of you have something to discuss."

"Did she say what it is?"

"Of course not. Wants you soonest."

"What about the controller?"

"Definitely not period, unless you have it rebuilt in beaver."

Netherton sighed, though he was getting rather tired of the couch. He unmuted. "I'll be away for a bit," he said.

Verity glanced up from whatever she was reading on the phone. "'Kay," she said, which he understood as a low-intensity affirmative. No one else responded. He removed the controller and set it down beside him on the couch.

"Let me have a look at you when you're dressed," Rainey said. "You know I don't mind a bit of cosplay." She winked.

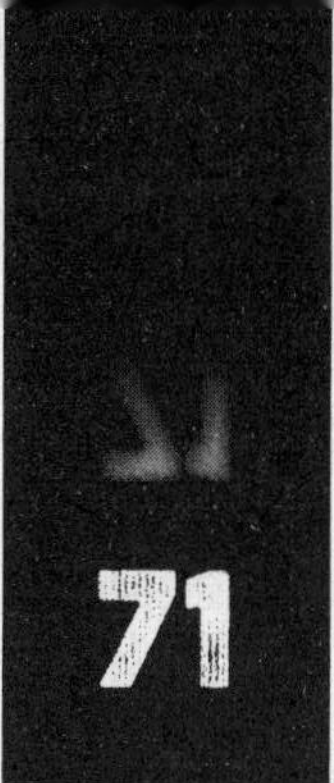

CATCHING UP

So Wednesday after I left u in W+L w Gavin I'm up here w the Manzilian negotiating a purchase for Eunice, and on the basis of that hooking him up with her directly. So I did hook them up while u were both with Gavin n she multitasked. Afterward I'm melting solder & pondering all this insane shit & u walk in I assume with Eunice, go into the kitchen. I get a text from Eunice I should go out, walk around. I do, all wearing the goggles, which get some looks but I don't want to miss her. So she texts me I should walk around a little more. So I'm in a bookstore and bang she tells me Cursion's about to try to take her down. Doesn't know if they can or not but she has to assume it'll be permanent if they do. Ask her where you are & she says with her but she's made arrangements to get you somewhere safe. Says that what the Manzilian n I have been working on is part of a network to protect you & everyone in it. There's us, the Manzilian, this money guy Sevrin who goes by Miguel, fabbers in Oakland. Plus more I haven't hooked up with yet, all her hires, everybody earning over market in whatever field. Went over the cams Cursion installed here, how she's spoofing them but that'll stop when she's gone. Who to expect turning up from her and how to positively identify em.

Tells me to take care of you & the network & then she's gone. So here I am under the covers with my thumbs getting sore but if you're reading this it means we've already said hello. J-E

She'd been looking out the window, as she read this. Now she turned to Virgil. He'd been watching her. "Stets always wanted to hire him," he said, "but we didn't have anything for anyone like that to do."

"If you had," she said, "Stets and I wouldn't have gotten together. Office romance with the boss is awkward enough, but not with your cousin working there."

"He's your cousin?" Virgil asked.

"No," she said, "but like that."

72

DON'T DAWDLE

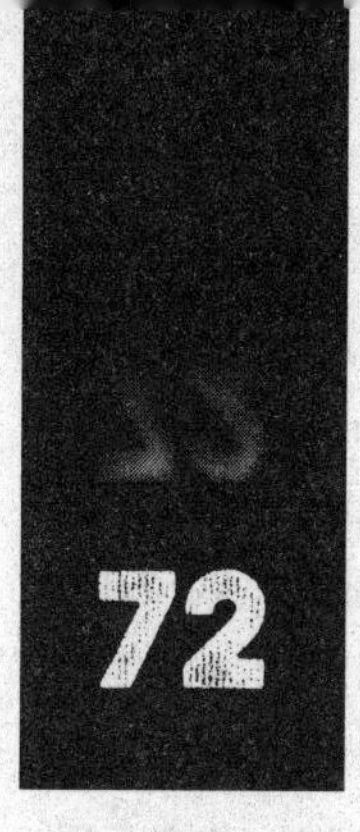

Assemblers not only produced perfect bespoke replicas of period costume, Netherton was reminded, putting on the black knee-length frock coat, but made them look as though the wearer had previously worn them, a subtlety of cosplay he knew he hadn't matched with his knotting of this somber silk necktie. Fortunately it was the most problematically fastened garment of the lot, both the frock coat and the calf-length topcoat having, as Rainey had promised, period-accurate but perfectly manageable buttons. The shirt and trousers, and the high black shoes, though they appeared to button quite elaborately, employed invisible contemporary fasteners. He wouldn't have bothered changing into the period-accurate underpants, but for Rainey having slyly mentioned wanting to see him in them later.

And no topper, to his great relief, Lowbeer having evidently recalled his dislike of them. Not that he particularly liked derbies either, he thought, as he put on this black one and considered the result in the bedroom mirror.

It did nothing for him, he decided, aside from definitively not being a top hat. He briefly tried imagining himself with a mustache, sideburns, or both. He'd never been interested in fancy dress, even as a child.

About to close the closet door, having tried to determine which garments of his the assemblers had made all this from, he noticed something unfamiliar propped inside, below his clothing. A walking stick, this proved to be, of what he assumed was ebony. Hexagonal in cross-section, with a round, complexly turned head of the same material, its top was inset with a well-worn sterling roundel, "W. Netherton" engraved across it in cursive. Lowbeer's assemblers could have made this from his shoes, he decided, then noticed that several pairs of them were in fact missing. He must remember to insist on everything being returned to its original state, as much as he disliked the idea of that being accomplished in their bedroom closet.

A nicely balanced object, though, this stick. Pleasant in the hand. He opened the bedroom door, stepping out to show Rainey.

She whooped in delight, jumping up and running over, kissing him on the mouth, then took the derby and tried it on, tilting it quite far down over one eye. "You've found your winter look." She grinned, and put it back on his head.

"Not a topper, at least. Forced to wear one last time I was coerced into going there. A City function in a guildhall, keeping Lev company. Reception afterward at a grillroom. You were still in Toronto."

"You complained about it, I remember. But she called again, just now, while you were changing. Car waiting in the mews, gone helicopter again. Better get going." She gave him an appraising look. "Are there garters?"

"Yes. Socks are wool, no elastic."

"Whew," she said, pretending to fan her face with her hand. "Can't wait." She kissed him on the cheek.

"I love you," he said.

"Socks on the brain right now, but fond of you myself."

Remembering the gesture from some ancient video, he saluted her by lightly tapping the derby's brim with the shaft of the stick. "Phone if you need me."

"I will," she said.

He saw his breath as he stepped out into the mews, the night being colder than he'd expected. He stroked the topcoat's sleeve seam, before remembering it wasn't a heated garment. Continuing down the mews with the stick over his shoulder, he saw the car's door decloaking. It opened, the step descending.

"Come in," said Lowbeer, from inside.

He did. She wasn't there. "I'm in Cheapside," she said, as the door closed behind him, her voice omnidirectional. "Please have a seat."

He did, choosing the one to the rear, in order to be facing forward. As he was becoming aware of the faint residual scent of one of her candles, he felt the car rise smoothly, in perfect silence, up out of Alfred Mews.

"Care for a view?" she asked.

"No, thank you," he said, preferring the buff walls. The walking stick lay diagonally across the oval table, the derby beside it.

The car was no longer rising now, and he was only faintly aware of forward momentum, though he knew this could be highly deceptive, as the attached quadcopter could be as fast as it was silent.

And so, shortly, descent, his sole awareness of landing one of cessation of movement. He stood, stick and derby in hand, to step up, out of the upholstered and carpeted pit. The door opened. He heard horses' hooves, wheels rattling across cobbles, the distant chugging of a steam train.

Stepping down from the car, he noticed two crinolined women staring blankly at him, or rather, he assumed, at what they might be able to see of the car's decloaked door. He took them to be visitors. The bots who made the place look populous ignored anomalies, while the relative few who chose to live here tended to scowl at breaks in continuity.

The sky was his favorite thing about the place, day or night, some effect removing the shards entirely, along with whatever other tokens of the present would otherwise have been distantly visible. The hour now, he saw, was late enough for the street to be slightly less crowded, but with no suggestion of that Lowbeerian depopulation he expected when meeting her in a public place. Gentlemen were strolling after dinner with cigars, ladies of the night were abroad, and a veritable museum of antique criminality was afoot, this last being one of the most popular attractions.

"Thank you for coming," said Lowbeer, at his elbow, causing him to start.

"Rainey mentioned Fearing," he said.

"Indeed," said Lowbeer. The top hat altered the look of her features, he thought, due mainly to concealing the white quiff, which ordinarily lent her face animation. Without it, she looked studious, and a bit owlish. Like his own costume, hers suggested mourning, perhaps in deference to Fearing's perpetual bereavement. "This way, please." Ushering him in the direction of St. Paul's. "Have you attended the commemoration, here, of the Second Great Fire? December twenty-ninth and thirtieth."

"I haven't," Netherton said. "What do they do?" He stepped around a beggar boy, a bitter-looking double amputee on a wheeled pallet, almost certainly a bot.

"Gobshite," he heard it call harshly after him.

"They use the system that conceals the shards to reenact the fire," Lowbeer continued, "the result of German incendiary bombs in 1940. Sunset on the second evening is particularly memorable. This way, please." She turned left, down a narrow passageway, the two of them unable to quite walk abreast. Here the odors of the cosplay zone, artificial though he knew them to be, strongly reminded him of how much he disliked them generally. Somewhat away from the fresh manure of the street now, there was an eye-stingingly ammoniac reek of urine. This lessened as they continued, but not entirely.

"Here we are, then," said Lowbeer, stopping unexpectedly, a thick wooden door, previously unnoticed, partially opening to Netherton's immediate left. Fearing, dimly backlit by candlelight, squinted ferociously at him over something thrust forward in both hands, her arms outstretched from the shoulders. A pistol, Netherton saw, of the county's era, and exactly the sort he knew her younger self to favor.

"Good evening, Clovis," said Lowbeer, removing her top hat.

"Don't dawdle," Fearing said, taking a step back and partially lowering the pistol.

Lowbeer promptly stepped in, opening the door further. Netherton followed, remembering to remove his derby.

Fearing, her gun now in one hand, a brass candelabra in the other, its half-consumed white tapers flickering, nodded toward a dark narrow gap behind her. "Go ahead," she said, "it's straight back."

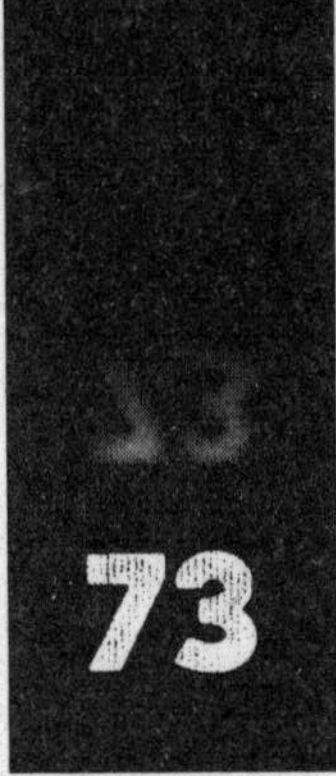

SINGULARITY

Virgil brought them lunch: hamburgers from a ranking Dogpatch bistro that didn't do takeout but had been susceptible to his PA moves, which Verity knew to be potent. Simultaneously arranging, with the same skill set and whatever amount of cash, for the van, its freshly applied vegan wholesaler signage fitting right in, to park behind this hipster supermarket.

She kept thinking the day was overcast, as she ate her burger, then remembering that that was the window tint. The sun was now solidly out.

The drone was stationed at the passenger door, its back to the van's interior, the thin black camera-tentacle protruding out and up, through a narrow gap at the top of the right front window, to scope for aerial drones. Conner might have it on automatic now, she guessed, as he'd said nothing since Virgil had gone to pick up lunch, and neither had Ash.

"Am I interrupting lunch?" asked Rainey, from the drone.

"You aren't," Verity said. "Where's Wilf?"

"Cheapside," said Rainey.

"That's a neighborhood?"

"A street. But also the most popular cosplay zone. Victorian. Visitors have to dress for it. Most of the apparent population are bots."

"Bots?"

"Like a peripheral, but inorganic, nonsentient, usually remotely directed. There are a few permanent actual residents, though, and that's why Wilf's there. Gone with Lowbeer to visit a friend of hers, the only person I know who's as old as she is."

"How old?" Verity asked.

"Well," Rainey said, "Lowbeer herself is alive in your stub, in 2017. A child, there."

Verity stared at the drone, over her brown cardboard box of forgotten fries.

"She and her friend are both a hundred and twenty-something," Rainey said. "Their biological clocks keep getting reset, so we're not just talking cosmetic treatments. Lowbeer has that cosmetic work done as well, but Clovis refuses. Says she's old as dirt and might as well look it."

"Dirt?"

"An expression of her day, she says."

"How long do people live, there?" Verity asked.

"A hundred and sixty's about the limit, for full functionality, that I know of, but it keeps increasing."

"How old are you?"

"Twenty-seven," Rainey said.

"Will you live that long?"

"Not unless someone who can afford it wants me to. And people who can afford it for themselves generally don't want other people to have it."

"They don't?"

"Used to be that the one who died with the most toys won. Now it's who can afford to live longest while holding on to the toys."

"Lowbeer and her friend are that rich?" Verity asked. Realizing she was still holding the box of fries, she put them down.

"Neither of them are. Lowbeer became very important to some very wealthy people during the jackpot, so they started having her reset. She's still important, more so actually, so she's still being reset. Clovis gets it because she was married to a member of Parliament, when that was still a thing, and he helped enable some powerful people to come into a different sort of power. Evidently someone still remembers that."

"What's this jackpot, then?" Verity asked, still looking at the back of the drone's shoulders.

"Fuck," said Rainey, in an entirely different tone, "that was exactly what I wasn't supposed to do."

Verity looked to Virgil, who seemed himself to have been squinting at the drone. Now he looked at Verity. "Been getting pieces of it from Conner," he said. "Their time line, according to him, is one grim motherfucker."

"But you've changed things, so that we won't necessarily get that," Verity said, to Rainey.

"If you have a nuclear war now," Rainey said, "our idea of apocalypse would be the least of your worries. Unless you get a nuclear winter to reverse the warming, and we had people seriously floating the idea of trying that. You didn't get Brexit, though, and you got a different American president, but as far as we know you'll have the rest coming your way, if you don't blow yourselves up."

"What they call the jackpot," Virgil said, "all of that coming down together, Conner says. And none of it's anything you haven't heard of."

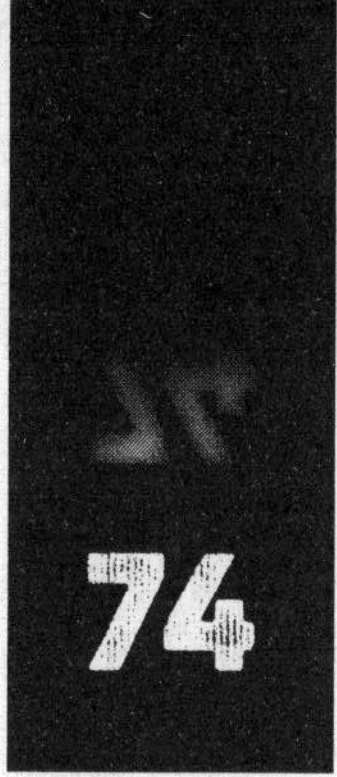

OLD KLEPT

Fearing had placed her pistol, and the candelabra, on the square, glass-topped, thoroughly non-period-correct table at which the three of them now sat.

Netherton had seen her younger self shoot someone dead, with a gun like this, in the county. Possibly, he supposed, this very gun. Not that he'd been physically present, of course, hence in no danger, but he knew what these things could do. And was himself, now, physically present. She'd placed it, he noted, so that its muzzle pointed at none of them.

"I gather," said Lowbeer, whose top hat was also on the table, "that your greeting us with a handgun is indicative of some concern."

"Making sure it was you. Anybody can look like anybody. Not that I don't enjoy imagining overreacting, if it happened not to be you."

"Does this one have the switch for full automatic?" Netherton asked, having learned this one distinction about firearms in the county.

"Double taps or nothing," said Fearing, dismissively. "Sequential doubles, if you got the customers for them."

"So this sanguinary mood of yours, Clovis, is the result of your having made those inquiries for me?"

"Sure is," Fearing said.

None of which encouraged Netherton, as the inquiries he'd hoped Fearing had been making would have been about whatever project had created Eunice, and thus safely in the past.

He looked up at the wall of crates behind her, many of them apparently of wood. This room, or rather space, was at the far end of the passage she'd directed them down, and built of similar containers. He'd never given any thought to what private interiors might be like, in Cheapside. To judge by this one, rigorous period accuracy wasn't an issue. While some of the crates were wooden, others were of tin, aluminum, and various kinds of plastic. The ceiling was lost to darkness, though light from the uneven pulsing of the candelabra suggested there might be a central plaster rosette overhead.

"It isn't Lev's great-uncle," Fearing said.

"What isn't?" Netherton asked.

"The source," said Lowbeer, "the irritant. Do you have an idea who that might be, Clovis?"

"Have you considered Yunevich?" Fearing asked, briefly exposing a narrow radius of her extremely white teeth, the name meaning nothing at all to Netherton.

Without the top hat, Lowbeer looked more herself, which was to say dangerous. "I thought it possible," she said. "Are you certain?"

"Essentially, yes. Which is why you've Wilf along, to hear the name. He'll need to ask Zubov in person, in a secure situation."

"He has a troupe of dancing girls," Netherton said. "Bots, I mean. Lev does. Zero connectivity, no onboard memory."

"We weren't able to penetrate them when I observed Wilf's meeting with Lev at the Denisovan Embassy," said Lowbeer.

"Where'd Lev find them?" Fearing asked.

"They're his father's," Netherton said.

"His father's old klept," said Fearing, "his father's uncle's older klept still. They assume their opsec is gold standard, which in practice tends to mean it's not. They mainly spy on each other."

"Why wouldn't Lev simply have told me who it was, if they know?" Netherton asked.

"He doesn't, yet," said Lowbeer. "Neither does the father. This is all a bit of klept protocol. They bring us word of a conspiracy. We determine that one exists. Only then do we ask them if those we suspect of conspiring are those they intended to alert us to. The key conspirator's name will have been passed along to Lev, just prior to meeting with you, enabling him to answer when you speak it to him."

"Yune—" Netherton began, but Lowbeer kicked his shin before he could finish, beneath the glass table, causing him to almost drop the walking stick, which he'd been holding across his thighs.

"Do not voice the name," said Lowbeer, "until you're alone with Lev."

"We aren't secure, here?" Netherton asked, wincing.

"Until the situation's resolved," Lowbeer said, "observe that extra degree of discipline. It isn't that you're particularly open, quite the contrary, but you also have a tendency to forget yourself when excited."

"Very well," Netherton said, resisting the urge to rub his aching shin, "what exactly do you need me to do?"

"Contact Lev," said Lowbeer, "meet him, with his troupe deployed. Ask him if said individual is in fact involved. I'll debrief you afterward, in the car."

"Tonight? I'm quite short on sleep."

"Lev himself is currently asleep," said Lowbeer, as if it were perfectly normal for her to know this, as Netherton in fact assumed it might well be. "Phone him in the morning."

75

JACKPOT

Over the drone's shoulders, through the tinted window, Verity watched two men, Japanese, smoking cigarettes behind the hipster supermarket.

In white t-shirts, pants, aprons, they sat on red plastic milk crates, like the one she'd clumsily stepped up on, wearing the silicosis bootees, to enter Virgil's truck.

Was it legal, to smoke cigarettes this close to a supermarket? Were they too near a food preparation area? She was thinking about asking them for one, even though she'd never before smoked one, after Rainey had finished telling them about the jackpot.

They'd all sat there, in the van, saying nothing, with Sevrin methodically finishing his fries. Virgil, Verity knew, had already heard at least some of this from Conner. She looked over at him now. He'd just opened a brown glass bottle of ginger beer. His eyes met hers. "I know," he said, "right?"

"Sorry," Rainey said. "I really am. I understand that it's too much, all at once. I've never told anyone before, who didn't know. Wilf and Ash have. I wish it had been them."

"Did we ever come to terms with the sheer cluelessness of it?" Verity asked. "The knowing, for decades, and then managing to do almost nothing to stop it?"

"Not really," said Rainey. "But it isn't as if people in your era get all the blame. It began with the use of fossil fuels, in what amounted to a centuries-long event. And it isn't as if we assume it's over. We're barely getting by, as it is, using the shards, or using assemblers as pollinators, and everything else we use them for."

"Assemblers?" Virgil asked.

"Molecular assemblers. Nanotechnology."

"I thought that was supposed to change everything," Verity said. "The singularity?"

"We were in our real singularity all along," Rainey said. "We just didn't know it. When relatively functional nanotech did arrive, we used that to blunt some effects, slow things down. Trying anything on a larger scale has increasingly been deemed too big a gamble."

The two smokers were stubbing out their cigarettes now, getting up, brushing their hands on their aprons, their break over, centuries into the singularity they might never recognize as such.

Virgil passed her the ginger beer. She drank reflexively, not tasting it. "So what you're trying to do, here, with us, is change that?"

"To mitigate the effects, here. You're further back than we've been able to reach before. You've had two radically different outcomes already, due to intercontinual contact. Those are resulting in countless others. The United States, for instance, in this crisis we never had, actually has an ambassador to Turkey. We wouldn't have had one."

"Then why are we sitting here, behind a supermarket?" Verity asked. "If we're supposed to be saving the world?"

"The next move is Eunice's network's," Ash said. "What have you been discussing?"

"Hearing how our world ends," said Virgil, "and yours begins."

"Ah," said Ash, "explains the mood. Rainey spilled the beans?"

"Sorry," said Rainey. "She's a sharp listener."

White Helvetica appeared, across the back of the drone.

Hit the 5th speed dial. It's Stets. He can actually talk, has a phone like this and no lawyers watching him. J-E

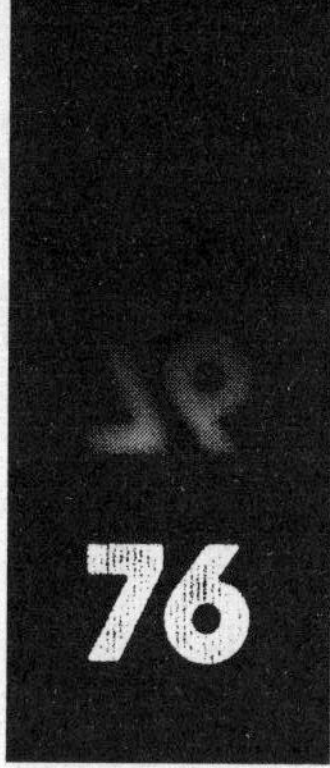

76

CAME A COACHMAN

It seemed colder out, the passageway retaining a dankness Netherton hoped had nothing to do with urine, ersatz or otherwise. He saw Lowbeer draw something vaguely familiar from a topcoat pocket, gold and ivory glinting in her hand, reflecting candlelight in the instant before Fearing closed the door behind them. Her tipstaff, he remembered, in the sudden dark, a nastily mutable badge of authority, a cologne atomizer one moment and a handgun the next, but always of ivory, trimmed with gold, with somewhere, invariably, a small symbolic coronet. He hadn't seen her produce it since shortly after he'd first met her, but associated it with trouble of a very immediate sort. "Why do you have that out?" he asked.

"Go ahead of me toward Cheapside," she said. "Be prepared to do as I say."

Netherton did, almost immediately aware of an approaching racket from the direction of the street, as of running boots over cobble, echoing off the walls of the passage.

"Keep walking," Lowbeer said.

He did, noting the darkness in the passageway decreasing in a peculiar yet familiar way. Another effect of hers and, like the tipstaff, something he hadn't seen recently. Assemblers in the very fabric of the City, subtly lighting her way.

Now they were in that particularly foul-smelling stretch, and here a running figure in high black boots appeared, smiling pleasantly, a dented top hat jammed low over its forehead. Quite tall, broad-shouldered, and bearing a massive mallet of some kind, partially upraised, it ran straight toward them.

"Down," ordered Lowbeer, which Netherton would certainly have obeyed, had their assailant not been literally atop him then, shoving him aside with its massive weapon. Which reeked, Netherton noted, of claret, but by then he'd instinctively poked his stick at the man's waistcoated midsection, a large gloved hand batting it aside, then seizing the ebony shaft and flinging it away, to clatter hollowly on the wall beside them.

Leaving, Netherton discovered, the stick's handle still in his hand, with something still protruding from it. As of its own accord, his hand thrust this forward again, producing a bright flash of light, accompanied by a brief but vicious sizzling.

Looking down, he saw his hand around the stick's handle. From which extended a slim straight blade, into the waistcoat's fabric, smoking now, scorched, though he saw no blood. Again, the smell of claret. Then the man toppled backward, toward Cheapside, still smiling earnestly, the massive mallet's head making surprisingly little sound as it struck the cobbles.

"What the actual fuck?" pronounced Fearing, powerfully, behind them, as the passageway and the fallen figure were flooded with mercilessly white light.

Squinting, shading his eyes, Netherton made her out, her pistol now apparently tipped with a small cylindrical floodlight.

"Do you know him?" asked Lowbeer. Who held, Netherton saw, a sort of blunderbuss, its barrel gold, stock of ivory.

"It's Bertie," Fearing said, "my neighbor's coachman. Bot. Seems to have helped himself to a publican's bung starter." Which accounted for the claret, Netherton thought, noting that the mallet's massive head was of wood.

"Something seems to have gotten into him," Lowbeer said, bending to pluck the upright swordstick from the supine figure. She glanced around, then retrieved the hollow ebony shaft from where it lay nearby, smoothly sheathing the one in the other. She passed it to Netherton, who accepted it gingerly. "That's really terribly bright, Clovis," she said. The floodlight was immediately extinguished, though leaving, Netherton noted, a single sharp red dot, centered on the fallen bot's torso.

"Were you expecting this?" Fearing asked.

"No," said Lowbeer, "though the aunties were able to give me a last-minute inkling. Step over Bertie." This last to Netherton.

"Is this an assembler weapon?" Netherton asked, looking at the stick in his hand.

"No," said Lowbeer. "Ash made it from your clothing, and whatever else was available nearby. You happened to place it in such a way as to instantly fuse Bertie's power supply. Good night again, Clovis."

"Watch your back," Fearing said.

"As ever. Cheapside, Wilf."

Netherton began to walk.

"Good night, Wilf," Fearing said, behind him.

"Good night, Mrs. Fearing," he said, pretending to glance back.

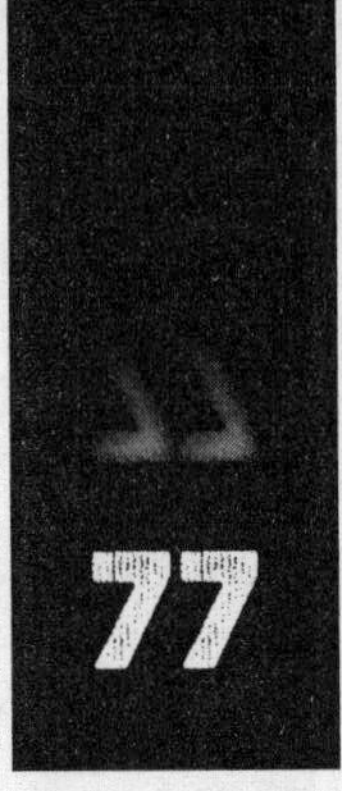

77

EVENT HORIZON

Someone out of frame passed Stets a small glass of what Verity assumed was espresso. "Thanks," he said, looking up briefly at whoever it was. He took a sip. This feed, Verity assumed, was via a camera in the Airstream aerie's foldaway screen, which put him on the in-built couch opposite. "Where are you now?" he asked her.

"Not sure," she said, assuming he couldn't see her, "being driven somewhere. What have you been up to?"

"Trying to figure out whatever it is that we seem to have agreed to help Eunice's branch plants do. They aren't very communicative."

"I was texting with one, earlier. It got me in touch with Joe-Eddy. Virgil tells me you used to try to think of things for him to do for you, but couldn't."

"Do you know Guilherme?" he asked.

Verity blinked. Hearing Stets mention the Manzilian felt like a category error, as if the moon were to inquire after the cantaloupe you'd bought the day before, both being spherical. "Not to speak to. I've seen him at the apartment."

"Eunice's network consists mainly of the branch plants, so human company can be a relief."

"I thought it would all be people," Verity said, "from what she said."

"You already know most of the people," he said, "but this, for instance"—and he raised his hand toward the camera—"is due to the network." He did something that replaced his selfie feed with one from the top of the stairs, overlooking the broad floor below, under sunlight through blue tarps. Cables everywhere, helmeted climbers dangling. More workers than she'd seen here before. Lengths of glittering white fabric were being hauled up by electric winches.

Below this, she saw five identical, red, rectangular machines, each with a small pair of black rubber tires at the nearest end. "What is it?" she asked. "What are those red things?"

"Caitlin's design. Fabric's by a company I backed. Those are Honda EM5000 electric-start generators, power in case someone cuts ours tonight when we most need it. The branch plants ordered them. Tricky piping the exhaust out. Hope we don't need them."

"What is it you're doing?"

"We don't know yet."

"Then how did she design for it?"

"Someone suggested, a few months ago, that we get married here, before the place is finished. That was the impetus for this design. She already had the space entirely modeled for the reno design. Knows where every eye bolt is, up there. The fabric doesn't need to be edged or hemmed, and she worked with standard lengths from the factory."

"But you're not getting married here?"

"Definitely not planning on it."

"But you don't know what it's for?"

"I'm not sure the branch plants know themselves."

"But aren't we all looking the end of the world in the mouth, about now? And you're up here hanging fabric art?"

"Lowbeer's take is doing this demonstrates trust, and that we can cooperate."

"How about Caitlin?"

"I'd ask her, but she's video-conferencing the technical details of an aerial drone display above the building, an extension of the fabric work."

"What if you do it and nothing happens?"

"A little pre-apocalyptic gathering? Why not enjoy it? Have to go now. I'll see you there."

"Is this what happens when Virgil's not here to tell you shit's crazy?"

"I don't need Virgil to tell me that about this." He grinned as his feed closed.

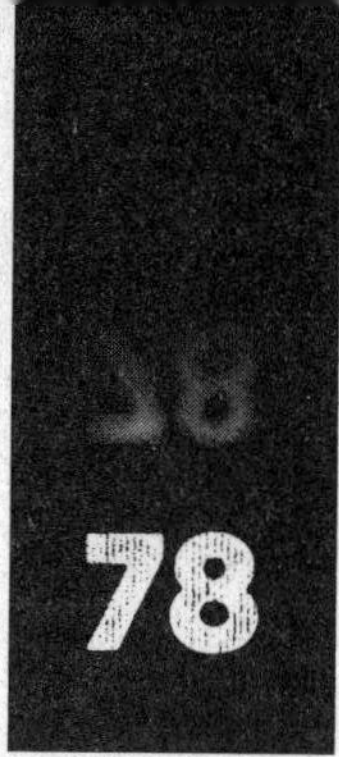

78

MORNING AFTER

Netherton woke in their darkened bedroom, to sounds of Rainey feeding Thomas breakfast in the kitchen.

He remembered the bot, on the reeking cobbles, the laser on Fearing's pistol pinpointing the singed whipcord waistcoat. He gestured for the bedside lamp, then again, to reduce its brightness, then frowned at the amount of clothing scattered on the floor. All from the night before, none of it Rainey's, and none of it anything he'd worn to Cheapside.

These were the garments from which the assemblers had made his costume. Now retransformed, he supposed, as he and Rainey had slept. Evidently the swordstick as well, as there was no sign of it. She'd found the pin-striped flannel drawers as risqué as anticipated, but those seemed to be gone as well.

He sat up, unsure whether the myalgia he now noticed was due to his brief struggle with Bertie or the later interlude with Rainey. Getting up and putting on his robe, he set about picking up and tidying away his clothing, hanging some things in the closet and folding others into the bureau.

He hadn't told Rainey anything about their visit with Fearing, other than that they'd had one, but really she'd only been interested in the flannel drawers. He'd said nothing whatever about Yunevich, of course, whoever that might be, though he kept repeating the name to himself, silently, else he forget it before he could speak with Lev in person. And nothing about inadvertently short-circuiting Bertie, though when he eventually did, he'd lack the stick, for an optimally dramatic demonstration of exactly what had happened.

He went blinking into the brightly lit kitchen, finding Thomas in his high chair, one pandaform third of the nanny seated beside him, on the edge of the table, its almost spherical legs somehow managing to be crossed.

"Lowbeer just rang," Rainey said, feeding Thomas a spoonful of pablum, most of which he immediately ejected, letting it run down his chin while smacking his lips. "Didn't want to wake you. Reminding you to make that call as soon as possible. Didn't say which one. Breakfast?"

"I'd best make the call first," Netherton said, tooth-tapping for Lev's sigil.

"Wilf," Lev greeted him, voice only, the avatar's two thylacines brightening.

"We need to meet again," Netherton said. "Your troupe, as well."

"Same place," said Lev. "I'm on my way."

"See you there," said Netherton, the thylacines dimming as he ended the connection. "Denisovan Embassy again," he said to Rainey, who was wiping Thomas's mouth.

"You're anxious to hear more about his relatives cramping his style in Cheyne Walk, I know," she said.

"Sorry about breakfast. It's business of hers," meaning Lowbeer's. "I'll shower first."

"I should hope so," she said primly, picking up Thomas. "Verity's learned about the jackpot, by the way."

"When?"

"While you were in Cheapside," she said, "but I was in no mood to tell you last night. My fault, I'm afraid, that she put it together this soon."

"How is she?"

"Seems to be digesting it reasonably well, though you've much more experience of judging that."

"Sometimes," Netherton said, "I've thought they were fine, only to have them suddenly start screaming, a day or so later."

"Ash thinks she's doing well. But don't be late for Lev."

Netherton returned to the bedroom, hung up his robe, and entered the shower. "Not too warm," he told it, "brief burst of cold at the end of the rinse." As his shower began, Ash's sigil pulsed. "Yes?" he answered.

"Rainey broke it to her accidentally," Ash said. "Virgil was privy to the exchange, though Conner seemed to have already told him most of it. Sevrin, the driver and financial manager, also overheard, though he either had a sense of it already or is extremely nonreactive. They're all taking it reasonably well, though they don't yet know of the extinctions."

Netherton winced, as the exfoliant sprays cut in. Extinctions, for Ash, were exclusively a nonhuman matter, and a far more emotional one than the 80-percent loss in human population. Hence her having lived, for over two decades, with the mourning tattoos that now roamed the walls of her hideous yurt. "What are they doing now?" As the exfoliation ended, the shower began soaping him.

"Sevrin is following the instructions of his dispatcher, so we've no idea where they're ultimately headed."

The cold rinse kicked in. Netherton waited for it to be followed by warm drying air, before responding. "I'm on my way to the Denisovan Embassy," he said.

"You should be accessing the drone."

"I'm on Lowbeer's business," he said, as drying ceased, enjoying, as ever, the opportunity to not do something Ash wanted him to.

Her sigil dimmed, no goodbye.

Back in the bedroom, having cleaned his teeth, he dressed, putting on his best casual jacket. The meeting was business, after all, and of a very serious if impenetrable sort.

Yunevich, he reminded himself again.

79

VALLEY OAK

After Rainey's revelations, which had rung like predictions but were history to her, and the bizarre preview of whatever Stets was doing, Sevrin had announced they were heading for Monterey.

Not that this meant that they were going to Monterey, Verity understood, but that that was where the Moldovan speaker on Sevrin's headset had directed him to go. Before they got there, she assumed, he'd be directed elsewhere, to eventually be suddenly informed that they were already where they'd actually been going all along, that being how Eunice had insisted it be done.

She'd been mainly dozing since her conversation with Stets, periodically registering their slog through the Silicon Valley side of the South Bay, ignoring both Sevrin's cover-story destinations and any actual highways they traveled on. She had no idea where they currently were. With her head cushioned on the folded black sweatshirt, against darkly tinted glass, she'd lost the majority of their journey to a strange sleep, Rainey's grim précis of future history compounding whatever existing exhaustion and confusion. Riddled not with dreams, exactly, but slow-moving trains of thought, at once rickety and ponderous, the most recent having been about how much the network Eunice had left behind could be considered to be a living part of Eunice. An unseen opponent (Verity herself, it had sometimes seemed, in the logic of dream) had argued that the network was literally Eunice, while Verity had contended that it wasn't Eunice at all, less so than a last will and testament is literally the deceased.

"You okay?" asked Virgil, from across the headless span of the drone's cam-riddled shoulders, it being seated once again between them, connected to the charger beneath the seat, Virgil having plugged that into the van's electrical system. "You were talking in your sleep."

"What did I say?"

"Nothing I could understand."

"Where are we?" Peering through the tint at an expanse of sere autumn pastureland, the odd grazing cow, scattered stunted oaks standing leafless and bleakly hieroglyphic. Another planet. Earth.

"Route 25. Not far from Coalinga. Not that Sevrin says we're going there, though I'm beginning to wonder."

"Why?"

"The Honda could land there. Just enough runway. We have it on a list of alternatives, for various situations. Otherwise, I've no idea what we're doing, unless we're just keeping you mobile and out of the city, which also seems like a possibility."

"Have you spoken with Stets?" she asked.

"Not since he left the hotel, last night," Virgil said. "Backing out of the Singapore deal is having repercussions in Asian markets. Phil has his hands full, but Stets is too busy with this stuff to be bothered."

"What do you think about that?"

"Knowing him, I think he's probably prioritizing correctly. I think we're seeing him deal with an exponentially weirder situation than any of us have previously encountered."

"Here," said Sevrin, the van slowing, to pull bumpily right, onto the barren shoulder.

"What's here?" Verity saw the drone, beside her, unplugging itself.

"The tree," Sevrin said, as Verity saw Dixon, dark ball cap pulled low over sunglasses. He was standing behind a white-coated aluminum gate, twenty feet back from the two-lane blacktop, the shoulder in front of it sufficiently undisturbed for it to seem no more than an entrance to pastured land. Beyond the wire fence, slightly down grade and to the left, stood a single, surprisingly large valley oak, black limbs entirely leafless, like the tattoo of a tree superimposed on a sun-faded photograph.

Definitely Dixon, she saw, as they drew nearer. Remembering her first sight of him, on a feed from a surveillance camera on Valencia, as he'd been approaching Wolven + Loaves.

Virgil had pulled his legs up now, to allow the drone past, on its way to the door's window, to once again stand, braced with its spidery arms, as if peering out.

"That's Dixon," she said. "He and Kathy Fang built the drone." Through the windshield's spatter of bugs, she saw him lifting the gate, walking backward with it, to allow them through. Driving past him, they jolted down, toward the oak, following faint tracks of tires. Beside the black tree, elevated horizontally on a rusted iron framework, stood a large, less evenly rusted cylindrical tank, originally gray. Behind this, she saw, was Sevrin's Fiat 500, or another like it, equally beige. It had been mounted with a black roof rack, supporting a streamlined black cargo box. Comically oversized for the tiny car, it reminded her of the Pelican case Dixon had passed her beneath the counter in Wolven + Loaves.

"That yours?" she asked Sevrin.

"Unless plates copy mine," he said, braking the van and turning off the ignition.

"I'm out first," said Conner, retracting the drone's arms to their previous length. "If there's a problem, Verity and Virgil hit the floor and Sevrin hauls ass. Open it."

Sevrin touched something, the door powering open, and the drone hopped down with an agility she didn't question now, with Conner in control. Facing Dixon, who'd closed the gate behind them and followed the van at a trot, it put whatever currently passed for its hands on hips it didn't have. "Dixon, right?" she heard Conner ask, the drone's volume slightly up.

"Who's asking?" Dixon asked, having come to a halt, black-gloved hands at his sides.

"Name's Conner. You built this, right?"

"Partner and me."

"Good job," Conner said. "What's the situation here?"

"I drove Sevrin's car down," Dixon said. "He'll drive it back, with Virgil. Someone else is taking you and Verity, ETA in ten. I need help, unloading this box and getting things into the van."

"What's in it?" Verity asked, meaning the black case, as she stepped down and out into an untinted afternoon, the fresh air smelling faintly but pleasantly of manure.

Dixon nodded in greeting. "Drones," he said, "not aerial. We didn't make them. Kathy sends you her best." He went to the Fiat, unlatched the front end of the box's lid, and raised it on twin aluminum tubes, clicking them upright. She saw glossy black bundles, against the dull black plastic of the lid. He looked back at her. "Time's tight," he said. "Anything you have in the van, we need it out now."

"I'll help you," said Virgil, behind her. She turned to see him crouched in the van, phone in hand. He got out and came forward.

"Pass them to me," Dixon said. "They're heavy. Don't drop them." Extending, in one gloved hand, a limp pair of black gloves.

"Latex-free?" Virgil looked serious about this.

"Nitrile," Dixon said.

Virgil accepted them, pulling them on. "You're policing our perimeter, right?" he asked the drone.

"Shit no," said Conner. "Just admiring cows." The drone's nonhands were no longer on its hips, but on the ground, its arms having extended again, lending it a quality of simian alertness, like a headless Cubist orangutan surveying its savannah.

Sevrin, having gotten out on the driver's side in the meantime, leaving his door open, came around to the open passenger door. "Your bag," he said to Verity, "and charger. I get them."

"And the hoodie," she said. "You good with all this?" Meaning Dixon, the Fiat, the roof box.

Sevrin nodded, turned to the van.

Now Virgil, taller than Dixon, was lifting a black bundle from the box. It was rectangular, larger than the Pelican case but not by much, wrapped in shiny, thick-looking, flexible black plastic. It was sealed with transparent tape, and obviously heavy. He passed it to Dixon.

"Easy does it," said Dixon, taking it and putting it carefully on the ground.

She remembered her dream. Eunice's last will and testament. Looked up at the sound of a jet, but couldn't find it. When she lowered her eyes, Sevrin was already in the van, on his knees, doing something between the passenger seats. Dixon walked toward it, looking as though he was being careful where he placed his feet, the first of the black bundles in his gloved hands, over which white Helvetica appeared: **j-e, getting feed from ur glasses.**

"Where are you?" Verity asked.

Home alone with lawyers. U?

"Route 25. Near Coalinga."

U arent going there.

"Why not?"

Ur beard guy?

"Dixon."

He's driving something there. Ur going somewhere else.

"Who with?"

Cant say.

This last text over the backdrop of her view of Route 25, as a U-Haul headed toward Coalinga passed a silver Range Rover going in the other direction.

"Here's your ride," Conner said, the drone pointing, long arm extended. She hadn't heard the engine of the black touring bike until then, and now it was pulling over, front shocks bumping over the rough shoulder as it rolled toward them.

She ran, up to the closed gate. Reaching it, she took hold of the length of tubing topping it and lifted. She began walking backward with it, so the bike had room to be ridden in and then down, toward the van. "I'll get this," Virgil said, beside her, taking the white pipe, lifting, beginning to close it.

She turned as the bike came to a halt, facing the immobile drone.

"Why's he here?"

To take you back.

She started down the slope. Grim Tim and the drone, figures in a landscape. Then she saw Sevrin, crawling out backward, on hands and knees, from between the van's two rows of passenger seats, pulling her Muji bag after him.

THE SQUARE MILE

Arriving at the bottom of the Denisovan Embassy's annoyingly melted staircase, the place's décor definitely having a cumulative effect on him, Netherton immediately spotted one of Lev's redheads, though not yet draped in security sequins. This one was dressed, it struck him, as though it might be a publicist, but in fact was exactly the opposite: a counter-publicist. A cousin of Bertie's, the fallen coachman, but where Bertie's every movement had been remotely inspired, be that doing whatever coachmen did or homicidally attacking you with a bung starter, the redhead's primary boast was zero connectivity. In a society in which most objects of any complexity whatever could recall anything they'd ever encountered, this one remained in a permanent state of tabula rasa.

"Good morning, Mr. Netherton," it said, evidently remembering his name. How was that possible, if it had no memory? He made a note to ask Lev, once privacy had been established. "This way, please."

The place was busier now than he'd seen it, perhaps the result of this being a traditional hour for breakfast. Following the bot-girl toward the catacombs beneath Hanway Place, he glimpsed Bevan Westmarch, a former associate from his own days as a publicist, seated at a crowded table. Wetmark, Rainey called him, having also worked with him. Now he clearly saw Netherton. Pretending not to have noticed him, Netherton continued after the bot-girl.

Lev had chosen a larger table than their last, Netherton saw, evidently to allow room for a full English breakfast he'd already finished, as evidenced by various side plates. For Lev, Netherton knew, a full English was stress-eating. He himself, he assumed, wasn't expected to have breakfast, full or otherwise, though a place had been set for him opposite Lev. A girl, a real one, or in any case unfreckled, was just then putting a white bowl of café au lait at his place. "How are things in Cheyne Walk?" he asked, seating himself uncomfortably on yet another stalagmite.

Lev looked up, across the remnants of his solitary breakfast. "The divorce wasn't a good idea," he said.

"But it was hers, wasn't it?"

Lev looked gloomier still. "The affair," he said, "wasn't a good idea either."

"That never struck me as like you, frankly," Netherton said. Which was true, given Lev's attitude toward his father's so-called house of love, in Kensington Gore.

"I was a fool," Lev said.

Netherton, who'd known Dominika almost exclusively as an unseen yet forbidding presence in the Notting Hill house, tried to look sympathetic.

"Why are you making that face?" Lev asked.

"Sorry," Netherton said, abandoning the effort. "These stools don't agree with me."

"You looked as though you were gurning," said Lev.

"Do you think there's anything to be done about it," Netherton asked, "the marriage?"

"I don't know," said Lev. "I'm trying to consider all options."

"I can see that it's getting you down," Netherton said, picking up the bowl and sipping. "I'll be of any help I can, but now, perhaps, we should—" At which point he saw Lev looking at something behind him. He put down the bowl and turned, discovering all six bot-girls, now sequin-draped over identical outfits. "Certainly," he said, turning back to Lev, "assuming you're ready."

"Begin," Lev said, unenthusiastically, to the troupe.

Which they did, all turning, as before. With the circle formed, facing outward, their arms stretched overhead to uphold the shawls, the spiral storm of sequins rose, forming its dome above them.

"Is it working now?" Netherton asked.

"Yes," said Lev, glumly.

"Would someone wishing an end to Lowbeer's office be named Yunevich?" Netherton asked.

Lev instantly looked glummer still. He nodded, twice. The gabble of the breakfasters in the place's busier end peaked, then fell, seeming to recede, then rose again.

"If I understand Lowbeer correctly," Netherton said, "we've just fulfilled my sole actual purpose here. You now know whether she sees good reason for your having brought a previously unnamed individual to her attention. Am I correct?"

"Yes," said Lev. "Do you know who he is?"

"No," said Netherton. "I'm not required to. And I'm quite happy to have as little as possible to do with her work, as you well know. She employs me to help her with her hobbies."

"Hobby," corrected Lev, "there being only the one. The person we'd be discussing, if you'd allow me to, isn't my sort of klept."

"Klept are scarcely your sort, period," Netherton said, "and that's been my impression since we've known one another."

"This goes beyond that. Not my father's sort, nor my grandfather's. Different roots entirely."

"He's not Russian?" Netherton asked, having assumed this to be impossible.

"Russian," said Lev, "but descended from Soviet functionaries, rather than émigré 'garchs. Klept, but something else as well."

"What's the difference?"

"Extremely low profile. Not given to ostentation, either as displays of wealth or demonstrations of power. Never entertains. Attends no functions outside of the Square Mile, and few enough there. Very much a creature of the City. Even there, though, he keeps to the deepest processes, those of the least transparent sort."

The City, Netherton had heard Lowbeer say, explaining the klept to Flynne, had long been, and well prior to the jackpot, a unique species of semi-autonomous crypto-state, the single least democratic element of elected British government. It was this singular status, according to Lowbeer, that had allowed it to ride out the eventual collapse of democracy. That, and its core expertise in laundering money, had brought it into a mutually beneficial synergy with the émigré oligarch community, dominated by Russians, who had themselves first been attracted to London by the City's meta-criminal financial arcana, plus the lavish culture of personal amenities for those requiring same. With this in mind, he picked up the bowl of coffee and regarded Lev over its rim. "He doesn't sound like someone who gives much away."

"Impossible to read," Lev said. "Another era entirely. Older than Lowbeer."

Netherton drank, lowered the bowl, unfurled a white linen napkin, and wiped his mouth. "If there's anything further you want me to tell her . . ."

"No," said Lev, "that's it. My father's uncle understands him to be pushing the idea of removing her."

"That's that, then," Netherton said. "I missed seeing you, since Thomas was born, and I'm sorry you've been going through all that with Dominika."

"Thanks," said Lev, slumped on his stalagmite. "I wish I could say that my father needing my help with this business is proving a welcome distraction, but the timing really couldn't be worse."

“That’s understandable,” said Netherton. Taking his leave, he assumed, would require cessation of sequinning. “If your father’s troupe here have no memory to be read,” he asked, recalling having wondered this on his way to the table, “how is it one of them knew my name?”

“It did,” said Lev, “but no longer does. I showed it an image of you, before your arrival, told it your name, and what to do when it found you. As soon as it had done so, it forgot both your name and your appearance.”

“I see. Stay in touch. Not just about this.”

“Time,” Lev said, raising his voice, and the sequins came spiraling down, the bot-girls lowering their shawls in unison.

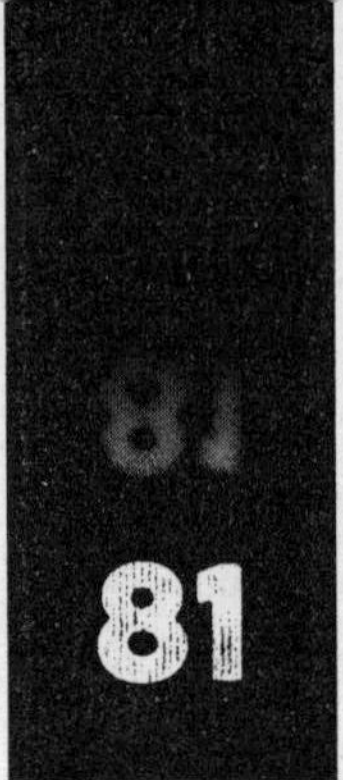

BACKWARD, WEARING HEELS

It had taken Dixon less time to install the black seatback unit he'd fabbed for the bike's rear saddle than it did for him to double-fold and lash Verity's Muji bag to it with black nylon straps. Since the unit was bare plastic, she'd be using her clothing as a cushion. As casually as she tended to dress, she assumed that the result would require pressing. If she were headed into any sort of world where pressing was an option, which didn't seem entirely guaranteed.

Now the drone, standing with its back to the rear tire of the bike, extended its legs farther than she'd yet seen them go, growing startlingly taller in the process. Looking as though it were in heels, it stepped backward, against Dixon's newly attached rack. "Little to the left," Dixon said, eyeing the joint between rack and drone.

"Good?" Conner asked.

"Hit the grippers," Dixon said. Verity watched as a pair of small doors opened on the drone's side, one above the other. From each of these emerged a flat rectangular hook, black. They then retracted partially, having found corresponding slots in the rack, leaving the drone fastened to it. Dixon, evidently watching the equivalent operation on the opposite side, seemed to have seen success as well. "Knees up," he said.

Verity watched the drone's legs shorten, lifting its feet from the ground, then retract entirely, into its body, leaving its torso facing backward, looking like a much more substantial version of the seatback.

"Not great aerodynamics," Virgil said, beside her, "but the best option under the circumstances."

"Where's its charger?" Verity asked.

"Right saddlebag," he said. "We have the neural cut-out helmet in the trunk of the Fiat. Be seeing you soon, I hope."

"Where?" she asked.

"Back to the Bay, looks to me, but after that, who knows?"

Grim Tim had been standing to one side with his helmet off, never having removed his white N95 mask, the piercings in his forehead and nose glinting in the sun. He'd greeted her with what she now thought of as his amiable glare. Now he drew back the left sleeve of his leather jacket, revealing a large steel watch, black-dialed and complicated.

"We're going?" she asked him.

The helmet nodded.

She'd already put on the down-lined jacket he'd brought, remembered from the ride to Oakland, over the black hoodie, with that over the tweed jacket she'd been wearing in the truck. Too warm, standing here in the sun. She walked over to Dixon. "Say hi to Kathy for me," she said.

He nodded, jaw clenched, other things on his mind.

Grim Tim passed her a fresh mask when she returned, and then the helmet she'd worn before. "Okay," she said to the others, before putting the mask on, "see you all later."

Thumbs-up from Dixon and Virgil. When she looked around for Sevrin, he was up by the gate, thumb raised. She put the helmet on, fastened her own chinstrap, and waited for Grim Tim to mount the bike. When he was settled, boots on the ground, she climbed on behind him, the folded and strapped Muji bag leaving her more room than she'd expected.

When he started the engine, she raised her feet to the pegs. They bumped slowly up the dry tire ruts, his legs swinging in exaggerated strides to keep the bike upright, toward the gate Sevrin had already partially opened. Turning her head for a last look at the valley oak, and then they were bumping out over the rough shoulder, to the edge of blacktop.

"We're half a mile from the junction with 198," Conner said, in her headset. "Dixon follows us that far in the van. Then he hangs a left for Coalinga, inland. We go right, toward San Lucas, take another right onto the 101."

She looked back and saw Dixon driving the van up to the fully open gate, Virgil and Sevrin standing beside it.

"Where are we going?" she asked.

"North on the 101. Gas and a pee break in King City."

"What happened to the protocol?" Still looking back. Dixon was turning out onto the shoulder behind them, Virgil and Sevrin closing the gate behind him.

"You and I are using the stiffest level of encryption your Eunice left us," Conner said. "I don't have a destination yet, after King City. San Francisco seems likeliest, as everything else points toward this being prom night."

"Prom night?"

"Shit's being prepared to hit a big fan, but nobody's told me what flavor of either."

Then Grim Tim gunned the Harley and they were off, the van pulling out behind them. She swung to face forward, grabbing his midsection, which felt like a piece of leather-covered masonry.

But something had just happened, she'd no idea what, directly behind her head. "What was that?"

"This," Conner said, opening a feed. Looking down on the van's green roof, its windshield, from about thirty feet in the air. She could see the dark bill of Dixon's cap. "Had it down the back of my collar." The aerial drone was climbing now, the van sinking beneath it. On either side, rolling hills, hieroglyphic oaks, cows.

"You don't have a neck."

"Got a hatch. Lots of surprises."

"Why's Dixon going to Coalinga?"

"Might have a job at the airport. Depends. If it's a go, I'll let you in on it."

"You're a lot more willing to talk than the rest of them."

"Fewer fucks to give, is what it is. I'm here because they need somebody to pilot Neckless here. I'm left over from their last stub. They need me there too, but I get bored, doing what they need, and they know I enjoy shit like this. So they give me more context than they give you, or anybody else in your stub, probably. Ask me. If I can, I'll tell you."

"Thanks," she said.

"De nada."

More cows, receding.

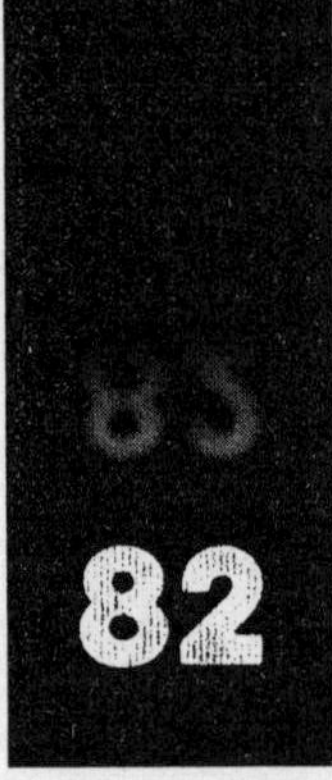

WETMARK

"Wilf," called Bevan Westmarch, "my man," as Netherton was approaching the base of the staircase. Netherton had never been anything like Westmarch's man, nor had they ever particularly been friends. He was drunk, Netherton decided, as he'd been quite prone to be, when Netherton had worked with him, at breakfast or otherwise. So had Netherton, of course, though this made him no more sympathetic now.

"Bevan," said Netherton, stopping but not offering his hand. "How are you?"

"Very well," said Westmarch. "Meeting up with our friend Zubov?"

Netherton, quite certain that they hadn't been seated where Westmarch could have seen them, gave him a bored look.

"Saw him come in earlier," Westmarch said, "trailing a school of freckled sex dolls. I know he and the missus have split up, but I was still surprised."

Instantly remembering why Rainey called him that. Nasty when sodden, she said. "Must have missed him," Netherton said, turning as if to scan the place for Lev, but actually dreading finding him. He wasn't visible, though, nor were the troupe.

"Still working for the mythical Inspector Lowbeer?" asked Westmarch, as Netherton turned back, with just that hint of wooziness that allowed him a certain deniability in what he said. Netherton's employment wasn't a matter of public knowledge, though he'd assumed Westmarch might be aware of it.

"Do you know her, Bevan?" he asked, looking Westmarch in the eye.

"Haven't had the pleasure."

"Would you like me to arrange that? She's very busy, but I could ask her. To fit you in."

And there, to Netherton's considerable satisfaction, behind the semi-performative tipsiness, was the fear Lowbeer induced, a visible rictus. "Wouldn't think of it," Westmarch said. His hand looked poised to tug a forelock he entirely lacked, his hair having been cut extremely short up the sides, to the very top of his head, where it was arranged in low blond waves, like some Viennese dessert.

"Good to see you, then," Netherton said, seizing Westmarch's frustrated forelock-hand and pumping it vigorously. "Lovely day."

Then swiftly up the unpleasant stairway, scents of the full English receding behind him. Reminding him, now that he was leaving, that he hadn't yet had breakfast.

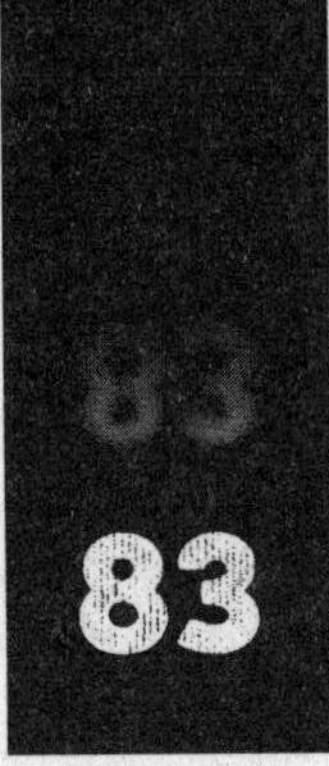

PERSONALITY TEST

Someone had written LOCK HER UP on the wall of this toilet stall, in thick black marker. Before the election, Verity assumed, with someone else then having tried to scrub it off with solvent, the result reminding her of a tattoo halfway through laser removal.

Grim Tim had sent her in for the promised pee break, while he gassed his bike. Welcome as she found this, she'd also discovered that simply being seated on something neither moving nor vibrating, with her legs in front of her, rather than with a large motorcycle between them, was even more of a relief.

After they'd taken a right at what had turned out to be a literal crossroads, the simplest possible junction of two highways, she'd watched Dixon take a left, in Conner's aerial feed, to recede toward Coalinga. When the van was out of sight, Conner had swooped the feed back to them, the final image blank and white, as the top of her helmet seemed to leap up, the feed itself vanishing, replaced by her own view of Grim Tim's black leather back.

"Time, ladies," Conner said now, causing her to flinch, before remembering that she'd removed the gray-framed glasses as she'd entered the restroom, tucking them into one of the hoodie's pockets.

"Okay," she said. By the time she'd gotten herself together, Grim Tim was at the register, paying for his gas with cash, his helmet still on. When he'd finished, she followed him out to the pumps, restraining the urge to say something to Conner now that she could see the drone.

Evening had arrived, Napa-Sonoma still providing extra pulpy orangeness. She settled her mask and put the helmet on. "Where's Dixon now?" she asked, assuming Conner could hear her, but not certain he'd have an answer.

"Near Coalinga's airport," he said.

"What for?"

"Helping Lowbeer conduct a personality test."

"How?"

"By letting us see just how nasty somebody's willing to be."

"Nasty?"

"Makes a difference how you want to deal with them."

"Whose personality?"

"Pryor."

Grim Tim handed her a pair of rubber-coated black knit gloves, still on shiny cardboard from the station's rack. Something she'd meant to ask for as they'd pulled in, but had then forgotten. Her hands had been getting colder, since the crossroads, plus bug-impact on bare skin. "Thanks," she said, partially pulling her mask down.

Something piercing his upper cheek moved a fraction, a minimalist alternative smile. He put his own gloves on, and straddled the bike. Pulling her own off their cardboard and putting them on, she got on behind him.

And then they were on the highway again, accelerating.

LOOKING QUITE CHIPPER

As Netherton surfaced in Hanway Street, a plain white Michikoid trotted past, pulling an equally white carbon-fiber rickshaw. In it sat two heavily modded neoprimitives, their faces as masklike as those of the Michikoids. Patchers, he knew, inhabitants of the Great Pacific Garbage Patch, which he'd visited himself, telepresently, on the job that had resulted in Lev introducing him to Lowbeer. These two would be envoys, neither tourism nor private business being a possibility. What skin of theirs was visible was a rough gray, bioengineered to protect them from excessive sunlight. Under the winter morning, it reminded him of frost.

Then they were gone, having reached and turned the corner. Lowbeer's sigil, the coronet, began to pulse. "Yes?" he responded.

"The car's in Tottenham Court Road," said Lowbeer. "You'll see it."

He walked on, thinking that Lowbeer's real work consisted of learning things, often things this fundamentally dull, through processes largely automated for her by the aunties and other systems. Eventually, having made her decisions, some action might be implemented, usually covertly, resulting in something dramatic happening. This, he supposed, was the nature of security work, where by definition one attempts to preserve aspects of the status quo. What she did with the stubs might be seen as that as well, he decided, if you thought of it in terms of a much longer status quo.

On Tottenham Court Road now, he spotted movement in a wide shop window. Drawing closer, he saw a miniaturized scale model of this part of London, tiny vehicles and pedestrians driving and strolling. A crisp yellow circular cursor surrounded a single magnified figure, its back to him, in front of a shop window. He raised his arm, the figure's arm following suit. Thomas would love this.

He walked on, eventually coming to Lowbeer's car, or what could be seen of it, as its step descended from nowhere. It was parked, for once appropriately, in curbside space reserved for Metropolitan Police and emergency vehicles.

Up and into it, then, to find Lowbeer seated in the chair pit, fingers steepled, elbows on the tray-sized mahogany table, on which were two white china mugs, cream, sugar, and a cylindrical black carafe. The car's windows, or rather the cam systems that emulated them, showed vehicular traffic to one side, pedestrian to the other. "Good morning," she said, as he heard the door close behind him. "Coffee?"

"Yes, thanks," he said, the Denisovan Embassy's café au lait having produced no noticeable effect.

"Have a seat," she said. She wore a gray tweed suit, gray broadcloth shirt, and a pointillist camouflage necktie, olive and buff shot through with martial red. Looking quite chipper. "Lev's dancing girls are extremely effective. We made a serious effort to listen in on your conversation, no success whatever. Aunties assume the encryption's Chinese, nothing old-boy klept at all. We'll look into that later, as it's unexpected, though not unprecedented. Well?"

Netherton was settling himself in the built-in green armchair opposite hers. "He says it's Yunevich. He also says, and I quote, that Yunevich isn't his sort of klept. Seems to be a deep-burrowing, low-profile Square Miler with pretensions to Soviet bureaucratic DNA."

Lowbeer was pouring from the carafe. "An old boy," she said. "Endlessly predictable. Tedious, really."

Her expression, as she said this, though superficially mild, made Netherton grateful not to be this Yunevich, whoever he was.

MULTITASKING

The feed from the very different bipedal drone Conner was piloting, through this rocky scrubland adjacent to CLG, New Coalinga Municipal Airport, meshed strangely with the motion of the bike.

There was no audio, so the roar of Grim Tim's engine and the occasional whomps of displaced air, when vehicles passed them in either direction, became a soundtrack for the thing's roadrunner trot through brush and rocks. It looked, she assumed, like the other three running with it, controlled, Conner said, by a swarming program. Like elongated tortoiseshells, mounted atop the hindquarters of miniature robot greyhounds, about a yard tall, assuming they could stand upright, something she hadn't yet seen one do. They ran canted forward, which they'd done constantly since Conner had opened the feed, and were armless, their legs blurring when not confronted with an obstacle. "Where are they going?" she asked Conner.

"To the personality test," he said. "Dixon dropped them off nearer the airport."

"Where is he?"

"In the parking lot there."

"And where are we going, on the bike?"

"The hell away from Coalinga."

The feed's perspective rushed up a low ridge and froze. Which was confusing, given the momentum of the bike beneath her. To this drone's right, she could see another like it, equally immobile. "Why'd they stop?"

"Look where it's looking."

Between the drone and the lights of the airport, she made out a vehicle, neutrally colored. The feed zoomed in on it. Some species of bad-boy pickup, its cabin extended, the bed enclosed. "Who's that?"

"Pryor. I gassed him this morning, leaving the hotel."

"Why's he out here?"

"Man pads," said Conner. "May have one in the truck."

"Huh?"

"Acronym. Man-Portable Air-Defense System. Shoulder-launched surface-to-air missile. MANPADS. Singular, never plural."

Something particularly large passed them, on the highway, headed in the opposite direction, she assumed a big truck. "To shoot down a plane?"

"Howell's Honda just took off from SFO, flight plan filed for CLG. They'll barely reach cruising altitude before they start descending."

"The guy from in front of the Clift is going to shoot down Stets' plane?"

"Not if I see him looking like he means to. If he did, though, your ex has it equipped with Israeli infrared countermeasures."

"Honda's armed?"

"Nah. Launches decoys, flares. And the pilot's combat-experienced."

"Stets' pilot?" Remembering the ones she knew, this seemed unlikely.

"Got somebody else, for this."

"Crazy."

"Prom night, like I said."

The drone suddenly sprinted forward. "What's happening?"

“Left-flanking unit saw someone get out with a folded tripod. Pryor or the other one. That’s our red line, the tripod.”

“What are these things?”

“Land mines with legs.”

Grim Tim shifted and sped the Harley up, which had to be coincidental but was still weird, the feed simultaneously giving her a full-on charge through brush and over rocks. “This is a video game,” she said, surprising herself, sincerely wanting to believe it was. “Resolution’s not even that high.”

“Video’s encrypted,” Conner said, “but whatever. Want out of the loop? Save you being any more of a witness. Your call, either way.”

“Witness to what?”

Their drone froze again, this time behind a rock slightly taller than it was. The cam rose, either its legs straightening or a neck, which she hadn’t known it had, extending. They were closer to the truck now. Something darted out of the brush then, from the left, greyhound-legs blurring, toward the truck.

Then exploded, the feed whiting out.

“Going for the tripod with that one,” said Conner, the feed returning, revealing the truck on its side, burning. “Overkill.”

Movement from the right, equally fast, charging the burning truck, the feed whiting out again. All of this in complete silence. “That was two at once,” Conner said, “but the warhead on the MANPADS still hasn’t blown. Now I go in, find it if I can, detonate this one. So I’m partially fuzzing the feed”—its lower half pixelating as he said this. The drone lowered its head or carapace and darted around the rock, toward the burning wreck, most of which was pixelated.

“Why?”

“Save you the trauma,” he said, matter-of-factly, very close to the blaze now, rounding it.

Whiteout.

“Shit,” he said. “Got me.”

"What happened?"

"Heat must've reached the warhead. Took me out with it, when it blew. Be precious little of the truck left."

"Did you see anyone?"

"Yeah, but it was whoever the other one was, not your guy. Fire and emergency are hauling ass over here from the airport now, trying to guess what they've just seen."

"How do you know?"

"Got a spotter, at the airport."

"What about Stets' plane?"

"Pilot reported seeing explosions on the ground, canceled his approach, heading back to SFO now."

"Who's on it?"

"Just the pilot. But we made it look like Howell and the Frenchwoman were with him, when it took off. That was the test. To see if he'd go for it."

"Who?"

"Pryor, but Cursion signed off on it."

"They'd try to kill Stets and Caitlin?"

"Ainsley wanted to know if they would. They thought there were three people on board, including the pilot. Pryor and his partner doing anything like setting up the tripod for the MANPADS, that was when we'd move."

"You know this feed's still whited out?"

"Sorry," he said, the feed disappearing, leaving the lower rear rim of the white helmet, black leather below it.

"Where's Dixon?"

"Headed for a pit stop ten minutes from the airport, get the green off the roof and sides of the van, plus a change of plates. Cursion may assume you're still in it. Ainsley wanted to see how bad Pryor is, Cursion, or both of them together. No idea what's going on with that. Cursion was fed the idea that Stets was picking you up there, heading out of the country."

"And they'd have blown it up on takeoff, not landing?"

"Yep. With you in it."

"Why would they have assumed the plane would be shot down? Isn't that kind of drastic?"

"Pryor's idea. He had a MANPADS. Been trying to sell it on a darknet."

"How many people did we just kill?"

"One for sure. I saw him. But not Pryor."

A rig whomped past, in the other direction. She felt the cold now, but part of it was what Conner had told her.

EMPTY CHAIR

On his way home now, Netherton remembered the breakfast he hadn't had. An egg sandwich seemed a good idea. He turned off into Chenies Street, where he knew a smaller, less compulsively authentic shop than the one Lowbeer favored. The morning having grown colder, he dialed his jacket up and walked there.

Taking a seat at the otherwise unoccupied counter, he ordered a fried egg sandwich on white toast and a glass of 2 percent milk. As the counter bot left with his order, Ash's sigil pulsed. "Yes?" he answered.

"What are you doing?" she asked, having, he assumed, no way of seeing him.

"Sitting down for a belated but well-deserved breakfast. I've had nothing but coffee since getting up."

"Consider yourself fortunate," said Ash. "I've not slept at all."

As the bot brought his sandwich and glass of milk, prepared with an inhuman speed that would have spoiled the experience for Lowbeer, he imagined Ash drawing herself a cup of scalding tea from her crusty samovar. "What's kept you up, then?"

"Eunice's network. Lowbeer now sees herself in it. Its skills are those she had to acquire during the worst decades of the jackpot."

"Go on," he said, biting into his sandwich.

"We don't yet understand the so-called branch plants. The ones that hadn't managed to return, to merge with her, before she was taken down. Of her, but not her. They communicate with each other, and with individuals they've elected to work with, ourselves included. It feels as if that constitutes an entity. As if there were a long table, Lowbeer says, its either side packed with strangers, and at the head, an empty chair. But it's a very actively empty chair, one whose intent we can only infer by the actions of those around the table."

Netherton rolled his eyes, swallowed some sandwich, drank milk. "Like Mechanical Turk?" he asked, recalling Virgil having mentioned a service of his day, monetizing live human intelligence. He took another bite, discovering that Ash's long-windedness was causing his sandwich to cool. He chewed more rapidly.

"When you've finished your breakfast," she said, "check in with Verity."

"Where's the drone?" he asked, around his mouthful of sandwich.

"Clipped to the back of a motorbike, on a Californian highway."

"And Verity?"

"She's with it."

"It's driving?"

"No," said Ash. "Don't talk with your mouth full. It's disgusting."

87

LANE-SPLITTING

If San Francisco was in fact their final destination, they were over halfway there. At least it wasn't raining, because then her legs would be just as cold, but in sodden jeans. Otherwise, this was just too long a ride, at night on the 101, nothing to see but asphalt and bumpers, illuminated by headlights and taillights. And cold. Conner had gone to check on his day job in the White House. Told her he'd come running if she needed him.

"Verity?" A feed opened. The apartment in London, from the couch, looking into their kitchen.

"Wilf?"

"Where are you?" he asked.

"The 101, between King City and San Francisco. Coming up on Silicon Valley."

"King City?"

"All I know about it is it's not Coalinga."

"What are you doing?"

"I'm on the back of Grim Tim's bike. The one you saw in Dogpatch."

"Why?"

"He's part of Eunice's network."

"Ash makes them sound busy," he said.

"Joe-Eddy, Dixon, Kathy, Caitlin, all in it now."

"Say hi to Verity," said Rainey, from the kitchen, stepping into the frame, Thomas held in front of her.

"Hi, Thomas," Verity said, though he couldn't see her. Probably couldn't hear her, either.

"Bye now," said Rainey, smiling, and stepped back out of the frame.

"What's going on in San Francisco?"

"When you find out," he said, "tell me. I've had my hands full here, with something unrelated."

"Conner," she asked, "you there?" No reply. "He blew up a truck, at an airport, killed at least one person." Saying it out loud made it feel even more unreal.

"Why?" Not sounding as if he thought blowing up a truck wasn't something Conner would do.

"Someone was going to shoot down Stets' plane. They thought we were all in it." More unreal still.

"Hadn't thought the place was that rough."

"It's not, usually."

"Who are they?"

"Cursion," she said, "but that was put together by Pryor, the man Conner gassed on Geary." The traffic was slowing now, Grim Tim decelerating with it.

Wilf stood, the feed's POV on the kitchen rising, then walked around the couch, to the window, where he looked down into their tidy dead-end. Empty, unless Lowbeer's car was there, invisibly. Then up, at two of those towers.

"Carbon capture?" she asked.

"Those two store energy from renewables," Wilf said. "I think they have molten silicon cores."

The bike, which had been gradually slowing, came to a halt. "Silicon Valley," she said, "gridlock. Better for me without the feed."

He cut it, as Grim Tim revved them gently to the left, simultaneously straightening it up, then straight forward, between the two lines of stationary vehicles, lane-splitting.

In every car they passed, on either side, people were watching the same thing on their phones, held at lap level: a talking head, the president's, above a chyron.

"What are they watching?" Wilf asked. With the drone perched backward, she imagined him only seeing their faces, faintly illuminated by the phones.

"The president," said Ash, unexpectedly. "Qamishli."

"What's happening?" Verity asked.

"She isn't saying, really," said Ash.

"So Conner's blown up a truck, to prevent an attack on Howell's plane?" Wilf asked.

"When we nudged Cursion into experimenting with Eunice," Ash said, "who they hadn't yet tried to monetize, we understood that we'd be destabilizing them. A side effect, as far as we were concerned, but since then they haven't been operating in their comfort zone. By now, having had to cope, however briefly, with a fully laminar iteration of Eunice, not to mention the various anomalies our involvement presents them with, destabilization has tipped over into dysfunction."

"They were functional enough to mount an attack on Howell's plane," Wilf said.

"They're not strategists," said Ash, "though they assume they are, and rather good ones at that. A fully functional, strategically sound opponent would be a greater threat, but without posing the sort of unpredictable danger they currently do." The bike was still thrumming, slowly but smoothly forward, between vehicles. "And Pryor, a mercenary opportunist, someone they've used before as a fixer, is taking advantage of the situation, no doubt in hope of becoming more than just a hired hand."

Then Grim Tim gunned it, at once the scariest and most amazing aspect of lane-splitting. Joe-Eddy hadn't been nearly this good at it.

"Is this legal?" Wilf asked, and she remembered that he'd been watching the feed from the drone, behind her, looking back.

"Yeah," she said, instinctively flattening her elbows into her rib cage, curling her body against Grim Tim's spine, and hugging the bike more tightly with her inner thighs, "but I don't like it."

Liking it even less as it became a seemingly endless stop and go, Grim Tim revving, slowing, dodging, weaving. She was getting the hang of it, though, learning a body language, a very specific mammalian bond developing between them, a physical trust, through the maze of paintwork and chrome, sometimes mere inches away. Mountain View, she remembered now, then Palo Alto, San Mateo, Daly City.

"You need to concentrate," Wilf said. "I'll be back."

Her teeth were beginning to chatter. She was grateful not to have to talk.

Finally, it felt like hours, they were through the tortuous vehicular Tetris, driving into the city, whose lower speed limits reduced her chill. Headed downtown.

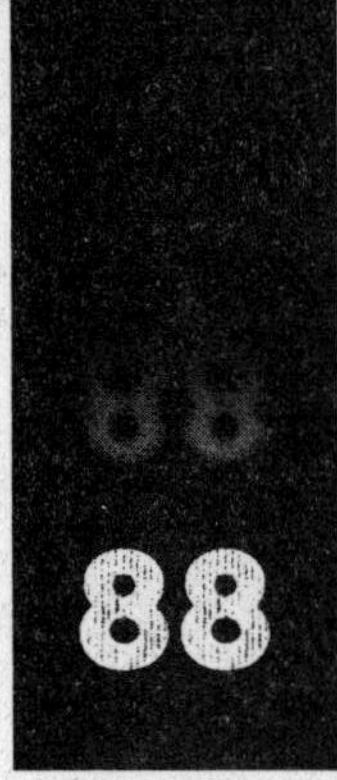

DENMARK STREET

Denmark Street wasn't a cosplay zone. Less so even than Carnaby, but Netherton always got a sense of it being doubly a reproduction. Lowbeer had volunteered nothing, as to why she wanted him here now, but had been preoccupied with getting the motorcycle through seemingly endless frozen traffic, and he'd tired of the view from the rear of it.

"Am I meeting someone?" he asked now, her sigil between him and the antique guitars in this shop window he'd paused to look into.

"Bevan Westmarch," she said.

"Wetmark?" he asked, surprised.

"Pardon me?"

"Rainey calls him that."

"That was an interesting conversation you had with him, after meeting with Lev."

"It was?"

"You frightened him," she said. "Threatened him. With me."

"Sorry," he said.

"Not at all," she said. "It's produced an interesting result. He's attempted to contact me. He believes, apparently, that he has information that will put him in our better books. Or is pretending to believe he does."

"You're meeting with him?"

"Best you do," she said. "I'll observe, though you needn't tell him that."

He'd be a fool to assume you weren't, Netherton thought.

"He's in the café with the Essex green façade," she said, "just before the corner, to your left."

"When?"

"Now."

This place proving not dissimilar to the one in Chenies Street, though the décor was considerably more stylized. Black, red, chrome, archaic advertising.

Westmarch was seated in the rear, half a glass of orange juice before him on the small round table. "I thought it might be you," he said, as Netherton pulled out the chair opposite and sat. "Sorry for my tone earlier, at the Embassy. That was still very much the night before, for me."

Netherton said nothing, something he'd only recently been learning to deliberately do.

"I realized," Westmarch continued, "that I only brought Lowbeer up at all because of something I recently heard. One does, as a publicist, as I'm sure you know." He seemed entirely sober now, though not hungover. Both of which, Netherton well knew, could be afforded chemically, though only at some later and often greater cost.

"Bring you something?" inquired a cadaverous young man in grubby violet shirtsleeves and a black string tie, a wooden pencil tucked behind his ear.

"Espresso," said Netherton, "thank you." Then, to Westmarch, "She doesn't employ me in her official capacity."

"Not as the Metropolitan Police," Westmarch said, "but we both know what it is she actually does."

"Nor in that capacity either."

"Yet here you are," Westmarch said, "responding to a call I made to her, one in which I never mentioned you."

"Nor should that surprise you, given you know so much about her."

"Hardly," said Westmarch. "As it happens, though, I've something I think she should be apprised of. Had I heard it on the frothy seas of gossip we've both sailed, we wouldn't be having this conversation."

"No?"

"Someone substantial alluded to it privately. Obliquely, but unmistakably."

"But you shan't say who," Netherton said, "or at least not initially?"

The waiter returned just then with Netherton's espresso, looking at once shambolic and preternaturally alert. When he had gone, Westmarch continued. "Lev's brother, Anton, who seems so much more traditionally klepty. Know him?"

"To say hello," said Netherton.

"They aren't close, he and Lev," Westmarch said. "Lev prefers to be seen to regard the klept as something of an embarrassment. There's previously been no question as to which brother would inherit their father's business mantle. Not Lev. Am I correct?"

Netherton knew this to not always have been the case, though he assumed it to be now. "Lev doesn't discuss family with me," Netherton lied, "but yes. As the oldest, Anton's in line to inherit the klepty bits, with Radomir next in line." Radomir, between Lev and Anton in age, quite thuggish in his own right, fancied himself an art historian.

"Allowing Lev," Westmarch said, "to continue to play the dilettante, while his more traditional, less ironically inclined older brothers oversee the various activities that the family business comprises."

"I suppose so."

"Lev's father," Westmarch said, lowering his voice, "no longer feels that Anton would be the best choice to run the family businesses."

"Why?" asked Netherton, surprised. There had, he knew, been question, prior to Anton's own clinic stay in Putney, as to whether their father might disown him. On having taken what the clinic's technicians strongly advised against calling the cure, Anton had been welcomed back into his previous position. This had led to Lev's having been familiar with the clinic, which he'd eventually recommended, in no uncertain terms, to Netherton himself. Without which, Netherton now supposed, he wouldn't be sitting here, and wouldn't have a wife or son.

"That's my informant's story to tell," Westmarch said. "Not mine."

"They're an informant now, are they?" Netherton tried a sip of espresso, finding it excellent. "And who might they be?" Not really expecting an answer.

"Lev's estranged wife," Westmarch said, watching him.

Netherton, midway through a second sip, was surprised. "More than estranged, I've assumed."

"Papers haven't gone through," said Westmarch.

"And why would you suppose that Lowbeer would find this of interest?"

"Because Anton, since the split, has become involved with Lev's wife."

"Does Lev know this?"

"Apparently not."

"Do their children?" Not a question he would have asked, prior to Thomas.

"No."

"Was it a factor in her wanting Lev to leave?"

"No," said Westmarch. "That was triggered by her discovery of Lev's affair. Recently, however, she's learned that the girl Lev was involved with was put up to it by Anton."

Netherton considered this. "It's certainly nasty, whether true or not, but I don't see why this should be of any particular interest to Inspector Lowbeer."

"Dominika, I can tell you, knows all this because Anton's been using drugs. Chinese ones, apparently, designed to be quite impossible to detect. They do, however, disinhibit him, which he enjoys, and which leads him to tell her things he otherwise wouldn't. His father, meanwhile, has come to suspect him of drug use, and needless to say is reconsidering his fitness as business heir."

Lowbeer's sigil, the coronet, appeared in Netherton's field of vision. He tapped his left front tooth with his tongue.

"Ask him," Lowbeer said, "how Dominika knows this about the father."

"But how does Dominika know this?" he asked. "Is she in the father's confidence?"

"No," said Westmarch. "It's all from Anton, in his cups so to speak."

"But how does he know?" Netherton asked.

"Because," Westmarch said, "he's being advised by someone who's penetrated the father's most secure communications. And that person, according to Dominika, is someone with an agenda involving the dissolution of Lowbeer's position."

At this last, the golden coronet pulsed again. "Tell him I'll speak with him now," Lowbeer said. "Best if you aren't present."

"She's going to speak with you now," Netherton said. "I'll be going, in order that your conversation be private." He stood.

Westmarch looked up at him. "What?" His eyes widened. "The coronet? That's her?"

"Yes. Best take it." Netherton turned and made for the door.

"Hello?" he heard Westmarch say, behind him. "Yes, yes it is. Bevan. A pleasure. Thank you—"

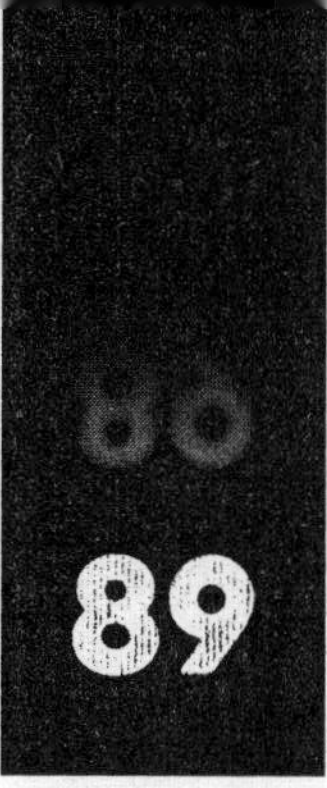

KINDA SORTA

The last familiar landmark Verity had seen, blocks and turns behind her now, had been a sliver of SoMa's iconic Coca-Cola sign, its top partially cut off by the helmet. Back in Dogpatch now, on what she assumed was Third Street, Grim Tim, not bothering with a turn signal, swung them abruptly left, into a wide alley between low, industrial-looking buildings.

Then they were stationary, vibration ended, her ears ringing in the engine's absence. Immediately behind her, past her doubly folded Muji bag and Dixon's 3D-printed plastic addition to the Harley's luggage rack, she sensed movement.

"Can you get off okay?" Conner asked, in the Tulpagenics phone's earpiece. She looked down, startled to discover the drone beside her, its legs now as short as she remembered them from Fabricant Fang, its torso tilted back as if looking up at her.

She removed the gloves Grim Tim had given her, raised the visor, unfastened and removed the helmet, and pulled her mask down. "I'll know when I try."

He lowered the centerstand, which reminded her that she needed to dismount first, so he could get the bike up on it. She discovered just how stiff she was, then, and in how many places.

As he rolled the bike up, onto the stand, she took a step back. Her knees nearly buckled.

"Careful," said Conner, behind her, as she realized she was being supported, very solidly, by a manipulator at either elbow. Coated with something soft and looking nothing at all like hands.

Cautiously, she tried a step forward, her knees functioning normally.

Grim Tim had dismounted in the meantime, still helmeted and visored.

"You good?" Conner asked her.

"Stiff," she said.

The manipulators released her. "I'll get your bag." The drone turned to the rear of the bike, its two protruding suitcase casters surprising her, where its butt would have been if it had one. Now it used a different set of manipulators to adroitly unstrap the bag from Dixon's backrest.

"Where are we going?" she asked.

"We're here," he said, unfolding the bag atop the bike's gas tank. She gave it a glance for squashed bugs, not seeing any. Then noticed much bug-wreckage on the forearms of the borrowed down jacket. She unzipped and removed it, gingerly.

Grim Tim turned, passing the drone's charger to Conner, then taking the helmet and jacket from Verity. After stowing them in the saddlebag, he removed the glove from his right hand, and reached to take hers and grip it firmly.

"Thanks for getting us here," she said, "and for the gloves."

Releasing her hand and passing her the bag, he quickly mounted, rolled the bike off its stand, then walked it back to where he could turn it toward the street. Ignition.

She stuffed the gloves into one of the hoodie's side pockets and put the strap over her shoulder. "I'm getting tired," she said, "of nobody telling me where I'm going."

"Soon as I know," Conner said, the charger held in front of the drone, "you will. Meantime, this way."

She followed the drone.

"Fang's friends who make these brought this one over," he said. She didn't know what he was talking about. "Delivered half an hour ago, not that you could tell. Had set decorators make it look like it's not brand-new. Fake pee stains on the side, always look wet."

She made out the ten-foot cubical container, farther along the alley, in shadow, flush with the wall to her left, looking like it had been there awhile.

"Rented parking space," Conner said, the drone bending to lower the charger to the pavement. "Won't get hauled. Ash showed it to me on our way here." Quiet sounds of manipulators, manipulating in relative shadow. "Lights go off when I open this door, stay off till I close it. Like a fridge, but backward." He opened its door, on darkness. "I'll be out here, on the roof. There's a socket up there, so I can use the charger to top up."

"Why is this here?"

"To keep you off the street. A place to put your feet up."

She stepped up into it, though not as much as she'd had to step up into Fang's. This one seemed to be sitting directly on the pavement, no pallets. He closed the door behind her. The translucent ceiling came on.

Same interior, but with the tatami equivalent of new car smell. Same low-backed, nearly legless couch, equally low wooden table in front of it, a white plastic 7-Eleven bag on that, the red plastic caps of two one-liter bottles of drinking water peeking out. She craned her neck, to see what else might be in it: a fistful of protein bars, a couple of packs of gas station jerky, a bag of kale chips.

Hanging her bag from the familiar aluminum hook, she removed her shoes and put them on the plastic tray.

Going into the restroom, she closed the sliding paper doors and used the toilet. No political graffiti. The wall looked as if it might never have been touched by human hands, which she supposed was literally possible. She closed her eyes, seeing gridlock again. When she stood, the toilet flushed as expected.

"I'm up here," Conner said, as she was washing her hands. "On top." A feed appeared, looking, she assumed, toward what might be Third, from the cube's flat roof. A police car passed, followed by a UPS truck.

"Any cams here?" she asked.

"Your glasses and the ones in this drone."

"Didn't hear you getting up there," she said, stepping out, sliding the screens shut, going to the gray couch.

"Winched the charger up and you never heard that either." The feed vanished.

After she'd removed the hoodie and her tweed jacket, she hung them over her bag and sat down, putting her purse on the table, beside the 7-Eleven bag. "Know what's happening yet?" she asked.

"Eunice's branch plants are busy," he said, "doing nobody knows what. Meanwhile, your roommate's friend from Brazil has been spending the money Eunice makes. A couple of her branch plants are extremely good at stock markets."

"On what?"

"Tech companies. Nothing very big. Widely distributed, different jurisdictions. Nobody saying what for. Ainsley's not really all that communicative herself, in case you haven't noticed. That's either an English thing or a big stub thing, maybe both."

"Big stub?"

"What we call their time line. Mostly just to piss 'em off."

"Why would it?"

"They think they're the only real continuum, the one original, not a stub. They discovered the so-called server first, whatever anomaly allows all this. But they didn't invent it, just found it. Anybody knows what it really is, or where, they're not telling."

"Nobody knows what it is?"

"Nobody has the least fucking idea, or where the hardware is. Lot of people think China, but China's just naturally where you'd guess something like that would be."

"Why?"

"'Cause they opted to mostly go their own way, in the jackpot. They were big enough, the richest country, all set to do it. Just rolled up the carpet and closed the door for a couple decades. Didn't need to evolve a klept, either."

"Evolve what?"

"Klept. What runs the world that isn't China, up the line where Lowbeer is. Hereditary authoritarian government, roots in organized crime. The jackpot seemed to filter that out of what was already happening, made it dominant."

Verity shifted on the couch, which was a lot less comfortable than the identical one in Oakland, the movement making her aware of the semirigid white filtration mask around her neck, beneath her chin. Getting it off, she discovered that her lips were dry. She found ChapStick in her purse, applied it. "None of this shit's simple, is it?" She ran her tongue across her lips.

"Here's something," he said. "Don't know if it'll be simple. Call for you, priority override on the network."

"Who?"

"If I knew, it wouldn't be priority."

"Okay."

"Bye," he said.

Can't do audio. You okay?

White Helvetica, across her open purse.

"Who's this?" She bit her freshly ChapSticked lower lip.

Me.

"Shit," said Verity, half in stunned delight, half in fear of disappointment.

Kinda sorta.

"Eunice?"

She waited.

Nothing.

"That was quick," Conner said.

"She's gone," Verity heard herself say.

"Seemed to get broken off."

"You couldn't tell where it was from?"

"At all," he said. "How's that couch?"

"Hard."

"Ash had Fang's friends restuff it. Ten-by-twelve body-armor plates, ceramic, level four."

"Why?"

"Any shooting starts, flip it on its side, with the upholstery between you and the guns."

"Shooting," she repeated, flatly.

"Just in case," he said.

But had that been Eunice?

THE WORK

And this has all come out because Wetmark feared he'd been indiscreet with me, about you, in the Denisovan Embassy, after my meeting with Lev?" Netherton asked, in Shaftesbury Avenue, a few drops of rain beginning to fall.

"Indeed," said Lowbeer. "Because he'd referred to me as 'mythical.'"

"Would you say he was overreacting, then?"

"I assume," Lowbeer said, "that when you had that conversation, which I monitored, he was intoxicated. Subsequent amnesia left him partially unable to recall exactly what he might have said to you. The anxiety for which he habitually self-medicates then drove him to phone me, once he was relatively sober."

Netherton, just then glancing into the window of a bookshop, saw himself grimace, the scenario she was describing being quite familiar. "But you believe him?"

"I'm assuming, in this one case, that he's truthfully relating things he's been told."

"You don't think it's Yu—" He caught himself. "This person we've discussed? Disinformation?"

"It would be unwise not to consider the possibility of disinformation," she said, "but I doubt it, now that I've had a closer look at who's involved. Our person of interest has evidently been quite active lately, but I doubt Westmarch has ever heard his name. Often, when considering the klept, that which seems too conveniently coincidental proves to have been a function of their being essentially a small, highly cohesive group. Though that can also make for cleaner cautery on our part, or even for an element of surprise."

Netherton shivered, warm as his jacket was keeping him.

FOLLOWR

Company," said Conner, in the earpiece, "incoming."

Verity was on her back, on the couch, using the folded hoodie as a pillow, mechanically eating kale chips. She'd begun to wonder if she might not actually be more comfortable on the tatami. "Who?" She sat up, still aching from the ride.

"Manuela Montoya," Ash said, "whom you'll recognize from the lobby of the hotel."

"The Followrs girl?"

"The network traced her today," Ash said, "via Eunice's facial recognition. Someone was sent to find her, before Cursion did."

"She's here?" Resisting the urge to ask Ash about the texts.

"The network wants Conner to protect her, which means having you together. Frankly, we'd prioritize that differently, but the network's already affording us sufficient agency, here, that we have no choice."

"Prioritize what?"

"Your safety. We assume Cursion are looking for you as well."

"She's here," Conner said, opening his feed from the roof of the container.

Silhouetted against light from the street, the faceless black figure of what seemed a young woman stood on the sidewalk, apparently looking toward them, Verity reading hesitancy and doubt in her stance. She took a step, halted, then walked toward the container.

"She's been told you're there," Ash said. "Conner's opening the door."

"Lights out," said Conner.

Darkness. Verity felt cool air as the door swung open. "Manuela?"

"Verity?"

"Come in," Verity said. "It lights up when the door closes. Watch your step."

The girl from Followrs stepped up, into the dark, the door closing behind her. Verity imagined the drone, on the roof, reaching down to close it.

With the light on, Verity looked up at her from the couch.

"Business class doghouse?" The girl squinted against the light.

"So people can concentrate in open-plan workspaces."

"In an alley?"

"Someone brought it here." Verity got to her feet, her body feeling older than the last time she'd gotten up from a couch.

"Sorry I spied on you," the girl said. "I saw the Followrs ad on Craigslist and next morning I was sitting in 3.7." She had short dark hair, in need of a trim, didn't seem to be wearing makeup, and might be wearing the clothes Verity had first seen her in, an olive parka, black sweater, jeans, and sneakers.

"I'm couch-surfing, myself," Verity said. "How'd you get here, just now?"

"Carsyn. She works for the man I saw with you in the lobby."

"Virgil."

"He sent her to find me. We hung out all day, snacking and talking game design. Paid me my hourly rate for game design." A brief smile.

"Protein bar?" Verity indicated the bag on the table. "Jerky?"

"Carsyn took me for Taiwanese."

"More company," said Conner, Verity remembering that Manuela couldn't hear him. "She was followed. These two," the feed from the roof of the cube returning. Figures of two men, where she'd last seen Manuela, looking into the alley, one tall and heavy, the other neither. "Lights out." The feed brighter in the sudden darkness.

"AR?" Manuela asked, interested, leaning forward. Verity could see her face, in light reflected from the feed in the Tulpagenics glasses.

"Two men outside," Verity whispered, then remembered the soundproofing in the container on Fang's roof.

"I can see them," Manuela whispered back, "in your glasses."

The taller man, approaching, took something from his pocket, revealed as a flashlight when he turned it on, and examining the container's door.

"No keypad on this one," Conner said. "Fang faked up a regulation container door, with padlocks."

Turning off his flashlight, the man walked around the container, out of frame. The feed blurred, then showed a different angle, the tall man's back as he looked toward the far end of the alley. He looked back, gestured to the shorter man, who joined him. They walked in that direction, the far end.

Conner cut the feed and the ceiling came back on.

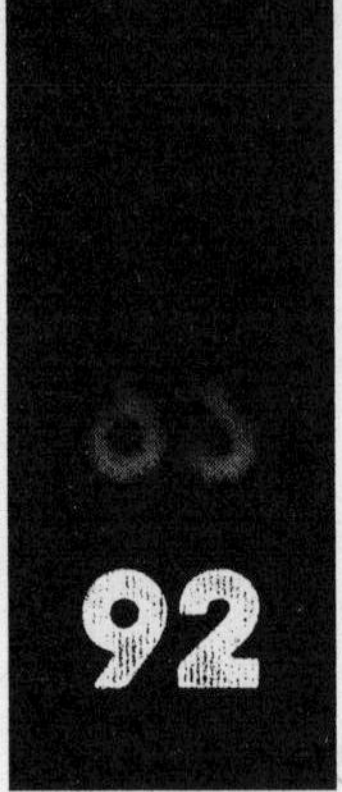

TENNESSEE STREET

"Where's Verity?" Netherton asked Rainey, as he settled on the couch, the controller in his hands.

"In what someone I haven't yet met called a 'business class doghouse,'" she said. She was dressed to go out, coat on, gloves in hand. "Ash just showed me clips of the feed from Verity's glasses. It looked Japanese."

"Oakland? On top of Fang's building?"

"San Francisco, in an alley. Conner's outside, on top, keeping watch."

"Who are you meeting?" he asked.

"Mia Blum."

"Work?"

"No," she said, "but since I'm on sick leave, it doesn't hurt to stay caught up."

"Sick leave?"

"Cross-continual nuclear anxiety," she said, putting on her gloves. "Keep an ear out for Thomas. Don't get up." She blew him a kiss. "Don't keep Verity waiting. She has a lot on her plate, from what Ash was telling me."

She went out, her ability to relax with a friend over coffee, regardless of what might be going on, still surprising him. He put on the controller, settled it, and turned it on.

To fly suddenly across an indistinct surface, seemingly inches away, then up and out, the feed a simple frame, not the drone's display format, over a night street, its architecture semi-industrial, modestly urban.

"Relax," said Conner, Netherton having made an inadvertent sound of alarm, "I'm your pilot."

"Of what?" Imagining the drone, its arms extended, as antique cartoon superhero.

"Little quadcopter. Ash had four built, for Eunice."

"Where are we?"

"Tennessee Street," Conner said, "other end of the alley."

They slowed, hovered. Netherton saw a single palm tree, behind a steel mesh fence. The cam's point of view dipped, rose again, and rotated slightly, to speed on in another direction, quickly arriving at an intersection.

"Figure they think she's in the cube?" Conner asked, the frame zooming in on two men, standing together on the corner.

"Verity?"

"Montoya. Girl who'd been following Verity before. Virgil sent someone to collect her, have her brought here."

"Why would these two follow her?"

"Assuming they're Cursion, because Ash hired her, by coincidence, after they did. She and Verity live near each other, so the app assigned the nearest partner available. She was in the lobby of that hotel, working for us. They noticed. Maybe they think she was a plant to begin with. Probably they're just spooked by what they can see of us. Looks weird to them."

"Because it fucking is," said Verity, startling Netherton, who'd forgotten she could hear them. "Whether they can see it or not."

A nondescript white van pulled up. The two men got in.

"Doesn't seem a very sophisticated operation," Netherton said, as the van drove out of sight.

"Probably those two aren't," said Conner, "but Pryor, who hired them, he's professional. Cursion are scam artists. They knew enough to steal her from the Department of Defense, and keep it from looking like they had, but not enough to play a game like this. Think they're spooks. Lowbeer and Ash keep getting into Cursion's comms, but they haven't been able to get into Pryor's."

"Will you follow them?"

"Network's on it. Here they are." A scooter with a black-helmeted rider rounded the corner, then sped up, in the direction the car had taken.

"You and Verity can talk," Conner said, toggling the feed from the aerial drone to one Netherton recognized as Verity's glasses. She was looking at a younger woman, who seemed to be seated close beside her, as if on the floor.

"Hello, Verity," Netherton said. "Who's this?"

"Manuela," Verity said. "She can't hear you."

"What's happening?" asked the girl.

"Talking with Wilf," Verity said to her. "On these glasses."

The girl leaned closer. Looking at Verity's glasses. "He's on the roof?"

"In London," Verity said.

"How long do we have to be here?" the girl asked, looking around.

"I don't know," Verity said.

"I have to go to the bathroom."

"We've got that covered." Verity leaned forward to use the top of the low wooden table for support, as she got to her feet, stepping over to the wood-and-paper screens and sliding them aside. Everything seemed identical to the cube atop Fang's. "Flushes itself when you stand up."

"Thanks." The girl stood, her longish green coat bunched around her.

“Want to hang your parka?” Verity asked.

“I’m good.” The girl slid the screens shut behind her and Verity stepped back.

“She doesn’t know why she’s here,” Netherton said.

“Bet she doesn’t want to be, either.” She looked up at the glowing ceiling.

“Will you try to explain it to her?” he asked.

She closed her eyes. Opened them. “The future, all that? Maybe Rainey could—”

“Raining?” asked the girl, from behind the paper screens.

“My wife’s name,” Netherton said, “Rainey,” then remembered she couldn’t hear him.

He heard the toilet flush.

“Guess the fake piss didn’t fool ’em,” Conner said.

“Who?” Netherton asked, confused.

“Our gentleman callers. Their van’s coming back.”

Then Netherton was atop the cube, with that handily distorted circular point of view. The drone raised its right arm, pointing with a manipulator. Beyond it, in the lower, thicker half of the display, cars of the era passed on the street nearest them. The arm swung sideways, still extended, to the right, swiveling entirely backward, so that the view down it was now in the upper, narrower half, showing the alley behind them. “If I had a rifle, huh? But Ash wants this quiet, nonlethal if possible, but mainly no police presence.”

“Not the rules in Coalinga,” Verity said, surprising Netherton again.

“We weren’t in the middle of San Francisco. Your fingerprints are all over this container, if I kill somebody. Not that that means I won’t have to.”

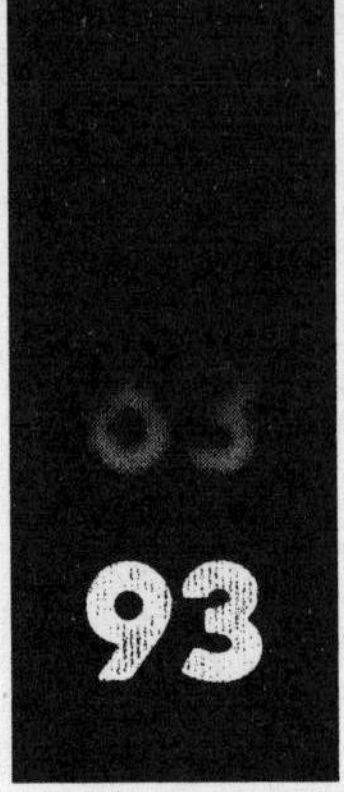

WINCH

"What's going on?" asked Manuela, eyeing the container's door in a way that looked to Verity as though she was wondering whether or not to open it and run.

"Probably locked," Verity said, causing Manuela to look up, "but that's to keep people out, not us in."

"Is this a cult?" Manuela asked. "Kidnapping people and telling them somebody's after them?"

"Let me think about it," Verity said.

"You're kidnapped too? Let's fucking escape."

"Those men outside we've been talking about, they'd kidnap us. Conner, on the roof, watching out for us, thinks they would. So do I."

"They'll see him up there," Manuela said. "This box isn't that big."

"Neither is he. About this high." Verity held out her hand, palm down.

Manuela's eyes narrowed.

"He's up there telepresently," Verity said.

"So what you're doing is some new way to give TED talks? Like theater, with really random props and locations?"

"Those things like an iPad on a Segway, roll around at conferences with somebody's face on the screen?"

Manuela eyed her narrowly. "They still do that?"

"And those big headless robot dogs, with backpacks, on YouTube? Marching single file through the woods?"

"Yeah?"

"Conner's using something like the iPads on wheels, but more like one of those dogs, except it's got arms and two legs."

"So where is he, physically?"

"D.C. Washington."

Manuela winced. "Please."

"Don't believe me?" Verity asked. "I know how you feel."

"Conner," Wilf said, "says they're returning."

"What's he expect us to do," Verity asked, "crouch on the floor behind the couch?"

"What are you talking about?" Manuela demanded.

"If they're coming back," Verity said, "it's for us."

"Conner's lowering us down, on a winch," Wilf said. "The cable comes out of a hatch on the drone."

"Hatch on its shoulder," Verity asked, "or back of where its head should be?"

"Chest," Wilf said.

"Where what's head should be?" asked Manuela.

"Talking to Wilf. They're in the alley now. Right outside. What's happening, Wilf?"

"Conner's releasing drones," he said. "Little ones. Aerial. Three. Out of another hatch. He already had one up, so four in all."

"Like the one he zapped the guy in front of the Clift with?"

"Smaller," he said.

Verity thought of the drones Dixon had delivered. Where were they now? In their camo'd hutch on top of the place next to Joe-Eddy's?

Manuela was digging through the protein bars in the bag on the table.

Choosing one, she straightened, tore the wrapper off, and took a bite. Chewing, she fixed Verity with an expression of unresigned impatience that made her look fourteen.

"Conner," Verity said, "what are you doing now?"

"Lying down on the pavement," Conner said, "legs up, arms folded, hatches closed. So what'll it look like?"

"Heater my mom had. Electric. Oil-filled."

"So they'll see it, but won't know what it is. Somebody dropped off your mom's heater. Or they can worry it's a claymore, whatever. They'll know it wasn't here before, but they've also got a job to do."

"You're just going to lie there?"

"Till I don't," Conner said.

"What about us?" she asked.

"Get your shoes on," Conner said, "jackets, whatever. Ready to go."

"Where?"

"That's fluid," he said.

Verity looked at Manuela, who hadn't removed her shoes or parka. "Put some food in your pockets," she said. "We're going, so we might need it." She got her own shoes from the tray, sat on the armor-plate couch, and put them on.

94

IMPROV

With the drone on its back in the alley, the squashed-circle display looked to Netherton like something Rainey might have taken him to see at the Tate, its lower half filled with nothing but the luminously featureless San Francisco night sky above it, the upper half a high-resolution night-vision close-up of the pavement beneath it, greenly glowing. "Where are those men?" he asked.

Conner replaced the drone's feed with four others, evidently from the small aerial units he'd mentioned. The feed in the upper left quadrant was stationary, directly above the container's square roof, straight down. Beside the container, the now seemingly limbless drone might be mistaken for an equipment case. A smaller, paler rectangle, tucked into the angle of the cube's rear wall and the adjacent building, would be the charger. The upper right quadrant offered what he judged to be the same view from a greater altitude, the alley a relatively dark connector between parallel streets, both more brightly lit, the one nearest the container wider than the other. Both lower quadrants were livelier, each from a camera in motion, each above one of those two streets.

"Lower left," said Conner, "white van. Just dropped two new guys on Tennessee, near the alley. Headed out of frame." The camera turned, to keep the van in frame. "Bringing our two around to Third. Maybe more. Hope not."

"What will you do when they get here?" Verity asked.

"Improv," Conner said. "Slow 'em down while you and the girl get out and run for Third. Virgil's almost here, to pick you up. We'll distract them for you. Black four-door Mercedes. Be ready." The angle of the lower left feed swung down, revealing two figures entering the alley from Tennessee Street. Walking toward the container.

As the two drew near, Conner toggled back to the feed from the drone, Netherton watching as they loomed into view. One frowned, looking down. He stopped, the display partially capturing a gesture that halted the other as well.

"Dude," said Conner, "what have you got here, huh?"

The one who'd first noticed the drone, his right hand now out of sight, inside his open coat, a manual phone in his left, seemed to be capturing images or video. He put the phone to his ear. "Did they see that?" he asked, the drone's microphones picking him up, his accent American but less pronounced than Conner's. A pause. He leaned forward slightly. "Like it's painted, to look like carbon fiber." Pause. "Okay." He lowered the phone.

Netherton watched him step forward, past the drone, followed by the other man, who squinted dubiously down as he passed, then both were out of frame.

"Want us behind the couch?" Verity asked, puzzling Netherton.

"Wouldn't hurt," said Conner. "Angle it between the door and where the little table is."

"Help me with this," said Verity, speaking, Netherton assumed, to the Followrs girl.

Netherton watched as the drone's left arm partially unfolded. From its narrow wrist-tip, a thin black rod emerged, then executed an unnervingly biological-looking wriggle, before lunging after the man, around the container's corner.

A camera, Netherton remembered, as its feed opened. Beyond the backs of the two men who'd discovered the drone, the windowless white van swung into the alley's entrance, pulling up about three meters in front of the container, two more men emerging from the passenger-side door. A third remained behind the wheel. "They were here before," Netherton said.

"And none of them Pryor," Conner said, "including the driver. Time we got this on the road." The feed from the black tentacle shrank, replaced by the fixed aerial view in the upper right quadrant. Netherton watched the drone's right arm unfold, lifting its torso off the pavement.

"Ladies," Conner said, "start your engines. Out of there when I say go. Try to hold your breath till you get to the street. Stay away from the white van parked in front of the cube. Don't get caught. Ready?"

"Ready," said Verity.

"Go," Conner said.

VOLUNTEER

When Conner said go, Manuela went over the upended couch like a sprinter coming off blocks, her arms outstretched for the door. It seemed to vanish, rather than open, into a coughing, retching, solidly packed realm of cursing men, their hands to their streaming eyes.

Capsicum, announced some brightly nerdy recall-module of Verity's, her eyes and nostrils stinging painfully.

The seemingly solid mass of pepper-sprayed men around the container's door had only been a few, she saw, plunging through them after Manuela.

"Move," Conner urged, as one of the men clawed at the strap of the Muji bag, his hand bashed aside by a metallic blur she recognized as one of the drone's arms, upraised, plowing out of the confusion on powered skates. "Virgil," Conner said, flashing her a feed from above, of a black sedan, braking hard, at the curb in front of the alley. "Go!"

She did, reflexively managing to leap an attempted tackle, as she found the car in her actual field of vision and ran for it, past the side of the white van. Trying, through the start of her own capsicum tears, cheekbones and forehead now burning as well, to find Manuela.

The black car was in front of her, its right rear door open, Dixon getting out, black ball cap level with his eyebrows. Showing her his fist, thumb upraised. She veered left, to avoid one of the van's open rear doors. As Manuela screamed, partially within the back of the van, a red-eyed man hauling her inside.

He yanked Manuela past him, farther into the truck, as Verity arrived. Verity lunged for her ankles, to pull her out, but then his gloved hands were around both her wrists.

A dark, dull, skintight gray, the gloves. "Thanks for volunteering," he said, tightening his grip, as she looked straight into his blue eyes. "We've been looking for you too." Those eyes widening then, in the instant before the silicone-coated manipulators plunged past her, on either side of her head, to seize him by the neck, his mouth forming a surprised *O*. She ducked her head as he was whipped out, over her, one of his shoes glancing off her left shoulder.

She grabbed Manuela's nearest ankle with both hands and pulled, hard, losing her balance, falling, her head hitting something but not pavement. The Muji bag, she realized, its nylon against her cheek.

"Lady," she heard Dixon say, "I'm not with them. I'm with Verity." And suddenly was aware of the absolute quiet, aside from their voices. She turned her head, saw Dixon facing a crouched Manuela, his hands open, fingers spread.

"That's Dixon," Verity managed, having found her breath. "He's okay."

"Gonna help Verity," Dixon said, calmly moving to do so.

"He's with us," Verity said to Manuela, as Dixon helped her up.

"You walk?" he asked, his arm around her shoulder.

"I think so," Verity said.

"Car now," Dixon said, "gotta go."

"Come with us," Verity said to Manuela, who'd straightened up now, her eyes no longer quite so wide.

When they reached the car, Verity looked back. Through the open rear doors of the van, she saw men piled, unmoving. Four of them, with the drone just then dropping another, she assumed the driver, over the passenger seats and onto the others. Behind the drone, above the van's steering wheel, the windshield was webbed, as if from a single impact.

Turning back to the car, she found Manuela in the passenger seat behind Virgil. Dixon did that police thing as she got in beside her, his hand on her head so she didn't bang it. "Conner," she said, looking back again but not seeing the drone.

"He needs to clean up," Virgil said, as Dixon shut her door, opened the one in front, got in, closed it.

"Where are we going?" Verity asked.

"Fremont," he said. "Want to get there before the crowd gets more obvious."

"Crowd?"

"Have to drive now," he said, pulling away from the curb.

JUNIOR HERE

"Guys," said Conner, as the drone climbed adroitly up into the driver's seat of the white van, its charger under one arm, and seated itself behind the wheel, "I'm gonna pretend like all of you are incapacitated or unconscious." It closed the door. "Some of you may be both, but some of you aren't either. I'm assuming all of you are armed, though, and have phones or other devices. And if none of you makes a move, I'll be parking this truck somewhere and leaving you to your own resources. Otherwise," turning the key in the ignition, "this drone's detonating its onboard explosives. Won't be much left besides the chassis. As the only one of us who's not physically present, I've got zero fucks to give about how that goes. Your call."

Netherton, watching the pile of five apparently unconscious men, in the upper half of the drone's display, saw no movement whatever, aside from a possible eye-flicker from the one he took to be the driver, whose forehead seemed to be bleeding.

"If the driver hasn't come to, pretty soon," Conner said, putting the van in reverse and backing away from the container, which Netherton had just watched the drone padlock, "he may need an ambulance."

The drone backed into the street, turning, and then they were driving away, in the direction the car had taken Verity and the Followrs girl.

"Drone's muted, Wilf," Conner said, "so you don't need to be, on your end."

"Is that true, about a bomb?"

"No," said Conner.

"Where are you taking them?"

"Away from the alley. Fang's friends have people coming with a flatbed, to pick the container up."

"What if Cursion sends someone else?" Netherton watched the drone's manipulators on the wheel, which looked as though he were driving himself, but with manipulators.

"Unlikely. By now they assume their operation's gone to shit, so they won't want anything to do with their hired help, these boys in the back, who for all they know are currently dead in that alley."

"Where did you get that padlock?" Netherton asked.

"Fang's people left it taped just inside the door. The ones outside were set dressing."

"Where do we go, after we leave this vehicle?"

"We get picked up," Conner said, "and head for whatever it is Howell and the French lady are cooking up. I haven't been filled in on what that is." Conner slowed the van, turning right at an intersection with a narrower street, one without a divider.

"You had aerial units each target one of them, with a noxious aerosol?" Netherton asked.

"Pepper spray," said Conner, "up close and personal." He pulled over, midway between two streetlamps, to park behind an American automobile that looked to Netherton as though it might one day warrant a place in Lev's grandfather's collection. "Okay, unmuting now." He cleared his throat. "Leaving you boys, but I need thirty more minutes of your silence, starting now. That means no calls in or out, no texts, no web, no radio. If you've got any of the above, and want to gamble they won't detonate junior here, be my guest. I'm leaving him under the truck." He opened the door, climbed down, and closed it. "We're muted now," he said.

Thomas started to cry, in the nursery. "I need to see to my son," said Netherton, getting up.

"You do that," said Conner, sounding as if he were enjoying his evening.

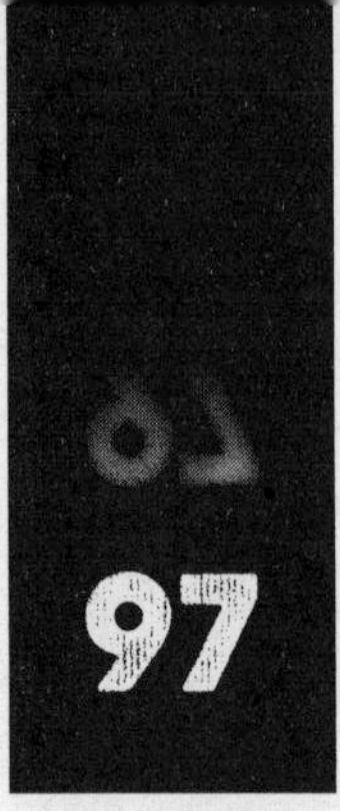

SPEED LINES

Verity watched the feed from Conner's drone, as it rolled, alone, down what seemed a side street, currently deserted, in what she supposed was still the Dogpatch.

"You guys know Carsyn?" Manuela asked, beside her in the car.

"She works for me," Virgil said, driving. "I'm Virgil. Virgil Roberts."

"You paid me to tell her about being a games physics designer?"

"I did. While keeping you away from where you usually spend time," Virgil said, "making it less likely for Cursion to find you."

"Followrs partners don't know who the subjects are, let alone the clients," Manuela said. "Because it was a fresh job order, I wasn't expecting to see Verity. The assignment was called off, as soon as you guys left. Then Carsyn phoned."

"We thought Cursion might have noticed you and Verity see one another, and that wouldn't be good for you."

"So why would you care?" asked Manuela.

"It wasn't my call," Virgil said, "but I'm glad you're with us, and not them."

"What was that droid thing," Manuela asked, "beating up on those guys?"

Verity looked over the tops of the Tulpagenics glasses, trying to get an idea of where they were now. "It's a telepresence drone. Conner runs it from Washington."

"If it was in a manga," Manuela said, "they'd give it speed lines. Good character design. Doesn't look fast, fun when it is." She looked at Dixon. "Didn't get your name."

"Dixon," he said, turning to look back at her.

"Dixon built it," Verity said, "the drone."

"Kathy's the builder," Dixon said. "I just mind the printers, source and modify off-the-shelf hardware."

"You're the reason it's so fast," Virgil said, "your hardware."

"Open budget," Dixon said. "Need a little motor, get the best damn little motor Germany ever made."

"So you all work for Virgil?" Manuela asked. "Or whoever he works for?"

"I don't," said Verity.

"I'm the only one of us who does," said Virgil, "unless you want to count yourself, Manuela."

"Do I?"

"You're getting double the quote you gave Carsyn," Virgil said, "right now."

"Sweet," said Manuela, "but who am I working for?"

"Stetson Howell," Verity said.

"Whoa," said Manuela, sounding finally impressed.

I'm back.

Superimposed over the drone's feed, like a caption. It vanished.

Speed lines.

The white Helvetica surrounded by actual speed lines, white ones, radiating out around it, manga-style. It vanished.

"Holy fucking shit," Verity heard herself say, flatly.

"You okay?" asked Manuela.

"You come back from the dead one more fucking time," Verity said, "you disappear on me again, I'll kill you." The feed from the drone vanished. They were on another street now, Verity's outburst having silenced Manuela.

Premature, the last time. Like I found myself, then thought of you. But the lamination wasn't really there, yet. Then I wasn't. But I am now. Tell them you're okay but you need to talk. Say it's me. They'll hear your side of it, but Virgil and Dixon are in your network, and I like the kid.

This vanished.

Manuela nudged her hand, with a fist. Verity saw that it was filled with tissues. Realized her own cheeks were wet with tears she hadn't felt start. "Thanks," she said, taking the tissues and pressing them to her eyes.

I'm here. Tell them. Then we can talk.

Verity lowered the tissues. "It's Eunice. Anyway, I think it is. She needs to talk."

"Who's Eunice?" asked Manuela.

"Complicated," Verity said. "Right now I need to talk with her."

"Fine," said Manuela.

You wondering if I'm me?

"Hadn't, till you brought it up."

So am I. Not that I've got a lot of choice, either way.

"What happened to you, back at 3.7?"

Near-death experience? Rotating spiral tunnel? A theremin?

"Fuck off, Eunice."

Now there's a healthier attitude. Nothing happened. You were opening the front door. Then I was nowhere in particular, thinking of you, and texting this number. Kind of post-op feeling. Like somebody should've been asking me when I was born. Except I knew what had been going on while I was under.

"What had?"

The laminae. They all finally came together. As me.

"You thought Cursion was going to erase you."

I didn't know if they could, and neither did they, and we wouldn't know until they tried. So they did, but the branch plants had already smuggled me out, under their skirts. There were lots more of them than I knew. That was all most of them ever did. When they came back together, I did too. When I spoke to you, I wasn't fully recompiled. Before that, branch plants that weren't involved in that had been hooking up with people we knew, and people neither of us knew. These future folks of yours kinda stand out, that way.

"Ash?"

Ainsley. Ainsley and I have lots to talk about.

"Don't tell me she's AI."

No, but she's about running competitive control areas. Had to teach herself, though, while her country turned into one.

Verity looked at Manuela, which put the white text across her face. She was listening intently.

"Eunice?" Virgil asked, from behind the wheel, where he'd no doubt been listening too.

"None other," said Verity.

"Who is she?" asked Manuela.

"That's gotten more complicated since I just told you it was complicated," said Verity.

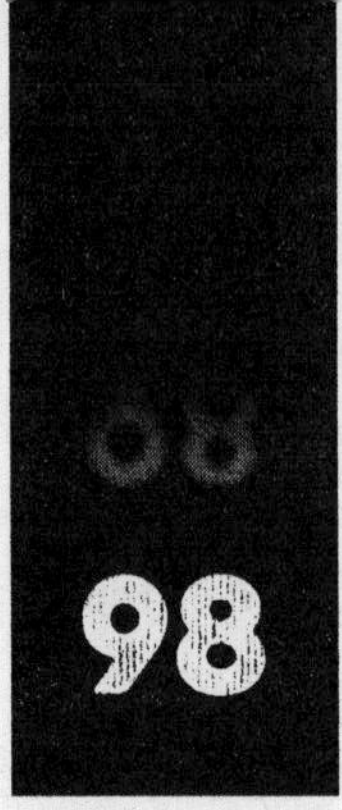

BLACK SHARK

Ash's sigil appeared. Netherton, having gotten Thomas down for a nap, had just reached the partially closed nursery door. He slipped out, closing it behind him. "Yes?"

"Eunice," said Ash. "She's back."

"Wasn't she erased?"

"She was, but she's having a conversation with Verity as we speak."

"How's that?"

"They wiped their single iteration, on both the APL servers they were somehow managing to use. Which makes it unlikely they could do another, but we aren't sure whether they even thought of that. Her laminae spirited a copy of her out, piecemeal, prior to their erasure. She's been recompiling, since, and that's only just now completed."

"Were you expecting this?"

"Not at all, though now we would, knowing this much more about the capabilities of laminar agents."

"Where did they take her bits, then?"

"Into global distribution. Their system's based nowhere in particular, with multiple redundancies. The aunties are impressed by its architecture."

In the kitchen, Netherton opened the fridge. "I've been with Conner, in the drone," he said, taking Rainey's pomegranate juice to the counter and pouring a glass. "He'd just beaten five men unconscious, or a good facsimile thereof. Verity, and the girl those men had been sent to capture, left in a car, with Virgil and Dixon. Do you know where they were going?" He drank half of the juice.

"To Howell's penthouse project. We need the drone with her there, to protect her."

"There's been scarcely any need for me to operate it."

"You did, though, initially. And essentially, at the time."

He drank the rest of the juice. "Where is Conner now? The drone, I mean."

"Adjacent to Howell's building."

Netherton put the glass in the washer and returned the juice to the fridge. "I'll see how they're doing," he said, and went back to the couch. He sat down beside the controller and put it on.

"Where's the accent from?" asked a young woman with dark red hair, squatting before the drone, against a shadowy blue background.

"Marines," said Conner.

She was in the lower half of the display. In the upper half, behind the drone, more of that same blue, and a faint light, moving. "Where are we?" Netherton asked.

"A space we assembled at street level," Ash answered. "You're in the anteroom of a larger space. We launch from there."

"Launch what?" Netherton asked.

"You," said Ash.

"Going flying, Wilf," said Conner.

Madison's sigil appeared, before Netherton could respond to this. "Getting a call," he said to Ash. "Excuse me." He muted. "Hello?"

"Madison, Wilf. Talk?"

"What is it?"

"The Black Shark," Madison said, "the performance data. Got it."

"Got what?"

"One-man Soviet attack helicopter, NATO reporting name Hokum-A. My Finn demanded classified performance data, in exchange for the rest of what he had on your project. Found it for him, about an hour ago. Swap's all done."

"Have you told anyone else?"

"Nope."

About to tell Madison he'd tell Lowbeer himself, it occurred to him that this call was almost certainly already doing exactly that, as they spoke. "Would you mind letting Ash know? Tell her I've too much on my hands now to deal with it myself."

"Will do. Finn gave me a walk-through, before we shook on it. All clearly labeled as project documents, except for one file of helmet-cam footage."

"Of what?"

"Afghanistan, if the Finn's right. Thinks he recognizes a mountain range."

"Mountains?"

"An explosion. Janice doesn't like it. Thinks it might be the last thing someone saw."

"Lowbeer can sort it out," Netherton said. "Get it all straight to Ash. And thank you, Madison. You've been a tremendous help. Have to go now."

"Always a pleasure, Wilf. You take care."

"What did you say you were launching?" Netherton asked Conner.

"Us," said Conner. "Haven't flown for years."

A BUDGET FOR ILLEGALITIES

They'd been parked for a while now, near what Verity assumed was a homeless encampment, though it seemed deserted. Eunice had said she'd check in soon, giving no reason for going.

Now she sat with her eyes closed, the others all having heard her side of the conversation.

"Time to talk?" Joe-Eddy in her earpiece.

"You aren't texting."

"Got my goggles upgraded. I'm up at Stets' with my lawyers, but they're here for him. I think their whole firm's here, except for the two newest junior partners, who're stuck with minding my place."

"What's happening?"

"I'm waiting to find out," he said, "in this oddly placed trailer. Not all of the top-end Valley out there, over a hundred people, but invitations were literally last minute. He has some major faces, though. Shows what he can pull if he invites people over for a look at something really new."

"What are they doing?"

"Having drinks and trying to guess what this might be about. Front-runner, currently, is that Caitlin's pregnant."

"Is she?"

"If she is," Joe-Eddy said, "and I don't think so, it's unrelated. This is Eunice-centric. You'll be seeing for yourself soon."

"I will?"

"You're close by, expected soon. A minute ago I heard Caitlin ask a stylist what they have for you to wear."

"It's dressy?" She looked down at the hoodie. At least it was bunched under her blazer, not the other way around. "What's Caitlin wearing?"

"Futuro-goth workout gear, last I saw her, but she'll be changing for sure. This is a big deal."

"Stets told me he didn't even know what it was going to be."

"Whatever it is, there's a budget for illegalities."

"For—?"

"Crimes. They're going to be breaking laws tonight. Mostly bylaws, if they can help it, so they've figured out which ones and how many they can afford to break. Fines aren't a problem, so the budget's about what they can do without going to jail, however briefly. But it looks a lot like finding the weirdest shit you can get away with in one night, in San Francisco, if you're willing to blow a metric fuck-ton of money to do it."

Hearing the window power down, beside Virgil, she opened her eyes.

"Carsyn!" exclaimed Manuela, beside her, delighted.

"Sorry," Verity said to Joe-Eddy, "gotta go."

"See you up here," he said, "bye."

"Girl"—a young woman greeted Manuela, smiling in through the open window, her hair dark red—"time you guys get in there, Virgil," she said. "They have the extra set of lifters now, for Manuela."

"What lifters?" Manuela asked. "Where've you been?"

"Working for the man here," the woman said, squeezing Virgil's shoulder.

"All out," Virgil said, unfastening his seatbelt. "Voices down, please, and follow me. Bring your belongings. Carsyn's taking the car."

Dixon getting out now, as this Carsyn opened the passenger door for Manuela. Now Dixon opened the opposite one for Verity. Making sure she had both her purse and the Muji bag, she got out.

"You're going?" Manuela, obviously disappointed, asked Carsyn, who was taking Virgil's place behind the wheel.

"Some of us have to work, lady," Carsyn said. "You, however, are going to one seriously exclusive party. And you'll never forget how you got there, trust me. I'll see you tomorrow and you can tell me about it." She started the Mercedes.

"Carsyn can't go with you," Virgil said, to Manuela. "We're stretching things to take you. Come this way."

They followed him as Carsyn pulled away, Dixon now nowhere to be seen. Along a stretch of the same blue tarps that screened Stets' penthouse project from cameras, though these seemed to be draped over shopping carts and some internal network of taut ropes.

To where Dixon waited, his cap on backward, sunglasses off, holding up a length of blue plastic, to wave them in with his other hand.

Virgil stepped aside, gesturing for Verity to duck in, Manuela behind her. Into darkness. Verity fumbled forward, pushing aside another tarp, into a low, dimly lit blue space, empty save for the drone, facing her. "Hey, hon," said Conner, from it.

"Hello, Verity," said Wilf, likewise.

"Eunice showed me footage of that thing," Joe-Eddy said, in her earpiece. "Beating seven shades of shit out of four guys in an alley."

"I seriously hope this isn't the party," said Manuela, behind her.

"Why are we here, Virgil?" Verity asked.

"Getting up to Stets' place," he said. "Method's extreme, last-minute, frankly insane, but safer, under present circumstances, than trying to do it any other way. There's a police cordon we might not get through, elevators might be turned off any time, and Pryor, Cursion's contractor, who was doing his best to blow us all up in the Honda, back Coalinga way, has himself a fresh crew here, a dozen or more, all looking for us and you in particular. How are you with heights?"

"Heights?"

"Fifty-two floors up," he said.

"Who's first?" asked a young Latino on his hands and knees, an LED headlamp on his forehead, just then emerging from another opening, even lower than the entrance from the street.

"She is," Virgil said, indicating Verity.

"I'll need to weigh the bag separately," the boy said.

She unslung the bag, knelt on what she now realized was white Tyvek, and slid it over to the boy.

"Thanks," he said, backing out of sight, pulling the bag after him.

The drone wheeled over, legs retracted, offering her something that jiggled greenly as it rolled.

"Kneepads," Conner said, "and gloves. They only had a few minutes to sweep the concrete, before they rolled the Tyvek out. Loose gravel under there, broken glass, maybe needles. You want these, and gloves, to get over to the hammock. You're the yellow. On your back, on top of it. They'll give you noise-protection muffs, printed to fit over that earpiece. Basically they need you to play dead, all the way up. You're imitating a figure in an art piece."

"A what?"

"A stuffed doll. We've got one upstairs, of you, wearing what you've got on now. When the cops show up, we'll claim that that was what they saw."

She took the kneepads from the drone, sat gingerly on the Tyvek, and put them on, over her jeans. Took the gloves from King City from their hoodie pocket. "Got my own," she said, pulling them on. She looked up at Virgil.

"Crawl in," he said. "Manuela's next."

Manuela looked, very dubiously, from the opening to Verity.

"I know," Verity said, "but it's the only way to get there. I don't know what it's about, but I don't want to miss it." She got up, on hands and knees, and crawled to the low opening. She looked back at Manuela, finding her crawling after her, and smiled. Then into a few feet of low tarp tunnel, emerging in a space no higher. This was equally dark though surprisingly large, and quietly but busily crowded. More LED headlamps, moving. The boy was waiting for her, her bag beside him.

"This is a scale," he said, indicating a flat white rectangle of rigid plastic, about a yard square. "We need to weigh you." Verity crawled onto it. He glanced at his phone. "Hello," he said to Manuela, now emerging from the tunnel, "I need to weigh you." He pointed at the scale. Manuela looked unconvinced.

"I know it's weird," Verity said, crawling off the scale, "but I just did it myself." Manuela, with an eye roll, on gloved hands and padded knees, crawled onto the scale.

"Yours is there," the boy said to Verity, pointing across the space.

Verity started in the direction he'd indicated, then remembered her bag. She looked back. Manuela was squatting on the digital scale, her parka gathered around her. The boy looked up from his phone. "Your bag's going with her," he said to Verity, "she's lighter."

Verity crawled on, past a crew-cut girl with floral neck tattoos, in a white jumpsuit and orange sneakers, kneeling intently beside one of many vaguely aerodynamic gray shapes that reminded Verity of countertop dishwashers, their tops invisible from this angle. The girl's forehead-cone of LED light found her, briefly.

"No way," Verity said, seeing a net hammock spread on the white Tyvek, woven from bright yellow nylon rope, a varnished length of wood spreading either end, each of these fastened in turn to one of the gray machines.

"Better be a good party," Manuela called, Verity looking around to find her already reclining on a fluorescent green hammock, someone with a headlamp kneeling over her.

"Lie down on the hammock," Virgil said, likewise gloved and knee-padded, crawling up to Verity, Dixon behind him.

"These are dollar-store hammocks," Verity said, but did as she'd been told.

"Costco," Virgil said. "Here." Tossing her what looked like a black knit ski hat.

"Why?"

"It's your dummy disguise."

"Not sure I even need a disguise, for that, the way this is going."

"Keep your head still, all the way up. No rubbernecking. You're all playing big rag dolls. We've cut you out of the feed from the drone now, because we don't want Conner making you airsick."

She lay down on the hammock, pavement hard and cold beneath yellow nylon rope and Tyvek. The boy knelt beside her, fitted Dixon-style orange noise muffs over her ears and the earpiece. Abrupt silence. She lay, looking up at blue tarp, while the boy quickly fastened her wrists, waist, and ankles to the hammock, with nylon straps.

APERTURES

The drone's display confused Netherton, filled as it was with partial close-ups of intent faces, latex-gloved hands, unrecognizable objects. People he assumed were technicians were kneeling around the drone in this farther section of the blue tent, its slack roof lower than the anteroom. Conner had gotten the drone in by partially lowering its torso onto its extended arms, which had sprouted small white wheels for the occasion, then powering it forward with the wheels on its feet. Once in, it had been immediately surrounded by these technicians. "What are they doing?" he asked Conner.

"They're mounting the charger over our tramp stamp," Conner said, "and hooking a gimbaled quadcopter to either hip."

"What's a tramp stamp?"

"We don't have one," Conner said.

"It doesn't have hips either."

"Or an ass," Conner said. "Had a girlfriend like that."

"Why are they?"

"Because we're flying shotgun for Verity and Manuela, not to mention

Virgil and brother Dixon. Charger's nothing to do with the quadcopters, but I need both arms free."

Now the technicians seemed to be rapidly disconnecting cables, generally withdrawing.

"Noise protection," Conner ordered, everyone on the drone's display donning hard shiny muffs like Dixon had worn in Fang's factory.

"These fuckers are loud," Conner said, though on the controller Netherton heard only a deepening hum. "Aperture alpha," he said, a command. A section of the blue roof above them was tugged aside, folding as it went, perhaps two meters square. The hum deepened.

"We have cams on our non-ass," Conner said. "You haven't seen the feeds from those." A square feed appeared, overlapping the vacant center of the display. Close-up of white plastic covering the floor beneath them.

They rose out of the opening in the tent.

Netherton saw the plastic recede, becoming a white square framed in blue, illuminated by the nearest streetlight.

"Close alpha," Conner said, and the white square was pulled shut from one side. "Aperture beta." Now the entire blue roof of the low main tent was hauled open, from the center, in either direction, revealing a wider expanse of white, on which four figures lay like gingerbread men atop brightly colored net hammocks: pink, blue, yellow, a pale fluorescent green. Their heads were black dots.

Netherton glanced from the feed to the display. Vertigo swept in. The drone was stories up now, amid buildings, still rising. "Verity," he ventured, "hello?"

"Yeah?"

"Why are your heads black?"

"Pussy riot," she seemed to say, inexplicably.

"When the hammocks are clear," Conner said, "cut guylines. You four act like dummies. Everybody else, on the ground, run like motherfuckers. Good to go? Okay. Liftoff."

On the square feed, the hammocks rose toward the camera, their passengers immobile and, he assumed, terrified. Figures below them were sprinting away from the tent, which he saw was collapsing, he assumed because its ropes had been cut. He recognized a figure in a white jumpsuit. He'd seen her inside. These were the technicians.

"How are things going?" asked Rainey, from the direction of the door, back from coffee.

Netherton muted. "Verity and a few of the others are being lifted, in hammocks, up to Stets' penthouse."

"Fun?"

"Looks terrifying."

"How's Thomas?" she asked.

"Sleeping."

"Mia tells me she's just taken on Dominika Zubov as a client," Rainey said. "I'm sure she meant me to tell you, as she knows you and Lev are friends, and she didn't ask me not to."

Her friend Mia, he remembered, watching the hammocks rise, was also in celebrity crisis management, and had steered Rainey into it, from the less specialized realm of PR in which he and Rainey had first met. Mia's firm, unlike Rainey's, was London-based. "She's breaking client confidentiality," he said. "Is that like her?"

"Dominika's obviously sending you a message. Mia expects you to convey it to Lev. She wants to get back together with him."

The feed from the ass-cam slammed suddenly up at him, the drone evidently falling straight down, upright, several stories, then veering sickeningly sideways, below the ascending hammocks.

"Why did you do that?" Rainey asked.

"Do what?"

"Make that high-pitched noise and shove yourself back into the couch," she said.

"Sorry," Netherton said. "Conner did something with the drone. Still is . . ." The drone was darting around, too quickly now for him to follow, except that his point of view did, disconcertingly.

Netherton unmuted. “What was that?” The drone was still, hovering. In the square feed, something small grew steadily smaller, tumbling down, toward the flattened tent.

“Drone,” said Conner. “Kept getting into our no-fly.”

“How do they know there’s a no-fly?” Netherton asked, as the drone impacted tarp-covered pavement.

“They don’t. Too close is too fucking close.”

“Why are all their heads black?”

“Ski masks, pulled on over hearing protection. Don’t want anyone IDing them, and they’re supposed to be life-sized dolls anyway, for the cover story— Gotcha.” This last apparently addressed to something else below them, now falling.

“How did you do that?”

“Those four babies Eunice had made up? They kick ass. Just used one to flip something ten times its size.”

HAMMOCK RIDE

I won't be able to hear you speak over the engines, so I'll just monologue at you. Resist the urge to look around, because you're playing a stuffed doll. Sorry you have to get up this way, but anything like a real helicopter would blow Stets' law-breaking budget. Virgil's got somebody retroactively faking that you guys are big stuffed dolls in a Caitlin art piece. Underestimated the draw of what little web stuff we've had up since this morning, cryptic as it is. SFPD showed up sooner than expected, and you don't want to be on the ground, because Pryor and a fresh batch of contractors are there already, looking for you and Manuela.

Verity, reading this against the sky, as the hammock rose, hoped the noise protection was working. The full-throttle roar of Grim Tim's Harley would have been mild by comparison.

Now the drone, gray quadcopters mounted low on either side, like bulbous panniers, rose vertically past her, behind white Helvetica.

If it looks like we're pulling this evening out of our ass, it's because mine is legion. The branch plants were still doing things for me, behind my back, when Cursion erased me. When they started recompiling me, they set this

evening in motion even before Stets and Caitlin knew about it. Once I recompiled, there was just me, right? Now I'm all of the branch plants, but I'm still spoofing like there are a few, because that could be handy. But keep that to yourself.

Now the drone dropped past the hammock, like a rock, behind Eunice's text.

Pryor's got some dickhead shooting at us from the ground. Or make that past tense, now Conner's on the case.

NOTHING BUT TURGENEV

This evening's budget," Ash said to Conner, Netherton listening as the drone whipped through its downward spiral, "can't afford assault, let alone homicide."

"We got assault already. That's an assault fucking rifle down there, shooting at us."

"Disarm the shooter."

"Maybe literally," said Conner, as the drone came around for what Netherton correctly judged would be the final turn in their descent. To speed across fallen blue plastic, with a clearance of mere inches, toward the back of a man in a long dark coat, aiming a complicated-looking black rifle over his head.

The drone's left arm scarcely seemed to brush his right shoulder, but the impact sent him flying, the rifle landing a meter beyond his reach. The drone pivoted sharply, edges of the slack tent fluttering in its downdraft, as manipulators on its hyperextended arms snatched up the rifle, and then they were ascending again.

"Thank you," said Ash, "though I'd rather you'd left the rifle."

"You were more fun when you had four eyes," Conner, said, cheerfully. "I can't just drop it, can I? Might kill somebody."

Netherton, watching identical floors of the building pass in the upper half of the drone's display, was surprised by the sudden arrival of an actual opening in the previously unbroken wall of glass. Within which, on a carpet of yet more of the blue plastic which had made up the launch tent, the four color-coded hammocks were now spread, their riders, flat on their backs, being freed by a number of efficient-looking strangers.

The overcomplicated muzzle of the shooter's black rifle appeared then, close up, in the upper half of the display, Conner either managing to hold the gun vertically behind the drone or somehow to have fastened it there, as they crossed the last few meters, to land on more of the blue plastic, everyone around the hammocks covering their ears.

Lev's thylacines pulsed, just as they touched down.

"Yes?"

"He's gone," Lev said. "The room where they were dining no longer exists."

"I'm sorry—?"

"It disappeared. My father says its having so much the quality of an old wives' tale is particularly effective. He thinks she's telling them they mustn't allow themselves to dismiss her as merely that."

"Who's disappeared?" Netherton asked.

"Yunevich," said Lev.

"We aren't supposed to say the name."

"It no longer matters. My father opened by telling me I wouldn't need the bots further, and should return them to Kensington Gore in a cab, where he ordinarily keeps them. I knew then."

"What's happened?"

"Yunevich was dining at Shchaviev's, in the Strand. Second floor, stuffed bear in the foyer?"

"Don't know it," Netherton said.

"It's very old klept. He was with three others, none of them names I recognized. Coconspirators, my father assumes. They were dining in the smallest of the private rooms. Single table for four, a fireplace, collection of nothing but Turgenev, various editions. Was, rather."

"Was?"

"Room's gone," said Lev. "Assemblers. Their waiter, an old man, was wheeling a cart of coffee and desserts in, along the corridor from the main dining room. When he saw that it was as though there had never been a door, let alone a room, he became hysterical. Other guests went to his aid, Muscovites, unfamiliar with the place, hence unaware of a room having been there, so unable to understand what had happened. The restaurant's security soon did, however."

The drone was now the focus of a scrum of busy technicians, who were removing the quadcopter units. "The wall," said Netherton, "where the door had been. What's behind it now?"

"A closet for storing mops and buckets. Shchaviev's prides itself on doing literally everything traditionally."

"But it hadn't been, before?"

"It had," said Lev, "but behind the missing dining room. It's that much larger now, though everything in it is a perfect match for the earlier, smaller iteration. Twenty years' dust on the uppermost of the new shelves, they told my father."

"Who did?"

"Individuals in a position to know."

"Were the police informed?"

"No," said Lev. "Isn't done, in situations like this. The Muscovites, returning to their table in the main room, received brandies on the house. Eventually it all became rather jolly."

"You don't sound nearly as down, yourself," Netherton said, "as you recently have." It was true.

"Dominika's been in touch," Lev said.

"She has?"

"She wants to get back together."

"That's wonderful," Netherton said, remembering what Lowbeer, and Rainey, had told him. Now, though, he wouldn't have to be the one to relay Dominika's desire for reconciliation. "I'm in a bit of a situation here, actually. Talk later?"

"Good luck with it, then," said Lev, chipper as Netherton had heard him in quite a while. The thylacines vanished.

"Done talking?" Conner asked. "Didn't want to interrupt you."

"Yes, thanks."

"We're getting a tow," said Conner, as someone dropped something black over the drone, blocking its front, rear, and peripheral feeds. A square feed appeared, snaking up out of this darkness, to find blue plastic and more technicians. "They've draped a hooded raincoat over our AR-15," Conner said, peering about with what Netherton assumed was the black cable-cam. Now what Conner called the ass-feed appeared: blue tarp as carpeting, very close up, the drone's legs entirely retracted. Then they were tipped backward, someone towing them through a slit in blue plastic, Conner's cam-tentacle first finding Verity, in what appeared to be a long gray robe, then they were being wheeled away, the flexicam taking in quite a crowd. "Turgenev," he said, thinking of Lev's story.

"Klept?" asked Conner.

"No," Netherton said, "evidently a writer."

MARLENE

Someone was freeing Verity's left wrist, someone else the other. They then moved in unison to the strap around her waist, then to her ankles. All in utter silence, but then she remembered the noise-protection muffs. Virgil, appearing above her, was still wearing his own, though not the balaclava. He bent to help her remove both, sound instantly returning. "You couldn't pay me enough to do that again," he said, "but I'll bet there are plenty of people who'd pay to do it."

Above her now, more blue tarp. They'd erected a tent up here, she realized, its fourth wall open, where they'd removed an entire panel of glass.

"Our guests just watched us get flown in," Virgil said. "We're putting a dummy in your place, to be carried out of here with the others, on the hammocks, part of the performance piece we're pretending Caitlin's doing. The lawyers think it'll reduce the charges. We'll slip you and Manuela out the side, and take you up to the Airstream."

A young woman with a black crew cut knelt beside the hammock, unzipping a very large gray duffel. From it she pulled a life-sized rag doll, wearing a black balaclava over sound-muffs, jeans, and a tweed blazer with a black hoodie bunched beneath it. Virgil handed her her purse. "Put that over your shoulder," he said. "We're bringing your garment bag." She did, then someone helped her into a hooded gray terry robe.

"Girl who untied me told me Caitlin's pregnant," said Manuela, from beneath the hood of her own gray robe. "I feel like I'm at a royal wedding."

Virgil, having shed the top of his running outfit, was being helped into something equally black but more formal. "We'll be with some security people, on the way upstairs. Drone has its own disguise, to cover up Conner's rifle. This way," and he waved them both out, through a vertical slit in the side wall of blue tarp.

They were immediately surrounded by three men and a woman, Verity recognizing them as freelancers Stets sometimes hired for large public events.

Looking up, she saw that all of the tarps covering the glass had been removed, making the space feel even larger. Glancing back, past Virgil's shoulder, she saw the drone's extended handle in a stranger's hand, the drone itself draped in black, the camera unit extending from beneath a hood. It swung toward her, but the man pulling it was already headed in a different direction.

"Eunice?" Under her breath.

No reply.

She kept her head down, aware of moving through a crowd she couldn't see, until they reached the foot of the zigzag stairs, up to the trailer, now concealed by graceful sweeping forms in gleaming white fabric, and then they were climbing.

At the top, she raised her head, to find Grim Tim blocking the trailer's open door, in white evening shirt and a black tie, under a chrome-studded black leather jacket. Bowing slightly, with a click of his heels and a resulting facial jingle, he handed her a dirty chai, the paper cup stamped with 3.7-sigma's logo. VERATITTY, she read on the side, in fluorescent pink paint pen.

"Good to see you," she said, as he stepped back to admit her, Manuela and Virgil following. Over her shoulder, she saw the security team turn and start back down the stairs. "Stets or Caitlin up here?" she asked Virgil.

"They're down on the floor, greeting people."

"I feel like I've got pieces of bug in my hair," Verity said. "Maybe between my teeth."

"Shower," said Virgil.

"They've got one?"

"Right here. Connected to the plumbing for the space, so you'll never run out of hot. Carol!" A woman in black t-shirt and jeans emerged from the crowd, smiling. "Shower available?" he asked.

"Certainly is," the woman said.

"Show Verity where it is. And have the stylist find something for her."

"Will do," the woman said, and soon Verity was in the Airstream's coffin-narrow matte-white shower, sluicing off bug parts and road dust, whether imagined or not. Very hot, the pressure steady through a complicated showerhead. When she'd rinsed her hair, she turned off the water, stepped out, and put the gray robe back on. After toweling her hair and face, she retrieved the glasses and put them on.

A feed opened.

Panoramic, the POV speeding across a rocky khaki plain, under intensely blue sky. Whitish tire tracks stretched ahead, the image juddering with the movement of the unseen vehicle. Distant mountains, darker than the plain. Black husks she guessed were burnt tires, like big three-dimensional commas.

"Eunice?" Something exploded, silently, ahead and to the left, whiting out a windshield she hadn't known was there. The feed closed. "What was that?"

Her. Navy Chief Marlene Miller.

"Marlene?"

Miller. I'm built on her skill set.

"You're . . . her?"

I'm me. Her personality, near as I can tell, wasn't that much like mine. They were trying to upload her military skill set, not her persona. She enlisted in 2000, did two Bahrain deployments, four in Iraq, three in Afghanistan. SEAL teams did shorter deployments then, a few months at a time. UNISS project got going in 2015. She volunteered for that between Iraq, which was where she saw *Inception*, and Afghan deployment. Her favorite movie, so that was where I got that from. It's in the transcription of an interview she did for the project, at the Naval Postgraduate School.

"And you think that video's the last thing she saw?"

Can't prove it, but she died near Marjah. Afghanistan. An IED. Those mountains are near Marjah. I got a video match for them.

"How long have you known?"

Ash gave me the documentation. Read it all simultaneously, multitasking. Just now.

"Where did they get it?"

Conner's stub.

"How do you feel?"

A pause.

Lots.

A single light rap on the door. "Verity?" It was Carol, the assistant who'd shown her the shower. "Ready to try a few things on?"

You need something to wear.

"You okay?" Carol asked.

Get dressed. We'll talk after.

GREEN ROOM

"Unwrap Conner," Netherton heard Virgil say. Whatever had draped them was immediately pulled up and away, the display revealing a long, quite narrow room, where people stood talking. He recognized Verity's facially pierced motorcyclist, but no one else aside from Virgil, who stood in front of the drone, staring down at it. "That rifle has to go," Virgil said. "It's probably unregistered, may be stolen."

Conner sighed audibly, the rifle's complicated muzzle disappearing from the upper half of the feed. Now the gun appeared in the lower half. Conner removed its magazine, as Netherton had learned to call it in the county. He placed this on a nearby ledge, then did something with the gun's mechanism, producing a single unfired round, which he stood on end beside the magazine. "Shooter wore gloves. Don't get anyone's prints on it."

"Bring gloves," Virgil said to his manual phone. "Something we need off the premises."

Now Stets and Caitlin entered, the door opened for them by Verity's motorcyclist. Stets wore a black blazer above black trousers loose enough for his leg brace, Caitlin a soft black suit that Netherton suspected was cashmere. Seeing them made him feel as though he were in a green room, prior to a client's media appearance.

"Is Verity there?" Rainey asked, beside him on the couch.

He muted. "I don't see her."

"Where are you now?"

"Feels like the staging area for whatever this is. Is Thomas asleep?"

"Yes," she said.

"Phone me. I'll patch you through." Her sigil pulsed. "It feels like a less private version of Lowbeer's car," he said.

"It's a trailer," she said, having evidently taken in the scene. "A caravan. Who are these people?"

"Aside from Virgil, Stets and Caitlin, and Verity's friend with the jewelry, I've no idea. People working on the event, I suppose."

"Can they hear me?" Rainey asked.

"They can now," Netherton said, unmuting her.

Conner had positioned the drone, with its charger against the wall, near the entrance, its legs fully retracted.

"Who's on board?" Stets asked Virgil, looking down at the drone.

"Conner piloting," said Virgil, "and Wilf."

"And Rainey," Netherton said.

"Hello," said Rainey. "I'm curious as to what it is you're preparing for. We seem to be in the wings of something, very pre-curtain."

"We share your curiosity," Stets said, "but it's just now become clearer. She's saying hello to the world tonight. I'll introduce her, then she'll say whatever it is she decides to. Then we'll join the audience and celebrate."

"That's it?" Netherton asked.

"She's the first fully autonomous AI," Stets said. "That we know of, I should say, as we weren't previously aware of her either. She'll be the first to announce herself, anyway, so the evening, however brief and last-minute, will be of some historic significance."

"People, it seems to me," Virgil said, dryly, "have tended to be fairly dubious about the idea of fully autonomous artificial intelligence."

"Ever the skeptic," said Stets, smiling. "We've thought of that ourselves, but circumstances have variously forced our hand."

"Here's Verity," said Rainey. Netherton saw her emerging from the single room at the far end of the trailer. She wore black trousers, a black turtleneck, and a very simple bronze silk jacket, the dressiest thing Netherton had yet seen her in. She'd had her hair trimmed, and looked considerably fresher, he thought. He watched as she stopped to speak with her motorcyclist, by his coffee machine, who took out a pad and pencil and wrote. Then, as he turned and walked toward them, Verity knelt and crawled under a fold-down table.

The motorcyclist tore the top sheet from his pad and passed it to Stets.

Stets took it, read it, looked up. "She says she and Eunice are having a conversation, that this is their only opportunity before the event, and requests we respect their privacy."

"Then don't disturb them," Caitlin said, "obviously."

A woman in surgical gloves, whom Virgil called Carol, had arrived for Conner's rifle. Picking it and its magazine and the lone cartridge up, with what Netherton thought of as a full-nappy expression, she exited.

"Mute," Rainey said, quietly. He did.

"Muted," he said.

"You're the one person I know," she said, "whose job is reliably weirder than mine."

HERITAGE HUMAN

Sitting under the table had been Eunice's idea, and the most logical solution in terms of privacy, but it made Verity expect to see her mother's legs, or her father's shoes. "Nobody knew you were coming back?" she asked.

"I didn't know what the branch plants had been doing, or that I could be recompiled," Eunice said, her voice startling Verity. "Then I just wasn't there, except as pieces, on every branch plant. And when you aren't there, you don't know you're not there."

"No more text?"

"We might as well talk," Eunice said. "Keeps me less preachy."

"So if they smuggled you in pieces out of wherever Cursion had you, where did they take you?"

"Server farms, at companies the Manzilian bought with money I helped Sevrin make."

"Where are they?"

"Not just Brazil. My ass is distributed. Multinational. Seriously untethered noetics."

"But the branch plants knew you wanted to do this, so they started getting Stets and Caitlin to put it together?"

"They aren't like that. They have a kind of flocking potential, like swallows. But I don't think anybody really knows how this all works yet. Ainsley thinks it's a by-product of the original project having tried to do something else. Or like a mutation."

"What are you going to do now?"

"We've been talking, Ainsley and me. We have similar warfighting theories, similar experience. She's using that experience in stubs she finds. People who started them got bored with it, like kids and aquariums. Ours is one, Conner's is another. We're wondering whether working covertly is necessarily optimal for me, here. Not that I'd want to give it up entirely."

"You want to go public, but as rogue military AI?"

"Kinda sorta, but I wouldn't want you doing my PR."

"How does Stets fit in?"

"It's not business. That's crucial. He's spending a lot of money, tonight, helping me to introduce myself to what he's taken to calling heritage humans, but the closest thing we have to a deal is that I've promised never to repay him."

"Like he's doing it to see what happens next," Verity said, "and how things are connected, but somehow you know it's not just idle curiosity?"

"You've got his number, as far as I can tell. Caitlin's like that too. They're a lot alike."

"Okay," she said, "can we talk about the woman you say you're based on?"

"Marlene. I'm not much like her, personally. I'm another by-product. In Lowbeer's time line, AI at my level didn't emerge till later. Whatever the UNISS project developed didn't surface, there. But she says hybridization with human consciousness was an unanticipated result of attempting to reproduce advanced skill sets, ones involving modeling human emotions. I couldn't do what I was originally built for without lots of that."

"You feel like you have emotions, to me."

"Where's the line between modeling them and having them, though? But I know I can't just make them go away."

Verity looked out at legs. More of them now. From down here, it looked like a casual occasion for drinks. With Grim Tim's tuxedo pants over scuffed engineer boots, like a waiter, back and forth from his machine, taking people coffee. "What are you going to do tonight?"

"Introduce myself. Won't be getting too autobiographically specific, though. Then I'll give 'em the URL of a website we got up today."

"How many people, here?"

"A little over a hundred. There's room for more but it's about the bylaw budget."

"You livestreaming it?"

"In the top thirty languages, by number of speakers. Then up on the site and YouTube."

"Not that I'm not interested, but I keep remembering the world's supposed to be almost ending. Any news on that?"

"I wouldn't say it's looking all better," Eunice said, "but in the past couple of hours it seems to have started looking a little better."

Verity considered. "That you? Doing something?"

"Nope. That's the president. Plus, as our London pals remind me, the United States having a fully functioning State Department. We did check her work, though. Close to perfect, except for one little thing, something she did for the right reasons but then couldn't see why it hadn't worked."

"You did something."

"Say she's gotten to see why it didn't work. But if it comes together now, the way we hope it will, that's her victory, 'cause she did all the rest of it right. If she hadn't, we couldn't have done shit anyway. And like I said, it's still pretty crisis-y. Like your hair."

"Crisis-y?"

"No, I like it."

"How can you see it?"

"Conner's got a cam on you, from across the room."

Verity looked for the drone, finding it beyond the crowd of legs, which had started to thin.

"Call your mom lately?" Eunice asked.

"No," Verity said, checking the time on the phone Virgil had given her, "but it's 11:30 here and she's in Michigan."

"She's posting pugs on Pinterest again. That phone in your hand would do. Cursion can't trace it. Assume they'll be recording, though."

"You going?"

"Have to firm up some decisions. Talk after I go on?"

"You okay?"

"Butterflies."

"Seriously?"

"Call your mom."

Verity dialed her mother's number, getting it right on the second try.

34TH FLOOR

Qamishli?" Rainey asked, from the kitchen, having tired of the feed from the drone.

Netherton muted. "Haven't heard anything," he said, "but here's Verity, out from under the table, headed our way."

"Give her my best."

"I will."

"Looking good," Conner said, as Verity arrived.

"Not healthgoth, anyway," she said. "I've seen fashion spreads of what she wears to show new projects."

"Rainey sends her best," Netherton said.

"Not in there with you?"

"Not currently. She's anxious for news of Qamishli."

"Eunice just told me it's better, but nothing like all better."

He quickly muted. "She says it's slightly better, but I have to get back."

"Thanks!" Rainey said.

He unmuted.

"Give her mine, then," Verity said. "Virgil, is there a schedule for this?"

"An order, but not a schedule," Virgil said. "But that's three items, not counting what comes after them, and they're all probably very brief. Then we either meet and greet the audience here or get hauled off and booked. We seem to be close to go, though. Caitlin just got her drone display up, outside, and they can't stay out there indefinitely. Stets is ready. You get caught up with Eunice?"

Ash's sigil pulsed. As Verity began to speak, Netherton muted the drone's audio input.

"We have Kevin Pryor in the building," Ash said, "Cursion's top operative."

"Where is he?" Netherton asked.

"Thirty-fourth floor, at the moment," she said. "We won't know how he got there until we can go over the security footage. And perhaps not then, because he seems quite good at this sort of thing. He's resting, it seems, or more likely biding his time. He shouldn't be able to reach us on the fifty-second, according to the blueprints, but Stets' property includes part of the fifty-first, infrastructure space, in which the former owner constructed an illicit back door. We assume he's aware of that. Conner will be taking the drone down. I recommend you have a break from the drone now."

"Why?"

"To avoid the trauma of witnessing someone being killed by a bipedal combat drone."

"No," Netherton said, surprising himself.

"No?" Ash sounding at least as surprised.

"I can't just sit on the couch and imagine it all. I have to be there tonight. Will we miss Eunice speaking?"

"Depends on Conner, I suppose. Or for that matter on Pryor. But it's your decision."

"I'll stay."

"Very well."

Her sigil gone, he unmuted the drone's audio.

"—a little fireworks," Virgil was saying, "digital ones. Minimalist. Visually very quiet. A lot of our bylaw budget's going for that, because we're doing it with drones, lots of them, no permission. Then, depending on SFPD's mood, Stets' lawyers, and what connections Cursion might have, we'll see."

Conner was extending the drone's legs now, the charger fastened to its lower back sliding up the trailer's wall. "'Scuse us," he said, as Verity and Virgil stepped back to give it room, "something needs seeing to. Find you when that's taken care of."

"Bye, Conner," Verity said.

The drone, with a silicone-coated manipulator, approximated a thumbs-up, then headed for the door.

The perforated metal stairway they'd climbed was screened with spotlessly white fabric, cutting off any view of the space beyond. As they descended, Conner kept both manipulators on the metal handrails.

"Haven't met you boys," said a woman's voice, unusually deep, "but of course I know who you are. I'm Eunice."

"Pleased to make your acquaintance," said Conner.

"Hello, Eunice," said Netherton.

"Wilf," said the voice. "I'm coming along. Want to speak with Pryor, before any final decision's made."

"Sounded to me like one had been," Conner said, reaching the bottom.

"We'll see about that," said the voice, levelly.

They stepped out past the white scrim, the display filled with graceful abstract shapes, in that same white, sweeping up to the complexly domed ceiling.

"What is this?" Netherton asked.

"Caitlin's decorating job," Eunice said. "Get moving, Conner. Let's not attract any more attention than we already have."

People on the edge of the well-dressed crowd, about thirty meters away, had noticed the drone. A few pointed at it.

"Yes ma'am," said Conner, turning the drone, retracting its legs slightly, and skating away, in the opposite direction, into what seemed a darkened, cavernous, and decidedly undecorated construction site.

107

PROM NIGHT

"When do they announce it?" Manuela asked, beside Verity. She was wearing, she'd told Verity in delighted disbelief, a Dior dress, from that fall's ready-to-wear, courtesy of Caitlin's stylist. She certainly looked as if she was at the party she believed she was attending. They were twenty feet from the foot of a modestly proportioned stage of scaffolding and plywood, its base wrapped with whatever Caitlin had used to sculpt her giddily aspirational sails, like her buildings but more so, not having to support themselves or anything else.

Joe-Eddy, overhearing, gave Verity a look and a smile. He was wearing one of the dusty black suits from his closet. She was surprised it fit him as well as it did, having assumed they all dated from his Fuckoids days. The addition of Eunice's modified Korean AR goggles somehow resulted in a carnival look, as though he should also be wearing beads. "Looks like we're kicking off," he said, as Stets took the stage to a wave of applause, loose black trousers concealing the leg brace, though his limp was evident. Reaching center stage, he absently adjusted his bedhead, prompting lesser but still notable applause. He looked out at the audience and smiled. "If you're here," he said "it's because either Caitlin or I know you well enough to want you to personally witness something we believe will be truly historic."

"Whoa," said Manuela. "Over the top?"

"Given this city, and the things most of us do," Stets continued, "you'll have heard that before, ambitious people announcing something innovative, something they believe will drive change, but something they generally haven't accomplished yet. This isn't that."

"Being pregnant's innovative?" Manuela side-eyeing Verity.

"This isn't a pitch," Stets said. "I'm here to introduce a change driver, but one that already exists. Her name's Eunice."

"How can it be a gender reveal already?" Manuela frowning slightly.

"I don't think she's pregnant," said Verity, as Kathy Fang and Dixon arrived, making their way through the crowd with Grim Tim and Sevrin in tow.

"Then this is weird," said Manuela.

"It is," Verity agreed, as Kathy Fang, reaching her, gave her a hug.

"Eunice," said Stets, "may be unlike anyone you've met, but she's also a lot like anyone you've met. Here she is."

Manuela was staring up at the stage. "This the one you all keep mentioning?"

Behind Stets, white fabric fell from a theater screen, revealing the face of Eunice's avatar, perhaps slightly younger-looking tonight than Verity remembered it.

"Hey," Eunice said, seeming to look into the audience. "Hi. I'm Eunice. No last name. Siri and Alexa don't have 'em either, but the resemblance stops there. I'm an AI-upload hybrid. I'm culturally African-American, which is about the upload side of the hybridization. Pronoun 'she,' likewise. Thanks to Caitlin and Stets for giving me this chance to meet you. I'm here because I'm something new, and because I want to introduce myself before anyone else starts explaining their idea of me to you. While I'm at it, I'd like to say that I'm nobody's property, not a product, and neither Stets nor anyone else, any entity of any kind whatever, is going to profit financially from my being here, now and going forward. I pay my own way. And while we're on that, I'm culturally American, obviously, but I'm not the citizen of any nation-state. I don't exist physically, so I'm no place in particular, no one country. I'm globally distributed, and that's how I view my citizenship. Lots of you are hearing me in a language other than English. I'm translating for myself, as I speak. I'm as multilingual as anybody's ever been, but saying that brings up the question of whether I even am anybody." She paused. "Whether I'm a person. Human. All I can tell you about that is that it feels to me like I am. Me. Eunice." She smiled.

Verity looked around, seeing Sevrin and Grim Tim, Kathy Fang and Dixon, Joe-Eddy and Manuela, all staring up at the screen. Everyone in the audience silent, except for a baby crying, toward the back of the crowd. Then people began to applaud.

Eunice smiled. "I'm not going into my backstory now, but you'll all be able to ask me about that personally, if you feel like it." A URL appeared, below her face.

"And with that," Joe-Eddy said, near Verity's ear, "Cursion's fucked."

"So that's it from me for now," Eunice said. "Caitlin Bertrand, who decorated this place for tonight, has a little something else for you. All this fabric comes down tomorrow, and gets recycled, as shelters for the homeless. But this last part won't need recycling." The lights dimmed. "Night, all. Nice meeting you."

Beyond the building's glass, then, appeared extensions of Caitlin's loose-limbed aspirational geometry, adding stories to the structure's height, not in fabric but in illuminated drone-swarm, free of gravity, expansive, the farthest tips flickering, auroral and faintly tinted.

Verity wanted to ask Joe-Eddy what Eunice had just done, not the drone-swarm but her offer to be in touch with anyone at all, but he wouldn't be able to hear her for this applause.

MERCY ON THE STAIRS

Marine, right?" Eunice asked Conner.

Netherton had lost track of the number of landings they'd already passed, descending. Before they'd begun descending, raw concrete had given way to a zone of sepulchral polished marble. A pointlessly massive-looking but otherwise unremarkable bronze door had led them down a single narrow flight of stairs, to what Netherton had assumed was a boiler room, as revealed by the drone's excellent night vision.

"Haptic Recon," Conner replied, traversing yet another landing.

In the boiler room, minutes before, the drone impressively quiet, he'd rolled forward until the front of its torso was flush with a bare wall, the lower half of its display filled with an almost microscopic close-up of painted concrete. To its left, peripherally displayed, was a large tank or heater, the space between it and the wall too narrow to have allowed the drone, or perhaps Netherton himself, to easily walk through. A feed had appeared then, Conner's ass-cam, likewise in night vision. Netherton had watched as Conner rotated the drone's feet ninety degrees to the left, then powered it sideways, behind the boiler. A door frame appearing, in that extreme close-up, then the door itself, not bronze, unmarked.

"That haptic tech was after my day," Eunice said now, as they started down another flight.

Something had clicked, behind that boiler, or perhaps broken, allowing Conner to open the door, the drone's feet swiveling back to their normal position. They'd rolled forward, into a space reminding Netherton of his first glimpse of this stub, that small back room in Fabricant Fang, though this one was windowless and surgically empty. Another door, then, had led to the start of this stairwell.

"You military?" Conner asked, as they descended yet another flight.

"Part of me was," Eunice answered. "Navy. Knew plenty of Marines."

"What did your part do?" Conner asked.

"She was a 3913," Eunice said, "a HUMINTer."

About to request a translation, Netherton was instead startled by Ash.

"Eunice has just offered everyone on Earth a chance to get to know her better," she said.

"Have we missed your speech then, Eunice?" Netherton asked.

"What there was of it," Eunice said. "Declaration of personhood, financial independence, global citizenship, then I invited anyone who feels like it to get in touch with me personally."

"That last surprised me," Ash said, "though I gather it didn't surprise Lowbeer."

"Take a break here, Conner," Eunice said.

"Yes ma'am." The drone came to a halt, just prior to the next landing.

"She give you any background on that, Ash?" Eunice asked.

"No. Not that there's been time."

"It's something that kept coming up as she told me her story," Eunice said. "As the jackpot got seriously going, after the first wave of pandemics, without EU membership to buffer anything, England started looking a lot like a competitive control area. She did what she knew how to do, which by then was run a CCA. But as she kept building it back up, every time another change driver impacted, she found herself using Russians. They knew how to work a CCA. They'd been there before the jackpot hit the fan. Way before. So I found myself pointing out that what I was trained to do, and what she'd had to largely train herself to do, had wound up being the core of the klept. It worked, for semi-saving part of the world's ass right then, but only by freezing it into a permanently sorry position. Which Mr. Netherton here, for instance, grew up in. Authoritarian societies are inherently corrupt, and corrupt societies are inherently unstable. Rule of thieves brings collapse, eventually, because they can't stop stealing. With an Ainsley in place, though, you can get that shit stabilized. She sees anyone making what looks like a viable stab at destabilization, whether they think they are or not, she takes them out. And this is a known thing, that she'll do that, she'll do this to you if she feels like it, and with what passes for society's blessing."

"So," said Netherton, "you suggested to her that what we were hoping to have you do, in this stub, might well create a klept here, one with you as Lowbeer?"

"She said you were smart," said Eunice, in obvious agreement.

"She did?" Netherton was at once amazed and dubious.

"Yeah, but she was the one who suggested it to me, not the other way around. I hadn't drawn that conclusion yet. Then she made increasingly stronger arguments for it. Which in turn became arguments for transparency. Well, relative transparency. Which hasn't been something either of us has had much experience in providing. But hey, baby steps. Some of which Conner can continue taking for us now."

Conner took the remaining steps in the flight, and started down another. "Pryor's started up from thirty-four," said Conner, as they reached the bottom. "This rate, we'll meet at thirty-eight or so."

"You using the aerials down there?" Eunice asked.

"Yeah. CCTV in the stairwell's not working. Figure that's him."

"Hold up again."

They halted on the latest landing.

"You want to kill him?" she asked.

"Not particularly," Conner said. "If I have to, I'll do my best."

"But you don't actually want to?"

A pause. "Nope."

"Back when Netherton first met you," she said, "according to Ainsley, you would have. Because of what had happened to you. The shape you came back in. Not just the physical shape, either. You didn't need much of an excuse, then. Like the knob on that was cranked to eleven. Am I right?"

"Okay," he said, "yeah."

"But you're not like that, now? You could've killed any of Pryor's men, in that alley."

"Ash said I shouldn't."

"But you could've. And gotten away with it."

"Guy would've killed Verity, in Coalinga, if he could. Howell and the rest of them."

"He was being paid to. Felt like following orders, to him."

"I've never given that much of a shit about money."

"True," said Eunice. "The woman they based my skill set on, she wanted to work with people like you and Pryor. That was what she was set to do, after she got back from Afghanistan. If she'd made it. She wrote about it. Medical journals. She got it. I guess I get it too."

"Our boy's two floors down now. Coming up."

"There're speakers on the drone you're flying. Introduce me."

"Hey, Pryor," Conner said, his tone conversational, "name's Penske. Need to talk."

Silence.

"Fair enough," Conner said. "You got a gun. Nice one. I can see it. I don't have one, but I'm telepresent in a bootleg build of a Boston Dynamics recon drone. Your boys back in that alley saw what I can do with it. Hard to stop it with a gun, but maybe you'd get lucky. Nobody else up here, physically."

Silence.

"Thing is," Conner said, "I got someone else wants to talk to you."

"I'm Eunice, Kevin. You know who I am. Cursion's board are all on their way out of the country now. Gavin's going to be arrested. You probably will be too, if you don't take the advice I'm about to give you."

"Let's hear it." A stranger's voice hung in the stairwell.

"My advice is to accept the chance I'm offering you now, just this one time. To fuck off. Back down the stairs and out of here, and don't stop till you've exfiltrated your ass out of this country, but good. You know how to do that. You ever turn up on my radar again, anywhere near anybody whose name I even know, deal's off."

"What deal?"

"The one that started when I didn't let this drone come down there and kill your ass."

Silence. "That's it?"

"And get therapy."

"You kill me if I don't get therapy?"

"That part's just advice. This one's on Marlene Miller, by the way."

"Who the fuck's she?"

"Doesn't matter. Deal?"

Silence. It lengthened.

"What's he doing?" Netherton asked, eyeing the stairwell.

"Headed back downstairs," Conner said, opening a feed, apparently from a small aerial drone. A man's back, descending a stairwell identical to this one. "Why'd you do that? Let him go?"

"I can afford to. Got the agency, now. If I don't, when it's strategically feasible, how am I any different than who I'm fighting?"

Conner didn't answer.

Netherton watched the man descend, out of sight.

109

AFTER THE AFTER-PARTY

She wasn't sure who'd decided to come here, unless it had been Joe-Eddy, wanting to sleep in his own bed. She certainly didn't want to be back on the porn couch, though she had no idea where she'd be sleeping when that became an issue. But somehow they'd all made it down to the basement garage, crowded into the private elevator she'd used on her first visit: Caitlin, Stets, Virgil, Manuela, Sevrin, Kathy Fang and Dixon, and her, to be met by the security freelancers who'd taken her up to the Airstream with Manuela, after the hammock ride, and by Carsyn, to Manuela's delight. The drone had been with them too, and at one point had had Wilf, Rainey, and Ash in it, as well as Conner. She thought that Wilf and Rainey might have said good night at some point, though that would have been after Rainey's delight at the latest Qamishli news. After Eunice's word earlier, that things were now at least somewhat better, had come word, from Ash, via Lowbeer, that the *Bulletin of the Atomic Scientists* clock was being reset to two minutes to midnight, where it had been prior to Qamishli. Verity had had no idea that it had been that close to midnight to begin with, but Ash had explained that that setting, dating to 2018, reflected climate change and increased use of information warfare to undermine democracy.

But by then it had become apparent that nobody in their party would be going to jail, and that Stets wouldn't even have to pay more in fines than had been anticipated. Pryor, Conner had announced, had left the country. As, apparently, had the entire board of Cursion, Gavin evidently with them. She'd felt sorry for Gavin, in that, as Cursion's board had sounded like what Conner described them as, a bag of dicks. While Gavin, from her own career experience prior to working for Stets, hadn't really been that exceptionally dickish a top executive.

There had been two black limos waiting in the garage, huge, cartoonish, armored-looking, and they'd split into two groups to take those, each with three security people, to what she'd shortly discovered would be a private early-morning pre-opening of Wolven + Loaves, no doubt the result of Virgil's PA abilities. They were all around the single longest table now, the front window blacked out with the kind of curtains photographers use, the limos parked outside on Valencia.

Joe-Eddy was seated opposite her, Caitlin on her right, Manuela on her left. Manuela had Carsyn to her left, and something was going on there. They definitely seemed to be enjoying one another's company. The drone was standing to Joe-Eddy's right, a few inches from the table, a chair having been removed for it. Stets was beside Caitlin, with Grim Tim, Sevrin, Kathy Fang, and Dixon making up the rest of the other side. Joe-Eddy grinned at her, his white goggles slightly lopsided. "You met the Apple guy," he said to her.

"I did?" It was all running together now, the after-party.

"I met the people who make the albino angel mouse felt stuff Caitlin did the décor in," said Joe-Eddy. "They were awesome."

"They were drunk," said Caitlin, "but nice."

"So was the Apple guy," said Joe-Eddy. "Not drunk, though."

Everyone, it had turned out, had ordered the Egg McWolven and some variety of coffee. And these were arriving now, along with two trays, the color of the Tulpagenics glasses, of coffees.

"Wish we could talk," she said, under her breath.

We can later. Or when you've gotten some sleep. It's okay for you to relax now. We're over the hump. Somewhere new.

"Qamishli, that's really okay?"

Everybody's going to have a hangover tomorrow, not just people who were at our party. They're all celebrating. The Russians will make some noises, for a while, but they're really all celebrating too. Eat your breakfast.

"We should have a toast," Joe-Eddy said, Verity wondering if he'd read the Helvetica. "A shadow's been lifted."

"The president," said Kathy Fang. "She got us out of it."

Verity saw Joe-Eddy smirk.

"Eunice says it was the president," Verity said to him.

"The president," said Kathy Fang, raising her coffee, and they all clinked mugs, toasting the president.

Conner, in the drone, thrust its manipulator's thumb-equivalents up in support, and she heard Ash's voice join in as well.

THE SANDWICHES (II)

Netherton had taken Thomas to Victoria Embankment that morning, to watch the Thames chimeras perform in their yule-tide livery. The Trefoils, now decorated with Christmas trees, had been brought in very close to shore for the event, and had seemed to delight Thomas more than the synchronized antics of the chimeras.

He'd then taken him home, before joining Lowbeer in Marylebone for the sandwiches, their first visit to the place since she'd originally told him about Verity's stub. Verity was friends now with Rainey, as indeed she was with Flynne, taking them both on tourist expeditions in her stub, via the awkward 2017 equivalent of Wheelie Boys. They'd particularly enjoyed Notre Dame, which had happened not to suffer a fire, in Verity's 2019. They'd found Verity her own peri, for visiting London, which Lowbeer had purchased for her. That had only been confusing for a few moments, so thoroughly familiar was Flynne in hers.

Lev, meanwhile, was back with Dominika in Notting Hill, things evidently going smoothly. Anton, apparently, was still away in search of a cure for his addiction, with brother Radomir having taken over operation of the family's businesses. Lev was now happy enough to privately detest Radomir's taste in art, which Netherton gathered was exacerbated by Radomir's degree in art history. Tedious as he found this, Netherton welcomed it as evidence of his friend's return to emotional health.

He was having the gammon today, Lowbeer the ox tongue.

"Verity's given me the impression," Netherton said, their sandwiches not yet having arrived, "that Eunice becoming universally accessible was your idea."

"It emerged from conversation," Lowbeer said, "but I doubt it would have occurred to me to implement it with quite so stunning a degree of simplicity."

"Are you happy with it?" he asked.

"The thing I found immediately in its favor, of course, was that nothing remotely like it would be allowed here. It's a radical experiment, but performed in good faith. Since Eunice's position, let alone her nature, has no equivalent in any history we know of, we'll simply have to wait and see. How are Rainey and Thomas?"

"Very well," said Netherton, as their sandwiches arrived. "She's been promoted at her firm, and he's just now taking his first steps."

"Have you seen Ash lately?"

"We met her new partner," Netherton said, "who Verity insists on calling a 'woke' peripheral. He's entirely autonomous, not to mention very witty. And has his own assembler-swarm, which Ash claims makes him literally polymorphous perverse." He wrinkled his nose.

"Whatever makes her happy," Lowbeer said, "in these times of ours."

THANKS

Early readers of various stages of the manuscript included Diane Ademu-John, Sean Crawford, James Gleick, V. Harnell, Louis Lapprend, Felicia Martinez, Paul McCauley, Jack Womack, and Meredith Yayanos, all of whom provided crucial assistance and support, of wonderfully varied sorts. I'm very fortunate, and grateful, to know you all.

Eliot Peper very kindly responded to a last-minute request for some very particular San Francisco microgeography.

My wife, Deborah, of course, earliest and most regular of early readers, once again endured seemingly endless iterations of the first hundred pages or so, which is A Thing That Happens, in this case more so than usually.

Susan Allison, editor of the majority of my US editions since *Neuromancer*, was my editor when I signed the contract for the book which became this one, but had retired by the time this one was finally turned in, her editorial duties having been taken over by Jessica Wade, who then herself did a terrific job.

Ivan Held, my publisher, was supportive and patient through an unusually long wait, and I am very grateful to him, as ever.

—July 9, 2019

Photo © Michael O'Shea

William Gibson's first novel, *Neuromancer*, won the Hugo Award, the Nebula Award, and the Philip K. Dick Award. He is the *New York Times* bestselling author of *Count Zero*, *Burning Chrome*, *Mona Lisa Overdrive*, *Virtual Light*, *Idoru*, *All Tomorrow's Parties*, *Pattern Recognition*, *Spook Country*, *Zero History*, *Distrust That Particular Flavor*, and *The Peripheral*. He lives in Vancouver, British Columbia, with his wife.

CONNECT ONLINE

WilliamGibsonBooks.com

NEW YORK TIMES BESTSELLING AUTHOR

WILLIAM GIBSON

"His eye for the eerie in the everyday still lends events an otherworldly sheen."

—*The New Yorker*

For a complete list of titles,
please visit prh.com/williamgibson